New York Times and *US...*
Caridad Piñeiro is a Jersey...
and is the author of nearly fi...
loves romance novels, superheroes, TV and cooking.
For more information on Caridad and her dark, sexy
romantic suspense and paranormal romances, please
visit caridad.com

Nationally bestselling author **Patricia Sargeant** was
drawn to write romance because she believes love is the
greatest motivation. Her romantic suspense novels put
ordinary people in extraordinary situations to have them
find the 'hero inside.' Her work has been reviewed in
national publications such as *Publishers Weekly, USA
Today, Kirkus Reviews, Suspense Magazine, Mystery
Scene Magazine, Library Journal* and *RT Book Reviews*.
For more information about Patricia and her work, visit
patriciasargeant.com

Also by Caridad Piñeiro

South Beach Security: K-9 Division
Sabotage Operation
Escape the Everglades

South Beach Security
Lost in Little Havana
Brickell Avenue Ambush
Biscayne Bay Breach

Cold Case Reopened
Trapping a Terrorist
Decoy Training

Also by Patricia Sargeant

The Touré Security Group
Down to the Wire
Her Private Security Detail

Discover more at millsandboon.co.uk

KILLER IN THE KENNEL

CARIDAD PIÑEIRO

SECOND-CHANCE BODYGUARD

PATRICIA SARGEANT

MILLS & BOON

First Published in Great Britain 2024
by Mills & Boon, an imprint of HarperCollins*Publishers* Ltd
1 London Bridge Street, London, SE1 9GF

www.harpercollins.co.uk

HarperCollins*Publishers*
Macken House, 39/40 Mayor Street Upper,
Dublin 1, D01 C9W8, Ireland

Killer in the Kennel © 2024 Caridad Piñeiro
Second-Chance Bodyguard © 2024 Patricia Sargeant-Matthews

ISBN: 978-0-263-32254-5

1124

KILLER IN THE KENNEL

CARIDAD PIÑEIRO

Chapter One

The chatter of restaurant diners bounced off the walls like marbles ricocheting off pinball machine flippers.

Shiny slabs of white and chrome gleamed from the spotlights beaming down on the walls and colorful splashes of carefully placed modern art.

Jose Gonzalez peered around the restaurant as the waiter brought over the first vegetarian dish of their tasting menu. The place was busy for midweek, likely because of the star the restaurant had recently earned and the sighting of a few celebrities dining there the week before.

He suspected that's why his date had insisted on coming here to eat the flowers, fruits and vegetables for which the restaurant had earned some fame. He'd met Marta a few weeks earlier at a popular hangout in the Fontainebleau where celebrities also liked to linger.

Marta was cover-model beautiful with her perfectly highlighted hair, pouty bee-stung lips and a body with all the right curves. So why did he feel like something was lacking?

As he chowed down on the salad of red and golden beets, arugula, pistachios and a vegan goat cheese, he had to admit it was rather tasty. But after another dish of nothing but vegetables emerged from the kitchen followed by a third, he glanced lovingly at a nearby table where a delicious-looking filet mignon sat next to golden roasted potatoes and Broccolini.

"Isn't this delicious?" Marta said, a false trill of delight coloring her voice and a piece of something green stuck to her lower lip.

"Delicious," he replied, hoping she wouldn't pick up on his boredom with the meal and surprisingly, with her.

Fail, he thought as she narrowed her gaze and peered at him. "Jose?" she said, voice rising in question.

His phone rattled against the hard, gleaming white surface of the table.

He glanced at the screen and saw that it was his cousin Trey calling on his office line. Jose normally avoided anything to do with his family's South Beach Security agency but taking the call this time was a welcome interruption.

"Who is it?" his date asked, clearly annoyed by the phone's buzzing.

Holding his hand up in a request for her silence, he answered.

"*Hola*, Pepe," Trey said, using his childhood family nickname.

"*Hola*, Trey. How can I help you?" he said, and hoped it would give him an escape so he could go grab himself a Cuban sandwich somewhere to satisfy the hunger gnawing at his belly.

"I need your help with a new project," Trey said.

Jose nodded. "Hold on a second. I'm on a date," he said, and placed his hand over the phone to muffle his voice.

"I'm sorry, but I have to take this," he said, shot to his feet and headed for the patio where the restaurant had a bar and outdoor dining area. It was quieter there, the sounds muffled by the verdant spill of plants down the exterior walls of the building.

"What do you need, *primo*?" he asked, and hoped it wouldn't be something that dragged him into the Gonzalez family business. For years he'd struggled to build his own path without his well-known family's influence as well as the dangers often faced by his cousins at SBS.

"This must be some date if you're taking my call," Trey teased.

Jose turned and peered through the glass door to where his date sat, her full lips thinned in aggravation at his absence. The bit of green gone.

"You could say that," he said, not wanting to be unkind. Marta was nice in her own way. She just wasn't his type, whatever that type was.

"You're not going to ghost her, are you?" Trey asked, the faintest hint of accusation in his voice.

"You know me better than that, *primo*. I'll let her down easy," he confirmed and pushed on. "So why are you calling?"

"We need your help—"

"You know I don't want anything to do with the agency," he interrupted quickly.

A frustrated sigh drifted across the line. "I know, Pepe. We need your help finding a property."

Finding a property? "That's it? Nothing else?" he said, surprised at the simplicity of the request.

"*Sí*, just that. Our K-9 business has been growing and we'd like to set up a training center for our people and dogs. We need to find a location for that center," Trey advised, and continued explaining what they wanted to have on the property and roughly how much acreage they would need.

"That's a nice-sized property," he said, and in his mind the dollar signs spun like the reels on a slot machine.

"It is, but I know you're the perfect person to find us a place," Trey said, rousing unexpected guilt.

"Why me, Trey? You know I try to avoid getting involved in SBS business and this sale… I don't need to tell you that my commission on a property like that—"

"Will be a very nice one. You're family and family sticks together," Trey said without hesitation.

Full-blown guilt erupted at Trey's words as if the trust Trey was placing in him wasn't deserved, but he intended not to disappoint.

"We *are* family. I'll find you the perfect spot. Don't worry."

"I won't. I know you'll do right by us," Trey said, and ended the call.

Jose lowered the phone and stared at it for a long time. Trey and his SBS cousins always managed to do right by whoever they helped.

He intended to do the same with SBS and after a quick glance at Marta, with his date.

Once they finished dinner, he'd end it like a gentleman. After that, he'd head to Little Havana for a tasty Cuban sandwich packed with roast pork, baked ham and Swiss cheese to satisfy his hunger pangs.

Finally, as soon as he was in his South Beach condo, he'd settle down in his home office and get to work on finding Trey a perfect property for his new venture.

TREY LAID HIS phone down and stared across his desk to where his siblings sat expectantly.

"He said yes?" his baby sister, Mia, asked, obviously surprised by their cousin's response.

"He did and I'm surprised as well," Trey admitted.

"Was it just about the money?" Ricky asked.

Trey wished he'd had Ricky on the line during the call. As a psychologist, his younger brother might have picked up on Jose's motivation, although Trey considered himself a good judge of people. He'd needed that a lot to survive his time in the marines and later as an undercover police detective.

Trey shook his head. "I don't think so. I got the sense he really wanted to help because we're family."

"Surprising," Mia said with the arch of a manicured brow.

"Pepe is a good guy and I understand why he wants to make his own way. It's tough being part of a family like ours," Ricky said, ever the mediator and sometimes the outsider since he was more of a feeler and not a doer like Trey and Mia.

Trey had no doubt about how hard it was to be part of their family. They had buried their roots deep into the Miami soil and flourished beyond expectations. But that success brought many demands, and Trey could understand Jose's desire to forge his own life and success removed from those demands.

Because of that, he said, "Now that we know Pepe will look for the property, do you agree Sara Hernandez is the best candidate to run the K-9 training center?"

He handed the résumé across the desk to Ricky to refresh his memory of their possible new employee.

"Her work history is impressive. She's responsible for the search and rescue teams in several state parks," Ricky said, as he in turn passed the résumé to Mia.

Mia took a quick glance at the paper and said, "I agree. She's very impressive and she's also a certified K-9 trainer. I'm all for asking her to take the job."

"Great. I'll reach out to her, and hopefully we can move on this quickly. The K-9 Division has really taken off, and I'd love to be able to train our own agents and canines," Trey said, and took another look at the résumé and Sara's headshot. She was pretty with that kind of girl-next-door look that was the antithesis of Jose's artfully groomed and manicured fashionistas.

Perfect, he thought, and picked up the phone to call her.

THE WOMAN CRASHED through the underbrush in the thick hardwood hammock he'd released her in earlier.

He always gave his women head starts to make it a fair fight.

This one was literally like the proverbial bull in the china shop, leaving a trail of crushed brush and broken branches, enabling him to track her easily.

He caught a glimpse of her bright red blouse as she darted behind a tree, probably thinking she could hide there until he gave up the hunt.

Laughing lowly, he picked up his crossbow and tucked it tight to his shoulder. It was lubed, loaded and ready to fire. He never took chances anymore because he'd almost lost one of his women when he'd misloaded an arrow.

Never again. If she'd gotten free…

Don't think about that, he told himself, and focused on the tree and the tiniest bit of red peeking out from the edge of it.

Waiting. Watching. Patient.

His mother had always told him to be patient. To take care of his things. To watch out for wicked women.

I'm doing just that, Mommy, he thought.

As the bit of red became a larger target, he let the arrow fly.

It struck flesh with a resounding *thunk*.

The woman dropped to the ground like a stone.

He walked over to where she lay face down, motionless. Blood leaked from the arrow embedded deep in her back, a darker crimson against the red of her shirt.

Laying a booted foot on her back, he tore out the arrow, wiped it clean with some leaves and slipped it back into his quiver.

Never let a good weapon go to waste, he thought.

Flipping the woman over, she stared up at him with sightless eyes. Blue like the sky above, but bloodshot and old-looking despite her youth. Drugs and hooking would do that to you, he thought. A wounded wasted life that he gifted peace with his benevolent kill.

After all, you wouldn't let a wounded animal suffer.

He knelt and slipped off her earrings. Cheap little wire ones with bits of fake crystals. Tucking them into his pocket, he was about to haul her off to her final resting place when the sound of a car engine intruded, loud in the quiet of early morning. A pricey car if he was any judge.

Sounds traveled far out here. It was why he used to do his hunting at night when the kennels had been open. In the years since greyhound racing had been banned in Florida and the kennels had closed, he'd had the entire property to himself.

Until today, he thought, and crept silently toward the kennels to see who had ruined his pleasure. It took him nearly ten minutes to reach the edge of the forest that bordered the abandoned buildings. He carefully hid in the underbrush to see who had arrived on the property.

He had been right about the car. An expensive Maserati SUV sat in the driveway in front of what had once been the kennel owner's home. Beside it stood what his mother would have called a "rather dandy fellow" thanks to her love of Regency romances.

Raising the crossbow, he used the scope to get a better look.

Handsome. Possibly Latino. Sharp dresser. If he had to guess, the suit was as pricey as the expensive Italian car.

A sinking feeling filled his gut as the man looked around and began inspecting the property.

This was not good. Having people here, in his playground, could only bring problems.

He told himself not to worry. Who would want these abandoned buildings way out here?

But as the fancy man smiled and nodded, he worried that trouble would soon be coming his way.

Chapter Two

The receptionist led Jose into Trey's office and when he entered, he realized it wasn't just Trey inside, but also Tio Ramon, Mia and Ricky as well as a twentysomething woman he would best describe as pixieish. At her feet was an immense black-and-tan bloodhound who raised its head as he entered and eyed him with somber deep-set eyes before lazily lowering its head again to rest it against huge paws.

Jose walked over to Trey and hugged him hard and then did the same with his cousins Mia and Ricky.

He shook his uncle's hand and said, "You look great, *tio*." In truth, his uncle looked years younger, as if the weight of the world had been lifted off his shoulders, and maybe that was the truth now that his son Trey had joined the agency and taken over many of its responsibilities.

"You look well also, *mi'jo*," Tio Ramon said, and clapped him on the back. A second later, his uncle swung his arm out in the direction of the young woman and what he assumed was her dog.

"This is Sara Hernandez. She's going to head up the new division and live at the facility. We were hoping you could show her the property and work with her to get everything up and running. You do know contractors and the like, right?" his uncle said with the arch of a thick, salt-and-pepper brow.

Tio Ramon looked so much like Jose's father that he suddenly felt as if he were five years old again and in trouble.

"*Sí*, I know contractors. I can recommend one as soon as Ms. Hernandez checks out the property and lets me know what's necessary."

SARA DIDN'T KNOW what to make of the very handsome man who was clearly being put on the spot by his family members.

His discomfort at working with her was apparent, but that didn't stop her from holding out her hand as she rose and said, "Sara Hernandez. It's very nice to meet you. This is Bongo, my K-9 partner."

He took hold of her hand and his gaze locked with hers. His eyes were the blue of the Caribbean Sea, and he had the same Roman nose and dimpled chin as his cousins. There was no denying they were family no matter how much this man might want to forget that.

"Nice to meet you also despite the circumstances," he said, and shot his family members a scathing glance before peering at Bongo with obvious reluctance. "He's big and… drooly, isn't he?"

She didn't blame him for not liking surprises. "It's a 'she' and yes, she is. A characteristic of the breed unfortunately. If today isn't good for you—"

"No, it's fine. I knew Trey wanted you to look at the property. If you want, I can drive you there and take you home afterward."

Pointing her index finger upward, she said, "I'm staying in the penthouse temporarily. We were hoping the owner's home on the property could be fixed up quickly."

Jose tilted his head from side to side, as if considering. "It didn't look too bad, but I'll let you decide. Maybe Mia could even help get it ready," he said, and looked in his cousin's direction.

"I'd love to help. Just let me know when you need me," she said with a broad smile and a quick look between the two of them.

"Great," Jose said, and clapped his hands as if to end any discussion. Facing Sara again, he said, "If you're ready to go…"

"I am," she said, and after bidding goodbye to all the family members, he and Sara walked out of the room and to the elevators.

Jose had his hands stuffed in his pants pockets and shifted back and forth on his heels as he said, "I don't mean to make this sound…negative, but I'm not normally this involved in my family's business."

Which she took to mean once again that he wasn't all that eager to work with her, and she was okay with that for a number of reasons. She'd grown up around men like Jose with their bespoke suits and fancy cars. Or at least what she assumed would be a fancy car, and she wasn't disappointed as they reached the parking level, and he directed her toward an elegant and sporty Italian SUV.

"I hope Bongo won't be an inconvenience for you."

Jose laughed and shook his head. "If I was worried, we'd have taken one of the company cars," he said, and tossed a hand in the direction of several vehicles in the garage that bore the SBS emblem.

Considering Bongo's size and drool factor, maybe that was a good idea, she thought. "Maybe we should take one of those," she said, and gestured toward an SBS SUV.

JOSE DIDN'T KNOW WHY, but he'd gotten the sense that she saw him as some kind of snob. He also didn't know why that bothered him. Shaking his head, he said, "No, that's okay. I think Bongo will be comfortable in the back seat."

Even if that meant having dog hair and drool all over his expensive Italian leather.

She hesitated, eyeing his pristine vehicle and then the SBS SUV, but gestured to his car and said, "If it's okay with you."

Hoping he wouldn't regret it, he opened the back passenger door so that the bloodhound, who was easily a hundred pounds of loose skin and ears, could hop in.

He turned to open the door for Sara, but she had already climbed into the passenger seat.

A liberated woman, he thought, and totally not the pampered type he normally had in his life.

He pulled out of the parking lot onto Brickell Avenue and as he checked for oncoming traffic, she caught his attention yet again.

She was dressed casually in a pale blue blouse that brought out the hints of blue in her gray eyes and embraced her generous breasts. As he slipped into the driver's seat, he noticed how the faded denim of her jeans clung to her shapely thighs.

His gut tightened unexpectedly, and he pushed away his awareness of her because this meeting was all about business. The last thing he wanted was to be involved with anyone connected to his family's SBS business. Reminding himself of that, he said, "I hope you'll like the property."

She shot him a quick look and nodded. "I think I will. Trey was kind enough to send me the photos you took of the location."

"Trey is a good guy. I think you'll like working with him," he said without hesitation.

"But *you* don't normally work with him?" she asked, head cocked to the side as she waited for his response.

He tightened his hands on the wheel and held his breath as he considered how to explain their awkward family dynamic. After a long exhalation, he said, "The longer you stay in Miami, the more you'll realize how well-known the Gonzalez family is and how much power they have."

"I gathered as much from some of the research I did

when I decided to apply for the job," she said, and nervously drummed her fingers on her thighs.

"It's normally a good thing unless you want to take your own path," he said, and shifted his hands on the wheel again as he turned onto the expressway that would take them to where the kennels were located. The property was forty minutes outside of Miami in an area mostly known as the home of various fruit orchards, flower farms and a racing horse stable that his SBS family had helped protect several weeks earlier.

"IT IS A good thing, but not necessarily easy," she said.

Sara knew all about trying to choose her own destiny. Her family, owners of a successful New Jersey financial investment firm, had wanted her to follow in the footsteps of her father and brothers and join the family business. Only Sara had no interest in stocks, bonds and finances or the kind of attention that came with such success. She'd almost reconsidered taking this job with SBS because of the attention it would bring. But from an early age she'd loved the outdoors and dogs, and this job was the way to follow her dreams.

She admired that Jose was of a same mind, and it made her reconsider her earlier thoughts that he was a lot like the men who'd orbited in her family's rarified circles. Their primary goal had been to take advantage of her family's success and connections to boost their way up the corporate ladder, but Jose was apparently trying to make his own way.

Jose shot a quick look in her direction, his gaze questioning.

"My family is…well-off," she said and left it at that. Let him draw his own conclusions about what that might mean and why she might not like it.

He did another quick peek at her and shrugged, but she wasn't sure if it was a shrug of confusion or acceptance. Since he turned the discussion back to the property, she sat and patiently listened as he explained the history of the location and the various buildings on it.

"I think it's perfect. There are already kennels for the dogs, a training ring, and a small oval track that you could maybe convert to an obstacle course. I understand that's a thing," he said and paused, as if waiting for her to confirm his understanding.

"That's a thing. I love training dogs on the obstacles, especially the little ones," she said with a laugh.

Jose chuckled and pointed his thumb in the direction of Bongo, who sprawled across his back seat, drooling. "I imagine you need some activity with a dog as laid-back as Bongo."

Sara shook her head and likewise laughed. "Actually, bloodhounds were bred to track scents for hours so they like being active despite their laid-back look. I normally exercise Bongo a lot to keep her in shape for assignments."

"Hopefully this job won't be so crazy that you won't have time to do that," he said, and turned off the expressway onto a small road that ran through flat fields and scattered homes and farm buildings on either side of the narrow street.

"How did you get started with the dogs and search and rescue?" he asked.

"I just had an affinity for dogs and I loved the outdoors. I loved helping people, so it seemed like a natural way to go," she said and quickly added, "What about you? Why did you become a real estate agent?"

A look filled with joy entered his gaze as he said, "I remember the day my family moved into their first home. It was so special. My parents had worked so hard for it. And I love architecture. Like you, it seemed like a natural way to go."

A few miles down the road, Jose slowed near a wooden blue-and-white sign that read Florian Kennels.

The bright Florida sun and damp humidity had taken its

toll on the sign over the years of abandonment. The colors had faded, and paint peeled here and there, exposing wood cracking from the elements.

She hoped the buildings and kennels wouldn't look as bad and was pleasantly surprised as they pulled up in front of a home and an assortment of other buildings.

HE'D BEEN TAKING a nap after tending to his garden earlier that day when the alarm tripped to warn that someone had come onto the property.

Since the fancy man's visit, he'd rigged a simple driveway alarm by the kennel sign so he would know when company was calling. The tall grasses there had made it easy to hide the device, especially since its green color blended in.

Grabbing a set of digital binoculars, he slipped on a long-sleeved camo shirt, snagged the remote for the surprise he'd installed the night before and headed through his fields to the hardwood hammock, careful to move silently through the woods to remain undetected.

He sneaked to the edge of the trees, crouched silently in the underbrush and raised his binoculars.

The man was back but with a woman this time who held the leash to a very large bloodhound.

A beautiful woman, he thought, and snapped off a few photos with the camera built into the binoculars.

He waited, patient, as the two and the dog entered the home, probably to inspect it.

It was a nice place. He'd visited a few times when the Florians had invited him to various events, but the home had reminded him of his mother too much. Made him too lonely and angry at the same time, so he avoided visiting. Luckily, he preferred his place with the peace and privacy that he needed for his games.

Barely half an hour later, the couple emerged, smiling, the

bloodhound trailing after them. The couple unfortunately seemed satisfied that the home would be suitable for them.

He hadn't been happy about that possibility when he'd seen the man, but this woman...

He might be able to have some fun with her. If she survived that was.

Watching, he followed them through the binoculars as they walked through the kennels and training ring and then visited the remains of the old racing track and outbuildings.

Holding his breath as they neared the outbuildings, he waited, finger rubbing almost lovingly across the remote.

That's it, he thought. *Just a little closer.* "Almost there," he said out loud, and held the remote up to make sure nothing would interfere with the signal.

Chapter Three

"The place is in good shape. Just some cleaning, fresh paint and minor repairs," Jose said as he gestured Sara in the direction of the small track once used to train the greyhounds for racing.

They strolled toward the track and paused at the low white fence surrounding the oval.

"This will make a great course. There's plenty of room for the different obstacles," Sara said, and pointed to one spot. "I could see a nice long tunnel tucked against that far side," she said, knelt and rubbed Bongo's ears. "Right, Bongo?"

The dog let out a low woof and shook her head, sending her floppy ears and drool flying into the air.

Sara wiped some drool off her jeans and laughed. The sound sparkled in the quiet of what was becoming a sultry afternoon thanks to the Florida humidity and heat.

Jose joined in her laughter, enjoying her easygoing nature and lack of guile. It was refreshing after the women he'd been around where every action seemed intentional and planned. But he reminded himself that she worked for SBS, and getting involved with her meant being drawn closer to the family business.

When she stood, she grabbed hold of Bongo's leash and pointed toward the outbuildings several yards away.

"What are those used for?" she said.

Jose peered in their direction and shrugged. "I don't know. I assume you can use them to store whatever equipment you'll need for the obstacle course," he said, and walked toward the outbuildings.

Sara and Bongo walked beside him, but he was only about ten feet away when something caught his attention. A strong smell. Like nail polish.

Something Trey had once said about a police raid on a meth lab ripped through his brain a second before a flash inside the outbuilding registered.

He wrapped Sara in his arms and hauled her to the ground as the outbuilding exploded, sending shards of glass and wood raining down on them.

Ears ringing and back stinging where shrapnel from the blast had torn into him, Jose slowly got to his feet and helped Sara to hers. Yards away, a fire was eating up one outbuilding and threatened to spread to the two nearby structures.

Bongo, who had apparently run off at the first hint of the blast, raced back to Sara's side.

"Are you okay?" he asked and peered from her to Bongo.

She nodded shakily. "I am thanks to you." Kneeling, she examined Bongo who had avoided any injuries.

Rising, brows knit together in worry, she said, "Are you okay?"

Jose looked back over his shoulder and winced at the sight of the blood leaking through the tears in his shirt. "Not really."

She raced around to examine his shoulder and gasped. "We need to get that cleaned up."

As another little explosion drew their attention, Jose said, "We need to stop that fire from spreading first. I saw a hose somewhere."

She nodded. "Back near the fence for the track," she said, and jerked a thumb in the direction of the old oval.

"I'll call for help," he said, and dialed 911.

They located the hose and water spigot and raced back to the outbuildings to wet down the two nearby buildings to try to save them. Barely minutes after they had started, the sounds of sirens filled the air.

A fire truck pulled into the driveway followed by a police cruiser.

The firefighters spilled from their vehicle and raced to work, reeling out yards and yards of hose. As the firefighters approached, Sara and he stepped aside to let them extinguish the flames threatening the remaining structures.

While they walked back toward the house and driveway, two police officers strolled up to them. One officer pulled her notepad from her duty holster and took out a pen.

"Mr. Gonzalez? I'm Officer Rojas. This is my partner, Officer McAllister," she said, and flipped a hand in the direction of the older man.

Jose nodded. "This is Sara Hernandez. She's a new South Beach Security K-9 agent."

"Nice to meet you. Can you tell us what happened?" Officer McAllister said.

Jose half turned toward the outbuildings, which earned an immediate comment from Officer Rojas. "We need to call some EMTs to take a look at you." She immediately jumped on her radio to call for medical assistance.

Jose peered at his back again, grimacing at the throb of pain that traveled across his body as he did so. "*Gracias*. I appreciate it."

"You mentioned on the 911 call that there had been an explosion," Officer McAllister said.

"We were approaching the outbuildings when I smelled something like nail polish. I remembered my cousin Trey mentioning acetone and a meth lab. He used to be a cop."

Officer McAllister nodded. "Detective Gonzalez. I've heard about him, and acetone *is* used in meth labs."

"And it's highly flammable. When I saw a flash through the window of the building, I knew I had to act," Jose said.

AND HE HAD acted to protect her over himself, Sara thought, and glanced over at Jose's back where several bits of wood had torn into his flesh.

She grimaced at the pain he must be feeling and how much worse it might get once the adrenaline of the moment wore off.

Standing beside him, she offered what little info she could as the officers continued their questioning. They were just finishing up when a team of firefighters came by, hauling their hose back to the truck.

One of the firefighters walked over to them. "Looks like a meth lab, kind of."

Officer Rojas said, "Kind of? What does that mean?"

"There's definitely some beakers, what's left of rubber tubing, clamps and stuff, but if it was a meth lab, it was a small one," the firefighter said, and with a nod of his head, he walked off to join his crew as they packed up to leave.

A second later, an EMT truck pulled in followed almost immediately by an SBS SUV.

"If you don't mind, my partner and I want to take a look at the damage, and you should have the EMTs work on your back," Rojas said. With a jerk of her head in her partner's direction, they walked toward the outbuildings.

From beside her, she heard Jose mutter a curse as he caught sight of Trey and Mia walking toward them. Shooting a glance at him, she said, "What's wrong?"

"This is exactly why I never wanted to get involved in SBS business," he muttered, and took off in the direction of the EMT truck.

She followed, clicking her tongue to get Bongo, who had been resting at her feet, to follow her to Trey and Mia as they stood by Jose at the EMT truck.

"Are you okay, *primo*?" Trey asked as Jose sat on the back ledge of the truck while one of the EMTs cut off his shirt.

"You know how much this guayabera cost?" Jose said, and tugged at the front of the Cuban-style shirt that was made from expensive linen. She recognized the pricey fabric since her father and brothers had often had custom-made linen shirts.

"I'll buy you a new one, but I'm more worried about your back," Trey said, and gestured to where the EMT had grabbed hold of some forceps.

"He's got about four or five wood shards in his shoulder. It won't take long to get them out and clean up the wound," the EMT said as she tackled the first of the splinters.

"*Gracias a Dios* it's not that bad," Mia said, and laid a hand on Jose's uninjured shoulder, but he shrugged it off.

"Easy for you to say, Mia. It's not your shoulder," Jose groused, but his complaint lacked any real sting. Unlike the splinters piercing his skin. Jose winced as the EMT removed each one.

"You kept me safe," Sara said, her mind traveling back to that fateful second when he'd covered her body to protect her.

With a shrug that had the EMT admonishing him to keep still, Jose said, "You should be thanking Trey. It was a story he told one *Noche Buena* that made me react."

Sara was impressed with Jose downplaying his role. In her earlier life, the men she knew would have been only too eager to take credit for something like that to improve their position with her family.

"The one about the meth lab? Is that what the police say was back there?" Trey asked, and peered in the direction of the two officers who were walking around the burned and broken shell of the outbuilding.

"The firefighter said it was likely a small one," Sara said, which earned a scowl from Trey.

"They must have been using the property while it was

empty. Very few people come out this way normally," he said, and looked around as if to confirm it.

"Hopefully they'll be long gone now that we're here," Mia said, and quickly added, "But for now, you should stay in the penthouse until we can secure this place. You too, Jose. We want to make sure you're okay since you were hurt."

A fleeting look swept across Jose's face. A combination of anger and resignation that she immediately understood from their earlier conversation and his comment just moments before.

Jose hadn't wanted to get involved in his family's SBS business, but with this explosion, she suspected he had no choice but to go along with whatever was happening until he could gracefully extricate himself.

And she had to brace herself in case the explosion made more than the local news. If it did, she knew her mother would be calling, worried about her chosen profession and pressing for her to leave her career for a safer life with the family business.

CROUCHED LOW, he kept an eye on the police officers and people gathered around the back of the EMT truck.

His explosion had gone off just as he'd planned, only the dandy fellow had somehow realized what was happening and kept them from getting close enough to be killed, or at least, severely wounded. But he was satisfied that the dandy had gotten a taste of pain.

It was all about the pain. The more he inflicted the less he felt it himself. It was what kept him going along with the belief that he was putting these women out of their misery and sending them to a better life. Ending the pain of their pitiful existences.

And these people weren't going to stop him.

As the police and EMTs left, the others lingered for only a few short minutes before heading to their vehicles.

He watched with satisfaction as the dandy got into the SBS SUV together with a man who had to be a relative. The resemblance couldn't be denied although from the looks of it this man was a warrior. The beautiful woman and the dog got into the vehicle with them while another gorgeous woman slipped into the pricey Italian SUV.

Having the men around was a problem.

Having the women around…

Well, that could be quite exciting, he thought, reconsidering just what he would be doing on this property.

But he had to be ready for them just like he would be for any hunt. And he had to protect his garden and hunting grounds at any cost. Any.

This group would soon find out that he wasn't someone to be messed with, and while he was busy showing them that, he intended to have his fun.

Chapter Four

It had been a surprisingly silent ride back to Brickell Avenue and the South Beach Security building.

Jose had expected Trey to pepper both him and Sara with questions about the explosion and the property, but he hadn't said much other than to ask how they were feeling.

"Achy," Sara said, making Jose feel immediately guilty.

"I didn't mean to tackle you so hard," he said, regretful about possibly injuring her.

"No need to apologize. You kept me from being hurt. How's the shoulder feeling?" she said, and leaned forward to see his face as he answered.

He turned slightly to meet her gaze and couldn't control the grimace of pain as he did so. "Tender, but it'll heal," he said, trying to downplay the injury, especially in front of Trey, who'd experienced far worse injuries during his service as a marine and a detective.

"I'll look at it in the penthouse. Wounds like that can be tricky," Trey said with a quick peek in his direction.

"Sure," he said, nodding as Trey pulled into the parking lot for the SBS building. Seconds later, Mia parked Jose's SUV right next to them.

"Sophie and Robbie are in the penthouse so we can discuss security at the location. Ricky will be coming by later—"

"Because you think we need some therapy to deal with our near-death experience?" Jose challenged.

With a reluctant nod, Trey said, "It might help to talk to Ricky."

Jose sucked in a breath to bite back another angry reply because underneath it all, he knew Trey was truly worried about them. "I appreciate it, but it's not necessary. For that matter, I'm not sure I'm really needed to discuss security and whatever else is happening at the property," Jose said as he felt himself being inextricably pulled into the SBS family business.

THERE WAS NO mistaking the mix of reluctance and anger spilling off Jose, and given their earlier discussion on the way to the kennels, Sara understood.

"I'm sure Jose would be better off going home and getting some rest," Sara said, not wanting to pressure Jose into something he clearly didn't want to do.

"Pepe does need rest, but we also have to find out as much as we can about what happened today. Plus he probably knows more about the history of the location than the rest of us, so it would be good to have him around until this all gets resolved. Isn't that right, *primo*?" Trey said, and eyeballed Jose in challenge.

Jose literally squirmed in his chair and was saved from answering as Mia rapped her knuckles on the passenger-side window.

"I'll meet you upstairs," she said, and pointed a perfectly manicured index finger upward before hurrying away while she took a call.

"We should go. The sooner we chat with Sophie and Robbie, the quicker they can work on a security plan for the location and the sooner you both can get some rest up in the penthouse," Trey said as he exited the car, brooking no disagreement.

But Jose delayed, making Sara say, "I'm sorry. I know you didn't want to get sucked into your family's business."

"I don't but Trey is right. I'm the one with the 411 on the property, although it might help to talk to the prior owners also," Jose said, and opened his door, clearly going along with Trey's plan despite his reluctance.

She followed his lead, left the SBS SUV, and Bongo jumped out beside her. They walked into the SBS building, badged themselves in, and over to the elevators that would take them up to the penthouse level that the agency used for clients' overnight stays or when one of their staff worked a late night or needed lodging, like she did.

"Hopefully we can get through the business quickly and get some dinner," Trey said, and used his badge in the elevator to unlock access to the topmost floor.

"That would be great," Jose said, but everything about his body language told a different story.

Jose had his hands clasped in front of him and he rocked back and forth slightly, obviously on edge.

The elevator swept straight up to the penthouse floor since it was well past the time when most people would be heading home at the end of the day. On the topmost floor, the doors opened into the luxurious suite that SBS was lending to her until the kennel owner's home was ready.

His cousins Sophie and Robbie, the SBS tech gurus, were setting the table in the expansive open space while Mia removed dishes from a large box. As she did so, the earthy aromas of beans mingled with the citrusy and garlicky scent of roast pork.

"Smells great," Jose said as he walked in and did a slow turn to examine the space. "Place looks great. You've furnished it nicely."

Sara had assumed that Jose would have been in the penthouse before, but clearly not. "It's very…" She hesitated, struggling to find the right word.

"Luxurious. Decadent. Over-the-top?" Jose said with a boyish grin.

"Definitely more than what I'm used to. Log cabin is more my style," she replied with a chuckle. She'd left luxuries like this behind when she'd opted not to join her family's successful business.

Trey stood next to them with his hands on his hips, also perusing the space. With a shrug, he said, "We like to be comfortable here."

"Especially since we use it when we need a place to chill," Mia said as she walked over and hugged Jose. "Sorry you were hurt, *primo*."

"I'LL BE FINE," Jose said, unable to say more, considering Mia had been shot months earlier during one of the SBS cases and had nearly died. His injuries couldn't even compare, making him feel lacking as he so often did around his SBS cousins.

Sophie and Robbie walked over then and likewise offered their regrets.

"Once the place is secure, we'll hopefully keep anything else from happening," said Sophie. Robbie and Sophie's mom was his dad's baby sister.

"I'm sure you will," he said, well aware that Sophie and Robbie had inherited the technological smarts that made their parents top NSA operatives.

"We will," Robbie said, and shook his hand before dipping his head and smiling in Sara's direction.

It was definitely a look of interest, which surprised Jose. Computer nerd Robbie had always struck him as asexual, so this was a new side to his cousin. On top of that, an unexpected pang of something reared up as well. He couldn't call it jealousy because he didn't really know much about Sara yet, although he liked what he did know.

"Maybe we should get to work," he said because the

sooner they did, the sooner he might get some rest and maybe even make an exit despite his cousins' wishes he stay overnight.

"Dinner first! I'm starved!" Robbie said, and wrung his hands eagerly.

"You're always starved," his baby sister Sophie said with a roll of her eyes, dragging chuckles from everyone in the room.

Jose followed Mia to the island separating the kitchen from the rest of the open space and was about to help her finish unpacking the dishes when Trey stepped out of a nearby room holding a sweatshirt.

Trey handed it to him and said, "This might be better than what's left of your guayabera."

He shot a look at his bloodied shirt and the cuts the EMT had made at his shoulder so he could clean and dress the injury. "You're not wrong," he said, and gestured with the sweatshirt toward the nearby room. "I'll be back in a second."

He hurried to the room, a well-appointed bedroom, shut the door, took off his shirt and shrugged on the sweatshirt, grimacing as the motion pulled at the wounds in his shoulder.

Muttering a curse, he walked back out to the kitchen and helped Mia uncover the last of the dishes they'd ordered. As he did so, Mia said, "We got these from our local Cuban place. I think you like it too, right?"

The restaurant Mia had chosen was located halfway between his cousin's office building and Jose's real estate company's home base.

"It's a good place and I like supporting local," he said, and placed a large dish of black beans next to a heaping plate of white rice.

"Local is always good," Sara said, and helped them uncover the rest of the dishes while Sophie, Robbie and Trey set the table. She must have fed Bongo since the dog had her head buried in a large dish and was busy chowing down.

In no time they had served themselves buffet-style and sat around the table, enjoying the food. Bongo lay nearby, her large head pillowed on equally large paws. Long ears flowed over her paws to almost carpet the floor.

"This is delicious. My mom would approve," Sara said as she forked up some roast pork.

"Your mom is Cuban?" Jose asked, wanting to know more about her.

"*Mami* is Cuban. *Papi* is about as Irish as you can get," she said, and faked a brogue as she tacked on, "Hails from County Clare."

Which possibly explained the hints of red in her golden-brown hair, like cinnamon dusted on hot chocolate. It could also explain the shards of green in her unique gray-blue eyes and the smattering of freckles across the bridge of her nose.

And oh damn, he was paying too much attention to her, he thought, and looked away as he ate some of the rice and beans.

"Tasty," he echoed, and decided to get to business in the hopes of making a speedy exit despite his cousin's desire that he stay overnight. "What are your plans for securing the place?"

Sophie shot him a puzzled look, clearly surprised by his question. "You want to know?"

With a shrug he regretted as pain flared in his shoulder, he said, "I'd feel more comfortable knowing Sara will be safe at the kennels. Especially after what happened today."

"We agree, Pepe. Sara won't be living there until we feel it's safe," Trey said, and lifted his chin in Sophie's direction, as if to prompt her to continue.

Sophie did so with a quick nod. "We can run through our plans *after* dinner."

"We also have a crew coming in tomorrow to clean, especially in the kennels. There are a lot of weeds and leaves that have piled up there over the years. The training ring also, although it wasn't as bad," Mia said.

"No, it wasn't. But I'd like to get some new artificial turf in there for better cushioning and footing if the budget allows," Sara said, and delicately picked up a piece of fried yuca to eat like a french fry.

The crunchiness of the yuca had him grabbing a piece, which he swirled through some citrusy mojo sauce before taking a bite.

"Will you need that surfacing for the obstacle course too?" Jose asked.

SARA NODDED AND popped the last of the yuca fry in her mouth. Hastily swallowing, she said, "That surface would be good for the obstacle course. That is if you want to have that kind of training at the location."

Mia and Trey shot a quick look at each other before Trey said, "Whatever you want or need, Sara. We told you that when we hired you. We want this to be a first-class facility for our people and if you'd like, for anyone who wants to have their K-9s trained."

"But the first thing to do is get it secured," Mia said, which had everyone around the table murmuring their agreement.

"For sure," Trey said, and looked at Sophie and Robbie. "I'd love to hear more about your plans *after* we finish dinner."

It was clear to Sara that Trey wanted the rest of dinner to be business-free. She had no doubt Jose wanted to finish the business part and rush out the door, but Trey clearly had other plans. Because she wanted to know more about the family in general, she said, "How long have you all been working together?"

The cousins peered at each other before Trey said, "I just

joined the agency several months ago. Like Pepe, I avoided being part of SBS for a long time, but when they helped Roni—"

"Your new wife?" Sara asked.

Trey nodded. "We weren't married at the time. She was a Miami PD detective and SBS helped us during a difficult case. I realized the good the agency does and that it was time to help out."

Mia added, "I was pretty much the same. My cousin Carolina and I were doing well as social influencers, but I felt like I needed to do more. Carolina and I still do some gigs, but SBS truly feels like home now."

Interesting, Sara thought before glancing in the direction of the other cousins. "What about you two?"

Sophie and Robbie shared a quick glance. "Our parents are with the NSA and were hoping that we'd follow them there right after college, but we had other ideas."

"Like creating some games and things at first, but like Trey and Mia, we eventually realized the good that SBS does," Robbie added.

Beside her Jose squirmed a little, understandably so. Feeling his discomfort, she said, "Not everyone's path is the same. My family has a successful financial company, but I preferred to go my own way especially after my family had some problems that made the news."

"You're talking about your dad?" Trey said.

It didn't surprise her that Trey knew. He'd probably researched her and her family before offering her the position. "Yes, my dad. He was accused of embezzling but was cleared. That didn't matter to the press. It's why I avoid that kind of publicity."

"It's not easy to do. We understand why Pepe steers clear of us," Trey said, and risked a quick glance at his cousin.

"It's not you, *primo*. It's the danger you're always in. We can't all be action heroes," Jose said, and there was no denying the anger and frustration in his voice.

"No, we can't, and we will try to free you from this as soon as possible," Mia said, her tone mirroring Trey's.

"Good. I'd appreciate that," Jose said, and dug into his food with some force, his fork scratching the plate beneath.

The exchange of words cast a pall over the meal, and silence fell over the table until the plates were empty.

"I'll clean so you can get started," Mia said, and sprang out of her chair.

"I'll help," Jose said.

Trey laid a hand on his uninjured shoulder and said, "No need. You should rest after that injury."

"I'll be fine," he said, and shot to his feet, but Sara caught the slight wince as he did so.

She helped as they all cleaned off the table, put away what was left of the takeout and Trey prepped a large pot of coffee.

In no time the table was clear, and Sophie and Robbie had popped open their laptops to demonstrate what they planned to do.

Sophie turned on the large television on the opposite wall of the room, and a second later an image from one of the laptops filled the screen: a satellite view of the kennels.

"If you're ready, we'll get started," Robbie said, and with a few keystrokes a dotted line appeared along the edges of the woods behind the main buildings on the property.

With a laser pointer, Sophie highlighted the line on the screen. "As we mentioned before, perimeter cameras should work here like they did at the *Buena Suerte* stables a few months back. I'm not sure we need security guards working the area at this time."

"I agree," Trey said, and gestured for Robbie to continue.

"We can place a driveway alarm on the new sign you plan on putting in," he said, and an X showed up by the entrance to mark the location of the alarm.

"Sounds good so far," Trey commented, and Robbie switched to a view that displayed the owner's home, kennels, training ring and outbuildings.

"For the house, glass break, entry and motion sensors as well as hazard sensors for smoke, fire and water leaks. Sirens, of course," Sophie said.

"Of course," Jose muttered beneath his breath, but Sophie pushed on with her suggestions.

"We'll also have security cameras and floodlights positioned to monitor the area around the house, kennels and training ring."

She stopped and glanced at Trey and seemingly knew what he was about to ask since she said, "We can get the house done tomorrow. The other locations will take a few days."

"Good. How about prepping the house so Sara can live there?" he asked Mia.

"As I mentioned before, we have a cleaning crew scheduled in the a.m. The house first and then the other areas," Mia replied and then continued. "Painters are coming tomorrow and once they're done, I'll call for the delivery of the furniture Sara and I selected."

"It seems like you've thought of everything," Sara said, grateful for their thoroughness in getting the location ready for her.

"We've tried. I just wish we'd thought about any possible dangers on the property before sending the two of you there unprotected," Trey said, regret in his voice.

"You couldn't have known," Jose said, his earlier anger and frustration missing.

"*Gracias*, for that, Pepe. It was probably a freak explosion, but we should have checked everything at an abandoned location like the kennels. From now on, we don't assume anything. We take every step as if we're on a case. Understood?" Trey said, and peered around the table at everyone.

Chapter Five

"Understood," Jose said half-heartedly, echoing what everyone else said and surprising Sara with his agreement.

With that decided, Mia, Sophie and Robbie went off to work while Trey hung back with her and Jose. "I want to take a look at that shoulder."

"What about Ricky? When will he psychoanalyze us?" Jose said with an arch of a brow.

Trey tightened his lips into a thin slash. "It didn't sound like you were too keen on talking, so I asked him to come by another night."

"You called him off?" Jose said, anger surging to the forefront at his cousin's controlling actions.

"Isn't that what you wanted?" Trey challenged.

Sara felt as if she was watching two rams in rut going after each other and so did Bongo, who raised her head in response to the vibes. Sara stepped in to lower the temperature of the discussion. "We appreciate that, Trey. I know I'd like to get some rest, and I'm sure Jose feels the same way. Right?"

Her words had the desired effect as the tension in their bodies melted before her eyes and Bongo laid her head back down on her paws.

"I'd like to get some rest. Maybe after you take a look at my shoulder, Trey," Jose said to further defuse the situation.

Trey nodded. "Sure thing. I have some first aid things in the bathroom," he said, and motioned in the direction of the room where she had been staying.

Because of that, she trailed after the two men to make sure she hadn't left anything too personal out in the bedroom or bathroom.

Luckily all was in order as the two men hurried into the bathroom where Jose peeled off the sweatshirt, revealing a nicely sculpted chest and lean six-pack abs.

Heat ignited in her core. There was no denying Jose was a very attractive man but at this point in her life, she wasn't interested. Her entire focus was on getting this K-9 center up and running. Nothing else, she thought, but couldn't pull her eyes away as Jose turned so that Trey could inspect his injuries.

"The EMT did a good job. There's a little swelling, but it should go down soon. I'll check again in the morning," he said and continued. "I keep some sweats and things in the other bedroom you can use tonight. I'll bring by more clothes for you in the morning."

"I'd rather head home tonight," Jose said, but Trey shook his head.

"And I'd rather we kept an eye on you until we know there are no other repercussions from the explosion," Trey insisted.

Jose hesitated, clearly not happy, but then relented and nodded. "Fine. I'd appreciate you getting some things from my condo," Jose said, and thankfully jerked the sweatshirt back on, hiding that too tempting masculinity from her gaze. Once he had done that, he reached into his pants pocket, took out some keys and handed them to Trey.

"We'll be at work for a while on the security details, but you can call me at any time if you need something," Trey said, and waved his cell phone in the air in emphasis.

"Anytime?" Jose said with an arch of a dark brow.

"Anytime. I am always here for you, Pepe," Trey said, and with that he rushed from the room, leaving the two of them standing there in awkward silence. Staring at each other through the reflection in the bathroom mirror.

"He sure knows how to make me feel guilty," Jose said, and faced her.

"I don't think that was his intent," Sara said, feeling as if she'd stepped into a minefield of family dynamics.

"Probably not. Trey has always been up front but that doesn't change how I feel whenever I'm around this side of the family," Jose admitted with a stilted shrug.

Not that she wanted to play psychologist like Ricky, but she wanted to know why this seemingly successful and handsome man had such issues with his cousins.

"How do they make you feel?" she asked as they walked out of the bathroom and back into the living room area.

Jose whirled to face her, a surprised look on his face. "You really want to know?"

She nodded. "I do. If I'm going to be working with them and you, I'd like to know what makes the Gonzalez family tick."

Jose shook his head and chuckled. "It may take all night."

"Then maybe I should get us some drinks," she said, jumped to her feet and walked to the wet bar at one side of the room.

Jose tossed out his selection as he settled himself on the couch. "Scotch over ice, if there is any, *por favor*."

There was definitely scotch, top shelf at that, as well as several bottles of other high-quality liquors. The Gonzalez family didn't skimp on anything for themselves or their guests.

She poured two fingers of scotch into a highball glass with ice and then a glass of wine from a bottle she'd opened the day before. She walked to the sofa, handed Jose the glass and sat opposite him in a large comfy chair.

He raised the glass and said, "To the new K-9 center."

Tapping her glass against his, she said, "To working together."

His lips quirked into a twisted smile as he said, "For now."

It bothered her he was in such a rush to leave, not that she should be bothered. After all, she barely knew him and yet... She wanted to know him better. He had possibly saved her life after all.

"For now," she echoed and pushed on. "So tell me. How do your cousins make you feel?"

A sharp blast of laughter escaped him. "Seriously?" he challenged and sipped his scotch.

"Seriously," she said, and cocked her head to peer at him, not wanting to miss any nuance of his answer.

He tilted his head from side to side, as if searching for an answer. But then the words burst from his mouth in a rush. "Guilty. Sad. Needy. Inferior."

"Wow," shot from her mouth before she could control it.

Jose shook his head and murmured. "*Sí*, wow. A lot to unfold, right?"

Since he'd shared and she got where he was coming from, she said, "I feel the same way sometimes. Guilty that I didn't go into the family business. Sad that they don't get me. Definitely inferior since I'm not hauling in some six or maybe even seven figure salary."

"But you're doing something you love, which means way more than money," Jose said.

Sara barked out a laugh. "Tell that to my bank account."

Jose leaned toward her, glass cradled between his hands. "Seriously, Sara. It does mean more, and you know it."

This close, she could see the rays of green in his amazing blue eyes and the dark stubble of an evening beard along the strong line of his jaw. As his gaze locked with hers, her stomach did a little flip-flop, and she took a sip of her wine to settle it.

"I know it does and so do you. It's why you have your own business instead of working with SBS."

"Well, that and the bullets," he teased and sat back.

She got it. Her dive into the family history before taking the job had warned about how risky SBS business could be in more ways than one. The bullets, of course, but also the regular exposure to the limelight with both their cases and the scrutiny that came from being that well-known. Such scrutiny had almost destroyed her family. But that worry hadn't stopped her from the opportunity of a lifetime. All she had to do was stick to her job and not get too involved with the Gonzalez family.

Or Jose, the little voice in her head warned.

"I was sad to leave my family in New Jersey, but I knew it was the right thing to do."

"Do you miss them? You're a long way from home," Jose said.

She nodded. "I do, but I'll go home for Thanksgiving in a few weeks, and I have some cousins in Miami. I'll visit them once I get settled."

"Because family is important," he said, sadness evident in the tone of his voice.

"Why does that seem to make you sad?" she asked.

He ripped his gaze from her to peer down into his glass as if it held the answer. With another awkward shake of his head, he said, "I sometimes wish I did want to be part of SBS. Work with them. Understand why they do what they do."

"Now's your chance." The words escaped her before she could bite them back.

Chapter Six

A chance? Jose wondered, and the words echoed in his brain, on and on and on. A chance he'd never wanted to take, only he'd promised his Tio Ramon he would help. But this woman presented another level of risk that had him reconsidering so much.

With a dip of his head in a semi-nod, he said, "I did sell them the property after all."

"You did," she said, and raised her glass in a toast.

"I will help you get the place ready. I know some good contractors who can assist with any work that needs to be done, like the new surfaces in the training ring and obstacle course."

She smiled, seemingly pleased that he'd remembered. "Help with the surfaces would be greatly appreciated."

He grinned and nodded. "A good real estate agency always remembers what a client wants."

Her smile faded, which made him quickly add, "Not that you're just a client."

"I'm not sure how to take that right now, but I'll assume it's a good thing," she said, and her smile brightened a bit.

"It's a good thing," he replied although he was still uncertain about what he was feeling around her. She was attractive, but not his usual type. Smart. SBS only hired the best, and he had to assume she fell into that category. Compassionate and maybe that came from dealing with animals and sensing what was going on without words being spoken. Or maybe it was because of what had happened with her father and the scrutiny she'd had to survive.

But as their gazes locked and his gut tightened with a very physical sign of desire, confusion erupted again about what was going on between them.

He shot to his feet and drew Bongo's attention with the sudden movement.

"I'm going to call it a night," he said.

She gave the dog a hand gesture, as if to reassure Bongo all was fine, and slowly came to her feet. "Good night, then. I'm going to take Bongo for a walk before we turn in."

"I'll go with. It's not as busy in this area at night, and I'd rather you didn't go alone," he said, and even though it was the truth, it was also in part that despite his earlier words, he wasn't ready to leave her just yet.

"*Gracias.* I'd appreciate that until I'm more familiar with the city," she said, and signaled to Bongo.

At the door, she grabbed a leash she'd set on an entry table and clipped it on. Using her security badge, she opened the elevator doors.

"Who else has a badge besides Trey?" he asked.

"Only Trey and Mia, and they've been really good about respecting my privacy after hours."

Good to know, while also being a challenge that the two of them were here alone with complete privacy.

Not that he was a hookup on the first date guy. Not that this was a date, which made him wonder what it would be like to take her on a date.

They rode down to street level, cleared the security desk in the main lobby and strolled out to Brickell Avenue.

MUCH LIKE JOSE had said, the area was not as busy as it had been during the day, Sara thought. "I guess this is mostly a business area?"

"Mostly although there are some residential buildings farther up," he said, and walked beside her and Bongo, matching his longer stride to hers. He'd tucked his hands into the pockets of his dress pants, which were smudged with dirt and grass from when they'd hit the ground earlier that day. Which reminded her of his injuries.

"How's the shoulder?"

"A little tender but getting better. How about you? Still achy?"

She had been sore immediately after the blast, but like him, the aftereffects were passing. "Better. Not so bad, but I suspect I may have a few bruises in the morning."

A wry smile crept across his lips. "You and me both. Hopefully tomorrow won't be as eventful as today."

"Hopefully," she said as Bongo sniffed at a spot on the curb and then paused to relieve herself.

She pulled out a poop bag but as she bent to clean up the mess, Jose said, "Let me."

He took the bag from her, secured the waste and tied the bag.

"*Gracias*. You didn't have to," she said as they walked back toward the SBS building.

"Not a problem. I do it for my *mami* all the time when we walk her dog," he said but held the bag gingerly, clearly not a fan.

Much like she wasn't much of a fan of being lumped in with his mother, who she assumed was a wonderful lady. It was as bad or maybe worse than being friend-zoned. Momzoned. So not good even though it was way too early to be thinking of him like that. Or maybe not too early as an image of him bare-chested filled her brain.

He dumped the bag in a trash can at the sidewalk's edge, they entered the lobby, cleared security, and went up to the penthouse. Once there, she unclipped Bongo's leash but her dog remained close, obviously uncomfortable with Jose, although bloodhounds were generally not protective.

Jose seemed uneasy around the dog since he kept some distance between them once they were in the center of the large living space.

"I guess this is good-night. Get some rest," he said, and with an awkward wave, he rushed off but then stopped as he neared her bedroom door.

"I never got where I'm supposed to sleep," he said sheepishly.

Sara pointed down the hall. "There are two bedrooms farther down. The spare clothes that Trey mentioned are in the one right past mine."

"Great," he said and walked off, leaving her alone in the immense space with Bongo.

She knelt and rubbed the dog's ears. "He's a good guy, Bongo. No need to worry," she said, and reached into her jeans pocket to pull out a treat for her dog.

Bongo quickly took the treat, leaving slobber all over her hand. She laughed and shook her head. "You are drooly, but you're my drooly baby. Let's get some sleep."

She signaled to Bongo who followed her into the bedroom where she'd set up a big circular dog bed for the bloodhound. As soon as she closed the door, Bongo went to the bed, circled around a time or two, and finally lay down, satisfied that everything was fine.

Except, of course, for the fact that Sara had nearly gotten blown up and still had a little soreness from being hauled to the ground. Soreness that a nice hot shower would help.

She went into the bathroom and turned on the hot water in the shower. Water spewed from not only a rain shower feature, but from the side walls and as she stepped in, the heat of the water soothed the physical remnants of the explosion.

The emotional remnants would be harder to handle.

She could have died. Jose could have died.

Jose had saved her life. Jose who didn't think he could be an action hero like his cousin Trey, and yet he had been just that this afternoon.

He was complex, she told herself while she showered, running soapy hands across her body, lingering at the tender spots.

Unfortunately, he was also a lot like the men she'd grown up with. Privileged and pampered. Part of the SBS family, no matter how much he denied it. Getting involved with him meant being more involved with the family, which had its own issues. But despite that, he was intriguing her more than he should.

But she reminded herself that he was only there because of a sense of obligation to his family. Once he finished doing whatever they expected of him, he'd be gone just like the boyfriend she'd had when her father had been accused of the embezzling. He'd run at the first hint of trouble.

That was a good thing to remember, she told herself as she let the heat of the water calm her jumbled thoughts about Jose.

When she finally left the shower, peace had settled over her. She slipped into her pajamas and bed, but as soon as she climbed beneath the sheets, her phone rang.

Her mother was calling.

She was tempted to ignore it, but knew she'd only keep on calling.

"*Hola, mami,*" she said.

"*Hola*, Sara. Your *Tia* Rosario called—"

Tia Rosario who was a terrible gossip and had likely seen the news about the explosion on the local Miami news. "I'm okay, *mami*. It was nothing big."

"It was an explosion, *mi'ja*. I thought this work was supposed to be safer than the search and rescue you were doing," she said.

"It is. It will be. Not to worry," she said, and quickly

tacked on the one thing she knew would placate her mother. "I can't wait to see you in a few weeks for Thanksgiving."

Her mother's harrumph burst across the line, but she'd been mollified by Sara's words. "See you soon, *mi'ja*. Love you."

"I love you too, *mami*," she said, and swiped to end the call.

She flipped on the television to relax, lay back onto the pillows and sleep slowly claimed her. But with sleep came unexpected dreams about Jose until the chirp of her phone warned it was time to start the day.

She brushed her teeth and hair, dressed quickly and rushed out to make a pot of coffee, but Jose had beaten her to it.

He stood by the counter, bare-chested in sweats that hung loosely on his lean hips.

When he saw her, he ran a hand through the rumpled locks of his hair and beamed her a smile. *"Buenos dias."*

And damn, she had to admit that waking to him there was definitely a good start to the day.

JOSE UNLOCKED THE door to the owner's home and did a quick look around the empty interior on the first floor as Mia, Sara, Bongo and a trio of cleaning people followed him inside.

A fine layer of dust covered everything along with some dirt on the floor. The air smelled musty, a testament to how long the home had been empty.

"The owners renovated about ten years ago to create this open space and a half bath," he said, easily slipping into real-estate-agent mode to describe the spacious ground floor, which was relatively clean considering it had been vacant for nearly three years.

"There is also a home office on the other side of this floor, a large, finished basement with a playroom and workshop downstairs, and three bedrooms upstairs with two bathrooms. They're not as updated as this area," he said with a wave toward the stairs.

Mia jammed her hands on her hips and did a quick look around the space. "This is a nice layout. Maybe we should start upstairs?" she said, and turned to the cleaning crew.

"Makes sense since we may track dirt through this area as we clean," replied an older woman with the cleaners. She gestured to the other two women to head upstairs, leaving him alone with Sara, Mia and Bongo, who sniffed around the edges of the room.

He held the keys to the home up in the air. "I guess you should get these. There are three keys to the front door. They also open the back door. You might want to change out the locks, though."

Mia nodded and took the keys. "That's a good idea. I'll call someone to come in today."

"*Gracias*, for everything," Sara said. She laid a hand on his arm and smiled.

"*De nada*. I'm sure the two of you have things to—"

A bloodcurdling scream cut through the air and echoed in the emptiness of the home's rooms.

One of the cleaners, a young woman barely out of her teens, ran down the stairs, stumbling so badly on the last one that Jose had to reach out to stop her from face-planting onto the floor.

"*Brujeria*," the young girl said, seemingly worried about witchcraft, and glanced back up the stairs as the older woman came down carrying a garbage bag filled with something.

"It was a few doves. A Santeria sacrifice probably. Nothing to worry about," she explained, and hurried out the door.

Jose was a little freaked out about the sacrifice but even more worried about the fact that someone had had the time inside the house to do it. "It's a good thing Sophie and Robbie will be securing this place," he said, and gave his attention to the young cleaning girl.

"No te preocupes. Todo estará bien," he said, telling the young woman not to worry just as her boss returned and commanded her to go back to work with a sharp jerk of her head.

The girl timidly went along, but not before shooting him a look mixed with gratefulness and fear.

"Sophie and Robbie should be here soon," Mia said and as if they'd heard her, his cousins entered with a duo of the SBS techs.

Sophie and Robbie came over to hug them all—family always came first even on a job—and then Sophie asked, "Is the cleaning crew here?"

Mia gestured with a perfectly manicured finger in Barbie-pink. "Upstairs."

Sophie nodded. "We'll start on this floor and then outside. We'll be done by the end of the day."

"Great. I'll feel better knowing this place is secured," Sara said, and signaled Bongo back to her side since the bloodhound had drifted toward the back of the kitchen with her sniffing.

Bongo hurried back and dutifully sat at Sara's side. The dog's head nearly reached Sara's waist, making Jose wonder how she controlled such a large animal, but clearly she was the boss, sparking admiration for her skills and that dangerous curl of interest again.

"Maybe we should tour the rest of the grounds so we can see what else needs to be done," he said, needing space. Despite the stale air inside the home, Sara's clean and flowery scent had drifted over to him, making him want to bury his head in the sensitive crook of her neck to see if it was either her skin or the waves of silky hair that smelled so good.

"That's a great idea," Sara said, and almost raced out of the house.

Mia shot him a wondering look and he shrugged, trying to play it cool as he held his hand out and urged Mia to follow Sara.

SARA SUCKED IN a deep breath, clearing out the dank smell inside the home and thoughts of what else besides doves might have been inside the garbage bag the cleaning woman had brought out and tossed by the back of her crew's van.

Being part Cuban, she heard about Santeria, and her mother had on more than one occasion done something that hinted to at least a passing belief in some things, like leaving a tasty treat for a patron saint during the holidays. But sacrifices were a whole different thing and the fact that someone had done it in the house...

She shuddered and hoped there wouldn't be more unwelcome surprises.

"You okay?" Jose said, and laid a comforting hand on her shoulder.

She nodded shakily. "Not a fan of animal sacrifice."

"I get it, but as awful as we think it is, it could have been done for good reasons. Maybe to help heal someone," he said, trying to relieve her worries.

"Still not a fan," Sara said, and Mia echoed her reaction. "Totally agree. Not a fan."

"Let's check out the rest of the grounds," Jose said.

"Let's," she concurred and glanced at Mia to see if she intended to join them.

"I'm going to hang back here in case Sophie and Robbie need anything or the painters arrive early," Mia said.

"Sounds good, *prima*. We won't be long," Jose said, and gestured for her to lead the way.

"I want to measure the training ring first since that's the most important thing for now," she said, then clicked her tongue to get Bongo moving and walked toward the building directly opposite the former kennel owner's home. As she did so, she caught sight of Trey who was directing a cleaning crew in the area.

Something pulled her in that direction, and she motioned to the kennels and said, "Do you mind if we check first?"

"Not at all. Whatever you need," Jose said, surprising her with his willingness considering how opposed he had been to helping his SBS family.

When they arrived, the cleaners were armed with rakes and brooms to clear out the debris in the enclosures where the dogs would be housed.

A man entered an enclosure and raked the leaves when a loud clang rang out in the empty kennels and was chased by his cry of alarm.

The man stepped back with the rake or rather, what was left of the rake as the head of it had been snapped off.

Trey urged the man aside so that Jose and she could see what had happened.

A large bear trap had bitten off the bottom of the rake. Fear shivered through her at what the trap might have done if the man had stepped into it.

"So not good," she murmured.

"Totally agree," Trey said, and then called out to the cleaning crew.

"Everyone please clear out until we can confirm it's safe in here."

"Are you worried about more traps?" Jose asked, face set in harsh lines.

Trey nodded. "There's no reason for a trap like that to be in here."

"Or for that Santeria offering to be in the house," Sara said.

"What offering?" Trey asked, worry coloring his tones.

"Some doves in one of the upstairs bedrooms," Jose said, and waved a hand in the direction of the house.

Trey shook his head. "This is not right. We need to get

everyone out of there," he said and took a step toward the house, but then a loud bang erupted from a chimney on the exterior wall of the house and smoke billowed into the air.

Chapter Seven

Before Jose's eyes the chimney crumbled, bricks raining down on the overgrown grass beside the house.

A second later, Mia, Sophie, Robbie and their crews raced out of the house, thankfully uninjured.

Trey and Sara took off in their direction, Bongo loping behind them, ears flapping.

Jose paused for a moment, frozen by shock, followed by his mind asking *Why?*

Why was this happening, he thought as he likewise rushed across the yard to where everyone had gathered outside the home.

Mia, Trey and Sara had peered at the pile of bricks that had once been the chimney. Sophie and Robbie drifted over after apparently giving their crew some instructions as they walked to the SBS vehicle.

He joined them and said, "I'm assuming this wasn't some kind of freak accident again."

Trey knelt and peered intently at the ruined chimney. He pointed to a blackened area close to the ground. "That's where the clean-out door for the ash dump would be. They probably put the bomb in there knowing it would take out most of the support for the chimney."

"If it was a bomb, does the same go for the outbuilding

that blew up?" Jose said, still trying to grasp that someone was working real hard to hurt them.

Trey slowly rose and faced them. "I'm going to call my contacts at the police department. See if they have anything else on that outbuilding explosion."

"HOOWEE," HE MUTTERED in low tones as he delighted in the destruction he'd wrought.

A pile of bricks was all that remained of the chimney, and he had to admit that he hadn't thought the small bomb he'd placed there could do so much damage.

He'd only intended that and his other little surprises to scare them off but if the looks on their faces said anything, it was that they had no intention of leaving.

Muttering a curse beneath his breath, he took a last look at the group gathered around the ruined chimney.

He was going to have to up his game with this crew, he thought, and skulked away back through the hardwood hammock, careful to hide his trail as he did so.

ALTHOUGH THE EXPLOSION had taken out the chimney, it had surprisingly done minimal damage inside the home.

To make sure there weren't any more surprises waiting for them, Trey had done a careful inspection of the home with Sara and Bongo trailing after him. Besides being great at search and rescue, Bongo had received basic training in locating explosives and cadavers and would hopefully pick up on any other dangers in the home.

After declaring it safe, the cleaning crew returned along with Sophie, Robbie and their team.

While the tech team secured the location, the rest of the team, including Jose, gathered on the first floor.

They all had their serious faces on, especially Jose whose arms were tucked tight across his chest, obviously in defensive mode. She understood. Everything that was happening was probably his worst nightmare since it made it harder to pull away from SBS. It was her worst nightmare also because it would bring media scrutiny and possibly put her in the spotlight. Maybe even revive stories about her father and his problems.

"They say the simplest explanation is usually the right one," Trey said.

"And the simplest explanation is that someone wants you off this property," Jose said, obviously getting where Trey was going.

"Can you think of any reason for that?" Trey asked, skewering Jose with his gaze.

Pursing his lips in thought, Jose nodded and said, "There had been a developer with some interest, but he lowballed the owners."

"Did he try to outbid us?" Mia asked and narrowed her gaze to consider Jose as he answered.

Jose shrugged and shook his head. "As far as I know, we were the only bidders after the owners turned him down, but I can find out."

Trey nodded. "When you do that, can you ask them if they had anything weird going on while they were here?"

"Do you think they would admit it?" Sara asked, fairly certain that a seller wouldn't reveal anything that could possibly dissuade a prospective buyer.

"They'd have to tell us about major issues, but minor harassment…" Jose said and dipped his head in doubt.

"Not sure explosions are minor harassment," Mia challenged, obviously worried about all that was happening.

"I'll find out," Jose told her, everything about his demeanor in defensive mode. Without waiting for any other comments, he whirled and strode out the door, his choppy strides matching the fact that he was clearly upset.

"It's not his fault," she said to the family members in the room.

"We know it's not," Trey said, but then wagged his head from side to side. "We get a little intense when we're on a case."

"Is that what this is now? A case?" she said, although she had no doubt that buying this property had somehow become more than just setting up the new K-9 center.

"It is, but don't worry. We will handle it," Mia said, and everyone around echoed her comment.

"And I will as well. I'm part of the team now, and I'll do whatever you need on this case," she said despite her worries about being in the public eye. She rubbed Bongo's head as her dog sidled up to her and bumped Sara with her head, sensing her upset and the tension in the room.

Mia reached out and laid a hand on her arm. "*Gracias*, Sara. We knew we'd hired the right person to join us."

"*Sí, gracias.* We appreciate anything you can do. In the meantime, I'm going to call the local PD and see what they have on the outbuilding blast," Trey said, and walked to the far side of the room to make his call.

As he did so, Jose marched back in, body set in stiff lines. Face all sharp angles. His gaze locked with hers, the sunny blue of his eyes now the stormy blue of turmoil.

He approached the group gathered there and said, "I spoke to the Florians. They confirmed a developer had put in a bid but dropped out once we expressed interest. As for anything funky, not a thing as long as they lived here."

"Unless they're not saying. Did you doubt what they told you?" Mia asked.

Jose shook his head. "Not at all. They struck me as honest people when we were negotiating, and nothing's changed my opinion."

"We trust your opinion. *Gracias* for reaching out to them,"

Mia said, mindful of Sara's earlier comments about Jose's role in what was now a case.

JOSE APPRECIATED MIA'S gratefulness and trust but that barely diminished the guilt he was feeling at getting his family involved in a property that was causing them so many problems.

"Whatever I can do, *prima*. We need to figure out what's going on."

"We?" Mia asked, her perfectly manicured brows narrowed in question.

"We, *prima*. I got you into this mess, and I plan on helping you get out of it," he said, feeling at fault for their current situation.

Trey returned to the group at that moment, face set in dour lines. "No fingerprints anywhere, but PD thinks they found the bits and pieces of a detonator as well as trace amounts of ammonium nitrate."

"Which is found in fertilizer, right?" Sara asked while Bongo sat dutifully beside her.

"It is, and I'm assuming we'll have traces of that in what's left of the chimney," Trey said, and glanced at Jose. "The simplest explanation is that this developer wants us gone."

"And any of his landscapers would have access to fertilizer," Jose stated.

"I guess we have our first suspect," Sara said.

"LET'S WORK ON securing the location," Trey said, and peered at Jose intently.

"Are you sure you want in on this?" he asked his cousin.

Jose nodded. "I'm in on this. I'll call around discreetly and try to find out more about this developer."

"That would be great, Jose. We appreciate anything you can do," Trey said, and there was no doubting the gratitude and support in his voice.

"I'll call the painters and hold off on any work until we secure this location," Mia said, and stepped away to phone the company.

"What can Bongo and I do right now?" Sara said, needing to do something while the rest of the team was at work.

Trey nodded and smiled, clearly pleased by her request. "I think the two of us should patrol the perimeter of the house and the remaining grounds."

"I want to go with," Jose said, earning a hairy eyeball from Trey.

"I need to know what's going on," Jose insisted.

"What about those calls?" Trey argued.

Jose raised his phone and said, "Mobile, remember?"

Trey sucked in a breath, as if preparing to challenge him again, but then relented. "Just keep back and don't distract us."

Sara knew he didn't mean the words to cut Jose down to size but as Jose drew his shoulders back and stood straighter, she had no doubt that's how he'd taken it. Despite that, Jose followed them outside, and Sara released her hold on the leash to let Bongo walk ahead and sniff around the outside of the house.

The dog moved decisively in the overgrown grasses, shifting from the foundation of the building to a few feet away under Sara's guidance.

Her dog did nothing to signal that there was something to worry about as they zigzagged from the house to the grass over and over until they reached the rubble of the chimney. There Bongo shifted to the bricks and took a long time to sniff before finally laying down close to the house.

"She smells the explosive," Sara said, and glanced past Trey to meet Jose's gaze.

"That's amazing. Did you train her to do that?" he said.

"I took classes with another trainer so that Bongo and I would be certified for that and cadaver location, but my main focus has always been search and rescue operations and training people to do that," she admitted, not wanting to misrepresent her skills.

"Still amazing," he said.

Trey repeated the compliment and pointed to the kennel area. "Do you feel comfortable checking the kennels?"

Sara examined the area. There was thick grass in and around the building, presenting the biggest danger if their assailant had laid more bear traps there, but otherwise the area seemed manageable.

"I do. Let's clear it so we can focus on the other buildings after," she said, and the three of them hurried there but slowed as they neared.

As she had before, she instructed Bongo to search, but kept her on a short leash and carefully perused the area before she let Bongo move in just in case.

Jose stayed close while Trey was a few feet away, inspecting the ground ahead of them. As he did so, he said, "We should get all this overgrown lawn cut down so it's harder to hide anything and to keep down the mosquitos."

"I have a landscaper we can call in once we know it's safe," Jose offered.

"Appreciate the help," Trey said, clearly trying to calm the waters with his cousin.

Chapter Eight

Jose tried not to take Trey's words as being condescending. His cousin had always been an upfront guy, and he took his statement at face value.

"Where do we go next?" he asked Sara.

She looked at the grounds and said, "Let's go near the woods and work our way back toward the training ring."

"I'll follow your lead," he said, not that he wouldn't be on his toes considering all that had happened in the last two days. He only hoped he wouldn't end the day with even more injuries.

They moved cautiously toward the line of trees surrounding the property. They were part of the parcel that SBS had bought as well as some farmland beyond the hardwood hammock. It made him wonder whether whoever was leaving them the little surprises was located in those woods or beyond.

Because of that, he said, "There's more land beyond these trees that belongs to the kennels. Do you think Bongo could pick up our suspect's scent and track it there?"

Sara peered over her shoulder at him and nodded. "If we can identify the suspect's scent, Bongo can track it for miles."

"Good to know," he said, and followed her as they slowly moved to the tree line, vigilant for any traps. When they neared the woods, Sara stopped and pulled Bongo back. Kneeling, she examined something, then rose and pointed to the ground.

He leaned forward and noticed a thin wire running about six inches above the ground. "Is that a trip wire?" he asked, not that he would know a booby trap from any old wire.

"Or a remnant of an electrical fence. Can you call the former owners to see if they had anything like that?" Sara asked.

"I can. What about in the meantime?"

Sara pulled a brightly colored waste bag from a pouch on her leash and tied it to a small branch near the wire. As she rose, she pulled out her cell phone. "I'll call the others to warn them."

He waited as she did so, and then they worked their way to the training ring.

As she had before, Sara kept a tight leash on Bongo until she had determined there weren't any dangers in the area. Everything went smoothly until Bongo reached a spot directly behind the building. The bloodhound hesitated at that point, eagerly sniffing around the foundation before tugging Sara away from the building to a spot several feet away.

"What's wrong?" he asked as Bongo circled around and around a spot, nose down in the thick grasses growing there. A second later, the dog lay down, signaling Sara that she had found something.

"WHAT IS IT?" Jose asked, a puzzled look on his face.

Sara didn't know what to make of Bongo's behavior unless a lot of fertilizer was in the area or worse, a cadaver was buried there.

She didn't discount that maybe someone had skipped the proper routes to bury a dead dog, but there was only one way to find out.

"Bongo is scenting either fertilizer or a decaying body. Did you notice a shovel anywhere?"

"I think the cleaning crew left one by the kennels. I'll go get it," he said, and carefully retraced their steps to avoid any surprises.

While he got the shovel, she cautiously parted the grass in the area Bongo had identified and noticed there was one section where the ground seemed slightly mounded, as if it had been dug up and patted back down.

Kneeling there, she rubbed Bongo's head and fed her a treat from a pouch on the leash. "Good girl, Bongo. What did you smell?"

Her dog let out a low woof and rubbed her head against Sara's leg before pawing the ground before her again.

Sara hoped it was just fertilizer, but the way the ground had been torn up had her worried about what they would find.

She stood, inspecting the area once more as Jose approached, shovel in hand.

"Where should I dig?"

She gestured to the spot where she had yanked away the overgrown lawn.

"Right there but be careful. It could be more than just fertilizer."

He drove the shovel into the ground gingerly and picked up a large clump of grass and the red clay prized by the farmers in the area.

Tossing it aside, he dug into the earth in small chunks mindful that it could be another bomb. He flung clumps of grass and soil to the side until he was about a foot deep. So far there had been nothing, to Sara's immense relief.

"Should I keep going?" he asked as they peered into the hole he'd made.

She wanted to call off the digging, only Bongo once again

pawed the ground and looked up at her with mournful eyes, as if to say, "Why don't you trust me?"

"Sara?" he prompted, waiting for her instruction.

"Bongo says we should dig some more," she said, and rubbed her dog's head almost apologetically.

Beads of sweat dotted Jose's forehead. Dark rings of perspiration marred the armpits of the new guayabera shirt Trey had brought him that morning to replace his ruined one. With a nod, however, he drove the shovel in again, wincing. Reminding her of the injuries to his shoulder.

"I can dig if you want," she said, feeling guilty, but he just shook his head and jammed the shovel in a little more forcefully.

A slight thunk, as if he'd hit wood or something, had Jose pausing and glancing down at the hole. More carefully, he used the shovel tip to clear the soil and after he did so, he reared back and muttered a curse.

Sara rushed to his side and peered down.

The empty orbital sockets in a skull peeked up at her from the dirt.

THE SBS CREW huddled around the excavation and the near dozen police officers working in and around the hole.

CSI officers, suited up to prevent contamination, carefully removed bones and placed them in evidence bags. Every now and then bits and pieces of fabric emerged from the soil that had kept its secrets for so long.

Beside him Sara wavered a bit and Jose wrapped an arm around her shoulders, offering support and comfort.

He understood how she was feeling. He felt as if the ground beneath his feet was disintegrating and threatening to swallow him whole.

"What do we do now?" he said, and shot a look at Trey, who stood beside him, body tense. Arms wrapped across his chest.

"We wait for the ME's report and see what they have to say about the victim," Trey said.

But then one of the CSI officers, possibly having heard him, called out, "Victims. There are two."

The man held up a second skull.

Jose's stomach turned and a sour taste filled his mouth.

As if sensing that it was getting to be too much for everyone, not just Jose, Trey said, "Let's head back to the house and brainstorm this."

The group ambled toward the home, heads occasionally turning to look toward the training ring and the police officers assembled there.

Inside the building, they drifted toward the kitchen. Trey and Mia leaned on one set of counters while Sophie and Robbie snagged stools at the island that separated the kitchen from the rest of the open concept space.

Sara and Jose stood opposite them with Bongo tucked close to Sara's side.

Trey motioned toward the bloodhound. "Bongo did a good job."

Sara nodded and rubbed the dog's head. "She did only… We just sit and wait for the ME's report?"

Trey tipped his head to one side, as if considering his answer, but then finally said, "Once we have information on the victims, we see what connection they have to the kennels."

Firmly settling his gaze on him, Trey said, "Pepe. You said you'd call the owners for info."

Jose nodded. "I will, not that they'll admit they know about a grave with two women."

"How do you know it's women?" Mia immediately challenged.

"It almost always is, isn't it?" he said sadly and quickly added, "But I also noticed one of the CSI people pulling out what looked like a bra."

"Good catch," Mia said.

"Let's run with that. Two women, and they've been missing for some time given the state of decay," Trey said.

"How hard will it be for the police to ID them?" Jose asked.

Trey shrugged. "It depends."

"On?" Jose queried.

"On whether anyone even cared that they were gone," Mia said sharply and as he met her gaze, he noted the mix of sadness and anger there.

Puzzled, Jose said, "I don't get it."

It was Sara who piped up with an explanation. "They could be runaways, maybe sex workers. Women living on the fringes of society."

"Women no one would miss," he said, finally understanding the sadness in Mia's gaze.

"Let's start with that," Trey said, and jerked his chin in the direction of their tech guru cousins. "Can you get lists and photos of any women who were reported missing in the last five years?"

"What about the sex workers?" Jose said.

"Harder to do without knowing where they might be strolling. Can you ask the owners about their former employees? Especially any young female workers who might have suddenly 'quit,'" Trey said, using air quotes on the "quit" part.

Jose nodded. "I'll call as soon as we're done here."

"*Bueno.* We'll leave Sophie, Robbie and their crew to finish up while the rest of us head to the office," Trey said, and pushed away from the counter.

The rest of the team flew into action, but Sara hesitated and said, "What if there's more than just these two?"

Chapter Nine

He wanted to howl out his frustration, but instead all he could do was mutter repeated curses as he stared through the scope of the crossbow at the crowd gathered around the garden home for his first two kills.

He shouldn't have planted them so close to the training ring only he'd been lazy, and when some plumbers had made the hole to fix a problem with the drain, he'd figured, "Why not?"

As soon as the plumbers had finished and gone, he'd dumped the women he'd been keeping at his place and filled in the hole.

No one had been the wiser.

Until now...

The stream of curses escaped him, audible only to him thanks to the distance to the property.

He had hoped that the little gifts he'd left for the dandy and his friends might have discouraged them from staying. Especially the traps he'd laid around the perimeter, only the pretty woman with the bloodhound had discovered one of them.

That was bad.

If they bypassed those traps and used that bloodhound to search the woods...

He couldn't let that happen.

As he watched one of the SBS equipment vans drive away, he leaned back against a tree trunk to wait them out.

Once the rest were gone and night had fallen, he'd work on protecting his garden.

SARA SCROLLED THROUGH the photos of the missing women that Sophie and Robbie had pulled together while also overseeing the techs working on the location's security.

So many faces, she thought. Young ones. Old ones. Every race.

So many lost souls.

The snick of a door opening had her staring toward the back bedroom where Jose had gone to call the former kennel owners.

When he exited the room, he wore a troubled expression, his handsome face all sharp lines, full lips drawn tight.

Smudges of reddish dirt marred his new shirt, and his hair was tousled, as if he'd been raking his fingers through it in agitation.

"How'd it go?" she asked, and stroked Bongo's head as the dog, possibly sensing her unrest, laid her large head in Sara's lap. It didn't take long for her to feel the wet of Bongo's drool as it soaked her jeans.

"Good, I think." He walked over and sat on the stool next to her at the large island in the kitchen.

He swiped his phone open and laid it on the quartz countertop.

She leaned over to see a photo of what looked like a crew of people in blue-and-white uniforms. At her questioning look, he said, "The Florians always took a group photo before the start of every racing season. This one was taken the last year greyhound racing was permitted in Florida."

Leaning close, he used two fingers to enlarge the photo and focused on a young girl in the second row. Tapping the screen with his index finger, he said, "That's Teresa Hansen. They called her Terry."

Something about the girl's face clicked with her, and she scrolled to the top of the photos she'd just been viewing.

"What did they say about her?" she asked.

"She was seventeen. A runaway who came to them through a halfway house that helps troubled teens. She was reliable and always willing to help, and then one day she didn't show up. They didn't worry at first, but when days passed without her, they reached out to the halfway house who said that Terry was missing."

Sara shook her head in disbelief. "And that's it? Terry goes missing and no one does anything?"

With a shake of his head, Jose said, "Apparently the people at the halfway house asked around, but no one knew where Terry might have gone. Her things were still at the house, which worried them, so they reached out to the police who told them to file a report."

Which could account for the photo she'd thought she'd seen. She raised an index finger in a stop gesture. "Hold on a minute."

Turning her attention to her laptop, she scrolled through the photos, those missing and lost faces tugging at her heart until she reached one she thought looked familiar.

She turned the screen so that Jose could see it. His shocked gasp confirmed that he also saw the resemblance to Terry.

He brought his phone close to her screen for a better comparison and that left no doubt in her mind.

They'd possibly identified the one woman and made a connection to the kennels.

Sara whipped out her phone and snapped off a photo showing the two screen images. She quickly sent it to the rest of the SBS crew and got immediate replies.

Fantastic! Mia texted.

Awesome! came from both Sophie and Robbie.

Great job. Let's convene in the penthouse for dinner and planning, Trey responded.

Dinner and planning? Was Jose in favor of that? Sara thought, and showed the response to Jose.

She didn't think it was possible for that knife-sharp slash of his lips to get even more severe, but it did. He looked away, shook his head and blew out a harsh breath.

Laying a hand on his arm, she said, "It's not too late for you to pull out of this. You've done what Trey asked."

With another abrupt shake of his head, he said, "No way. I'm not leaving you alone to deal with this."

Something in her heart trembled at his words, but she worried this was way out of his comfort zone. Hers as well. "I'm not alone. I've got the entire SBS crew with me."

"And now you have me as well. I got us into this mess—"

"There's no reason for you to feel guilty," she said and stroked his arm, trying to reassure him.

"I recommended this property, Sara. Maybe I should have done more due diligence."

"You know better than that. There's no way you could have known. None of us could have, not even Trey with all his experience," she said and at that, the tension left his body like a balloon losing its air.

He nodded. "I'm not leaving. Not until we figure out what's happening, and I know you're safe. Plus, I imagine you would rather not be plastered across the news," he said, and cupped her cheek.

"I wouldn't. People don't understand how hard that is," she said, and leaned into that caress, drawing comfort from it and something else. That something else that she'd been feeling about him since the moment she'd laid eyes on him.

"I do. I understand," he said as she reached up, cradled his jaw and ran her thumb across his lips, the gesture as intimate as any kiss.

He smiled and leaned close. Ran his thumb across her lips as his gaze traveled over her face. "You feel it too," he said.

At her nod, he shifted closer, so close his warm breath spilled across her lips, but just then the whoosh of elevator doors had them jerking apart guiltily.

JOSE SUCKED IN a breath, savoring her fresh floral scent as he slipped off the stool and jammed his hands in his pockets to keep from touching her again.

Trey's observant gaze drifted between the two of them as the elevator doors opened and he led the rest of the South Beach Security crew into the penthouse. But joining them this time were Mia's new husband John Wilson and Trey's pregnant wife Roni, whose baby belly was really showing. He guesstimated she was at least six months pregnant by now, and wondered how she handled being pregnant and actively working as a detective with Miami Beach PD.

To avoid Trey's continued observation, he hurried over and hugged Roni, and then shook John's hand. "It's good to see you. What brings you two tonight?"

A wry smile slipped across Roni's lips, and she grabbed hold of Trey's hand and swung it playfully. "With the hours we both work, it's sometimes the only time we get to spend together."

"Ditto. The new start-up is consuming me so I try to sneak time with Mia whenever I can," John said, wrapping an arm around Mia's waist and dropping a kiss on her cheek.

"And we want to help. Too many women go missing and their families never know what happened to them," Roni added, her smile fading.

"We think we identified one," Jose said, referring to the photo they'd sent to the team earlier.

Trey whipped out his phone and took another look at his text message. "It definitely looks like the same girl. First thing to do is check in with local PD to see if anything they have so far might help confirm that."

"But first, dinner. I'm always hungry lately," Roni said, and stroked her hand across her baby belly.

"And all that digging makes for a hungry boy," Jose said as his stomach growled loudly, earning a big woof from Bongo, as if in agreement.

"Sorry, girl. It is time for me to feed you," Sara said, and with a hand gesture directed the bloodhound toward the fridge.

While Sara dished out fresh food and filled Bongo's water bowl, the rest of the team shuffled around menus for the restaurants in the area before settling on a local Mexican place.

Once the order had been phoned in, the team settled in around the table and shared reports on what they had accomplished that day.

"All the windows and doors on the house are secure. We've got the cameras on the house installed and will finish connecting them tomorrow," Sophie said.

Robbie added, "We couldn't access the training ring, but did finish securing the kennels. Tomorrow we'll add the driveway alarm and perimeter cameras."

"Great. We'll assign an agent to monitor the feeds until we feel it's secure and Sara can move in," Trey said.

"And that 'we' includes Sara feeling it's safe," Mia said, and shot a quick look at her.

"That sounds good," Sara said, but Jose wasn't convinced she was serious. He knew what it was like to be railroaded by his SBS family and feel trapped.

Laying a hand on hers beneath the tabletop, he squeezed and focused on her. "Are you sure that's what you want?"

She nodded emphatically. "I came here to do a job and I intend to do it. I trust the team, and if they say it's safe, I'm ready to move in."

"We won't push Sara to do anything she's not ready to do," Trey said, obviously reading his vibes.

He bit back the question about what they would push him to do. In truth, he could have extricated himself from this investigation, but he was committed now. Committed to Sara and exploring what he was feeling about her, he told himself.

"I'm good, Trey. You're doing everything you can to make sure the kennels will be safe for me and for everyone," Sara said.

"Unlike the two people in that grave," Mia said with a sad shake of her head.

"We will find out what happened and bring peace to those women," Trey said.

Jose had no doubt the SBS team would do just that. It's what had made them Miami's premiere security and investigative agency.

Trey's cell phone chirped, and he answered. "Sure. I'll be down in a second."

Skipping his gaze across everyone gathered at the table, he said, "Food's here. I'll go get it."

Jose joined the others as they went into action, splitting up to get sodas, cutlery, napkins and plates. All of them acting as if this was an everyday thing, and maybe it was for them. He hoped it never got to be that everyday for him. Which reminded him why he shouldn't let whatever he was feeling for Sara go any further. This was her world now, and he didn't want any part of it.

Minutes later Trey returned, and they settled around the table to eat and plan what they would do the next day. Sophie and Robbie would resume securing the location. Trey was going to coordinate with the local PD on the autopsies and any evidence they had gathered at the scenes of the explosions.

"I'll find out what I can about… Terry Hansen," Mia said, and peered at Sara. "Since you're worried about other traps because of the trip wire you found, let's bring in our other new K-9 agents, Matt and Natalie, to help search. Are you okay with that?"

"I am. I've got a sick feeling there are more surprises there and don't want to search alone," Sara said, and shot him a quick look from the corner of her eye.

"I'll go with you," he said despite all his earlier reservations.

Trey immediately jumped in with, "*Gracias*, Pepe. Hopefully with all of us working on this we'll secure the kennels more quickly. I can join you once I finish with local PD."

Jose did a slow nod in appreciation. He had expected Trey to single him out as not being capable enough to be part of the investigation. He'd always thought his cousin saw him as somehow inferior, unable to be an action guy like he was. It was why Jose had always felt closer to his younger cousin Ricky, a psychologist who had also been trying to make his own way before being sucked into the family business.

Meeting Trey's gaze across the table, he realized now that he'd been mistaken. And when Trey nodded, as if saying "I know you can do this," the years of feeling that inferiority, that insecurity, fell away.

"That sounds like a plan," Jose said.

Chapter Ten

Everyone had filed out of the penthouse except Trey. He kissed his wife and said, "I'll meet you downstairs in a few minutes."

Sara, apparently sensing Trey wanted a moment alone with Jose, excused herself. "Have a good night, Trey. I need a shower and I should call my mother to explain what's happening before my Tia Rosario beats me to it."

When she was gone, Trey flipped a hand in the direction of Jose's dirt-stained shirt.

"Looks like I owe you another one, Pepe," Trey said with a laugh and shake of his head.

Jose narrowed his gaze and examined his cousin carefully. "Why do I think you're liking this way too much?"

"Maybe because I like you. I've always known you had it in you," he said, and tapped the back of his hand across Jose's midsection.

"What? Tacos?" Jose teased, not wanting the mood to get maudlin or too serious.

But Trey was having none of it. "The Gonzalez backbone. Courage. You've got it and I appreciate you helping us."

Jose blew out a harsh laugh. "As if you couldn't handle this on your own."

Trey shrugged broad shoulders and wagged his head from side to side. "Probably. Maybe. Like Sara, I worry those two are just the first ones we'll find. It'll take all of us to solve what's happening at that location. A location you convinced us to buy," he said, his tone teasing.

"Way to make me feel guilty," he said, earning another chuckle from his cousin.

Trey turned and tapped his badge against the elevator access screen before pointing a finger toward the bedrooms. "Sara is an amazing woman, Pepe. But she has her own issues. Remember that."

Before Jose could respond, the elevator doors opened, and Trey walked on.

Jose barely had time to wave goodbye before the doors closed to take Trey down to where Roni would be waiting.

Much like Jose was waiting for Sara to finish her phone call and shower, looking forward to spending what was left of the night together.

But as he sucked in a deep breath, imagining whether they would continue what they had started earlier, he realized Sara wasn't the only one who needed a shower. The stink of the day clung to him, and he wondered why no one had mentioned it earlier while they were eating dinner.

He hurried to his bedroom, stripped off his clothes and quickly jumped into the shower. The heat of the water chased away some of the soreness from the digging. But as he ran soapy hands across his arms and torso, it reminded him of the moment the shovel had hit something hard and white.

Something human.

How long had the two women been there? A year? Two? He didn't know enough about dead bodies, but it clearly hadn't happened recently.

Had it happened while the kennels were open? he asked himself, and the answer came to him instantly: yes.

If one of the women in the ground was Terry Hansen, it had to have happened while she was working there.

She'd been seventeen at the time. Terry had only just begun her life, and someone had taken it from her.

Anger filled him, and he quickly finished his shower, determined to find out as much as he could about Terry. Determined that she wouldn't be forgotten.

In that brief instance, he finally realized why Trey and the rest of his cousins did what they did: so people would get justice. Justice that they possibly didn't receive from the usual law enforcement channels.

He towel-dried himself and tossed on the sweats Trey had brought him along with the other clothes from his condo. When he exited the bedroom and walked into the spacious open area, Sara was seated at the table, working on a laptop. Bongo lay at her feet but raised her head to eyeball him as he approached. Recognizing him, the dog laid her big head back on her even larger paws.

"What are you doing?" he asked and walked to the table to lean over her shoulder.

The action brought him so close he smelled her shower freshness and that brought an immediate reaction as he hardened, enticed by that flowery perfume and her natural scent.

He straightened to give himself some space as she said, "I'm just scrolling through this list of missing women. So, so many."

"Too many," he said, wondering why no one had cared or if they had, why the women had remained missing.

"And it may not even be Terry or any of these women," Sara said, and flipped a hand in the direction of the laptop screen.

"My gut says one of those bodies is Terry," he said, but quickly tacked on, "Not that I'm any expert."

"You're not and I'm not either, but it's just too much coincidence that she was working there and just disappeared," Sara said, and closed the laptop.

"Done for the night?" he asked but got his answer even before she spoke as she pulled over a notepad and pen.

She peered over her shoulder at him, the gray of her eyes the color of a stormy winter sky. "Would you mind calling the Florians again?"

He shot a quick look at his watch. The night had flown between dinner and their showers. It was nearly ten. "I don't, but maybe in the morning. I'm not sure they'd welcome a call at this hour."

Nodding, she said, "You're right. I lost track of time. I should take Bongo for her last walk of the day."

"Easy to do when so much is happening. I'll go with you."

She leashed the bloodhound and together they hurried downstairs, let Bongo do her business, and then returned to the penthouse, where Sara gave her a treat and unleashed her. The dog immediately sat near the table where they had been working earlier.

He gestured to the pad and pen and then over to the nearby sofa. "I know you're not done for the night. Why don't you get comfortable, and I'll get us something to drink while we work on those questions together."

"That sounds nice. A finger of that aged rum neat would be appreciated," she said, and slowly rose from the table, pad and pen in hand.

When she walked to the sofa, Bongo followed and sat by her feet.

At the wet bar at the far side of the room, he poured a finger of a twenty-three-year-old rum, took some ice from the small fridge there and poured himself a scotch. He walked over to the sofa, handed Sara her rum and sat close, wanting to be able to read what was on the pad as they worked together.

Sara sipped her rum but then set it aside so she could write down their questions. "Did the Florians notice anything different about Terry in the days before she disappeared?"

"Did she hang out with any of the other workers and who were they?" he said.

She raised an index finger. "We should get a list of everyone working there at the time."

"If they'll give it to us and the police. I'm guessing some people might want a warrant before they do that," he said, recalling what little he knew based on the police dramas he'd watched.

"Hopefully it won't take that. Like you said, the Gonzalez family has a lot of pull—"

"And the Florians won't want to piss us off," he said.

SARA HELD BACK from commenting on it being an "us" now.

"No, they won't. What else can we ask them?" she said, and they rattled off a few more questions that Sara jotted down on the pad before finally setting it aside and grabbing her glass of rum again.

She sipped the rum and the heat of it traveled down her core, but it wasn't as comforting as the warmth of his body along her side. It seemed almost natural to lean into him, and he reacted by wrapping an arm around her shoulders to hold her close.

They sat there in companionable silence, sipping their drinks. Each lost in their thoughts about today's gruesome discovery and what it might mean.

"This wasn't quite how I pictured my first few days at work," Sara finally said, needing to share the questions racing around in her brain in the hopes of quieting that unrest.

"What did you picture?"

"Puppers. Lots and lots of puppers," she said with a laugh and rough shake of her head. She reached down to the floor, where Bongo lay by her feet, and rubbed the dog's head. "Right, Bongo?"

A low woof answered her, as if the dog knew exactly

what she had asked, and sat up to lay her drooly head on the edge of the sofa.

"How long have you been partners?"

"About six years. Before Bongo I had a German shepherd but when she died, I decided to get a bloodhound because they have more scent sensors than other breeds," she answered, and stroked the dog's head and ears.

"Was it hard to train her?"

Sara eyeballed him, as if to judge if he was truly interested. Satisfied that he was, she said, "Not too hard. Bloodhounds are quite smart."

"Is she protective?" he asked, and from the tone of his voice, she sensed that he thought that the dog wasn't all that keen on him.

"Not really. Bloodhounds are very easygoing, and they think everyone is a friend," she said, and almost as if Bongo knew they were talking about her, the dog raised her head and looked at him.

JOSE TOLD HIMSELF it was a friendly look even though he felt like Bongo was their very determined chaperone. He sipped his whisky, falling silent as he considered what to do next.

Sara spared him by asking, "I'm sure this isn't how you pictured this sale going."

"You can say that again," he said with a rough laugh and rattle of the ice in his glass. But the emotions that had been building in him reared up and he blurted out, "I sure didn't expect you."

Her hand trembled as she set her glass on the coffee table in front of the couch, and she shifted to face him.

"Me? You didn't expect me?" she said and tapped her chest with her finger.

He nodded and caressed her cheek. Ran his thumb across the creamy skin there and then drifted it lower to trace the edges of her lips. "I didn't," he said, before leaning forward to finally do what he'd wanted to do for hours.

He kissed her.

Chapter Eleven

His lips were hard and mobile. Soft and demanding. Needy and gentle all at the same time.

Her head spun with the whirlwind of emotions swirling through her, as conflicted as the vibes she was getting from him.

That was confirmed as he expelled a rough breath against her lips and shifted away slightly as he said, "Like I said before, I didn't expect you. This."

"I didn't either. It's…confusing. There's just so much going on," she admitted, but even as she did so, she slipped into his lap, straddling his legs so that they were face-to-face because she didn't want to miss any nuance of what was happening.

He smiled, a lopsided smile, and cradled her jaw before easing his hand around to cup the back of her skull. Tangling his fingers through her hair, he applied gentle pressure to draw her close.

"It is confusing. It's hard to separate the craziness of this situation from what I'm feeling," he confessed, and his warm breath spilled across her lips. This close, it was impossible to miss the crystals of darker teal in the aqua of his eyes or the stubble of his evening beard on his face.

"What are you feeling?" she asked, raising her hand and

running it across that sandpapery stubble, and then dipping her thumb to rub it across his lips.

IT TOOK ALL of Jose's willpower not to cup her buttocks and draw her against the proof of what he was feeling.

He was too much of a gentleman to do that, and he had no doubt Trey would whoop his ass if he did. He tempered that need and instead stroked his hands across her back, gentling her as he said, "I'd be lying if I said I didn't want you, but that want is way too soon."

And it was way too complicated because of her connections to his family and SBS.

"It is. I'm not the kind to just hook up," she said, and quickly slipped off his lap. "And I'm not a tease either."

This was going from so nice to so wrong so quickly, and he tried to smooth things over. He faced her on the sofa and said, "I know you're not. I'd like to see if this—" he paused and pointed back and forth between them "—can go somewhere. If that's what you want."

She nodded her head shakily. "I think it's what I want only… Being involved with you and your family—"

"And the business."

"And your business. When I first heard about the job posting, I did an internet search and you came up a lot also at a number of events."

He tipped his head from side to side, considering what she said and finally said, "I hit a lot of social events, but a lot of them are for charities I support."

"What kinds of charities?" she asked, as if hoping the cause was worth the publicity.

"Ones that help renovate homes for injured veterans and people in need."

"Good causes," she said, but then quickly tacked on, "But I just want to train the dogs and stay out of the news. I've already lived through that."

And he knew it hadn't been a good thing based on what Trey had said earlier. "Mind telling me more about what happened?"

"My father was wrongfully accused of taking a client's funds. My family…there was a lot of media coverage until he was cleared of wrongdoing."

"And now you're in the news—"

"Again. I'd rather live a low-key life, but first we have to work on this investigation."

"You're right. The sooner we finish that, the sooner we can explore whatever it is that we're feeling," he said, and cradled her cheek again, the caress meant to comfort and not entice.

She covered his hand with hers and offered him a regretful smile. "First thing in the a.m. you call the Florians and we take it from there."

With a last stroke of his thumb across her smooth cheek, he said, "I will. Maybe that will help us decide what to do."

She nodded. "I'm a little tired and need to be alert tomorrow. I'm going to turn in."

"I agree. I'll see you in the morning," he said, then shot to his feet and held his hand out to help her from the couch.

She slipped her hand into his and rose. With a slight hand gesture to Bongo, the dog came to her feet and tucked herself tight to Sara's leg.

Sara and Jose walked hand in hand to her bedroom door where she paused and faced him, hesitant. "Good night," she said, then dropped a quick kiss on his lips and rushed into her room. She would have slammed the door in his face, but Bongo's big body was in the way. As soon as her dog was inside, she closed the door.

Jose stood there, staring at the polished wood, teak he guessed. As a Realtor he noticed those kinds of things, and maybe he should think about how to use those skills to help Sara and the SBS team in the future.

Or maybe even now, he thought, doubling back to the sofa to grab the paper and pen to review the questions they'd come up with and maybe add some more.

Later in his bedroom, he lay on the bed and turned on the television to see if there was any coverage of today's discovery. Flipping from one local news show to a hyper local cable news channel, he listened as one reporter after another gave only the barest info on what the police had found at the kennels.

Possibly not surprising since the police probably had very little so far.

Trey had said it would take a few days at least to determine cause of death, much less identify the two bodies.

Although Jose was sure that one of them was poor seventeen-year-old Terry. Since he knew from all those TV crime shows that the killer was most likely someone Terry had known, he was going to press the Florians to find out who had been Terry's friends and more importantly, who hadn't been.

He added a question to the list to find out who might also have after-hours access to the location and how someone could have dug a grave without anyone noticing.

A grave filled with bones, he thought, as the image of what he'd found that day rocked him. The off-white skull against the reddish-brown Florida soil. A few inches away, thin finger bones poking upward, as if trying to claw free of their prison.

Shoving away those images, he forced himself to think about what he'd seen on the property, trying to remember if there had been anything that had seemed out of the ordinary on his various visits to the location before recommending that Trey buy it.

Or if there had been anything unusual about the sale itself. There had been interest from that other buyer, but he hadn't thought anything about that since it wasn't unusual to have multiple bidders on a project. But maybe this buyer hadn't liked losing the property. Maybe because they had been hiding the bodies at the kennels? he thought.

That and so many other ideas came to mind, and he jotted them down, determined to help find out what had happened to those two women and why someone clearly wanted SBS off the property.

SARA HAD TRIED her best to fall asleep and get a good night's rest, but sleep hadn't come easily. The images of the last two days had tumbled over and over in her brain, rousing more questions than answers.

Answers that wouldn't come easily, she thought as she placed the espresso pot on the stove, needing the caffeine that a good cup of Cuban coffee would provide. Hopefully it would help make up for her restless night.

The coffee was just bubbling up in the pot when she heard Jose's door open and his soft footfalls as he walked down the hall.

Bongo raised her head as he came in and barked a "Good morning."

He walked over, knelt and rubbed Bongo's head and ears. "Good morning, Bongo. Sara," he said, and beamed a smile in her direction.

She shut off the stove and raised the coffee pot. "Do you want some?"

"Sí, por favor," he said, and strolled to where she stood by the stove. He laid a hand on her waist, bent and dropped a fleeting kiss on her cheek.

She placed the coffeepot back on the stove, rose on tiptoes and brushed a kiss on his lips as she said, "Good morning, Jose."

"I think I like starting the morning like this," he said, and deepened the kiss, but a second later her phone chirped, shattering the moment.

"I have to get that," she said, and snagged her phone from the counter.

"It's Trey," she said and answered. "Let me put you on speaker. Good morning, Trey."

"Buenos dias. I was hoping the two of you could come down in about an hour."

She met Jose's gaze and he nodded and said, "I just need to call the Florians, and then we can come down."

"Bueno. We're bringing in some breakfast, so don't worry about making your own," he said, and ended the call.

Sara laid the phone on the counter and Jose said, "I'll go make that call."

She nodded. "I'll bring in your coffee."

"Sounds good," he said, and hurried off to phone the former kennel owners.

THE SBS TEAM sat around the conference room table.

Trey had already given them a brief on what the police had so far, "brief" being the operative word, Jose thought again.

"Hopefully PD will have something in the next few days. Roni will keep on them to give us any info, and we promised to keep them updated," Trey said, and peered in Jose's direction. "Do you have anything, Pepe?"

Jose nodded. "I spoke to the Florians this morning. They weren't too keen on me waking them that early, but they co-operated once I explained what we'd found."

"Did they have anything useful to add?" Mia asked.

He nodded again and provided his report. "Apparently there was some kind of plumbing issue that forced them to dig up the area behind the training ring. The contractors had fixed the problem and were supposed to fill and grade the area but when they arrived the next day, someone had already done the work."

"Like whoever killed those women," Trey said, and glanced around the table where everyone nodded in agreement.

"How long ago was that?" Trey asked.

"About three years ago. Around the same time that Terry Hansen disappeared."

"Any idea who Terry's friends were? Enemies?" Trey said.

"I have some names. I assume someone can check them out," Jose said, ripping a piece of paper from the pad and passing it to Trey.

"Robbie and I can do that while our crew finishes up the security details," Sophie said, and took the paper from Trey.

As she did so, Jose said, "There's one name I think we should focus on—Barry Metz. He was a caretaker of sorts. Lives in a cabin at the far side of the woods. He's been watching the property since the kennels closed and was supposed to move after the sale. The Florians aren't sure that he did."

"Let's hope he did, otherwise it might be an issue. I don't like the idea of kicking anyone out of their home, even if they are a squatter," Mia said.

"I agree. If he's still there and not a threat, we can consider how to handle it," Trey said and finished with, "Our other K-9 agents, Matt and Natalie, will meet us there to finish the search of the property. If there's nothing else—"

"Just one thing. The developer who was bidding against us is…a little shady. Nothing concrete, but I heard he had connections to some underworld types," Jose said, earning a sharp look from his cousin.

"Talk about burying the lede," Trey said with a shake of his head that ruffled the longer strands there.

"His name is on that sheet as well, Sophie. Just be careful who you talk to about him," Jose said, worried about what might happen if the rumors were true.

"Got it. We'll keep the search to our sources for now," Sophie confirmed.

"If the developer is dirty, maybe the bodies are connected to him, which would explain why someone wants us off the property," Mia said, connecting the dots to a possible motive.

"Or he could just be pissed off we outbid him, and he wants to make us sell," Robbie said, offering a different explanation.

"Seems to be a lot of trouble when he could have just bid more for the property," Jose said, not feeling Robbie's motive for what was happening.

"Or maybe whoever buried those bodies wants to keep his secrets safe," Sara suggested.

"My money is on that reason," Mia said.

Trey echoed his agreement and said, "I think so too, which worries me because like Sara said, I think we're going to find more bodies."

Chapter Twelve

Sara had met the other SBS K-9 agents a few days earlier when she'd first arrived. Matt was now engaged to the owner of the *Buena Suerta* stables whom he met on an earlier SBS case. Natalie had likewise met her new fiancé, an Everglades tour boat owner, and his son on another investigation. Both agents lived close to the kennels and with their past military experience in addition to their K-9 partners, they would be a big help in defusing any dangerous situations.

She walked the perimeter with Matt, Natalie and Jose and identified five possible trip wires along the edges of the woods. They'd carefully marked the areas with bright yellow caution tape and were just finishing up the last one when Matt said, "We should trip it from a distance to see what we're facing."

"How will we be able to do that?" Natalie said, peering at the wire and then back toward the buildings that were a good thirty yards away.

Jose tracked her gaze and said, "I used to be a pitcher. I think I could nail that wire from sixty feet away."

Matt shook his head. "*Mano*, that would be quite a feat. I think thirty feet is more than enough."

"Done," Jose said, and looked around for something

he could toss. Several feet away were two baseball-sized rocks. He walked over, picked one up and hefted its weight in his hand.

Satisfied, he walked about a dozen yards away with the rest of the team. Matt and Natalie stood off to one side, and he waited until Sara and Bongo were slightly behind him.

"Ready?" he asked.

"Ready as we'll ever be, but maybe we should let the others know," Sara said. She tightened her hold on Bongo's leash, and called Trey to warn him they were tripping the wire.

After Sara finished with the call, he nodded, and slipped into his familiar pitcher's stance. Focusing on the yellow tape around the wire, he went into his wind up, then released the rock.

It sailed just high of the trip wire.

"Close but no cigar," Matt teased.

"Next time," Sara and Natalie said, almost in unison.

He didn't intend to disappoint. Picking up the second rock, he tested its weight and assumed the position, wound up and hurled the rock.

It nailed the wire.

A second later, a semideflated volleyball studded with sharp wooden spikes sailed down in an arc that would have nailed anyone tripping the wire.

"Wow," Jose said, and took a step toward the area, but Natalie swung out her arm to hold him back.

"Wait. Sometimes a booby trap has a delayed secondary trap."

Barely a few seconds later, a small explosion sent shrapnel peppering the trees and ground in about a ten-foot circle.

Jose let out a low whistle. "Whoever this is means business."

THE SOUND OF the blast reverberated across the land, pulling him away from tending to his garden.

He lay down the hoe at the edge of a row of onions and looked toward the kennels in the distance with a smile.

Someone had tripped one of his surprises.

Eager to see the damage it had done, he raced to his front porch and grabbed the loaded crossbow he kept by the front door while he was working the land.

Racing across the fields, he threaded his way through the trees, moving as quickly as he could without disturbing his other garden or setting off any of the traps he'd set in the area to chase off trespassers. It made his passage slower than he would have wanted, but he had to be patient.

Whoever had tripped the booby trap would still be there, delightfully shredded if he'd devised the mace-like device and explosive correctly.

But as he neared the area, he noticed the duo of men walking around in bright white hazmat suits. Raising the crossbow, he peered through the scope.

No body even though he'd heard the explosion, and the spiked volleyball was still swinging back and forth in a deadly arc.

He gritted his teeth at his failure and shifted the crossbow to look toward the group gathered several yards away from what he guessed was a CSI team.

Three beautiful women stood there along with another woman he hadn't seen before and a Labrador retriever. They were chatting with the warrior and dandy. There were also two other men, a nerdy looking one and another military man who had a shepherd at his side.

The pleasure he'd been experiencing with the sound of the blast and the expectation of carnage slowly ebbed and was replaced by anger at his failure.

A failure just like his mother always told him he would be.

His finger tightened on the trigger as he contemplated the arrow burying itself deep into the luscious flesh of one of the women.

Pleasure slowly returned with that image, but he had to be patient.

Before pleasure, it was time for fear.

THE SOUND OF the blast had ripped the CSI team from the training ring and had also brought his cousins and the rest of the SBS crew hurrying in their direction.

As soon as the head crime scene investigator arrived, Jose said, "We need to call in the bomb squad. Maybe they can defuse the other traps and collect evidence as well."

"How did you trip it?" Trey asked and skewered the four of them with his gaze.

"You forgot I could throw a strike from the outfield," Jose said with a laugh.

Trey shook his head and patted Jose's flat midsection. "Good to know you haven't let yourself go to flab."

"Glad I could help, but I'm not sure what else I can do now," he said, watching the CSI team split up, one group heading toward the tree line to collect evidence while another returned to finish their work at the training ring.

"You can help brainstorm. The installation team found an alarm by the kennel sign. Combined with these traps, the explosions and the bodies, we need to regroup. You were always good at thinking on the fly, Pepe," Trey said, and clapped him on the back.

THE TENSION IN Jose's body was undeniable, but Trey was clearly not about to give Jose an excuse for bailing, not that Sara thought he would. It surprised her again, as many of the men she'd met through her family would have run by now, including the man who had been her boyfriend at the time her father's problems had become so newsworthy.

"We'll do whatever you think is best," Jose said.

"Great. Matt and Natalie have to head to their current

assignments, but the rest of us can convene in the house," Trey said.

But as they turned to go, something flew through the air and an arrow embedded itself in the ground at Sara's feet.

Jose immediately stepped in front of her while Matt and Trey urged Natalie, Mia and Sophie behind them.

The two CSI officers reacted, moving toward the forest, but Trey called out to them in warning.

"There are other booby traps," he yelled, which made the CSIs stop in their tracks.

Sara peeked around Jose's body, searching the forest, but she didn't see anything. But the arrow was something that might be useful.

Loosening her hold on Bongo's leash, she let the blood-hound sniff the arrow, hoping she could pick up some kind of scent.

The CSI officers came over at that moment. "We'll have to take that as evidence. It may have fingerprints or DNA," one of them said.

Sara gestured for him to take it, hoping Bongo had gleaned what she could from the arrow.

"Let's go plan," Trey said, and looked over at Matt and Natalie.

"You have your assignments, but we may need your help later if you're up for it."

"Whatever you need," Natalie said, and Matt echoed her words.

"Good," Trey said, and with a quick look around to the others that said so much despite its brevity, they all walked toward the house.

At the driveway, Matt, Natalie and their K-9s peeled off to their cars while the rest of the team entered the house.

As Sara walked in, she realized someone had brought in a foldable six-foot table and chairs so that they would have a workspace.

Sophie's and Robbie's laptops were there along with a map and a greenish rectangular box.

"What is that?" she asked, peering at the box and trying to figure it out.

"It's a driveway alarm," Sophie said, and pointed to a sensor on it. "This detects motion and heat. I'm guessing it sends a signal to either a phone or laptop once it's tripped."

"Our team found it hidden by the weeds near the old sign when they went to install our driveway alarm," Robbie explained.

"And since someone just shot an arrow at us, I think it's safe to assume we're being watched," Sara said, and a shiver traveled through her body.

Jose laid a hand on her shoulder and gave a comforting squeeze, but it did little to calm the fear running through her body.

"And they always seem to be one step ahead of us," Mia said dejectedly.

"That just means we have to step up our game," Trey said, and leaned over the table to gesture at the map. "We've secured all the buildings except the training ring. We have one perimeter camera installed but have to put in more once we defuse the traps."

"Do you think the camera picked up whoever shot at us?" Jose asked and stroked his hand across Sara's shoulders, sensing her continued discomfort.

Sophie shrugged hesitantly and shook her head. "Not sure. The camera is intended to record anyone coming onto the property."

"We'll check and let you know," Robbie said.

Sara hoped they had gotten something. Anything really because as Mia had said, they seemed to be one step behind whoever was causing these issues.

"I'm hoping Bongo picked up a scent from the arrow, but it's a long shot," she said and quickly added, "No pun intended." The arrow shaft was narrow, and she suspected their assailant had been smart enough to wear gloves.

"It's worth a try. It's also worth it to explore those woods and see why someone wants to keep us out of there, but first I'd feel better knowing more about our possible suspects. Sophie and Robbie have been doing some digging around," Trey said, and held his hand out to invite the two tech gurus to provide their information.

Chapter Thirteen

Sophie whipped out a mini projector, and a second later broadcasted an image from her laptop onto the wall.

"This is Anthony Delgado, the developer who was trying to buy the property. Rumors say he paid off local politicians to change the zoning to permit residential housing on this property," Sophie began.

"Rumors also have it that Delgado has connections to local mobsters. They've apparently invested in his projects in exchange for what no one knows," Robbie added.

"Maybe in exchange for burying the bodies," Sara said, the image of the women's bones still vivid in her memory.

"Easy enough to do when you're doing major construction," Mia said with a shrug.

"But is there any connection to the contractors working to repair the training ring problems? The owners said they seemed surprised that the hole had been filled," Jose asked.

Sophie smiled and held up a finger. She flipped another image onto the screen. "This is Guy Sasto, the owner of the contracting company. He used to work for Delgado before he went out on his own. He occasionally works on Delgado's projects."

"So, Delgado's suspect number one," Trey said, and it was clear to Sara that he felt there were other possibilities as well.

"Who else do you have in mind?" Sara asked, worried that they weren't getting any closer to solving this investigation.

"Before we move on, do we all agree Delgado might be responsible for those bodies and any others in those woods?" Trey asked.

As everyone around the table nodded, he gestured for Sophie to continue.

JOSE HAD HEARD the rumors from his colleagues about Delgado but having them confirmed by his SBS family was a completely different thing. Knowing what he did now, he had no doubt Delgado could be behind the attacks, but he tried to keep an open mind as Sophie pulled up another photo.

He recognized the face from the photo the former kennel owners had previously sent.

"This is Barry Metz. He's the one the Florians let live in the cabin on the other side of the woods," Sophie said, and with a tap of the keys, a mug shot featuring Metz displayed on the wall.

"Four years ago Metz was arrested for the sexual assault of a thirteen-year-old in nearby Homestead," Robbie said, tag-teaming with his sister.

"So why was he free a year later and working for the Florians?" Jose asked.

A tight smile flitted across Sophie's face. "The parents of the girl didn't want to subject her to a trial and the media attention."

"He wasn't prosecuted?" Sara asked, just to confirm.

Robbie nodded. "He wasn't prosecuted. Homestead PD kept an eye on him for months, but he kept off their radar."

"And came to murder here," Jose said with some bite.

"It's easy to judge, but women get victimized twice in cases like this. First when they're attacked and then after, when the defense attorneys go at them," Mia said, obviously sympathetic to the parents' decision.

"It's a big escalation to go from sexual assault to multiple murders," Sara pointed out.

Trey dipped his head in agreement. "It is. That's why I'm asking Ricky to look at this and give us his opinion."

While Ricky was a psychologist, Jose didn't think this was generally in his cousin's wheelhouse, but maybe he had added it to his specialties with all the work he did for South Beach Security.

"What do we do now?" Jose asked, troubled by everything that was happening and the fact that they were only a little closer to solving the puzzle.

"We need to talk to Metz and Sasto," Trey said with no hesitation.

"Not Delgado?" Sara asked.

Jose stroked a hand across her back as he said, "That's the last person we want to talk to, trust me. To be honest, if I had known it was Delgado, I would have pulled out of this buy."

"But you didn't know and that's okay. We will get to the bottom of this," Trey said.

Mia added, "This is a great location, and in a weird sort of way, I'm glad about what's happened. Those two women, and any others if we're right, deserve justice and their families need to know what happened to them."

Jose understood what she was feeling. "Agreed. No one should be tossed away like trash."

With that, Sara looked at him, smiled and slipped her hand into his. "You're both right. We will get justice for those women."

"I guess it's time for us to go talk to Metz and Sasto," Jose said.

"Do you know Sasto?" Trey asked, obviously aware that he worked with a lot of different contractors on behalf of his real estate clients.

"I do. I can set up an appointment with him," Jose said with a dip of his head.

"After we talk to him, we'll see about meeting Metz," Trey confirmed.

"Sophie, Robbie and I will mind the fort here. The CSI team said they'd be releasing the training ring to us later today," Mia said, and skipped her gaze over to her tech cousins.

"Robbie and I will keep trying to get more info on our suspects," Sophie said.

"*Bueno.* It seems like we've got our work cut out for us," Trey said, and with that the team went into action.

SASTO WAS OUT of the office when Jose called, but his assistant said he'd be back shortly and arranged for the meeting.

"Why does it bother me that he's out of the office at the same time someone is shooting arrows at us?" Sara asked as they drove to Sasto's location in nearby Homestead.

"And that he can make the trip to the kennels in only about fifteen minutes, maybe less in the early morning or late at night," Jose said.

"Too much coincidence," Trey added.

It was a short distance to Sasto's office, and as they pulled into the parking lot, a fortysomething man was stepping out of a large white pickup that had a company logo on the door that read Sasto Contracting Company.

Jose pointed in the man's direction. "That's Guy Sasto. His father founded the company, and he took it over about ten years ago when the old man retired."

The man hesitated as he noticed them parked a few spaces away. When he spotted Jose in the front seat, he waved and smiled, but that smile dimmed as Trey slipped from the car.

Sasto sauntered over to them, shoulders pulled back in a way that reminded Sara of a bantam rooster trying to appear bigger.

Jose got out of the car and so did she, taking Bongo with

her in the hope she'd sniff around Sasto and maybe pick up a familiar scent.

Approaching the contractor, Jose held out his hand and said, "Good to see you, Guy."

Sasto's gaze moved from Jose to Trey before giving her only a cursory glance. "I wish I could say the same. What do you want?"

The contractor ignoring her and Bongo was maybe a good thing, she thought as she maneuvered so that the dog could nose around Sasto's legs.

Finally taking note of her and the bloodhound, Sasto got spooked and stepped away.

Sara bent to rub Bongo's head and said, "Don't worry. She's friendly."

"Not a fan of dogs," Sasto said and then returned his attention to Trey and Jose. "I'm in a rush. My assistant set up a meeting this afternoon."

"With us," Jose said.

Sasto narrowed his gaze. "You need some work done?"

"We do. We need you to fill a hole for us. Heard you did the original digging for the Florians," Trey said, his voice as tight and tense as his body.

"I did some work at the kennels. Is that a problem?" the contractor said and lifted his chin in a defiant gesture, but he was several inches shorter than both Trey and Jose and with a waist going to flab. He wasn't going to scare off either of the two men or her and Bongo either.

"They pulled two bodies out of a hole. A hole you dug and filled in," Trey said.

Sasto's face turned a sickly green and he waved his hand back and forth. "No way. I had nothing to do with that."

"But you did the work, didn't you?" Jose said, his tone friendlier and sympathetic.

"We had to fix a broken drainpipe causing backups and weakening the foundation. My guys did the repair but when they went back in the morning, the hole had already been filled."

While the men had been talking, Sara had loosened her hold on Bongo's leash again to let her get close to Sasto, who had been too upset to notice. Bongo had nosed around his legs, but then returned to calmly sit at her side.

She rubbed Bongo's head as Trey continued with the interrogation. "You had access to the equipment that night, right? Easy enough for you to go back—"

"I had nothing to do with those bodies," Sasto insisted, not that it dissuaded Trey.

"What about Delgado? He have anything to do with them?" Trey challenged.

Sasto turned that unhealthy seasick color again, leaned close to Trey and in low tones said, "You don't want to mess with him. I know your family has clout, but Delgado. He's one scary guy."

"Scary enough that you would do whatever he asked? You can tell us. Like you said, our family has clout. You know my dad is with the DA's office," Jose said, his voice also pitched lower so only their small group could hear the exchange.

Sasto made the sign of the cross against his chest. "On my kids' lives, I had nothing to do with those bodies. Delgado either."

Sara was inclined to believe him. Only a sick man would swear an oath on his kids' lives.

That seemed to placate Trey and Jose as well since Trey said, "If you find out anything, will you let us know?"

Sasto nodded and Jose shook his hand, clearly wanting to keep things friendly.

"We'd appreciate that," he said.

As she was climbing into the SBS SUV, she noticed something hanging from the pickup's rearview mirror. Something that looked like it had been made by a young child. On the back window of the pickup were vinyl decals depicting a mom, dad, two kids and a cat.

Sasto was likely telling the truth, but if he was, where did that leave their investigation? she thought.

Chapter Fourteen

By Jose's guesstimate, the cabin on the far side of the property was a little over a mile away from the other buildings at the kennels. A wide swath of a hardwood hammock offered privacy. There was also another fairly large stretch of land beyond the cabin that was part of the kennel property but leased to a local farmer.

When they pulled up in front of the cabin, the door slowly opened, and a large overall-clad man walked out cradling a shotgun. From what he could remember of Metz's mug shot, it was him although way older and heavier.

As Trey killed the engine, he shot a quick look back at Sara and Bongo.

"Can Bongo restrain him if we need her to?" he asked.

Jose faced Sara, who was shaking her head vehemently.

"No. Bloodhounds are too friendly and gentle to be trained to attack. She's more likely to lick him to death than anything else," Sara said, and rubbed Bongo's ears. The dog immediately licked her hand as if to prove her point.

Trey muttered a curse just as the man called out, "You've got to the count of five to either leave or tell me why you're here."

Trey opened the window of the SUV and called out, "We're the new kennel owners. We just want to chat."

Metz rocked on the balls of his feet and mumbled something to himself that Jose couldn't quite make out.

A second later, Metz laid his shotgun against the side of the cabin, but close enough to reach it if he needed to.

"Stay here," Trey said in a low tone, but Jose shook his head.

"Where you go, we go," Jose said, and Sara joined his chorus with, "We're going too."

Trey looked from him to Sara and Bongo, then nodded. "No quick moves and don't get too close."

"Got it," Jose said, carefully opening his door and stepping out.

Sara joined him a second later with Bongo at her side, not that the bloodhound would be of assistance.

Trey took a step toward the cabin, but stopped by the front of the SUV, maintaining a few yards between himself and Metz. Hands held slightly upward, as if in surrender, he said, "I'm Trey Gonzalez. My family bought the Florian kennels."

"I heard. I have until the end of the month to vacate," Metz said, and spit out a stream of something brown that landed on the floor of the cabin porch. That action probably explained the splatters of indeterminate shades of brown on his overalls.

"I hope that move won't be problem," Jose said, trying to be conciliatory in the hope of defusing the situation.

"I still got a week to go," Metz said, and jammed his hands in his pockets.

Jose raised his hands as if pleading. "We're not here to rush you. We just want to ask you a few questions."

Metz hesitated and then pointed at Bongo. "What's with the dog?"

"She's my K-9 partner. She's going to help me train other dogs," Sara explained and rubbed Bongo's head and ears. "She's friendly," she added, as if also trying to calm any unease that might make Metz act violently.

Metz grunted and then glared at Trey. "You're a cop, aren't you?"

Trey shook his head. "Not anymore. I work with my family now."

"If you're not a cop, why are you here and asking me questions?" Metz said, narrowing his gaze as he focused on Trey.

Since it seemed that Metz had an issue with cops, Jose said, "You used to work for the Florians, right?"

Metz shifted his gaze to Jose and said, "And who are you?"

"I'm Jose Gonzalez. I'm the real estate agent," Jose said, hoping it would continue to defuse any tension.

Laughing, Metz said, "A real estate agent? That's a good one. I'm afraid now. Real afraid."

Jose's gut tightened with anger at being so easily discounted but forced a smile to his face. "Just a real estate agent. You worked for the Florians?"

After another slight hesitation, Metz nodded. "I did. Just some general handyman stuff around the kennels."

"They let you stay here once it closed?" Sara asked.

Metz dipped his head and said, "They wanted to make sure nothing happened to the place since they weren't around."

"Did you notice anything out of the ordinary?" Trey asked.

Metz shook his head. "Nothing. It's pretty quiet out here."

Jose peered at Trey, needing his confirmation to continue. At the slight nod of Trey's head, Jose faced Metz and said, "Do you remember Terry Hansen?"

Metz frowned and peered upward, as if searching the sky for an answer, but then he nodded with some conviction and said, "Pretty little thing. She was around for a while and then just up and left."

"Left? Where did she go?" Sara asked, playing the innocent even though they were all well aware of Terry's fate.

With a casual shrug, Metz said, "Got me."

"Did Terry get you? You like pretty little things like her, don't you?" Trey challenged, getting an immediate reaction.

Metz jabbed his finger in Trey's direction. "I didn't touch Terry just like I didn't touch that girl. She lied about her age and lied to the police because she didn't want her parents to know she liked it."

"She liked it? She was thirteen!" Trey shot back.

Jose knew his cousin well enough to know Trey would like nothing better than to lock Metz up, but to do that they needed evidence.

To lower the temperature again, Jose said, "We found Terry, Barry. We know where she is."

Metz smiled and pointed in Jose's direction this time. "You hear that, Trey? Why aren't you asking her about what I didn't do?"

In a deadly calm tone, Trey said, "Because we found her in a hole in the ground."

METZ ROCKED BACKWARD and Sara feared he was reaching for his gun, but then the man just collapsed into a rocking chair on the porch. The wood of the chair creaked with the weight of him and crazily tilted back, worrying her that it might crash to the ground, but Metz stabilized it with his feet.

If she read his face and actions correctly, Metz seemed truly shocked by what Trey had just said. He either was an award-worthy actor or an innocent man.

"You knew Terry. You liked her. You want us to figure out what happened, don't you?" Sara said, exploiting what she was reading in the hopes he might reveal more.

"Where did you find her?" he asked and peered at Trey almost pleadingly.

"You know where, Metz. Only one hole big enough on the property around the time Terry left," Trey said.

Metz's eyes widened as if the answer had suddenly come to him. It struck her again: actor or innocent?

"The contractors dug a hole to fix a drainpipe," he said, his tone almost defeated, she thought.

"And you filled it up after putting Terry in there, didn't you?" Trey said, charging into cop mode the way he might have in an interrogation room.

Metz slapped his hands on the arms of the rocker. "I didn't kill Terry. Like I said, she just up and left."

"Right around the time the contractors were doing the work," Jose said and then added, "Who filled up the hole, Barry?"

With a shrug and shake of his head, Metz said, "I thought the contractors did it, but they acted surprised that it was filled."

Which confirmed what Sasto told them, Sara thought.

"Who else had access to the property?" Trey prompted.

Metz spread his arms wide. "Look around. Not much here. Almost anyone could come and go on that property without anyone noticing."

Sara peered around and hated that he was right. Between the wide-open spaces and the woods, it would be easy, especially at night, for someone to enter the property and not draw much attention.

"Was there anyone else working at the kennels who was friends with Terry? Who maybe showed too much interest?" Jose asked.

Besides yourself, Sara thought, and somehow wasn't surprised by Metz's answer.

"Everyone loved Terry. She had her issues, but she was a good kid," Metz said.

"What kinds of issues?" Jose asked, his tone sympathetic once more.

"Rumor had it she did some hooking in the South Beach

area. Heard her pimp wasn't too pleased with her coming to live and work out here," Metz replied.

"Know his name?" Trey asked.

Metz shrugged and shook his head. "No. Are you done now? I got some packing to do."

Trey nodded and said, "We appreciate your help."

He was about to turn and walk back to the car when Jose asked, "By the way, do you own a bow of any kind?"

Chapter Fifteen

Jose braced for Metz's reaction, but the man merely gestured to the shotgun and then raised hands with knuckles swollen by arthritis. "Do these fingers look like they can use a bow? I can barely pull the trigger."

Jose's grandmother had suffered from the disease, so he recognized how debilitating it could be. But that didn't necessarily eliminate Metz from the earlier killings.

"If you think of anything—" Jose began, but Metz cut him off with a barked laugh.

"Yeah, sure, I'll let you know."

Jose shared a look with Trey and then Sara. Together the three of them turned, but before they headed back to the SUV, Sara swung back toward Metz and said, "Do you mind if I walk Bongo? She's been in the car too long."

Metz delayed, but then did an almost regal wave of his hand. "Walk away. It's your property after all."

Jose was surprised by his easy acquiescence and pleased by Sara's quick thinking.

With a click of her tongue, she strolled with Bongo to the stand of trees. The dog was active at first, but then paused to lay on the ground. Sara seemed surprised by that and urged Bongo to her feet to let her sniff some more. Bongo lay down again, forcing Sara to tug on her leash and get her working her way toward the cabin. As she did so, Metz rose to watch, appearing a little more anxious as the dog nosed around the edges of the small cabin. Luckily, Bongo stopped at one point to relieve herself and Sara responsibly picked up the waste.

Once she did so, she walked Bongo toward the front porch where Metz stood at the edge, peering down at her.

Bongo stopped to scent him, and he stumbled back from the bloodhound.

"Don't worry, she's friendly," Sara said again, but Metz kept his distance.

Sara walked toward them and once she was at their side, they all hopped back into the SUV, but remained silent until Trey had turned out of the driveway and onto the narrow road that ran along the edges of the kennel's property.

Jose swiveled in the seat. "Bongo scented something close to the cabin?"

Sara nodded. "She did. Something dead."

Whipping his head around to gaze at Trey, he said, "What do we do now?"

Trey tightened his hands on the wheel, knuckles white from the pressure of his grasp. "The police need probable cause to search Metz's home and I'm not so sure that we have enough right now."

"But you own the property. Can't we give them what they need?" Jose asked, unsure how things like that worked in Trey's world.

Sara laid a hand on his shoulder and squeezed. "It's a fine line to walk. We don't want a defense attorney claiming we were acting on behalf of the police and doing a warrantless search that violates Metz's civil rights."

"What about the rights of those women? And any others that may be buried in that forest? Don't they have rights?" Jose shot back, angered that the criminals had more rights than their victims.

"You're preaching to the choir," Trey said, and turned off

onto the road leading to the highway. "Let's head back to the offices and regroup. Discuss how to proceed."

JOSE SHOOK HIS head in disgust. "How to proceed? I'm all for finding out what Bongo is smelling," he said, and glanced back in Sara and Bongo's direction.

Sara was all for that also, but it wasn't that easy, she thought, and rubbed Bongo's head and ears. "If there is a dead body there, we don't want to compromise any evidence that might be in that location," she explained, and at his exasperated sigh, she added, "But maybe we can consider identifying areas where Bongo scents something."

Trey nodded and said, "That's a possibility but only if we proceed with extreme caution. For all we know, there are other booby traps in those woods."

Sara had no doubt there were other surprises waiting for them. Because of that, she said, "Safety is a top priority. We don't want any of the team to get hurt."

Jose and Trey were silent for long moments, and it worried her.

Trey was likely running through all the scenarios for how the SBS team should proceed as he drove them to Miami and the SBS offices. As for Jose, was he reconsidering his involvement? Had this gotten to be more than he bargained for when he'd agreed to help?

She leaned back in her seat, also thinking about all that had happened and how different it was from what she thought she'd be doing in her new job. She'd thought she'd be comfortably settled in the former owners' house and getting the place ready for a new batch of agents and their dogs.

Not this, she thought, and sighed as it brought worries about the kind of exposure she'd had with her family's earlier problems.

Beside her Bongo also sighed, laid her head on Sara's lap and looked up at her with those mournful brown eyes.

Sara smiled and stroked her hand across the dog's smooth loose skin, shifting the folds with her caress. "It's going to be okay, girl," she said, more to reassure herself and not the dog.

"It is," Jose echoed from the front seat. "We will figure out what's going on."

His words alleviated her earlier worry since it didn't sound as if Jose was going to run from whatever was happening, impressing her again with his resolve.

It eased some of her anxiety as did running her hand back and forth along Bongo, taking comfort from that connection to her partner and to the man who was proving to be more than she imagined when she first met him.

As for Trey, although he kept quiet, she had no doubt he was mentally running through all the likely scenarios for how to find out who had murdered Terry Hansen and the other woman in the grave, as well as any other bodies they found.

When they reached the SBS building, they hurried up to the office where Mia had arranged for assorted sandwiches to be brought in so they could work through dinner.

Sophie and Robbie were already in the conference room as well as Trey's pregnant wife, Roni, and Mia's multimillionaire tech husband, John Wilson.

At nearly six months, Roni's baby belly was well-pronounced, and she looked pale and a little tired. It made Sara wonder how she was handling the demanding job of being a Miami Beach detective and helping out the SBS team as well.

Trey immediately went to her side, hugged her and then rubbed his hand across her belly in a tender caress. "How are you feeling?" he asked, worry alive in his gaze.

"Tired and I have a backache. I just need to get some rest," Roni said with a forced smile.

"Maybe you should head home," Trey suggested, but Roni shook her head.

"I've got some info from local PD. Not much, but some," she said, and sat.

Mia walked over and rubbed her hand across Roni's shoulders. "Help yourselves to the food and drinks so we can get this meeting going," she said, and eyeballed everyone to get them moving along.

Sara did as she asked, grabbing some lean ham and cheese as a snack for Bongo until she could feed her later. Setting that on a plate for her dog, she then grabbed a sandwich, chips and a soda for herself and sat.

A second later Jose joined her, offering her a weary smile. Once the rest of the team had settled down, Trey started the meeting.

"Why don't you go first so I can get you home, Roni."

"Your suspicions about the identity of the one woman were accurate. The local police were able to ID Terry Hansen thanks to dental records her family provided," Roni said.

"What about COD?" Sophie asked.

Jose gave her a puzzled look that vanished as Roni said, "The ME couldn't be sure about the cause of death, but both women had bone damage indicative of being shot by a broadhead arrow. There was also a piece of a shirt that the ME could match up with the skeleton, and the damage on that was also indicative of an arrow wound."

"Like the arrow someone shot at us today?" Jose asked, brow furrowed with worry.

"Very similar to that arrow. By the way, the ME found traces of human blood on the arrowhead, but no viable prints," Roni said, and peered in Sara's direction. "I understand Bongo scented something."

Sara nodded. "Possibly, and if we're relying on that, Sasto is not a suspect any longer."

"I ran the suspects through my probability program, and it confirms that. The probability for Sasto to be the killer is only 35 percent," John Wilson said, and passed around copies of a report his program had generated.

Jose peered at it and said, "This is what your secret program does?"

With a shrug, John said, "Not so secret anymore since I've offered a version of it to Miami Beach PD to test."

"A version of it?" Sara asked, also wondering what the program did and why someone had almost killed John and Mia in order to get it.

John peered around the table and at Trey's nod, he explained. "A scaled down version. My program sucks in data from pretty much everywhere and uses that to determine probabilities on who might be a crime victim or who might have committed the crime."

JOSE SCRUTINIZED THE report that John had provided, trying to make sense of what he was seeing based on what John had just said. Waving the paper in the air, he said, "According to your program, Sasto is out and the probability that Metz is our suspect is only about 65 percent. Failing grade, isn't it?"

John nodded. "A failing grade because Metz is on disability due to his RA."

Jose confirmed it, saying, "I saw his hands today. They were in pretty bad shape."

"And he didn't stand for long. He plopped down in that rocker really quick but it could have been because of what we said about Terry Hansen," Sara added.

"Plus no bomb-making experience," Roni said, then winced and rubbed her belly, in obvious discomfort.

"Which leaves us back at square one," Trey said, with a frustrated sigh before turning his attention to his wife. "Maybe I should take you home."

Roni shook her head, and the shoulder-length strands of her sun-streaked light brown hair shifted with the action. "I'm okay. Let's just finish up."

"Let's," John said, and whipped out more copies that he handed to everyone.

As Jose peered over the report, John explained. "This is a list of sex offenders in a sixty-mile radius who have some kind of experience with explosives and/or military tactics."

Jose's eyes widened at how many names were on the list. It seemed like way too many but beside each name was a number. He gestured to the number and said, "Is this the probability of them being connected to the murders?"

"It is," John said and quickly added, "And I don't need the program to know that this is probably a serial killer and there will be more bodies on that property."

"Bongo thinks so too," Sara said, and hearing her name, Bongo sat up at Sara's side. She rewarded the dog with a rub of her ears and a treat from her jeans pocket.

"What do you want us to do?" Sophie said and laid down the list she had also been perusing.

Trey smoothed his hands across the report as it sat on the tabletop. "You and Robbie should take the top five suspects on here and do a little more digging. No pun intended."

After, he looked toward Mia and John. "This is great, John. *Gracias.* We have a list of missing women, and maybe you can do something to see if any of them have interacted with our suspects."

John nodded. "I can run their data, locations, etcetera and see where they intersect."

Trey turned his attention to Jose and Sara. "I guess we can work with Matt and Natalie in the morning to identify any areas in our woods where we think we might have a body. But just identify and not touch. We don't want to jeopardize the evidence."

"Or trip a booby trap," Jose added.

With a dip of his head, Trey said, "Or trip a booby trap. Is there anything else to discuss?"

Robbie held his hand up, drawing Trey's attention. "What's up, *primo*?"

"Sophie and I were thinking that we could also send up one of the lidar drones to map the area. See if it's showing any irregularities belowground."

With an affirmative nod, Trey said, "That's a great suggestion. It could confirm whatever the K-9 team locates, and help the local PD once we call them in."

"When will we call them in?" Roni asked, weariness evident in her tones and the droop of her shoulders.

"We can have one of them join us in the morning if you think that's appropriate," Trey said.

"Detective Ray Espinoza is the lead on the murder case. If it is a serial killer, the faster he's in on this, the better," Roni said and quickly added, "I can let him know if you want."

"Call him, *por favor*," Trey said, rose and held his hand out to Roni.

She slipped her hand into his, her actions slow and pained. Trey clearly noticed as well since he eased his arm around her waist to offer support and comfort.

"We'll meet back here at 9:00 a.m. to head to the kennels." When they all nodded, he continued. "John, thanks for your help. If you and Mia have anything else—"

"We'll let you know. Why don't you get Roni home now?" Mia said, also picking up on the other woman's discomfort.

"I'm okay," Roni said, not that you could tell from the look on her face and the almost stiff way she was moving.

"*Amorcito*, let's go home," Trey said, and kissed her cheek, which dragged a hint of a smile from Roni.

"Time for all of us to get some rest," Mia said, shooting to her feet and grabbing hold of John's hand.

"I guess we're going," John said with a laugh, and followed his wife as she nearly raced out the door.

Sophie and Robbie snapped their laptops close and likewise stood, but Robbie said, "We've still got some work to do. We'll be in our offices if you need us."

"Buenas noches," Jose said, and waved at his two cousins as they left the room, heads bent together while they chatted about the tasks left to finish that night.

He glanced at Sara. "You ready to go? Want to grab some chips and things for the penthouse?"

"I'll never say no to a chip. Bongo either," Sara said with a laugh, and playfully rubbed behind the bloodhound's ears. Leaning close to her dog and wrinkling her nose, she said, "Maybe after a nice bath."

Leaving the table, they grabbed a few bags of chips, strolled to the elevators and badged themselves up to the penthouse, but as they did so, Sara said, "Don't you want to go home?"

With a shrug, Jose said, "As much as I want to go home, it makes sense for me to stay close during this investigation. Unless you want some privacy."

She waved her hands in refusal. "I like the company, especially with all that's happening."

As the elevator stopped and they entered the penthouse, lights from under the kitchen cabinets spilled golden beams onto the countertops, but the real light show was outside the wall of windows that faced the city and Key Biscayne.

SARA WALKED TO the windows and stood there, Bongo tucked beside her.

"Beautiful, isn't it?" she said.

Jose walked to her side and murmured, "Beautiful," but as she met his gaze, she realized he wasn't talking about the sights outside the window.

Heat flared through her and rushed to her cheeks. She ripped her gaze from his and focused on the beauty beyond. The harshness of the man-made buildings was juxtaposed against the moonlight glittering on the calm waters of the bay.

"I pictured you as a nature girl. It made me wonder why you would come to a place like this," he said, and pointed out the window.

"I'm more comfortable in the wilderness but there's beauty in so many things," she said, and sneaked a peek at him from the corner of her eye.

"There is. Ugliness too, like what we found at the kennels," he said, his tone filled with anger and disgust.

"We will get justice for those women and for anyone else out there," she said, and turned away from the window. "I need to tend to Bongo. Feed her, take her for a walk, and then give her a nice bath. It's important to keep all those folds clean."

He glanced at Bongo and arched a brow. "That's a lot of folds. Need help?"

"Sure, but first food. She's got a healthy appetite," Sara said, and hurried to the fridge for the fresh food she gave Bongo at night.

The bloodhound devoured it, and after taking her for walk so she could relieve herself it was time for the bath, a necessity to keep Bongo clean and avoid any issues with the loose skin on her body.

In the bathroom she prepped a bath, adding a special shampoo to the water.

Bongo licked her face and Sara laughed at the dog's antics. "I know you love your baths," she said, and the dog didn't hesitate to jump in, splashing water over the edges of the tub.

Sara chuckled and washed Bongo, scrubbing her down with the lather. Carefully checking her skin for signs of any irritation and washing beneath any folds to keep them clean and avoid nasty doggy odor.

She had just finished rinsing off the soap and pulled the

plug on the bath to empty the water when Jose came in with an armful of towels.

He sat on the toilet seat cover and handed her one.

"Thank you," she said, and toweled down Bongo who helped her by shaking her head and body, sending droplets of water flying across Sara and the tiles of the shower.

Jose laughed and handed her a fresh towel. "Looks like you might be needing this."

"Thanks, again." She grabbed the towel and wiped the water off her face. Dabbed at the spots staining her blouse and jeans.

Bongo hopped out of the tub, wetting her again as she brushed past Sara on her way out of the bath.

"Looks like you may need to clean up too," Jose laughed, and pointed a thumb in the direction of the open concept space. "I'm going to go shower. Meet you out there after?"

Chapter Sixteen

"Definitely." She liked spending time with him and was excited about where it might lead but also worried about how she might fit into a world like his, filled with so many events and people.

She hurried from the bathroom and after cleaning up from Bongo's bath, showered. The warmth of the water spilled over her, chasing away the tension of the day. Helping to prepare her for what she might face tomorrow when they searched the woods.

She worried they'd find a body in the woods between them and Metz's cabin.

Rushing from the shower, she slipped into an oversize T-shirt and loose shorts, her typical nighttime casual wear. They were comfortable and more so, they wouldn't give Jose the idea that she was throwing herself at him although in truth, maybe that's what she wanted to do despite her misgivings.

Jose was already on the sofa when she exited her room, Bongo sitting at his feet. As she approached, she noticed the highball glass with rum sitting beside his scotch. Scattered around the glasses were the few chip bags they'd snagged from the conference room.

She sat next to him, grabbed a bag of chips and opened it. "Thanks."

Hearing the ruffle of the bag, Bongo came to her side, clearly expecting a treat. "Just one. You know they have too much salt."

Bongo whined but didn't budge so Sara gave her the one chip, and seemingly satisfied, Bongo drifted a few feet away to lay by her bedroom door.

"Really? Just one?" he said as he munched on his chips.

"Just one. She's learned that, and I give her healthier treats when she's working," she said, and tossed a chip into her mouth. The saltiness of it had her reaching for her rum and taking a small sip.

"Maybe I should limit myself too," she said with a laugh, and set the bag down, but kept the rum, holding the glass between her hands, steadying herself. Being close to Jose created too many unsettling feelings.

He held his scotch glass in one hand and eased his arm around her shoulders, drawing her closer.

She snuggled into his side, savoring the warmth of his body and the strength of it. Of him. Of his character.

Most of the men she'd known growing up would certainly have run after the explosions much less the discovery of the bodies. They were men unaccustomed to physical dangers. They lived their danger in the stock market and business ventures.

She'd thought Jose was like them in so many ways but as the days passed, he set himself apart from them in unexpected ways, including hanging in unlike her boyfriend had done.

"You've been a surprise," she admitted, then brought her legs up, knelt and faced him.

He seemed taken aback. "Really? How?"

She scrutinized him, dipping her head before cradling his jaw. "You're still here, for one."

A half smile lifted his lips, yanking free a boyish dimple. "You expected me to run?"

A rough laugh escaped her. "Maybe. When my dad got in trouble, my boyfriend at the time tucked tail and ran. And what's happening now sure isn't what either of us signed up for."

"It isn't, but we're going to see this through, right?" he said, and planted a kiss in the center of her palm.

"We are." She set her glass on the table and slipping onto his lap, she said, "There's something else we need to do."

JOSE HADN'T WANTED to push and certainly hadn't expected that Sara would.

"Are you sure?"

She shook her head and laughed. "No. I'm not normally a risk-taker."

"I'm not either," he said, but didn't hesitate to cradle her against him, his hands stroking the long line of her back as she straddled him.

"What have we gotten ourselves into?" she asked and ran her fingers through the short strands of his hair before dipping her hand down to trace the edges of his lips with one finger.

He watched her, seeing the gray of her gaze deepen to charcoal and her pupils widen as she focused on his lips. "Murder. Mayhem," he said seriously, but then added in a lighter tone, "Romance?"

She smiled, her full lips tilting up playfully at the corners, making it impossible to resist them and her any longer.

He kissed her, savoring the warmth of her lips. Loving the taste of her, especially as she opened her mouth, almost shyly. She danced her tongue out to meet his as they kissed over and over until they were both breathing heavily, and he needed more.

Reaching up, he cupped her breast, her nipple hard against his palm.

She lowered her head to watch him as he caressed her.

Moaned and shifted against his legs, settling him at her center. The heat of her bathed him and from somewhere deep inside him came something like a growl and an emotion he'd never felt before with any other woman.

"I want you," he whispered against her lips.

"I want you too," she answered, and with that, he shot to his feet with her cradled in his arms.

He marched with her to her room and paused by the door as Bongo raised her head and eyeballed him guiltily.

Or at least that's how it looked to him, which made him kick the door closed for privacy from the bloodhound's too alert gaze.

Hurrying to the bed, he gently laid her on the comforter and eased beside her as he noticed a few scattered bruises on her creamy skin. He traced one on the tanned skin of her arm and said, "I wish this wasn't how we met."

She ran her fingers through his hair again and cradled the back of his skull, drawing his attention to her gamine face once more. "Tell the truth. I'm not the kind to spend time in one of your typical clubs or parties or all those big social events."

He chuckled and shook his head. "No, you're not and I'm glad for it," he said, bent and kissed her again, rejoicing in that difference. At the honesty of her and her beauty.

Sara stroked her hands up and down the powerful line of his back. Held him close as they kissed and he slipped his hand beneath her T-shirt, caressing her again. The tug of his fingers dragged a surprised gasp, and he tempered his touch until she laid her hand over his and urged him on.

He lost his carefully held restraint, deepening his kiss. Breaking away from her only to ease off her T-shirt and then his so they would be skin-to-skin.

She was so smooth against him, so tender and yet strong.

When she shifted her hips, pressing upward, he dipped a finger beneath the waistband of her shorts and eased his hand between her legs to build her passion until there was no stopping where they were going.

He slipped off her shorts and his sweats, muttered a curse. "Hold on. I'll be back."

Hurrying to his room and his wallet, he ripped the condom out of it, tearing the foil and rushing to roll it on before he fell back onto the bed with her laughing, and urging him over her. Into her.

Dios, he thought as he slipped into her. It was like nothing he'd ever felt before. It was like coming home.

HE STILLED ABOVE HER, confusing her.

She met his gaze and his amazing aqua eyes, normally like Biscayne Bay on a sunny day, were a dark, intense teal. "Jose?" she asked, puzzled by his hesitation.

"You're so beautiful. So special," he said, and bent his head to whisper a kiss against her lips, his touch tentative.

"So are you, Jose. So special," she said, knowing that at times he felt insecure about his place in the accomplished Gonzalez family. She wanted him to know there was no reason for that. He was as special, maybe more so, than his cousins.

He moved then, drawing in and out of her, making her tremble from the surge of passion he roused by that simple movement.

She dug her fingers into his shoulders, struggling for control. Needing his strength as he surged into her again and as desire built, it drew them up higher and higher until with one last thrust, he took them over the edge.

Afterward, they lay there silently, holding each other. Stroking and caressing as they savored the peace and joy that came from their union.

"I won't ever be sorry we met like this," she said, and rose on an elbow to gaze at him.

He grinned and faced her. "I won't either."

"What if we find what I think we will tomorrow?" she asked, worried about what the future might bring.

With a determined dip of his head, he laid a hand at her waist and said, "Then we'll deal with it together."

Chapter Seventeen

She woke wrapped in his arms and greeted the morning with his loving, dawn's hopeful rays bathing their bodies through the wall of windows.

After showering and making a quick breakfast for themselves and Bongo, they took her dog for a walk around the block. Bloodhounds needed a good amount of exercise and activity, and she worried Bongo hadn't gotten enough the last few days.

But she would today, Sara thought, thinking about the search they'd have to conduct and what it would reveal.

"I can see the wheels turning," Jose said, and playfully tapped his temple in emphasis.

"Racing might be a better adjective," she said with a smile and toss of her head.

He nodded and said, "It's going to be a busy day."

As they rounded the last corner before the SBS office building, Jose's phone chirped.

Brows furrowed, he said, "It's Trey."

He answered and his look turned even darker. "Don't worry. We can handle things on our own. The important thing is to make sure Roni is okay."

Fear gripped Sara at the mention of the pregnant woman, and she recalled how she'd looked the night before. Too tired and pale, she thought.

Jose ended the call. "Roni's spotting. Trey's taking her to the hospital."

She laid a hand on his arm, trying to reassure him and herself. "She's going to be fine. These things happen sometimes."

"I hope so. They're both so excited about the baby," he said, looked away and muttered an expletive. "Trey said to go with Sophie and Robbie. He'll meet us there later. Matt and Natalie will be there at ten."

"Let's find Sophie and Robbie," she said, and with a click of her tongue, instructed Bongo to walk with them back to the SBS offices. Inside they found Sophie and Robbie packing the drone equipment to map the woods.

In no time they were on their way to the kennel location. Once they arrived, Jose and she waited while their tech gurus prepared the drone and computer equipment that might confirm whatever Bongo and the other canines found during their search.

"I've heard about using lidar drones to find hidden objects, but I've never had firsthand experience," Sara said as Sophie did a final check on the equipment.

"We've used it several times and I still find it amazing," the other woman admitted.

"Thankfully we have John's supercomputer to process the data. That really speeds things up," Robbie said, and walked over with the remote.

The crunch of tires on the driveway gravel drew their attention.

Matt and Natalie had arrived.

They parked, exited the van and seconds later, their two K-9 partners bounded out of the SUV and raced over to Bongo. The three dogs eagerly sniffed each other and tussled playfully until their human partners instructed them to sit.

Matt spoke up first. "Natalie and I were discussing that

while our dogs are good trackers, they haven't really had much experience with cadavers."

"We thought we should shadow you and let the dogs get acquainted with the smell if we find anything," Natalie said, and rubbed her Lab's head.

Sara nodded. "Good idea. Honestly, searching for cadavers isn't something Bongo and I usually do, but she's been trained for it."

JOSE HAD BEEN letting the K-9 agents and his tech cousins run the show. But it seemed to him they were losing sight of something important and with Trey's absence, he felt he had to say something.

"I know you're all ready to search, but don't forget someone may have set some booby traps out there," he said, and gestured toward the woods and the caution tape they'd tied around the trip wires they'd already located, and had been defused by the bomb squad the day before.

"You're right. We have to move cautiously and be alert." Sara seconded his warning, earning murmurs of agreement from the other SBS agents.

At their seeming acceptance, Jose said, "I can be a second set of eyes if you want."

"That would be great," Sara said, and stroked a hand down his arm.

"We should get going. The police and CSI units are waiting on us to continue their investigation," Sophie said, and lifted the drone out of the SUV cargo area.

"We've programed this to survey the wooded area and just beyond, to the cabin where Metz is living," Robbie said, cradling the remote in his hands.

"You may hear a buzzing sound as it flies overhead. Don't let it distract you," Sophie warned, and pulled some yellow stake flags from the cargo area.

She handed them to Jose and said, "Can you mark anywhere you get a hit?"

Jose nodded. "I think I can manage that," he said with a self-deprecating chuckle.

"Let's go," Sara said, and with a quick hand signal to her dog, Bongo jumped to life, bounding ahead of her.

Jose fell into step beside her while Matt and Natalie followed, their dogs on a tight leash as they approached the woods.

Sara paused there, searching the edges of the tree line where bits and pieces of the shrapnel in the booby trap peppered the ground. Other pieces had embedded themselves in the bark of the trees along the perimeter.

Jose's gut tightened and grew cold at the thought of what might have happened if they had tripped that trap.

He shared a look with Sara before she drew in a long breath and nodded. "I'm ready."

He wasn't sure he was, but he'd never run from a challenge.

With a slow dip of his head, he confirmed he was ready and walked by her side, his gaze glued to the ground and trees in their path. For safety's sake, he grabbed a long branch and used it to poke and prod at the ground before them.

As he did so at one spot, the leaves scattered there gave way, revealing a hole big enough to swallow up a man. Mindful of the risk of a secondary trap, they all quickly retreated the way they'd come in and waited, but nothing happened.

Retracing their steps, they peered into the hole. At the bottom, sharpened sticks would have seriously damaged anyone who fell in.

"Vietcong used traps like this," Matt said.

"Whoever this is, they mean business," Natalie said.

At Sara's side, Bongo whined and tugged on her leash.

SARA WOULD HAVE normally given Bongo free rein to follow the scent, but with the surprises the killer had rigged, she drew Bongo close and kept a keen eye out for dangers.

Bongo tugged her about ten feet away, focused on a scent. As they neared an area a little more concave than the rest of the ground, Bongo jerked on her leash harder, nosed around the leaves and underbrush, and then sat down.

Sara raised her hand and motioned for Matt and Natalie to come forward. Pointing at the ground, she said, "Let your partners scent this area and reward them."

She knelt and rewarded Bongo with praise, her favorite ear rub and a treat. The other SBS agents mimicked her actions as their dogs smelled the area and sat down, copying what Bongo had done.

Satisfied they had located a possible cadaver, Sara motioned to Jose who stuck a yellow stake flag into the ground.

They continued through the woods, allowing Bongo to search and the other dogs to train. Carefully minding the areas for traps.

They found two other spiked pits and marked them as well for the safety of the police and CSI crews who would gather evidence.

After Bongo's third hit, the other two K-9s had seemed to get the hang of it, sniffing and sitting down to notify their handlers of a hit.

"They're quick learners," Sara said, pleased by how well the other dogs had caught on. But then again, Belgian Malinois and Labradors were great dogs for cadaver searches.

"Do you think you can do it on your own?" she asked, examining the large swath of trees they still had to cover. As she did so, she caught sight of the drone flying overhead, also searching the area.

Matt and Natalie shared a look before nodding. "I think we can. We'll keep an eye out for booby traps, go to the top end of the woods, and work our way toward you."

"That makes sense. Call if you need anything," Jose said, and waved his cell phone.

Natalie nodded. "We'll keep you posted."

Matt and Natalie carefully worked their way back to the tree line and hurried to the top of the hardwood hammock to start their exploration.

Jose and Sara resumed their search, Bongo in the lead. As Jose tapped the ground with the stick, a loud snap split the air.

She caught a blur of motion from the corner of her eye and a second later, Jose grabbed her, his hands hard on her shoulders, pulling her against his chest.

Another spiked volleyball split the air in front of her, passing dangerously close to Bongo.

"Down," she called out, and the bloodhound instantly lay flat.

Jose wrapped his arms around her, and they dropped to the ground, Jose protecting her body against any secondary attack.

She held her breath, waiting for an explosion.

Chapter Eighteen

What seemed like an eternity passed, but nothing happened.

Jose raised his head to peer around.

Nothing. *Nada*, he thought.

Despite that, he warily rose to his feet, peering around the area again before he offered Sara a hand up.

She stood, her blouse and jeans stained with dirt and grass.

"Sorry," he said, and brushed away an errant leaf from her shoulder. "I've messed you up again," he said, regret slamming into him that he'd triggered the trap.

She cupped his cheek. "You kept me safe. Again. I owe you twice now."

Turning, she urged Bongo to move away from the spiked ball arcing back and forth, back and forth.

But Bongo refused to move.

She gave Bongo both verbal and hand commands, attempting to move the bloodhound, but her dog wouldn't budge.

"She's scented something there, right?" Jose said and at Sara's reluctant nod, he plunked a stake into the ground.

Seemingly satisfied with that, Bongo came to her feet, and they continued their search, identifying two other areas before their path intersected with that of Matt and Natalie.

Jose jammed his hands on his hips, sweat pouring off him

from the heat and humidity beneath the canopy of trees. He did a slow swivel, taking in the sight of the traps they'd identified and worse, the almost dozen flags marking the spots where their dogs had identified possible remains.

No, not just remains. Burial sites. Graves, he thought and met Sara's troubled gaze.

"Is this possible?" he said and waved a hand in the direction of all the bright yellow scattered around the forest.

Sara, Matt and Natalie likewise scrutinized the grounds, disbelief on their faces until Sara locked her gaze with his and in a soft tone said, "It is. Sadly, it is."

THERE WAS LITTLE exuberance around the conference room table that night as the SBS team gathered.

Trey sat at the head, hair rumpled from the constant way he ran his fingers through his hair, clearly troubled.

"Roni will be fine, but the doctors have put her on bed rest. The stress of her job might be what's causing the spotting," Trey said, and skipped his gaze around the room. "Detective Espinoza will be our liaison in her absence."

"We're glad to hear Roni's going to be okay," Sara said since it was clear to see how worried Trey was about his wife.

"*Sí*, she is. She's going to be okay," he said, but woodenly, as if he didn't quite believe it.

Mia took hold of his hand and squeezed reassuringly. "She is, Trey. Believe it."

He nodded and quickly launched into the purpose for the meeting. "What you identified today...if you're right, we're dealing with a serial killer."

"We're right," Sara said without hesitation.

Sophie added support for her statement. "The map we produced from the drone footage confirms there are anomalies at the spots identified by the K-9s," she said, and passed around copies of the computer-generated map.

"The lidar is pretty accurate, isn't it?" Trey asked, and glanced in John's direction as he sat next to Mia.

"It is. It's a proven technology in the right hands," John said.

"And we're the right hands. We did this as carefully as we could," Robbie said to eliminate any doubt.

Trey pursed his lips and nodded. "We'll turn this over to PD who may or may not decide to call in the FBI."

"There's going to be a fire storm of publicity. We should prepare a press release about it. Maybe even do a press conference," Mia said.

Sara cringed at the thought of that, the publicity, and explaining to her mother since she was sure to call again if she heard the news. But she had no choice since she was now part of SBS and was not about to quit her job—or leave Jose—over the public exposure she so dreaded.

Trey blew out an exasperated sigh and dragged his fingers through his hair again. "I'm not sure I'm up for that. Maybe you can do it. Or Pepe," he said, and tossed a hand in Jose's direction.

Sara waited for Jose to say he wasn't part of SBS, but he surprised her with, "Whatever you need. We're all here for you."

Her estimation of him rose ever higher if that was even possible. He'd proven himself time and time again over the last few days, showing her that he was the kind of man you could count on.

"If we're sure about this map and what the K-9s discovered, it's time to move on to the suspects. Do we have anything else?"

John drew out some papers from a pile in front of him and passed around copies.

"We've cross-referenced our list with other data to eliminate suspects. Some were in prison, others were not in-state. Others are dead," John said.

Sara glanced at the list, seeing that many of their original suspects had been scrubbed. "This doesn't leave that many people," she said, disheartened.

"Unfortunately, you're right. Only a few. Hopefully our investigation and any evidence PD finds in those graves will help solve this case," Trey said.

JOSE WASN'T FEELING as confident as his cousin while he reviewed John's report.

"What do we do with this now?" he asked, unfamiliar with what his family would normally do to investigate.

"We continue to dig into their histories," Trey said and glanced around the table, settling his gaze on John, Sophie and Robbie. "Is there anything you can do to eliminate any more of these suspects before we go knocking on doors?"

The trio shared a quick look and then John nodded. "We'll work on it."

"That's it?" Jose blurted out, shocked that's all Trey could suggest. "What about Metz? He's literally living feet away from those bodies. He's been living there the entire time!"

"His RA makes him an unlikely suspect, but you're right about Metz," Trey said, his tone conciliatory despite Jose's disbelief.

"He can't be that close and not have seen something," Sara said, filling in what Trey hadn't said.

"Something or someone. While they scrub the data," Trey said, and jerked a thumb in the direction of the tech gurus, "we'll pay Metz another visit at the same time PD and the CSIs scour those areas you identified."

Guilty that he'd pushed Trey, especially since his cousin had his wife's medical issues on his mind, he said, "I didn't mean to step on any toes, Trey. I'm sorry."

Trey held his hand up and waved it off. "No worries, *primo*. With so much on my mind, all ideas are welcome."

Trey's easy attitude only made him feel guiltier until Sara

laid a hand on his and squeezed reassuringly. "It seems like a good time to break."

Everyone nodded and Trey shot to his feet. "I'm going to go see Roni. You're free to have dinner brought in—"

"John and I have a dinner date with Carolina and her new boyfriend. I haven't seen much of her lately and would hate to cancel," Mia said as she likewise hopped to her feet, tugging on John's hand.

Jose glanced toward Sophie and Robbie who waved him off. "We've got work on another case," Sophie said.

He didn't think his family was matchmaking, but regardless, it left him and Sara alone for the night. "It's just you and me," he said, and peered at her.

With a smile Sara said, "Sounds good to me."

THEY REACHED THE penthouse in record time, happy to have time alone and not think about the investigation.

"Do you want to order in dinner or go out?" she said, hoping he'd want to stay in because she was tired after the day they'd had. Also dirty, she thought as she ran a hand across the smudges of dirt and grass on her blouse and jeans.

He took note of her action. "Why don't you clean up and I'll make dinner. The fridge is pretty well-stocked."

She arched a brow in surprise. "You're going to cook?"

Jose laughed and shook his head. "Did I strike you as someone who only makes reservations for dinner?"

With an apologetic shrug, she said, "Sorry to say that you did." Most of the men she'd known, including her father and brothers, would have already been on the phone placing an order.

Raising both hands as if in surrender, he said, "Let me prove you wrong. I'll prep dinner and take care of Bongo while you take a shower."

Bongo had been patiently sitting at her side and at the mention of her name, the dog barked and walked over to

Jose who bent and rubbed the dog's head and ears affectionately. In response, Bongo licked his face, making Jose grimace playfully.

"Not sure I'll ever like doggie kisses," he said, and pointed toward the bedrooms. "Go. Shower. Relax."

Pleased that Bongo and he were getting along, Sara went to the bedroom and took a very long and very hot shower, savoring the heat of the water that chased away memories of the day. But as the aromas of what Jose was cooking wafted into the bedroom, her stomach growled.

Steak if she had to guess, and it smelled delicious.

Raking her fingers through the wet strands of her hair, she hurried out to where Jose had already set the table.

Bongo lay near her bowls. There was fresh water in one and evidence that she'd scarfed down the food Jose must have set out for her.

Jose was at the stove, an apron tied around his lean waist. Drops of water marked his T-shirt and the edges of the sleeves, as if he'd scrubbed his arms to wash up.

Cuban-style steaks, thinly pounded and marinated with lemon, minced onions and parsley, were cooking on the stovetop griddle. There were two pots on the stove beside it, and as she lifted the lids, she realized he'd made rice and beans.

"Smells delicious," she said, wrapping her arms around his waist and pressing her head against his back.

He stroked his hand across her arm and said, "You'd better stop distracting me if you want dinner."

After a tight hug, she said, "I'll get some drinks."

"I opened some red to let it breathe," he said, and jerked his chin in the direction of a bottle sitting on the counter.

She grabbed glasses from a nearby rack and poured them generous portions. They needed it after the day they'd had and what they would have to face once the PD and CSI teams began their investigations.

It made her feel helpless in a way because she'd come to jump-start a new K-9 division and that was all on hold with what was happening.

Jose reached out and ran his index finger across the furrows on her brow. "I can tell they're not happy thoughts."

With a twisted smile, she said, "Not happy. Selfish possibly."

"Why is that?" he said and flipped the steaks onto plates. A second later, he was piling on rice and beans before walking with the plates to the table.

She grabbed both wineglasses and he removed a bowl from the fridge and brought it over to the table: an avocado salad.

"You went all out," she said, but he held up a finger as if to say, "I'm not done yet."

Grabbing a potholder, he opened the oven door, and returned with a plate of fried ripe plantains he'd been keeping warm.

"Wow, I'm impressed," she said as she glanced at the meal, a typical Cuban one much like her family might have had.

"I cheated and used canned beans and frozen plantains, but it works," he said.

They sat to eat, and hunger took over, making for a quick and silent meal. Bongo wandered over and lay down between them, wanting company. As pack dogs, bloodhounds didn't like being alone, and Bongo was used to being at her side for most of the day and night.

As Jose finished his rice and beans, she snagged the very last *maduro*. The ripe plantain was sweet in her mouth with the fried crunchy and caramelized bits.

Jose eyeballed her and jabbed his fork in her direction. "That was *la verguenza*."

She laughed at his reference to the Gallego's curse, namely, taking the last bit of food that should be kept in case company came. In her family, they also teasingly said that whoever took the last bit was bound to be an old maid.

But as Jose's teasing look heated and ignited warmth deep inside her, she didn't think that was going to be her fate.

Voice husky, she said, "You cooked so why don't I clean, and after we can take Bongo for her last walk of the night."

He nodded. "Sounds good."

Rushing off, she cleaned and got ready for the rest of the night, eager for what might happen. Especially if it was a repeat of the night before.

Chapter Nineteen

Night had fallen hard, an almost moonless evening with the barest sliver in the sky sprinkling light through the trees down onto the bright bits of yellow.

The flags almost looked like daffodils poking their heads out of a spring ground, but the stake flags were anything but flowers in his garden.

He tightened his hands on the stock of the crossbow, anger riding high.

Those damn dogs had done their job well, he thought as he counted the flags and noted the caution tape wrapped around his surprises.

A stream of obscenities escaped him.

They'd ruined his garden. His beauties.

They'd also ruined the fun he'd planned to have with the beautiful women who had shown up to work at the kennels.

Now he'd have to redo his plans because he intended to have his revenge, especially after what they'd done to his beautiful space.

But before he did that, he had one other thing to do.

Inching along the edges of the forest, he crept toward the cabin, careful to keep quiet because Metz's hearing was way too keen.

It was how the man had found out about his little games after Metz had moved into the cabin several years earlier.

Metz had been only too eager to remain silent if he got to take part in the fun before he added the woman to his garden.

His willing partner was now nothing but a loose end.

Creeping toward the cabin, he kept an eye out for signs of anyone else because now that Metz had the attention of SBS, someone could be watching.

He didn't see anything or anyone.

Rising on tiptoes, he peered in through a side cabin window.

Metz was asleep in a rocking chair in front of the television. Luckily for him and unluckily for Metz, the television volume was turned way up, but he didn't take any chances.

The first porch step always squeaked and so he skipped it, placing his booted foot on the second. Another step had him on the porch where he avoided another creaky spot until he was at the front door.

He'd have the element of surprise, but not for long.

Making sure the crossbow was ready, he took hold of the doorknob and twisted it slowly. Silently.

You should always lock your door, he thought as he raised the crossbow to his shoulder.

Metz roused then, a surprised look on his face, and started to stand, mouth open as if to ask what was up.

The arrow embedded itself deep in his thick chest.

Metz dropped back into the rocking chair, which groaned from his weight and rocked violently from the force of his fall.

The old man stared from the arrow in his chest to his attacker. He reached up and tried to remove it, but his gnarled fingers could barely grasp the shaft.

"Why?" he managed to say on a strangled breath as the last vestige of life escaped from his gaze.

"You failed me, Barry. You let them ruin my garden," he said, and the calm that had filled him as he had planned his kill fled.

He pulled a knife from his belt and drove it deep into his lifeless partner, venting his rage again and again until both he and the room were splattered with blood.

Only then did the red haze in his eyes fade.

Time to go, he thought, and hurried from the cabin, but not before preparing another surprise for whoever decided to visit.

Once he was done, he walked to the woods and cut a leafy branch from a nearby pine tree. Retracing his path, he carefully used the branch to brush away his footsteps until he was in the underbrush.

If the SBS team thought it would be easy to track him, they'd be wrong.

Dead wrong.

"SHE'LL NEVER LEAVE you alone if you keep feeding her bacon," Sara said as she caught Jose sneaking Bongo a piece. "Besides, the salt and grease aren't healthy for her," she teasingly chided since she'd been guilty on more than one occasion of giving Bongo a similar treat.

Jose popped the last bit of bacon into his mouth. "Or for us but boy is it tasty," he said with a boyish grin.

She walked over, grabbed his empty plate and skimmed a kiss across his temple, but he wrapped an arm around her waist and hauled her down onto his lap for a deeper kiss.

A rough cough jerked her back to reality, and she pushed to her feet to find Trey standing by the elevator.

"I'm sorry. I didn't mean to intrude," Trey said, an amused flush on his face.

"I'm sorry if we're late," Sara said, and hurriedly grabbed the rest of their breakfast dishes to place them in the dishwasher.

"You're not late. I'm a little early," he said, and skewered Jose with a questioning look.

"We won't be long," Jose said, and picked up the remaining glasses to take them over to the sink.

"No problem. I wanted to warn you that word got out about what we found. I expect a gauntlet of reporters once we get to the kennels, but I know you've handled reporters before," Trey said, and turned his gaze on Sara.

Her stomach knotted at the thought of dealing with the reporters like she had when her father had been accused. She'd dreaded it and even afterward, when one of her and Bongo's searches had become newsworthy. She'd hesitantly dealt with reporters and their questions. But none of those searches could possibly compare to what they'd discovered on the kennel property or the attention it would bring.

Despite that, she acknowledged his statement with a dip of her head. "I have. I can handle them."

"Good. I can use all the help I can get this morning," Trey said, weariness dripping from his words.

JOSE HAD NO doubt his cousin's head wasn't completely in this game, and he understood why.

"How is Roni doing?" he asked.

A barely there smile slipped onto Trey's lips. "Much better. The spotting has stopped, and she'll be home either later today or tomorrow, but will have to continue her bedrest."

Jose walked over and squeezed Trey's shoulder. "That's good to hear, *primo*."

"It is. It'll make her crazy to just lie there, but it's what's best for the baby," Trey said, with a bob of his head.

"We're here for you. Whatever you need," Jose said, and Sara echoed his comments.

"A to-go cup of Cuban coffee and you driving so I can grab a quick nap would be greatly appreciated."

"You got it," Sara said, and while she prepped the coffee, Jose directed Trey to the sofa where his cousin plopped down tiredly.

"Roni and the baby will be fine," Jose said, trying to reassure his cousin.

"It's just...scarier than anything I've ever faced, and I've faced some scary things," Trey said, and after another shake of his head, drove his fingers through his hair.

Trey had faced drug dealers, mobsters and murderers not to mention enemy combatants during his tours of duty. That this scared him more spoke volumes about his love for his new wife.

"We're here for both of you," he said again and patted his hand on Trey's thigh in commiseration.

Trey glanced toward Sara who was just finishing up in the kitchen. "Is it a 'we' now, Pepe? Are you sure about what you're doing?"

With only a quick glance back in Sara's direction, Jose nodded and said, "I'm sure."

Trey blew out a long breath, raked his finger through his hair again, and finally said, "It's not going to get any easier, *sabes.*"

In his mind's eye came the image of the yellow flags waving in the slight breeze of afternoon like grisly flowers rising up from the ground.

No, it wouldn't be easier, he thought.

"I understand, but I'm here for the long haul, hard as it may be," he said just as Sara came over to join them.

She sat in a chair across from them and handed Trey the to-go cup of coffee.

He took a sip and sighed with pleasure. "*Gracias.* It's delicious."

Sara smiled. "Glad I could help."

Trey leaned forward, the coffee cup cradled in his hands. "I know this isn't what you signed up for, Sara. I appreciate everything you've done so far."

IT WASN'T ANYTHING like she imagined her first days on the job would be, but she had no hesitation about what needed to be done.

"The women in those graves deserve justice. I will do whatever it takes to make sure they get that," she said, leaving no hesitation about her determination to finish what had been started.

He offered her a grim smile and nodded. "We will make sure they get justice. The first step is to face the press and after, visit Metz. Are you ready for that?"

Chapter Twenty

Trey had warned them there would be a gauntlet but nothing could have prepared them for what awaited their arrival at the kennels.

What seemed like a battalion of news trucks lined both sides of the road, making it almost impossible to drive to the entrance of the property. A police car, lights flashing their warning blue and red, blocked the driveway.

As they drove up, reporters and camera operators swarmed like angry bees around their SUV. The police officer guarding the entrance had to push his way through and once he identified them, he radioed his partner to move the cruiser so they could pass.

A few of the reporters tried to follow them through, but the officer chased them like a beekeeper herding worker bees back to the hive.

In front of the kennel owner's home there was a phalanx of police cars and medical examiner and CSI team trucks as well as ambulances to transport the bodies.

As they pulled up in front of the house and exited the SUV, someone peeled off from a group of CSI people in hazmat suits by one of the ME's trucks.

"That's Sandy Gonzalez, no relation. She's one of the MEs for Miami-Dade," Trey said as they waited for the woman.

When she approached, Trey introduced them. "I wish I

could say it was good to see you, Sandy. This is Sara Hernandez, the new head of our K-9 Division. Jose Gonzalez, my cousin who's helping us out."

They shook hands with the woman who didn't seem all too pleased to be there. That was confirmed with her next words.

"I was hoping your team was wrong, but we've already found human remains in the first area you've marked. I hope you didn't mess up the scene."

Trey's lips thinned into a tight line. "My people are professionals. We preserved the scene as best we could."

"Let's hope so. While we work, Detective Espinoza wants to chat with you," she said, and walked away without waiting for their reply.

"Is she always that friendly?" Jose said with a sarcastic laugh.

"If you've been murdered, she's the one you want on your case," Trey said just as an older man in a rumpled dark suit and wrinkled shirt walked up. His top button was undone, and his tie had come loose from its knot. Everything about him screamed "cop" at Jose.

"Gonzalez," the cop said, with a dip of his head in Trey's direction.

"Espinoza. You're looking good," Trey said, and clapped the man on the back.

"I'd be looking better if I hadn't been here since dawn dealing with the press," Espinoza groused, and faced Sara and Jose.

Trey introduced them. Espinoza pulled a pad out of his inside jacket pocket and immediately started taking notes and asking questions.

"What made you search the property?"

"We had several incidents once we arrived. You should have the records about the explosions, but we also had someone shoot at us," Trey said.

"With an arrow?" Espinoza said just to confirm.

"With an arrow much like the one that killed the two women we found. Your CSI people have the arrow," Jose said, already impatient with the detective's questioning.

"How did you find those women?" he asked, and peered directly at Sara and then Bongo, who was patiently sitting at her feet.

"Bongo," she said, and rubbed the dog's head before continuing. "We were searching the property for any traps and Bongo scented something. We started to dig and found the women."

Espinoza nodded, jotted something down and then motioned with his pad toward the woods where a legion of law enforcement had spread out to recover the remains and any evidence.

"What about the woods? What made you look there?"

"We noticed some wires. We thought they might be part of an old electric fence, but we tripped one and realized that someone wanted us to stay out of the woods," Sara told him.

The detective peered at the dog again. "And your K-9 scented something."

Sara once again rubbed Bongo's head in an almost nervous gesture. "She did."

Espinoza hesitated, tipping his head from side to side as if tumbling around what he'd heard, and then looked at Trey. "You sent over a list of suspects. Wilson help you get that?"

Trey nodded. "He did. Our team is running down those leads right now. We plan on speaking to Metz again."

A low "Hmm," hummed from Espinoza. "You think he's still a suspect?"

Trey dipped his head. "Possibly. At a minimum, he knows more than what he's saying and Bongo smelled something close to his cabin."

Another low hum erupted from the detective before he slapped his notebook against Trey's chest. "You were the best detective on the force, so you know why I'm telling you this. We need to do everything by the book. Whoever killed all these women," he said, and waved the notebook around in the direction of the woods and training ring, "they need to pay for this."

"We know, Ray. That's why you're here," Trey said, and mimicked the detective's gesture, waving an arm at the police activity at the scene.

"*Bueno.* I'll leave you to issue a statement to the press. Keep it short and sweet," Espinoza said, and then quickly added, "We'll all go talk to Metz as soon as you're done."

The detective briskly walked away to join the ME and CSI teams.

"Keep it short and sweet?" Jose asked, wondering what it was the detective wanted.

"He doesn't want us to give them any info that could compromise the case."

"What's there to tell?" Jose said with a shrug.

"For starters, how many bodies there are," he said.

SARA QUICKLY ADDED, "If it bleeds, it leads. The press just loves sensational stories like this."

She'd only been involved in one murder case, and the press had turned it into front page news for days much like they had milked the accusations against her father for as long as they could.

"Are you ready for that? For them?" Trey asked and at her nod, they walked up the long driveway and past the police car where they were immediately swarmed by the press.

It was almost a physical attack as bodies crowded around her and Bongo, who hugged tight to her leg, overwhelmed by the assault. Jose wrapped an arm around her shoulders and used his other arm to block those who were trying to push closer with their cameras and microphones.

"Please give us some space," Trey said, and held his hands up as if to shove them away and then to ask for quiet.

Two police officers stepped in to offer assistance, shooing away reporters until they were at a reasonable distance.

Once they had some quiet and calm, Trey reached into the pocket of his guayabera and pulled out a piece of paper. He had clearly prepared a statement for the press in anticipation of the circus that was happening.

"*Buenos dias.* I'm Trey Gonzalez, the acting head of South Beach Security. I have with me Sara Hernandez, the new head of our K-9 Division and Jose Gonzalez, my cousin and the real estate agent who secured this property for SBS."

The reporters started tossing out questions, but Trey kept to his prepared statement.

"It came to our attention that this location might be the site of a crime. We immediately called the police to investigate. They are doing that at this time and will provide you with further reports when they deem appropriate. I ask you for patience as they conduct their investigations and that you address any questions to Detective Ray Espinoza, who is heading up the inquiry."

"Is it true your dog found multiple bodies?" one reporter called out.

Sara glanced at Trey who nodded to confirm she should answer, but she kept it discreet. "My K-9, Bongo, scented something unusual. Based on that, we called in the police."

"But is it true it's more than one woman?" another reporter shouted and shoved his mike in her face.

"No comment. You can check with Detective Espinoza for additional information."

The newspeople peppered them with more questions, but Trey ignored them and walked toward the kennel owner's house.

Jose applied gentle pressure on her shoulders, urging her to follow. He leaned close and whispered, "Are you okay?"

As she looked at the crew of people searching through the woods and thought about what they might find, she wasn't sure she'd ever be okay again. But they had to push forward for the sake of those women.

"I'll be okay as soon as we find out who did this."

DETECTIVE ESPINOZA INSISTED on going with them to interview Metz.

Jose stood by Sara and Bongo as Trey and the detective walked toward the cabin.

It struck him as odd that Metz hadn't exited as soon as they'd pulled up. He had to have heard the SBS SUV as it crunched its way up the gravel of the drive.

Beside Sara, Bongo whined and tugged on her leash, seemingly upset.

Hearing the bloodhound, Trey stopped and turned to look at them.

Espinoza stepped onto the porch and time seemed to slip into slow motion.

A sound, like a branch hitting the ground, split the air and the hackles rose on the back of Jose's neck.

Chapter Twenty-One

Trey whirled, wrapped his arm around Espinoza's body and jerked him off the porch.

The action sent the two men tumbling onto the ground with a resounding thud.

Worried about a secondary attack, Jose stepped in front of Sara and Bongo, but nothing happened.

Well, nothing if you ignored the arrow now embedded in one of the porch columns, Jose thought.

Sara, Bongo and he rushed forward to help Trey and Espinoza to their feet. The detective's eyes widened at the sight of the arrow that might have hit him if Trey hadn't acted so quickly.

"I owe you, Gonzalez," Espinoza, said and brushed red clay from his suit jacket.

"You need to watch every step. This guy is determined to take out anyone trying to find him," Trey said, and a second later he walked to the side of the porch to examine the trap that had been set.

Jose and Sara ambled over, and Trey gestured to the make-shift bow and trigger made from a branch. "Basic and rudimentary, but it did the trick."

At Sara's side, Bongo was still antsy, tugging at her leash.

"She smells something," Sara said as Bongo fought to go up the steps to the cabin.

"Let her go, but be careful," Trey said.

Sara gave Bongo a little more leash and followed her up the steps and to the front door.

Jose stayed close behind, ready to act if there were any other surprises left behind by the killer.

At the door, Sara hesitated while Bongo pawed the area near the entrance.

Jose moved forward but stopped dead at the sight of what looked like a bloody boot print.

He waved over Trey and the detective and motioned to his discovery.

"You two stay back while we go in," Espinoza said, making Trey repeat his earlier warning.

"Move slowly and carefully, Ray. There could be other traps."

The two men stood to either side of the door, and the detective grabbed the handle, turned it and threw the door open as they all held their breaths.

Nothing happened as the door flew open and rebounded against the inside wall of the cabin.

Espinoza stepped into the doorway and as Trey, Sara and he moved forward, the detective held his hand up to stop them.

"Stay back. This is now an active crime scene, and I don't think Sara and Jose should see this."

Trey stepped to his side, peered into the cabin and nodded. "You two should step away. Look around for other evidence."

Jose slipped his arm around Sara's shoulders and urged her off the porch, but Bongo continued to fuss, making her issue a sharply worded command.

"Heel, Bongo," she said, and the bloodhound finally responded, walking with them to the ground in front of the cabin.

At his questioning look, Sara said, "It was the blood. With her sense of smell, it hit her right away."

They both looked toward the cabin and while Trey and the detective were still in the doorway, it was impossible not to see Metz's feet as he sat in a rocking chair and the blood painting the floor of the cabin red.

His stomach turned and cold sweat bathed his body at the thought of what could have made so much blood spill onto the floor.

As he faced Sara, her face was a pale, almost ghostly white. "I've never been good with this kind of thing. It's why I always stuck to search and rescue."

Like him, Sara had been forced into something well out of her wheelhouse, but he wasn't about to let that stop him from this challenge.

"Let's look around," he said, and together they walked back to the trap that the detective had triggered.

As Trey had said, it seemed very basic. Someone had cut branches off a tree and fashioned them into a bow and a trigger that would release the arrow once someone dislodged the wire.

Bending, he noted the fishing line that had been strung across the front porch to act as the trip wire.

"Most anyone has fishing line around," he said to Sara as she let Bongo sniff around the branches.

"I don't see you as the fishing type," she said with a raised eyebrow.

"I have a boat and I like to fish. I'll take you out some day."

SARA SMILED, liking the sound of that since it hinted at something more permanent. "That sounds nice, but I warn you now. I don't clean fish."

Jose grinned and playfully tapped her chin. "That's okay because I do, and I make a mean ceviche."

"I'm game," she said, and gestured toward the arrow embedded in the porch column.

"It's a lot like the arrow someone shot at us, and there's blood on it."

Jose examined the arrow, but then looked toward the cabin. "I'll wager it's Metz's blood."

"Probably," she said, and once again let Bongo sniff around the porch in the hopes of picking up a scent.

Bongo sniffed and then shook her head back and forth, sending her long ears and drool flying every which way.

"Find," Sara commanded.

Bongo glanced back at her as if to say, "Find what?"

"She doesn't look too enthusiastic," Jose said, hands jammed on his hips.

"Not enough of any kind of scent, but sometimes it's not just the K-9 that is responsible for finding someone," she said, and gestured to the ground.

"Someone stood there. See the slight imprints. The ground is too hard and dry for anything more pronounced and…" She paused and pictured the route someone might take into the woods. Gesturing to the ground again, she said, "The dirt there looks brushed smooth. See how different it looks."

Jose peered at the earth intently but shook his head. "I can't say that I do, but I trust you. If you see it, let's check it out."

"But stay clear to not wreck any evidence," she warned, keeping a wide berth of what she thought was the killer's trail while also trying not to lose it.

As with the dirt in front of the cabin, there was a decided difference in a narrow path of grass leading into the woods.

Nearing the tree line, something lighter caught her eye and she gestured to a pine tree.

"Someone cut some branches off that tree. I'm sure CSI can confirm whether it's one and the same as the branches used for the booby trap."

"I'm no expert but it looks the same to me," Jose said, with a nod.

"He went into the woods here, so my guess is he knows his way around and he either has a place nearby or parked his car close."

"And set more traps along the way?" Jose said, gaze locked on the woods where the happy yellow of their flags and caution tape was a stark contrast to the somber crime scene.

Sara shrugged, unsure. "Maybe, unless he was in a rush or more concerned with hiding his tracks."

Searching the area, she took note of the CSI agents working the scene and then glanced toward where their killer had entered the woods. Shaking her head, she said, "We'll have to keep a close eye out. Are you with me?"

"I'M WITH YOU," Jose said without hesitation. He'd come this far and intended to see it through, no matter what.

Sara loosened her hold on Bongo's leash, giving her bloodhound a freer rein to nose around the underbrush. As the dog entered the woods, they followed at a discreet distance, but as Sara had warned, Jose kept a close eye, vigilant.

They moved slowly, cautiously, and as they did so, the cool of early morning evaporated like dew under the glare of sunlight. In the woods the shade provided some relief, but it was dank, humid and buggy as they trudged along, searching for any signs to point them in the killer's direction.

"He kept to the woods, but along the edges probably because it might be easier to track him in those fields over there," she said, and gestured to the farmland where there were rows of harvested cornstalks and beyond that, an orchard of some kind.

"Is that part of the SBS property?" she asked.

Jose nodded. "About another twenty-five acres or so belong to SBS. It's been leased to a local farmer for quite a long time, and we agreed to let them keep farming. Even dropped the lease price so they could keep it as farmland

and avoid developers like Delgado from turning this area into suburbs."

"I'm shocked that a real estate agent like you would be opposed to more development," she said as they started walking again, trailing behind Bongo's lead.

"I'm all for reasonable development, but this area should stay rural. There's already too much encroachment close to the Everglades," he said, determined to protect the fragile area threatened by nearby civilization.

"You are a constant surprise," Sara said with a chuckle and a shake of her head.

Bongo tugged hard on her leash, nearly upending her.

"Easy, girl. What did you find?"

They followed Bongo as she finally emerged from the woods and into an almost five-yard-wide patch of wildflowers. Beautiful and utilitarian since the colorful flowers drew pollinators to help improve the productivity of the crops.

"Heel," Sara commanded as she noted a trampled path across the flowers and into the nearby field of cornstalks.

"Don't you want to follow?" he asked and pointed to the obvious trail.

"I do, but I also want the CSI team to preserve the evidence. Hopefully there's more boot prints. Maybe even fiber and blood to confirm this is the way the killer came."

He nodded. "Got it. I'll call Trey and let him know what we've found," he said, and made the call.

"Good work. We'll have a crew there in a few minutes," Trey said.

Jose stood next to Sara and tracked her gaze as it roamed over the fields in front of them. She raised her arm and pointed into the distance before glancing back at him.

"Is that an orchard?"

He nodded. "Mangos. Also, avocado trees. Good money nowadays thanks to all the hipsters," he said with a chuckle.

"What about a farmhouse? How far away would that be?" she asked, her mind clearly racing with possibilities.

He stood akimbo and peered out, imagining the farmhouse he'd visited while working out the details of the purchase. "Probably about a mile or so to the farmhouse. I could take you there later if you want."

"I want," she said, and her gaze skipped from the fields to the woods behind them.

"A mile or so there. Another mile of woods. Maybe less than that from the woods to the kennels," she said, and it was clear what she was thinking.

"A few miles isn't all that far. Typical walking pace is like fifteen minutes a mile, right?" he said, thinking that he could cover the distance in far less time.

She must have read his thoughts since she said, "You look like a runner. How long would it take you?"

"I do a six-minute mile, but not through brush like that and not while trying to avoid booby traps," he readily admitted, peering at the thick underbrush in the forest and how it might trip up anyone trying to rush.

"Unless you were the one who set the traps. But let's say you started near here. Parked on the road close by. You could easily make it through the woods in twenty minutes and then bam, you're at the kennels."

Definitely bam, you're at the kennels, he thought, and nodded. "The farmer wasn't on our list of suspects."

"He wouldn't be unless he'd committed a crime, but think about how many serial killers were just 'ordinary people,'" she said, emphasizing the words with air quotes.

"I'm almost afraid to ask," he said, deferring to her knowledge of the kind of evil that could commit such crimes.

"BTK. He was even president of his church council. The Butcher Baker. An apparently well-liked small-town baker who hunted his women down in the wilderness, much like what this killer is doing," Sara said, with a toss of her head in the direction of the woods behind them just in time to draw his attention to Trey, Espinoza and a duo of CSI agents.

"What have you got?" Trey asked, and searched the area around them, quickly picking up on the trampled wildflowers in the nearby patch. "Boot prints?"

Sara nodded. "Possibly."

The CSI duo did a closer inspection and the one agent, a thirtyish woman, nodded and said, "Definitely some kind of boot print." Looking around, she said, "Ground is softer here thanks to the irrigation system."

"There may be another one here," Sara said, and swept her arm in the direction of a dirt row along the edge of the cornfield.

"We didn't want to push on to keep from compromising any evidence," Jose said, but quickly added, "Sara has some thoughts on this though."

Chapter Twenty-Two

Sara gave Jose credit for giving her credit. Once again, he was proving himself to be unlike the other men she used to have in her life. But then again, the Gonzalez men were breaking the mold in many ways. Even Trey with all his alpha ways regularly surprised her with his caring and compassion.

Trey peered in her direction and said, "What are you thinking?"

"Whoever is doing this is well familiar with this area and either lives nearby or has easy access. I'm leaning toward lives nearby because while the road leading to the kennels is small, it has a fair amount of traffic."

Trey shook his head. "But not at night, and I'm willing to bet that's when he does his hunting."

Sara nodded. "I agree, but it would be less obvious if he came on foot, and Jose tells me there's a farmhouse not all that far from here."

Trey mulled over what she said, delaying for a bit before turning to Jose. "We met the farmer to discuss the lease terms. Anything rub you wrong?"

Jose's shoulders rose and dropped in a noncommittal shrug. "Can't say that it did although he did seem worried when we said we were buying the property."

"Logical considering you might want to boot him off, right?" Espinoza offered for discussion.

"Logical," Trey said to Sara. "I hired you because of your skills. That includes your ability to read people. Why don't you and Jose go to the farmhouse? Do a meet and greet as if it's just a neighborly visit."

"Makes sense," she said with a quick dip of her head.

"It does. You'd be seeing each other around. It's a perfect excuse," Jose said.

"But don't do anything stupid. If there's anything weird going on get out of there and call us. Understood?" Espinoza warned.

Jose held his hands up in surrender. "Real estate agent, remember?"

That seemed to satisfy Trey and the detective. Trey handed Jose the car keys and they hurried back to the cabin. Along the way she paused to let Bongo relieve herself and gave her a treat along with a good ear rub.

"You did great, girl," she said, and the bloodhound licked her face before they pushed on toward the cabin.

As they approached, it was impossible to miss the yellow crime scene tape surrounding the area.

Through the doorway she could see two agents working on Metz, gathering evidence.

"He was in on it," she said while they walked to the SUV, Bongo hugging her side.

"Had to be. It's why he's dead and I can't say I'm sorry," Jose replied, sweeping out his arm and drawing her close.

The shiver that wracked her body was so strong, he stopped and wrapped both arms around her in comfort.

"It's no way to go," she whispered against his chest.

Bongo, sensing her upset, leaned close and rubbed her head against Sara.

Jose reached down and petted the bloodhound's head, trying to ease her distress at her owner's anguish.

Long moments passed as they stood there, bundled together, letting overwhelming emotions ebb so they could continue with their investigation.

When Sara shifted away slightly, she wiped tears with a shaky hand.

"You good to go meet your new neighbor?" Jose asked, clearly not rushing her in case she still needed time to compose herself.

"Ready as I'll ever be," she said, and got into the SUV for the short ride to the neighboring farmhouse.

AN OLDER BLACK pickup truck sat in the driveway as they drove up to the farmhouse.

Sara hoped it was a sign that someone was home.

Jose hopped out, walked around to Sara's side, and waited as she unharnessed Bongo and leashed her once she was on the ground.

The building had the clean lines and large front porch typical of many of the older farmhouses in the area. Fresh white paint gleamed in the sunlight while colorful impatiens lined a pea gravel path leading to the front door. Terracotta pots sat on the steps to the porch, filled with cascading bright pink petunias.

A painted white porch swing in pristine shape boasted comfy pillows decorated with cheerful, purple pansies. A coir mat emblazoned with the word *Welcome* sat by the front door.

Certainly not a home that screamed serial killer right off the bat. Until she reminded herself of how well people could be at hiding what was really going on inside their heads.

They had just taken a step up the stairs when the front door, which also boasted a floral wreath matching the pinks and purples prevalent in the garden, opened wide.

A handsome older man with a leonine head of white hair and neatly trimmed beard stood behind the screen door.

Dressed in an immaculate white shirt and pants, he held a glass of lemonade, and looked like Colonel Sanders had just sprung back to life.

"Nice to see you again, Mr. Gonzalez. How can I help you?" he asked in a cultured voice with the barest hint of an accent that she couldn't quite place.

Jose forced a smile. "It's good to see you again, Mr. Guidry. I wanted to introduce SBS K-9 agent Sara Hernandez since she'll be your new neighbor at the kennels."

Guidry hesitated for the barest second, then stepped out from behind the screen door and held his hand out in greeting.

She shook his cold wet hand and told herself the chill was from the glass of lemonade he'd been holding just seconds before. His touch created an unsettled sensation that made her gut somersault with disgust.

Hiding her reaction, she slapped a smile on her face and said, "It's a pleasure to meet you."

He held on to her hand a little too long if you asked her, and smiled. She imagined it was what a shark looked like a second before it bit you, eyes dead behind that wide grin. As Bongo nosed around his feet, Guidry grimaced and shuffled back a bit, as if to discourage the bloodhound from continuing to sniff.

"The pleasure is all mine, my dear," he said, and slowly released her hand.

When Bongo sniffed Guidry's feet again, he escaped toward the front door.

She urged Bongo back to her side with a hand signal. A second later, Guidry faced Jose. "I understand you've had a bit of excitement at the kennel."

Jose tipped his head from side to side, delaying until he finally said, "Nothing the SBS team can't handle."

"Of course. How could I forget the famous South Beach Security team now owns the kennel? I'm sure they deal with this kind of thing all the time," Guidry replied, his tone so unctuous she imagined him sliding off the porch from its oiliness.

"What kind of thing is that Mr. Guidry?" she asked, wondering what it was that Guidry imagined was happening on the property.

With a careless kind of shrug followed by a slurpy sip of lemonade, he said, "The explosions. A murder? Maybe two?"

"You're right that SBS is handling it," Jose said, his words clipped with anger.

A low hum seeped from Guidry as he digested Jose's words. "If you need anything, just let me know. It's the neighborly thing to do, right?" he finally said.

"Of course, Mr. Guidry. We'll be sure to call if we do," Sara said, and with a gentle tug on Bongo's leash, guided the dog down the steps, but as they hit the pea gravel path, Bongo stopped and looked back toward the house.

Guidry lingered on the porch, sipping his lemonade. As he realized he had their attention again, he raised the glass, as if in a toast. The action struck her as challenging rather than friendly.

"Sara?" Jose asked, placing a soothing hand at the small of her back, and likewise peered toward the other man.

"Bongo picked up on something," she said softly, and with a click of her tongue, commanded the bloodhound to move.

At the SUV, she bundled Bongo into the back seat and harnessed her in with a playful rub of her body. "You're a good girl, Bongo."

The dog nuzzled her face and Sara laughed, the dog's loving action wiping away how dirty Guidry had made her feel.

When she hopped into the passenger seat and buckled up, Jose said, "What do you think?"

"He's condescending and gave me the willies."

"The willies, huh? Is that a technical term?" Jose teased,

then started the SUV and did a K-turn to drive away from the farmhouse.

"Definitely," she said with a chuckle, and quickly added, "There's something not right about him," she said, and swiveled to take a final look at Guidry.

He was still on the porch, following them with his gaze, and that earlier sharky grin faded into a knife-sharp slash.

Yep, something was definitely not right with her new neighbor, but did it mean he was a serial killer?

Chapter Twenty-Three

The team had gathered around the conference room, plates with food from a local Asian fusion restaurant sitting in front of them as they discussed the information they had gathered.

"The police have found at least a dozen women, but it will be more since they're still digging. The bodies were in various states of decay, and their best guess is that the earliest of them go back about four years. There are also two victims who are recently deceased, including one that was buried only days ago," Trey said and passed around photos.

Jose peered at the crime scene photo of the woman. Dirt smudged a pretty face with too much makeup that had been smeared in spots. Fake blond hair with obvious roots and a mismatch to her pubic hair. Fake boobs too and a cheap tattoo of what he guessed were butterflies on one ankle.

"We have a tentative ID from a fingerprint—Maisy Moore. Nineteen," Trey said.

"She looks way older than that," Jose stated.

"Makeup can do that. So can a hard life, and Maisy had a hard life," Trey replied, picking up a piece of paper and started summarizing from it.

"Ran away from home at fourteen because she was being

sexually abused by her father. Ended up in foster care but also had issues with another of the males in the home."

Mia jumped in. "Issues? You mean he was also abusing her?"

Trey shrugged. "Possibly. He denied it, and she left before the investigation could be completed."

"So, her abuser possibly skates free?" Sara said, clearly upset by that possibility.

"Possibly. We can check him out once we've finished this investigation," Trey said, and continued. "Maisy ends up on the streets after that. Multiple arrests for prostitution. The killer probably picked her up near one of the strip clubs."

"Maybe like he did Terry Hansen, although the only person who said she was a sex worker was Metz. This girl even kinda looks like Terry," Sara said as she peered at the photo.

"He has a type," Jose said as he examined the photo again. Something about the photo made him ask, "If she died so recently, is there a better chance of getting more evidence from her?"

Trey nodded. "Police immediately identified the fatal wound," he said, and reached over his shoulder to gesture to his back. "Broadhead arrow straight through, which likely hit the heart and a nearby artery. There's also evidence of sexual assault and piquerism."

"Piquerism? What's that?" Jose asked, puzzled by the term.

"Some killers need to stick people to experience arousal. Usually with knives, but it could also be pins or razors," Trey explained.

"But the sexual assault means we have DNA, right?" Jose queried, trying not to be shocked by the need to stick someone to get aroused.

"Killer could have worn a condom and sex workers can be problematic because they may have had multiple partners prior to the killer," Trey replied.

He felt like a fool that he hadn't thought about that complication, but then again, sex workers weren't normally the kinds of people in his life. Although he'd met a high-priced escort or two at some of his clients' parties, he thought.

"We'll know more about the exact COD and other evidence once they've finished the autopsy. As for the other victim, no positive ID on her yet, but PD speculates she's been dead for about a month."

Missing for a month and no one cared, Jose thought sadly, thinking that his parents would have been calling other family and friends within an hour if he failed to show up.

"Using facial recognition software on the internet, we think we found the second victim using her profile on Facebook. We've sent the info to PD," Sophie said, and flashed a side-by-side of the police photo with the image from her social media account on a nearby television.

"Tina Rodriguez left home two years ago and took up a life on the streets to support her drug habit. That's also when she stopped posting to her account," Robbie said.

Jose's heart hurt with sadness as he looked at the picture of the seemingly happy and pretty young woman in the Facebook photo and saw what her troubled life had led to. But something struck him at the same time and lightened the sorrow weighing down his heart.

"She's not just some nameless body anymore," he said, and peered around the table, his gaze settling last on Sara, who slipped her hand into his and squeezed.

"She's not," Trey said, and they pushed forward with their review of the case, discussing the additional steps they'd be taking.

"Terry, Maisy and Tina have many similarities. Sex workers. Age. Physical appearance. Those are obvious, but there may be other things we're not seeing. I'll run any info about them through my program to identify additional similarities," John said.

"We'll also refine the list of missing women to try and ID who's in those graves," Mia added.

"We're analyzing satellite photos taken over the last decade for changes in that forest area to hopefully pinpoint when each of those graves was dug," Sophie said.

"If we can do that, we'll match those dates with the list of missing women, again so we can ID the dead," Robbie said.

"What can Jose and I do?" Sara asked, obviously eager to help.

"How did you feel about Guidry?" Trey asked, narrowing his gaze as he peered at them.

"First time I met him, I didn't really get any vibes, but I was only focused on closing the deal," Jose readily admitted.

"And now?" Trey asked with an arch of a dark brow.

Jose glanced at Sara for a hot second before saying, "Smarmy. Off but I can't say why."

Sara quickly jumped in. "I got bad vibes and Bongo seemed drawn to him. Maybe she scented something, and he clearly wasn't too happy about Bongo being near him. Right, girl?" she called out to the bloodhound who had been quietly resting at one side of the room.

"Do you think it's enough of a scent for her to follow?" Mia asked.

Sara peered at Bongo, grimaced and shook her head. "I don't think so. But as far as I'm concerned, he should be a suspect. He's close by and there's something off about him."

Trey sighed heavily. "I get that Bongo didn't have enough scent, Sara. I know you're not a miracle worker and I appreciate your opinion on Guidry."

SARA WISHED SHE was a miracle worker because these dead women deserved justice. Even Metz deserved it, which made her think about the scene of his death.

"Whoever went at Metz left evidence behind. We know there's a few boot prints. Maybe we can match them to a certain kind of shoe," Sara said, and at that, Trey nodded, yanked a photo from his pile of papers and passed it to her.

"There was a partial print in blood on the porch steps and a full boot print in the field. They were enough to confirm the killer wore some kind of work or duck boot. As wet as the land can get out here, it's a common kind of shoe but the soles can be unique," Trey said.

Sara had seen her share of duck boot soles over the many years they'd done search and rescue. Gesturing to the imprint in the dirt, she said, "L.L. Bean duck boots are some of the most popular, but they have a sole with a chain-like tread. Sperry soles are more circular, like little pods. Sorels have deep herringbone-like ridges."

She ran her hands across the lighter ridge pattern on the photo, trying to recall other boot prints she'd seen over the years but couldn't quite place the soles. "These ridges are lighter. Not as deep as Sorels," she said, and traced the ridges in the photo with her finger.

"It'd be easier to wipe off mud with ridges like this, right?" Jose asked as he also examined the photo.

"It would," she said with a quick nod.

"Mud like a farmer would have on his boots? Just like Guidry might wear," Jose said, eyes opening wide as that occurred to him.

"Definitely more like a work boot a farmer would wear rather than a duck boot. We should start searching the internet to see what we can find on the boots and also on Guidry," Sara said.

Sophie and Robbie added, "We'll do the same."

"Great. Do you think the police will let us into Metz's cabin so that I can take Bongo around. See if she can pick up any kind of scent?" Sara said, eyeballing Trey as he sat at the head of the table.

"I'll reach out to them. In the meantime, the police have released the kennel owner's home, so I'd like for you to run Bongo through there to see if there's anything else," Trey said.

"If there isn't, and if Sara still wants to live there, I'll arrange for the painters to come in," Mia said and looked at her intently, as if trying to gauge how she felt about living in the house.

With a shrug, she said, "The Florians lived there for over thirty years without a problem. I don't see why I can't live there as we had planned to get the K-9 center running. Our K-9s might help stop murders like this from happening or help PD solve them, right?"

"That's why we wanted to start this division. Even civilians might want to train their K-9s for protection or just obedience. This new center might be able to fulfill all those needs," Trey said, his voice sporting the kind of eagerness she'd heard when he'd first approached her about the project. He'd understandably lost that enthusiasm in the last few days with the weight of the murders and Roni's troubled pregnancy dragging at him.

"Are you sure?" Jose said, and tightened his hand on hers, offering support and comfort.

She nodded. "I'm sure. This is what I was meant to do. What *we* were meant to do," she said, and skipped her gaze across everyone seated at the table.

When no one contradicted her, she smiled and Trey said, "Seems like it's time to call it a night so we can be fresh in the morning. I need to take care of my wife."

He shot to his feet and pointed at each of them. "And I meant it when I said get to work in the morning," he said, emphasizing the last few words. "*None* of us can be sharp if we're tired."

"Got it, *jefe*," Robbie said teasingly, and offered up a mock salute.

"Go home. Get some rest. Fresh eyes may make the difference," he said, and without waiting for the rest of them, he made a beeline for the door.

Mia and John were next, arms wrapped around each other. "We'll see you in the morning. Like Trey, I'm looking forward to some time with my new wife."

Sophie laughed and with a sad shake of her head, she said, "It's just you and me and our cold beds, *hermanito*."

"We need to get a life," Robbie teased as he and his sister slipped from the room, leaving her and Jose at the table.

"Time for us to go and get some rest," he said.

She inched up a brow and shot him a knowing smile. "Only rest?"

He leaned close and brushed a kiss across her lips, whispering, "Sex can be restorative, *sabes*."

She didn't know why it bothered her that he'd said "sex" and not "making love." But then again, their attraction had been fast and furious. Had there really been time for love?

He sensed her upset and pulled back, danced his gaze across her face. "Are you all right?"

"I'm fine. Just fine," she said, snatching up the papers Trey had passed out earlier and signaling Bongo to come to her side.

Chapter Twenty-Four

It was impossible not to see that whatever he'd said had upset Sara, Jose thought.

Much like she had done, he grabbed the papers and followed her to the elevator. Once it arrived, she quickly used her badge to access the penthouse, silent the entire time. Bongo was plastered close to her leg, also sensing her mistress's mood.

He let Sara have that silence, hoping that her upset would fade by the time they reached the penthouse a few floors up.

It hadn't.

She walked straight to the table, tossed the papers on it and said, "I know what Trey said, but I don't think I'll be able to get much sleep until I do a few more things."

He chalked her upset off to that restlessness and said, "How about some coffee?"

She nodded. "Sure, but I need to walk Bongo first. I really should have done it before now."

"I'll go with you," he said, but she held her hand up to stop him.

"I need some time alone," she said, and without waiting for him, she grabbed Bongo's leash and rushed toward the elevator.

Not good, he thought, but recognized she needed space. Because of that, he busied himself with making coffee and searched the refrigerator to see if there were any desserts. Maybe something sugary to sweeten her mood, he thought. Something sweet always cheered him up.

Whoever stocked the fridge for Trey must have thought so too because there were homemade flans on one shelf as well as a container of chocolate chip ice cream in the freezer in case you wanted to get chip-faced.

Hoping that would do, he poured himself a drink and sat to wait for Sara.

JOSE'S WORDS SHOULDN'T have bothered her as much as they had, Sara thought as she walked Bongo along the curb in front of the SBS building. Bongo did her duty quickly, but Sara wasn't quite ready to return to the penthouse. Plus her partner hadn't really had any good exercise over the last few days.

She told herself that was the reason she walked right past the entrance and to the corner, and then turned to walk down the block.

The South Beach Security building was primarily in a business area, so foot traffic was light. Just a few office workers either rushing home or out for some late-night food.

She passed the Cuban deli they'd ordered from the other night and considered stopping in for something sweet, but passed on it to keep walking Bongo, who seemed to be enjoying the longer stroll. Rounding the block, she was just past the entrance to the building's garage when Bongo stopped and jerked her in the direction of the entrance.

A heartbeat later, a masked man raced at her from the shadows, wrapped one arm around her waist and pressed a hand across her mouth.

She lost her hold on Bongo's leash, not that her partner would be of much use.

Years of instinct and training took over.

She stomped her assailant's foot hard, grinding his toes into the sidewalk.

Her attacker yelped and lifted her body to keep her from stomping down again.

Jabbing her elbow sharply into his midsection, one, two, three times, loosened the hand at her mouth. She bit down viciously on his gloved hand.

He released her and she stumbled back from him, but he came at her again, tackling her to the ground.

JOSE GLANCED AT his watch for what had to be at least the tenth time in the last ten minutes.

She was taking far longer than when he had gone with her to walk Bongo.

It worried him that something was wrong.

Hopping to his feet, he rushed to the elevator, bouncing on the balls of his feet inside in his haste to find Sara.

It seemed like forever until the elevator arrived at the ground floor.

He rushed past the security desk and through the lobby, almost jogging out the door and to the sidewalk.

It was then he caught sight of Bongo racing toward the corner and his heart stopped cold.

He broke into a run and grabbed hold of Bongo's leash before the dog could rush into oncoming traffic. Bongo hopped up and laid big paws on his shoulders, but he urged the dog down, searching for Sara.

A sharp scream dragged his gaze midblock, and it took him a second to register what he was seeing.

Sara and someone all in black wrestled on the ground.

He muttered a curse and sprinted toward her, dragging a barking Bongo along with him.

The man pinning Sara to the ground looked up, surged to his feet and raced off.

Sara was just sitting up as he dropped to his knees beside her to make sure she was okay.

She pointed to her escaping assailant and commanded the bloodhound, "Find, Bongo. Find."

Jose released Bongo's leash and the dog took off.

Jose scrambled to his feet, chasing after the bloodhound to the end of the block and around the corner, but in just those short few seconds, Sara's assailant had vanished.

He called Bongo to his side, secured her leash and jogged back to where Sara was slowly getting to her feet.

She wavered a little, shaky, and he eased an arm around her waist to offer support.

"Take it easy. I'm here," he said, and she leaned into him, burying her face against his chest. Her body trembled as one shaky breath after another escaped her as she tried to regain her composure.

He stroked a hand up and down her back, offering comfort.

Bongo leaned against their legs, the weight of her also supportive.

With one long controlled breath, Sara straightened. Meeting his gaze, she said, "We need to let Trey know what happened."

He nodded and was reaching for his cell phone but hesitated. "He's got enough on his plate with Roni. We can handle this for now."

Sara hesitated, her gaze troubled. Reluctantly, she agreed. "Let's call Sophie and Robbie. Get them to pull up any video in the hopes we can ID this guy and where he went."

Jose nodded and dialed his cousins. Sophie answered and said, "What's up? I thought Trey said to take the night off?"

"Sara was walking Bongo when someone attacked her right outside the entrance to the parking garage," he said, and turned on the speaker.

"Is she okay? Do you need me to call an ambulance?" Sophie immediately asked.

"I'm fine," Sara said, even though Jose had his doubts about how fine she was.

"Can you pull video from around the building? Maybe we caught him on the CCTV?" she said.

"Robbie and I will work on it. We'll call you as soon as we have something," she said and hung up.

He faced Sara and ran a hand down her arm. It came away wet and bloody.

"You're hurt," he said, and examined her, noticing the angry and bloody scrapes on both her elbows.

She half turned to also inspect the damage, wincing as she did so. "It must have happened when he tackled me."

"Let's go upstairs and get you cleaned up."

When she took a wobbly step toward the corner, he slipped his arm around her waist again, shoring her up.

She leaned on him heavily as they walked back into the building and through the lobby. At the security desk the two guards jumped to their feet, seeing her condition.

"Can we do anything? Do you need us to call the police?" one guard asked.

Sara held her hand up in a stop gesture and offered the guards a weak smile. "I'm okay. We're handling this internally."

"If you need anything, we're here," the guard said.

By the time they reached the penthouse, Sophie was already calling. "We have video. He's masked in all of them, but we think we can calculate his height and weight from the videos. We'll let you know what we find."

"*Gracias*, Sophie. Hopefully you'll have something by the morning," he said, and hung up.

"They will," Sara said more optimistically. "Sophie and Robbie are amazing at what they do."

"Let's hope you're right," he said, and motioned to the sofa. "Get comfortable while I round up some things to clean your elbows."

Chapter Twenty-Five

Sara didn't have the energy to fight with him. The attack had drained her. Shaken her.

A few minutes more...

She wouldn't think about what might have happened if Jose hadn't come along when he did.

Bongo walked up to her then and laid her head on Sara's thigh. She stroked Bongo's head, rubbed her ears and said, "Why do you have to be so friendly, dog?"

As if to prove that point, Bongo licked her hand and drooled on Sara's jeans. She wiped it away with a chuckle and shook her head. "Go lay down, girl."

With another lick, Bongo ambled away to rest by her bedroom door.

Jose returned, hands full of cotton balls, adhesive bandages and bottles. "This may sting," he said as he wet a cotton ball with disinfectant.

She braced herself but still jumped as he gently swiped at her scraped elbows.

"I'm sorry. I didn't want to hurt you."

"I know," she said, and in the second that followed, it became about more than the abrasions on her arms.

He cradled her chin and applied gentle pressure until she faced him.

"I care for you, Sara. It's not just a hookup," he said, sea-colored eyes bright with the light of his happiness.

"I want to say 'I know' only…it's hard to know whether what we're both feeling is real with all that's going on," she admitted, not wanting to place blame on either of them for the confusing emotions.

The light in his eyes dimmed and darkness crept in, stealing his earlier joy. "You need time. I get it. I'll give you all the time you need," he said, and with a butterfly light brush, swiped his thumb across her cheek.

The caress, simple as it was, felt like a kiss goodbye, but she tried to take his words at face value and remain optimistic.

"I know Trey said to get some rest, but I'm too wired. I was going to work on tracking down the boots and finding out more about my new neighbor," she said, then popped to her feet and nervously rubbed her hands across her thighs.

He hesitated, clearly trying to decide what to do, but finally flung a hand in the direction of the bedrooms. "I'm going to shower and then check out some things. Check in with my cousins on what they've got before I bother Trey."

"Sounds like a plan." She stood there, rooted to a spot by the sofa until he walked out of the room. She finally released the breath she'd been holding. A breath that had wanted to call him back and step into his arms. Arms that could excite or comfort. Arms she had come to rely on way too much in the last few days.

Shaking her head to clear away those thoughts, she walked to the table and shuffled through the papers there to find the one with the boot print.

Opening her laptop, she searched various websites recommending footwear for farmers like what Guidry might wear. She whittled down her list to the most popular boots at the websites. The only problem with that was that too many people might own them.

In reality, the only person she was interested in was Guidry. If he owned a similar boot, it increased the likelihood that he was the suspect they should focus on.

Hopping from one list of "best boots" to the other, there were several manufacturers that made each of the lists. In addition, the same models kept popping up. Grabbing a pad of paper, she made a list of those models and then went to the companies' sites to check out the soles.

The first three boots were no goes. The ridges were either too deep or ran the wrong way.

On the fourth try she got a possible hit, only there were slight discrepancies between the prints. So slight that she guessed the boot had to come from that manufacturer.

Searching through the company's work boots, she finally hit on one that seemed identical. Just to be on the safe side, she printed out an image for a better comparison.

As she laid that image against the CSI photos of the boot prints, she had no doubt she'd gotten the right brand and model.

"I found the boot, Jose. I found it!"

But as she kept reading on the company's site, some of her enthusiasm dimmed.

Jose hurried over and glanced at the photos she had laid out on the table. Picking up the print from the company website, he compared it and nodded enthusiastically. "You did. You found it."

"There's just one problem. It's the company's bestselling work boot for farmers, and it's a big boot manufacturer. That means there could be thousands of pairs out there," Sara said, slumping against the chair dejectedly.

"But we don't have to track down thousands, Sara. All we have to do is find these boots in the suspect's possession. Once we have another suspect although Guidry is on my list," Jose reassured her.

With a dip of her head, she said, "Maybe it's time to call Sophie and Robbie. See what they have."

He nodded. "Sure," he said, then dialed his cousin and put the phone on speaker.

As soon as Sophie answered, she said, "Let me bring in Robbie."

After a slight hesitation, Sophie said, "We have some news."

"So do we. I've tracked down the model of the boot Metz's killer was wearing," Sara said, and met Jose's gaze over the phone sitting on the table.

"That's great. We should send that over to PD," Robbie said.

Leaving that alone for the moment, she said, "What's your news?"

Another uneasy silence followed before Robbie said, "We were able to determine the height of your attacker from the CCTV footage. He's roughly five feet eight inches tall."

"That sounds about right for Guidry. He was shorter than my six feet," Jose confirmed.

Sophie immediately countered with, "But that info doesn't match up with what we got from Florida DMV."

Jose and Sara shared a puzzled look before Sara said, "What do you mean it doesn't match up?"

"DMV records indicate that Guidry is six feet two inches tall," Robbie stated.

"No way. The man we spoke with today was several inches shorter than me," Jose insisted.

"People do shrink with age, but not that much. Plus Guidry is only forty-eight according to the records so he's not of an age to be getting shorter," Robbie said.

"Guidry had a whole Colonel Sanders vibe going on so he looked older than forty-eight, but he could just be prematurely gray," Sara said, recalling how their possible suspect had appeared when they visited.

"Or he could not be Thomas Guidry," Jose said, stating the obvious. "Can you send over a copy of his DMV records so we can see what Guidry is supposed to look like?"

"Sending it right now," Sophie said, and a second later a ding on her phone confirmed she had received a message.

Sara opened her phone and displayed the photo.

The air left her lungs as if someone had punched her in the gut. With a shaky hand she held the phone up so Jose could see the license.

His eyes opened wide, and a curse exploded from his mouth. "That's not Guidry."

"What do you mean it's not Guidry?" Sophie asked.

Jose took the phone from Sara and enlarged the photo with a swipe of two fingers. "It's not the man we met today, although…there are some similarities."

He laid the phone back on the table, and Sara leaned over to take another look at the enlarged photo. "They do look alike," Sara said.

"Enough to be related?" Robbie asked.

Jose tilted his head from side to side, examining the photo and considering the similarities. "Definitely. I'm guessing they could be brothers and close in age. The Guidry we saw could be an older sibling to the man from the license."

"But if the man we saw isn't Thomas Guidry, who is he?"

Chapter Twenty-Six

"You should have called me," Trey said the next morning as they gathered in the conference room to discuss what the team had found after a night of research.

"Blame me, *primo*. I decided you needed the rest and time with Roni," Jose said to avoid Trey ripping into the cousins.

Trey inhaled deeply and ran a hand through hair that was still shower damp. Blowing out the breath, he admitted, "*Gracias*. It was good to have a night off with Roni."

He clapped Trey on the shoulder and said, "How is she doing?"

The first smile he'd seen in days erupted on his cousin's face. "Much better. No more spotting and she's feeling stronger."

"Good to hear," Jose said and with another pat on Trey's shoulder, he walked over to pour himself a big cup of coffee. He needed the rush of caffeine and sugar after the night they'd spent trying to figure out who was posing as Thomas Guidry.

As he turned to go back to the table, he caught sight of Sara hugging Trey and felt an immediate pang of jealousy, which made no sense. Trey was head over heels in love with his new and very pregnant wife, and Sara…

He didn't know what was really up with Sara, only what he wished for and what he'd royally messed up with his thoughtless words the night before. He wasn't sure that his attempt to apologize had worked since they had gone to sleep in separate beds.

He wanted to fix that. Somehow, he would, he thought as he strolled to the table and sat next to where Sara had placed her papers. Bongo lay on the floor a few feet away and at his approach, the bloodhound got to her feet and came over to greet him.

He rubbed the dog's head and ears. "Good morning, Bongo," he said, and after a lick of his hand, the dog went back to her earlier spot.

Making believe he was reviewing his own notes, he nevertheless kept an eye on Sara as she left Trey and got some coffee and pastries.

When she returned to the table, she placed the dish with the pastries in a spot between them.

At his questioning look, she said, "I know you have a sweet tooth."

"I do. *Gracias.*" He grabbed a glazed doughnut from the plate and gobbled it down in a few bites.

At the head of the table, Trey clapped his hands to start the meeting. "Let's get going. I understand you have a lot to share with me," he said, and shot an accusatory eye at his tech guru cousins.

Sophie was not about to be cowed. She lifted her chin a determined inch and said, "We're not apologizing. You looked like you were ready to face-plant yesterday."

"Fair enough," he said, and pushed on. "What did you find out?"

"The man at the farm who claims to be Thomas Guidry isn't. We think it's his brother, Shawn Guidry," Sophie said, and handed Trey the photos they had unearthed the night before.

"This is a very old photo of Shawn," Trey said, eyes narrowed as he examined the image.

"It is. Shawn has managed to avoid notice for a long time, but we ran age progression software against it and made him gray," Robbie said, and handed Trey another photo.

Trey immediately nodded. "This is the man I met to discuss the lease. Jose? Sara?"

"Definitely who we met," Sara confirmed with a swift bob of her head.

"What do we know about Shawn and where is Thomas?" he asked, peering around the table.

"Where Thomas is we can't answer right now. But we do have some info on Shawn," Jose said, and dipped his head in Sophie's direction to ask her to report.

"Misty Waters married Shawn Guidry Sr. in Baton Rouge. Within a few months Shawn Jr. was born, and Thomas followed two years later," Sophie said, and passed Trey some photos they had dug up from an ancestry site.

"Shawn Sr. seems to have abandoned the family when the boys were ten and eight respectively. Two years later, Misty sent Shawn Jr. to a boarding school for troubled children," Sophie said.

"Any indication of what kind of trouble?" Trey asked.

"We plan on calling the school this morning to see if anyone is willing to talk," Sara said.

"What about after? College? Employment?" Trey prompted, eager for more information.

"Shawn was bright enough to land a scholarship to Tulane. Finished with honors and was employed by an investment firm in Miami. Lost the job within a year and from what we can see, he went from job to job for years and then disappeared off the radar," Sophie admitted with a sheepish shrug.

"His falling off the radar coincides with the Guidrys taking a lease on the farmland," Jose said, reading off the notes he'd taken the night before.

"It was too late last night to talk to neighbors, but we plan on doing that this morning," Sara added.

"Mia had a meeting this morning with a prospective client, but once she's free, she can help with that," Trey said, and once again turned his detective's eyes on his team. "What is it you're not telling me?"

Jose blurted out, "Sara was attacked last night."

"We think it was Shawn Guidry based on his general height. Nothing else from the footage since he was wearing a ski mask," Sara said.

"Are you okay, Sara?" Trey asked, his gaze filled with concern.

"I'm okay," she said but that didn't seem to satisfy Trey.

"Are you sure? Your safety is what's most important," he stressed.

"I'm okay. I had Bongo and Jose to help," she said.

Seemingly persuaded, Trey said, "What about Guidry's car? He had to have driven here from the farm."

Sophie pointed toward the large television at the far side of the room. "We got these clips from the CCTV. The same white panel van went around and around the block a few times just before the attack on Sara."

Jose watched as the clips played on the television, but it was impossible to see who was driving, and the license plates had been obscured with the reflective license plate covers used to block red light and speeding cameras from capturing a plate number.

"There is a DMV record for a white van in the name of Thomas Guidry," Jose said.

"That's just too much coincidence in my mind. Shawn was probably scouting the location," Trey said.

"And waiting for me, which means he's been watching us for the last few days, and I didn't see it," Sara said, and pursed her lips in obvious frustration.

Jose laid a hand on her shoulder and offered her a reassuring squeeze. "There was a lot going on. Anyone could be distracted."

"It's my job to see things others miss," she reminded him, still beating herself up about the attack.

"In a forest during a search and rescue. This is not the same thing," Trey offered to ease her upset.

"It won't happen again," she said.

"I know it won't," Trey said, once again reassuring her with his calm, uncondemning presence.

It surprised Jose in a way. The Trey he'd known all his life hadn't seemed that understanding and composed. He'd always imagined him as someone who kicked ass first and asked questions later. But then again, Trey had been a successful leader on the battlefield and as a detective.

Leaders thought about the consequences of their actions, much like Trey was doing now as he said, "It seems like we have our jobs cut out for us to contact teachers and friends and learn what happened in the Guidry family. I trust you all to work together and with Mia. In the meantime, I'm heading to the kennels to coordinate with PD and their CSI teams. I'll keep you posted on anything new."

When he stood, the others around the table did the same thing, but a second later Mia walked in, dressed to the nines in a coral-colored suit that screamed Boss Lady.

Trey strolled to Mia, gave her one-armed hug and said, "The team will fill you in. I'm off to the kennels."

With that Trey left and Mia took over, studying all the materials and information they'd gathered and assigning each of them tasks.

Much like he'd felt with Trey, Jose was likewise impressed with the way Mia handled herself and the team. As they finished, he paused on the way out to share a private moment with her.

"I've never said this, but...you guys are pretty amazing. I never really understood that," he said, awed at the discovery of what his family actually did to help others.

Mia's full lips tilted up in a wide smile. She laid a hand on his arm and said, "We're glad you're here with us."

"I'm glad to be here," he said, surprised by the words as they escaped him and their truthfulness.

"Good. Once you find out more about Shawn, you may want to reach out to Ricky for some advice on his personality traits. That may help us deal with him better," Mia said.

"We will." He hurried out to where Sara waited for him in the reception area, Bongo patiently lazing at her feet.

Mia joined them and motioned down the hall. "There's a smaller conference room where you can work. Make your calls," Mia said.

Chapter Twenty-Seven

Sara was still upset with herself that she hadn't noticed that someone was tracking them.

As Trey had noted a day or so earlier, she was a good read of people and preferred talking to neighbors up close and personal to get a better idea on what they thought of Guidry.

"If you don't mind, I'd rather interview the neighbors in person," she said.

"I'm okay with that if Jose is," Mia said, and peered at her cousin.

"Whatever Sara thinks is best," Jose replied, and ran his hand down her back, offering his support.

"Thank you," she said, appreciative of his agreeing with her decision.

"Just keep me posted and if Sophie and Robbie find anything, I'll keep you in the loop," Mia said, and with a wave, ran off to handle her share of the chores they'd defined during their meeting.

"Are you sure you're okay with going back out to the kennel and farms?" she asked.

He nodded. "I think it's the best way. We're both good judges of people, and there are things you just can't see over the phone or during a video call."

"I agree. Let me just take Bongo for a quick walk and then we can go," she said, and in no time, they were on their way out the door. As she had over the last few days, she walked Bongo in front of the SBS building only now she was vigilant, searching the crowd and the passing vehicles for signs of a white panel van or anything else that was out of the ordinary.

Satisfied, she joined hands with Jose and tugged him toward the entrance to the parking lot but as they approached, she hesitated, uneasy. Beside her leg, Bongo shifted closer, picking up on her vibes.

"I'm here. You don't need to worry," Jose said, and his words immediately relieved her discomfort.

"I know," she said without hesitation. Jose had her back in so many ways that it filled her heart until it felt like it might burst.

With a smile, he wrapped an arm around her neck and drew her close. Completed the hug by wrapping his other arm around her back, holding her tight, and rocking to reassure her.

Bongo thrust her head against Sara's leg, wanting to join in. It dragged a laugh from her and as they stepped apart, Bongo quickly moved into the gap between their legs, wanting some love also.

They both stroked and rubbed Bongo's head, ears and body, earning happy licks and a series of contented barks before they walked into the parking lot, located their SUV and secured Bongo in the back seat.

After they were moving, she reached over and stroked her hand down his arm, grateful.

He looked her way for a quick second, smiled again and twined his finger with hers.

Hands resting on the console between the seats, they made the half an hour or so drive to the street leading to the kennel. The homes along the road were sparsely laid out, but Guidry belonged to a local farmers' group, and they had pulled up a list of members the night before. Several of them lived along this road and would be the first ones they approached to find out more about Guidry.

At the first farmhouse, a man and woman were in the front yard, heads tucked beneath the hood of a vintage blue Ford tractor. As they drove up, the couple poked their heads out and the seventysomething man pulled a handkerchief from his pocket to wipe his hands clean.

The woman swung around to stand next to him. She was also in her seventies with carefully coiffed gray hair and a smudge of what looked like grease on one cheek.

"Can we help you?" the man said as they walked up after exiting the SUV, Bongo taking the lead, head down as she nosed the ground. Nothing about her behavior hinted at anything off, and she sat calmly at Sara's feet.

Jose held his hand out and said, "I'm Jose Gonzalez with Gonzalez Realty and this is Sara Hernandez, an SBS K-9 agent."

The man's gaze slitted against the sun as he examined them. "Are you the people who bought the Florian kennel?"

"We are. We're just introducing ourselves to our new neighbors," Sara said, and shook both their hands.

"It's a pleasure to meet you," the woman said, and jerked a thumb in her husband's direction. "This is George, but everyone calls him Pappy. I'm Tillie," she said, and laid a hand on her chest.

"I understand you've been here for nearly fifty years," Sara said, recalling what she'd read about Guidry's neighbors to break the ice.

"We have," Pappy said with a bright smile and hugged his wife close. "Came here as newlyweds."

"I imagine you've seen a lot of change in all those years," Jose said, earning a hairy eyeball from the man.

"We have and can't say we like some of what the developers have been doing, so we were glad to hear the kennel property and farm weren't going to change all that much," Pappy said.

"It won't. We plan on sprucing up the kennel to use the location as our new training center. Mr. Guidry will continue to lease the nearby farmland," Sara stated.

At the mention of Guidry, their smiles faded into looks of disgust.

"I gather you're not fans of your neighbor," Jose said, also picking up on the couple's sudden change of attitude.

"He's a bit..." Tilly began, but shrugged and held her tongue.

Pappy chuckled and shook his head. "Tilly's way too nice, but I'm not. He tries too hard to be charming and he's a liar."

"I don't trust him," Tilly added, with a decided bob of her head and jabbed an index finger in Sara's direction. "Especially you. Keep an eye on him."

"We will," Sara said, sensing what Tilly wasn't saying, namely, that Guidry couldn't be trusted around women.

Pappy peered at them intently once more, cocked his head to one side, and said, "Is it true you found bodies in the woods?"

Sara didn't see the sense of lying. "Bongo picked up on a scent and our team located them."

"The police are here now?" Tilly asked and wrung her hands together.

"They are. They'll be removing the bodies to try and ID them. They're also gathering evidence," Jose explained.

Pappy and Tilly shared a look before Tilly blurted out, "Do you think it's possible there are more bodies on our farm? We have woods close to where they're searching."

JOSE WAS TAKEN aback by the question because it hadn't occurred to him that the killer might have been burying bodies beyond the boundaries of the kennel property.

Facing Sara, he said, "Do you think we could search in that area for them?"

"We'd be willing to pay you for your services," Pappy quickly offered.

Sara instantly held her hands up to wave off his proposal. "That's okay. We'd love to help our new neighbors."

"That would be greatly appreciated so we could have some peace of mind," Tilly said, hands clasped in gratitude.

"We understand. We have some more stops to make, but once we do, we'll call to arrange for the search," Jose said.

The older couple's demeanor relaxed with his promise, and they hugged Sara and him effusively.

Once they had bundled Bongo into the back seat, they hopped in and drove off to the next farm down the road. Unlike Pappy and Tilly's avocado and mango orchards, this farm specialized in growing orchids and other exotic flowers. Much like Pappy and Tilly, the owner of the property welcomed them and had little good to say about Guidry.

That same experience occurred at the last two farms, leaving them to report to Trey on what they'd found out and the request for a search of the woods.

When they arrived, Trey was standing by Detective Espinoza and a trio of CSI agents. Trey and Espinoza intently listened to whatever was being said by the CSI folks, but their gazes flitted to a gurney as it wheeled past them.

They waited in front of the kennel owner's home until Trey was done and then hurried over to speak with him.

"How did it go?" he asked.

"Not much love for Guidry from the neighbors. Most think he's not to be trusted," Jose said, consolidating the various comments for his cousin.

"More than one also warned me to watch out, so it's clear they think it's not safe for women to be around him," Sara added to his assessment.

Trey nodded. "Good work. We should run that by Ricky when we get a chance."

"There's something else," he said, mindful of the request from Pappy and Tilly.

"Sure, what is it?" Trey said.

With a quick glance at Sara, he raised his arm and pointed in the direction of the woods. "That hardwood hammock continues across the road into a neighboring farm. Those owners are worried that whoever did the killing didn't stop at the road."

Trey jammed his hands on his hips and glanced at the tree line. With a shake of his head, he said, "The last of the graves stops well short of the road."

"It does, but Pappy and Tilly are very upset about the possibility," Sara said, pleading their cause.

Trey hesitated but as his gaze searched Sara's face, he recognized how important it was to her and to the neighbors. "If you think it makes sense, arrange to do it tomorrow."

"Thank you," she said, and Jose echoed her gratitude.

"It will give them much-needed peace of mind," he said, but at that, Trey muttered, "I wish I had peace of mind."

"What's up?" Sara asked.

"That was the last of the bodies, but it will be another day or so before they'll be finished searching for any additional evidence," Trey stated.

Jose motioned in the direction of where his cousin had been standing earlier. "Is that what you were discussing?"

Trey shook his head. "No. One of the CSIs thinks there's a bit of an anomaly in the last grave."

"An anomaly?" Sara questioned, brow furrowed over her troubled gray eyes.

"The team dug up a pelvis that's clearly masculine. Pelvic cavity was smaller as was the pubic arch. The pelvis was narrower with a higher iliac crest and denser bone," Trey explained, using his hands as well to demonstrate the differences.

"Thomas Guidry?" Jose suggested for consideration.

Pursing his lips, Trey did a reluctant shrug. "Possibly. Once they get all the bones, they'll be able to tell height based on the leg bones. A visual inspection of the bones and bone age test will give us an age range."

"And after that we'll be able to take a better guess if it's Thomas, but if it is, where's Misty?"

Jose barked out a laugh. "My guess is in the grave with Thomas."

"I agree," Trey said. With a last look at the woods, he said, "Let's head back to the offices to discuss what we've got so far."

"Sure, but if you don't mind, I'd like to stop to let Pappy and Tilly know we'll do the search in the morning. Their house is on the way back," Sara said.

Trey smiled and nodded. "Sounds good. I'll see you back at the office."

Chapter Twenty-Eight

Dusk descended over the farmlands, painting the sky in blues, pinks and purples as the sun fled in late afternoon.

Jose turned into Pappy and Tilly's driveway so they could give them the good news about tomorrow's search.

He was almost at the farmhouse when a blur of something big and blue registered in the corner of his eye.

"Hold on," Jose shouted and violently jerked the wheel to the right, trying to avoid being T-boned by the blue tractor the couple had been working on earlier.

The plow on the tractor clipped the left front quarter panel, sending the rest of the SUV smashing against the side of the farm vehicle. The tractor wheels chewed up the side of the SUV with a sickening crunch and screech of metal on metal and the shattering sound of glass as the side window exploded.

Looking up at the driver on the tractor, all he could see was a dark shadow at the wheel. The driver was all in black with a black ski mask.

He struggled to keep the car from being crushed by the wheels as the black-clad driver jammed the tractor against the SUV again.

Realizing he'd never overpower it, Jose slammed on the brakes, sending him, Sara and Bongo reeling back and forth in their seats.

The tractor shot forward, heading straight for a tree to one side of the yard.

The tractor driver jumped off a second before the vehicle slammed into the tree with a sickening thud.

Jose tried to open his door to give chase as the driver sped to the woods, but there was too much damage to the door.

He looked toward Sara to make sure she was okay, but his vision blurred for a moment as wet warmth dripped into his eyes.

"You're hurt," Sara said, and turned in her seat.

He swiped his fingers across his brow, and they came away wet with blood.

Sara tore a piece of fabric from her T-shirt and held it against his brow to stem the flow.

Bongo was barking and shifting from one side to the other in the back seat, making Jose's head pound with the sound.

"Sit, Bongo. Quiet," Sara called out and Bongo whined until she issued the command again and the bloodhound finally fell silent.

The door to the farmhouse opened and Pappy and Tilly came running out.

"Are you okay?" Tilly asked at the same time that Pappy said, "What happened? Damn, look at my tractor!"

"I'm calling the police," Tilly said, and pulled a cell phone from her apron pocket.

"Do you think you can stand?" Sara asked.

"I'm fine, but this door is shot. You go first and I'll crawl out after you."

She did as he asked, exiting the SUV, and then reached back in to help him crawl over the center console. Once he was out, he leaned against the car as Sara got Bongo out of the back seat and did a once-over to make sure the dog hadn't also been injured during the incident.

Pappy walked over to inspect the tractor. Hopping up into

the driver's seat, he shouted back, "Someone hot-wired it. Darn front end is toast."

"Don't touch anything in case there are fingerprints or DNA," Sara called out to the older man.

Pappy lifted his hands as if in surrender and hurried back to wrap an arm around Tilly's shoulders as she finished up the call.

"Police are on their way," she said.

Despite the pounding in his head and the chill fear filling his core, Jose forced a smile for the older woman. "Thank you, Tilly."

As if on cue, the scream of sirens rent the air and within a minute, the strobe of red and blue lights traveled across the farmlands as the police cruiser approached.

Sara shifted to his side and laid a hand on his shoulder. Bongo took up a spot at his feet, the dog's weight comforting.

The cruiser cut off its sirens as it came down the driveway and pulled up to the wreck of their SUV. Two officers slipped from the car, and he recognized them from the day of the blast.

He nodded his head in greeting. "Officer Rojas. Officer McAllister."

Rojas shook her head in almost disbelief and said, "Mr. Gonzalez. Ms. Hernandez. I wish I could say it was a pleasure."

McAllister examined the ruined side of the SUV and let out a low whistle and shake of his head. "Who shredded the car?"

Pappy shot an arm out in the direction of his vintage tractor. "Someone hot-wired it. Ran it into the kids' car."

Jose hadn't been called a "kid" in years, but it fit perfectly coming from a character like Pappy.

Rojas pulled her notepad from her utility belt. "Did you see the driver?"

Jose shook his head. "He had a black ski mask on."

Rojas pointed her notebook in the direction of the tractor. "Let's see if we can find anything over there."

With that, McAllister and she walked to the crashed vehicle and began examining it, searching for evidence. Their flashlights bounced across the vehicle and down to the ground as they explored in the growing dark.

The sound of wheels crunching on the gravel driveway had him looking to where an SUV—another SBS vehicle— was coming down the drive.

As it approached, he realized it was Trey behind the wheel. Seconds later, his cousin parked and hurried over to them.

"Are you okay?" he said as he took note of the blood on Jose's face.

He removed the makeshift bandage, but immediately felt blood welling and reapplied the fabric and pressure to the cut, wincing at the tenderness at his brow.

"Let's get a butterfly bandage on that," Trey said, and hurried back to the SUV. He returned quickly with a first-aid kit and went to work on Jose's injury.

"How did you know to come here?" Jose asked.

"I was listening to the police scanner on the way home," Trey said without hesitation.

"Because that's what normal people do while they drive," Jose said facetiously.

Trey blew out a rough laugh and partially lifted his gaze toward Sara. "Do you think Bongo can pick up any kind of scent off that tractor?"

SARA MURMURED A curse beneath her breath because it was something she should have done right off the bat only she'd been too worried about Jose's injury.

"As soon as the police are finished, I'll move in," she said, and turned her attention to watching the two officers as they scoured the scene. When they shut off their flashlights and walked back toward them, she went into action.

With a hand signal to Bongo, the dog leaped into action, leading the way as she sniffed along the ground. At the tractor, she urged Bongo up into the driver's seat and instructed, "Find, Bongo. Find."

Bongo nosed around the pedals and when she patted the seat, did the same there before hopping up and scenting the higher portions of the seat.

"Find, Bongo. Find," she commanded again, and at that, the bloodhound dropped to the ground and sniffed the area before seeming to find a scent.

Head bent close to the earth, Bongo shifted her head back and forth, a clear indication she had something. She moved quickly, tugging the leash as she followed the odor, but it didn't take long for Sara to realize Bongo was leading them straight back to where Jose, Trey, Tilly and Pappy waited.

Barely a minute later, Bongo was sniffing all around Pappy's feet and sat, telling Sara that she had found the source of the scent.

"I'm sorry, Trey. Pappy's scent was way too strong," she said, disheartened at her failure.

Jose immediately came to Bongo's defense. "The guy had on gloves and a mask. No skin visible anywhere so how could he leave behind any evidence."

Sara raised a hand to stop him. "Bongo might have been able to pick up the driver's body odor from the seat even through his clothes."

"Is there anything you can remember about the driver?" Trey asked as Rojas and McAllister returned.

Jose shook his head. "Only that he was all in black and hiding his face. The gloves," he said.

"Leather or something else?" Sara asked.

Jose seemed puzzled for a moment and then said, "No,

not leather. Plastic of some kind. And black, but… I could
see his wrist. He was white."

She shared a look with Trey since it kept Guidry as a possible suspect. Officer Rojas must have picked up on it since
she said, "Is there something you want to share with us?"

"Not at all," Trey said with a shake of his head.

Although Rojas obviously didn't believe him, she held
back, instead saying to her partner, "CSI will be here shortly.
As first on the scene, we have to preserve any evidence, but
you're all free to go."

"*Gracias*, Officer Rojas. If you can, please keep us
posted," Trey said, and handed the officer his business card.

She barely shot it a look, held it up and said, "And I'm
sure you'll share anything you have when you're ready."

Trey smiled and without missing a beat said, "We will."

They walked to Trey's SUV and piled in with Jose in the
front passenger seat and her and Bongo in the rear. She had
just finished strapping in Bongo when Trey started the vehicle and did a K-turn to leave.

"Why didn't you say anything to them about Guidry?"
Jose asked as soon as they were off the farm property.

"Because the last thing we need is them spooking Guidry
into running," Trey said with a quick look in Jose's direction. Wincing, he added, "You're probably going to have a
shiner in the morning."

Sara peered at Jose in the dark of the SUV's interior and
could see that beside the cut at his brow there was some red-
ness along his cheekbone as well.

"Did you hit the side window?" she asked, worried Jose
was hurt worse than it seemed.

He shook his head. "I don't know. All I remember is trying to keep away from those huge tractor wheels and suddenly there was an explosion of glass."

Sara met Trey's gaze in the rearview mirror. "Maybe we
should take Jose to the hospital to see if he has a concussion."

"I'm fine. Just a headache," Jose admitted.

"Which is a sign of a concussion. Sara's right. We should have a doctor check you out," Trey said, and immediately programed the SUV's navigation to a nearby hospital in Homestead.

Barely ten minutes later, they pulled up in front of a large Mediterranean-style building dressed in shell pink walls and topped with terra-cotta tiles along all the roofs and porticos.

Trey drove them up to the ER entrance, turned around in his seat and said, "Do you want to go in with Jose while I watch Bongo?"

It made sense since she couldn't leave the dog alone and the hospital might not allow Bongo in since she wasn't technically a service dog.

"That would be great," she said, and hopped out of the car to meet Jose, who was already standing there, waiting.

"This is a waste of time," he murmured as they walked into the ER.

Luckily it was a quiet night at the hospital. A doctor was soon examining Jose, asking him a variety of questions while checking his vision and hearing. Once he finished with that, he had Jose do a series of balance and strength tests. The doctor finished by checking his reflexes.

"The headache is a clue you might have a mild concussion, but all the other tests are good. I don't think it's necessary to do any imaging," the physician said, and glanced in her direction.

"Make sure your boyfriend takes it easy for a day or so including screen time. Your brain needs to rest."

"Got it, Dr. Wright. I'll make sure he gets some rest," she said.

Jose hopped off the examining room bed, came to her side and wrapped an arm around her waist. "Thank you. My girlfriend and I are grateful for your help," he said, playfully emphasizing the "girlfriend" part.

"Come on, babe. Let's go home," he said, and planted a kiss on her temple.

"Remember, rest," the doctor admonished as they walked out of the examining room, stopped by the nurses' station to finish with his health insurance and pay. Once they were done, they strolled out of the ER, arms wrapped around each other.

Trey was standing beneath the portico, Bongo at his side. "I took her for a walk. She seemed a little antsy, but she didn't do anything so you may need to walk her again."

Sara nodded and accepted the leash as Trey handed it to her. "She was probably restless because she's not used to me leaving her alone."

"How did it go?" Trey asked and directed them toward the SUV parked several yards away.

"I'm fine, just like I said," Jose replied.

Trey checked in with her. "Is that what the doc said?"

"Pretty much. He does have a mild concussion and needs to take it easy for a day or two," Sara said, repeating the doctor's instructions.

"And that's what you'll do. No work for you," Trey said, and clapped Jose's back, offering what she supposed was man-style comfort.

"I'm not an invalid. I can help out with the case," he said, but she wasn't surprised.

Despite what he'd originally told her a few days ago, which now seemed like ages ago, Jose was without a doubt part of the SBS team.

Trey nodded. "You can. From behind a desk or the penthouse until we know what that hit did to your head."

Jose was about to argue with him, but Sara laid a hand on his arm to stop him. "It's what makes sense. Let's go home and get some rest."

WITHIN A FEW minutes they were on the turnpike and heading back to the South Beach Security offices. With the detour to the hospital, it was nearly an hour ride back, and Jose found himself drifting off to sleep.

Trey reached over and gave his thigh a shake. "Try to stay awake. I want to make sure there's nothing bad going on."

While he understood, the wear and tear from the crash and all their running around that day was dragging on him. It was a battle to stay awake, but between Trey and Sara, they kept him alert with a shake or questions he tried to answer quickly, not wanting to worry them.

Their actions distracted him to the point that he didn't even realize they were back at the SBS offices until Trey parked in one of the spots reserved for the SBS team.

"Why don't you two head to the penthouse? I'm going to check in with Sophie and Robbie—"

"We'll go with you," Jose immediately said, not wanting to be babied, especially in front of Trey who was the kind of man who would push on in a fight even if severely injured.

Trey met his determined gaze, and something clicked between them. There was recognition of Jose's strength there. Acknowledgment that he too was a man who would do what he had to no matter the cost to himself.

With a nod, Trey said, "Sure. We'll convene in the conference room and order in some food since I'm sure you haven't had a chance to have dinner."

"We haven't," Sara said as she unbuckled Bongo and quickly added, "I should walk her again before we go up since she didn't go earlier."

"I'll go with you," he said, and followed her as she let Bongo stroll up the ramp of the parking lot and onto the sidewalk.

As he walked beside her, she was silent for a long time until she risked a quick glimpse at him and said, "You don't need to prove anything to anyone."

She'd clearly picked up on that unspoken exchange between Trey and him. "I'm not backing down. Trey's handling a lot right now, and I'm not going to add to that."

Chapter Twenty-Nine

Sara couldn't argue that Trey had a lot on his plate, including multiple murders on the property he'd just purchased and the reality that a serial killer was still on the loose and attacking them.

But that didn't excuse Jose's stubborn insistence on ignoring the doctor's instruction to get some rest. "No one is going to think less of you if you take it easy for a day or two."

He jabbed his chest forcefully. "I will think less of me."

The way he had for so long in a family filled with so many successful and courageous people.

She cradled his jaw, went up on tiptoes and whispered against his lips, "I won't."

He groaned as if in pain, hauled her tight against him and deepened the kiss, his hand tunneling through her hair to cradle her skull.

When they broke apart, they were both breathing heavily and he leaned his forehead against hers and said, "No matter how crazy this all has been, I'm grateful for meeting you."

"I am too," she said, thinking that Jose had shown more than once that he was the kind of man who could handle being in a life like hers.

"Let's head upstairs. They're probably wondering why we're taking so long," she said.

"And playing matchmaker," Jose said, a wry smile drifting across his lips.

She narrowed her gaze to gauge if he was being serious, and seeing that he was, she said, "You think your family is matchmaking?"

He nodded and held open the lobby door for her. "I think both Trey and Mia were pushing us together although Trey seemed worried at first."

As she walked with him and Bongo through the lobby, she thought about that first meeting and couldn't argue with him.

"I guess now that they're both happily married—"

Jose interrupted with, "And don't forget Ricky is also engaged."

She hadn't spent much time with Trey and Mia's psychologist brother although they had planned on speaking with him for help with the killer's profile.

"They just want you to be happy," she said, and slipped her hand into his as they cleared the security desk.

While they waited for the elevator, he tugged on her hand to draw her in for another kiss.

"Had to have this before we got upstairs. I don't want to encourage them," he said with a laugh.

She chuckled and shook her head. "Like I said, they only want you to be happy."

HIS HEAD WAS POUNDING, and his face was sore. There were several dead bodies on the property he had just convinced his cousin to purchase, and the serial killer responsible for them had just tried to kill him and Sara. And he hadn't been home in days. He was staying at the penthouse because he wanted to be close to Sara and help his cousins with the investigation.

Somehow, despite all that, Jose was happy, surprisingly. And a lot of it had to do with the beautiful woman standing beside him with her big, drooly dog.

When badged into the now-closed SBS offices, he walked with her to the conference room, slipping his arm around her waist in a very loving and possessive gesture that was not missed by his cousins.

Trey, in particular, let his gaze linger on that caress, but said nothing.

Jose could swear that Trey forced away a smile before he schooled his emotions. It confirmed that he hadn't been wrong to think his cousins had been matchmaking when they'd thrown him and Sara together.

Mia said, "I've ordered in Cuban sandwiches again. Figured it was something we all like."

Like clockwork, one of the deli employees walked in with a big cardboard box and at Mia's instruction laid out sandwiches, assorted sides and sodas on the credenza at one side of the room.

"Sounds good, *prima*," he said, although in truth, he wasn't really hungry since he was nauseous. The ER doctor had warned him that was something he might experience because of the concussion.

The SBS crew must have been hungry since as soon as the deliveryman left, most of them headed straight to the credenza to grab sandwiches.

He hung back, letting those with appetites fill their needs first before Sara and he walked over. Grabbing half a sandwich, he then also scooped up some rice, beans and avocado salad.

As soon as they were all seated, Sara took apart one of the sandwiches and placed some pork, ham and cheese on a paper plate so Bongo could eat before they went to the penthouse.

While she did that, Trey began the meeting. "A couple of hours ago someone attacked Pepe, Sara and Bongo by driving a tractor into their SUV. Luckily, they were unhurt although Pepe has a mild concussion."

That prompted a chorus of questions and commiserations from his other cousins.

"*Gracias*, but I'm fine. Just a little headache," he said, wanting to downplay the injury.

"We're sorry you were hurt. We know you worried about working with us," Mia said.

"Like I said, I'm fine but the sooner we can solve this case, the quicker I can go back to my regular life," he said, with a little more sting than he intended.

Beside him Sara fidgeted, and he could guess why. With the state of their relationship unsettled in some ways, the end of the investigation might mean more distance between them. To reassure her, he laid a hand on hers as it rested on the table.

As he had before, Trey zeroed in on that gesture as did Mia, but neither said anything.

"Do you have any updates, Sophie? Robbie?" he asked, shifting his gaze to their tech guru cousins.

"We've done a lot of digging around and as best we can tell, Misty Guidry disappeared off the face of the earth about four or so years ago. No calls on her cell phone. Her bank account was drained in the months before that," Sophie said.

"We called Misty's brother in Baton Rouge who said they were never close, so it wasn't unusual not to hear from her or her sons," Robbie added.

"We have normal activity on Thomas's cell phone and bank account. In fact, some of the withdrawals from Misty's account match deposits on Thomas's account," Sophie said, using air quotes when she mentioned Thomas since they all suspected Shawn had been posing as his brother for some time.

"We know now that one of the bodies is male. I think we

all agree that it could be Thomas," Trey said, and peered around the table to see if anyone disagreed.

"And if it is, I'd put money on Misty being in one of the graves as well," Sophie said.

Murmurs of agreement filled the room just a second before Trey's cell phone rang. "It's the police."

He answered and after a brief back-and-forth, he said, "We appreciate that info. We have some as well that may help you confirm the approximate TOD. We'll send it over shortly."

After he hung up, he addressed the group. "PD has confirmed that the one skeleton is that of a male. Approximately fifty years old and six feet two inches tall. The woman in that grave with him was older. Approximately eighty years old and five feet four inches tall."

"Thomas and Misty. I guess we were right that the man claiming to be Thomas is actually Shawn Guidry," Mia said.

"They were close in age and looked enough alike that Shawn could pass for him with little effort. Except for their mom knowing who was who," Jose said, shaking his head in disbelief at what the man had done.

"It's hard to imagine someone doing that to family," Sara said, and squeezed his hand to offer comfort.

"It seems that was the reason he was sent off to the boarding school," Sophie said, and at Trey's prompting, she elaborated.

"We spoke to the current head of the school who had been there as a teacher when Shawn was admitted. It turns out there were several instances where Thomas was hurt as a young child. Apparently, Shawn Sr. thought junior was responsible, but Misty staunchly defended him. That was part of the reason Senior left."

"What about his behavior at the boarding school?" Jose asked, wondering if his actions there confirmed the father's suspicions.

"The school was highly regimented. Students had little free time and because most were troubled children, there was constant supervision," Robbie said.

"Sounds like a prison," Sara said, and he couldn't disagree.

"What would that kind of environment do to a young boy?" Jose pondered aloud.

Mia suggested, "Might be a good time to call Ricky."

Chapter Thirty

Trey did just that and once Ricky answered, he said, "*Hola, hermanito.* We were hoping to pick your brain. Why don't you fill him in?" he asked, addressing his techie cousins.

Sophie and Robbie reiterated the facts they'd been able to gather about Shawn Guidry and once they'd finished, Ricky said, "It sounds like you may be dealing with an undiagnosed Antisocial Personality Disorder. The parents' rejection and neglect. Their choice of one child over another."

"But it started before he was sent away," Sara said, wondering what could have caused that early behavior.

Ricky immediately provided an answer. "There is strong evidence that both genetics and prenatal environmental factors can cause that kind of behavior."

"So antisocial personality traits are set in stone at birth?" she queried, shocked that it could start that early in a person's life.

"It could be but not everyone with ASPD is bad. It all depends on how they channel those traits. In addition, recent studies on interventions show that certain therapies are effective in curbing antisocial behavior," he explained.

"What about the kind of intense discipline he got at the boarding school?" Jose asked.

A long hesitation followed before Ricky said, "That likely

only helped repress the behaviors instead of teaching the individual how to deal with their emotions."

"What would happen once they're out of that kind of environment?" Sara asked, recalling what the cousins had said about Shawn's later life.

"They might be in control for a little while, but in general, people with undiagnosed ASPD have trouble relating to people, holding jobs, and they can be impulsive. But they are highly intelligent and can be very charming," Ricky said.

"Which means he could have charmed his way back into his family's life," Sophie said.

"Very much so when you consider the guilt his mother may have felt at sending him away. He could easily manipulate that guilt," Ricky confirmed.

"Thanks. We appreciate your analysis," Trey said.

He was about to hang up when Ricky said, "I wouldn't just focus on what's happening at the kennels, Trey. You should look into the time immediately after he was fired. It's another rejection that could have set him off."

Trey nodded. "We will. *Gracias*," he said, and finally ended the call.

"We'll work on it. We'll call his employers over those years to see what they'll share. Check for any indications of violence in and around where he was living," Sophie said.

"Perfect. We sent over the boot info to the police as well as our suspicions about Guidry's true identity. They didn't think it was enough to get a search warrant, but maybe now that they have bones that possibly match Misty and Thomas it may be enough," Trey said.

"If it is, when do you suppose they'll ask for the warrant?" Jose asked.

"Probably first thing in the a.m. Until then, we should all get some rest, especially you, Pepe," Trey said, and pointed in Jose's direction.

It was obvious to Sara that Jose wasn't happy about being

singled out, but she understood Trey's concern. "You need to get some ice on that cheek and the doctor said to rest."

Although Jose's lips were in a firm disapproving line, he nodded. "We should go. This headache is getting worse."

She noticed then that he'd only eaten half his sandwich, and she worried he was also having some nausea as the doctor had warned. Because of that, she said, "Let's head out. I need to feed Bongo and take her for her last walk of the night."

He didn't argue, only stood, and said, "We'll see you in the morning."

"First thing and feel better, Pepe. We're all proud of how you're handling the mess we pulled you into and thankful as well," Trey said, obviously reading his cousin's earlier distress.

With those words the tension in Jose's body melted away. She slipped her hand into his and grabbed Bongo's leash. The bloodhound immediately came to her feet and followed them out of the office and to the elevator. It barely took a minute for it to arrive and deliver them up to the penthouse.

"Why don't you relax while I feed Bongo?" she said.

JOSE LEANED ON the kitchen counter to watch as she filled one of Bongo's dishes with fresh food and another with water.

Bongo inhaled the food and lapped up some water before the bloodhound trotted off toward the sofa, did a circle or two before settling down to one side of it.

"I'm not sure you're supposed to drink—"

"I'm not, but you go ahead," he said, and waved in the direction of the bar.

She shook her head. "I'm not really in the mood."

He was getting mixed signals from her and decided to clear the air. "What are you in the mood for?"

She smiled, a sexy siren's smile and held out her hand. "Bed. With you."

"Are you sure?" he asked, worried about the tentative state of their relationship, if you could even call it that.

"After all that's gone on today, I don't want to be alone."

He wasn't sure that's why he wanted her to want to be with him, but in truth, he didn't want to be alone tonight either. He wanted to be with her.

Slipping his hand into hers, he said, "Let's go to bed."

They strolled to her bedroom, Bongo following them, but at the door Sara gave the dog a "down" command, and Bongo immediately took a spot by the bedroom door.

"Good girl," Sara said, and closed the door to give them privacy.

Once inside, they rushed toward the bed but slowed once they were there, not wanting to hurry what was about to happen.

SARA TOOK HER time undoing the buttons on Jose's guayabera, which bore traces of the blood from his head wound. It was a glaring reminder of what had happened earlier, but also of his injuries after the explosion. Because of that, as she peeled off his shirt to expose his beautifully sculpted body, she slipped to his side to gently inspect the wounds on his shoulder.

The injuries had scabbed with no sign of any infection, and she said, "They're healing nicely."

She ran her hand up his arm to his shoulder and then faced him. The bright white of the butterfly bandage at his brow coupled with the increasingly black-and-blue area on his cheekbone was a scary reminder of the danger they'd been in that night.

"Does it hurt?" she said, and lightly danced her fingers over the purpling mess on his face.

He grinned, laid a hand on her waist and said, "Only when I smile."

She shook her head and chuckled much as he must have

wanted her to. But she understood he hid behind that self-deprecating humor and wanted there to be no doubt as to how she felt about him. "Don't ever think you're not a hero."

His full-lipped smile thinned and grew harder. "I'm just a regular guy."

With a dip of her head, she said, "You're *my* regular guy but the doctor said you need to rest."

HE HATED THAT she was right. "Let's get some sleep," he said.

"Are you sure?" she said, obviously worried that the night wasn't going as they'd expected.

"I'm sure. I'm here, Sara. I'll always be here for you," he said, more certain of her than he had been of anything else in his life.

She smiled and cradled the side of his face. "I love you."

He grinned, taking in those words. Relishing them as he replied, "I love you too."

That released something between them. Something wild and joyful and life-giving.

He may have faced death twice with her, but more importantly, he knew she would be at his side to savor life.

It roused a peace unlike any he'd ever experienced before. Satisfying and rich as they lay down together and then cuddled close, happily tucked in each other's arms.

He was just slipping off to sleep, contentedly lying in her arms when she said, "I don't regret what brought us together."

For so long he'd avoided working with his SBS family exactly because of all that had happened in the last few days. But like Sara, he had no regrets because it had brought them together.

"I don't regret it either," he said, and dropped a kiss on her forehead.

She snuggled closer and he smiled, content. Hoping that contentment could survive whatever was coming their way in the next few days.

Chapter Thirty-One

Sophie had some surprising news the next morning as they gathered at the kennels to finish up security and get the buildings ready. The police had released most of the areas to them since they were finished with their investigations.

As Sara looked around, she noticed that the only areas restricted to them were marked off by the yellow tape around the edges of the woods.

"I reached out to Guidry's past employer. It turns out he was fired from that investment job because of complaints that he had gotten a little physical with one of his female colleagues, but there's more," she said, glancing around as she dropped a literal bomb into the discussion.

"Shortly after Shawn's last known job, 'Thomas' Guidry joined the army and eventually became an Explosive Ordnance Disposal—EOD—specialist. The training for that takes about three years," Sophie said, making it clear that it wasn't Thomas who'd suddenly gotten patriotic.

"Which explains how Shawn seemed to have disappeared for all those years," Robbie added.

"And how he knew to bomb the outbuilding, chimney and set all those booby traps," Sara said with a shake of her head.

"We need to get this to PD. If this doesn't sway a judge into issuing a warrant, I'll be shocked," Trey said.

"I'll email the info to Detective Espinoza," Sophie said.

"While they prepare the warrant, let's work on getting this place ready for Sara and the K-9 center," Mia said, and peered at Jose intently. "Are you feeling okay?"

"Just a headache," he said, downplaying it, but his voice and body were tight, and she had noticed earlier that morning that he seemed a little pale.

"Maybe you can stay here and help out with the painters," Mia said.

"I'm okay," he insisted, and shot a quick look in her direction.

"Mia and I are just going to take some measurements for the flooring, and then we'll be back," she said.

That seemed to mollify him since he nodded. "I'll wait for you and the painters here."

"Great. The rest of us will finish up the security installations," Trey said.

Sophie gestured to the yellow tape along the edges of the woods. "We haven't been able to install the perimeter cameras because of the restrictions."

Trey stood, arms akimbo, and examined the wooded area. With a nod, he said, "We'll finish once they're gone. In the meantime, let's secure what we can."

With that the team went into action, but Sara hung back with Jose, wanting to make sure he was okay.

"Are you fine with staying here? I won't be long," she said, and rubbed Bongo's head as the dog bumped against her leg.

"I'm good. I'll just wait inside for the painters," he said, and without waiting for her, he walked to the house and stepped inside.

Sara stood there for a long minute, a weird feeling in her gut. She was torn between following him and going with Mia to measure for the new floors in the training center and track area.

"Do you want to stay?" Mia asked.

She was being silly. The painters would be here at any

moment and Jose would be fine. "No, let's do the measurements," she said, and they walked off toward the training ring.

JOSE STROLLED INTO the house, grateful to be out of the morning sun whose glare had just been making his headache even worse.

Although the doctor had advised against caffeine because of the concussion, he needed a jolt to get going since he felt lethargic even though they'd gotten a nice night's sleep.

He smiled as he thought about the night and how they'd fallen asleep in each other's arms. Woke wrapped together, he thought as he entered the kitchen in search of a coffee machine and hopefully coffee, even if it might be stale after years in the cupboards.

He opened one cupboard, and it blocked his view of the hallway, but sudden motion had him turning in that direction.

A mistake. Something sharp drove into his side, sucking the breath from his lungs.

He looked down to see the short knife buried between his ribs and in a blur of action, Guidry was behind him with an arm around his neck.

"Move or call out and I'll cut your throat," Shawn said.

"What do you want?" Jose said, words choppy since each breath seemed to create fire at the spot where Guidry had the knife buried in his side.

"Satisfaction. You and your friends have ruined my special place. Someone has to pay for that. Maybe those two pretty women I saw walking away," Guidry hissed against the side of his face.

"Leave them alone," Jose said, and pain erupted as Guidry delivered a little twist of the knife.

"Big hero, aren't you? We'll see how much of a hero when

I get you alone," he said, and applied pressure at his neck to shuffle him toward a side door in the kitchen.

With a shove, Guidry said, "Open it."

He did, and Guidry led him out the door and through the newly mowed grass behind the house.

Jose almost wished they'd left it longer since it would have created more of a trail to follow. He stumbled on a bit of uneven ground, bringing intense pain as the knife punched into his side again.

"Move," Guidry commanded.

Jose did, hoping the SBS crew would quickly notice his absence but also thinking about how he could save himself, especially since with each step he took, he was feeling weaker, and it was getting harder to breathe.

He was in so much pain coupled with fear, he hadn't really paid attention to where they were going. But as they stopped, he realized they were in the middle of a field that had once held a crop of corn. Now there was only the refuse of chopped cornstalks, leaves, and here and there, verdant vines from a pumpkin patch.

"On your knees," he said, and Jose readily complied, in part because his knees were already crumpling from the loss of blood. It was warm and wet against his side and down toward his waist.

Before his fading eyes the ground opened up, exposing a large four-by-four-foot hole. His surprise was short-lived as with a shove, Guidry pushed him in.

He landed hard and it drove out what little breath he had left.

As he rolled onto his back, his last view was of a crystal-clear Miami fall sky and the ground closing above him.

His last thought was of Sara.

"WHAT'S UP?" Mia asked as Sara stared toward the house through the open door of the training ring.

Sara couldn't say what it was, but she had an unsettling feeling in her gut that warned they had to rush back. "We're done, right? I'd like to make sure Jose is okay. He was looking a little pale this morning."

Mia nodded. "Sure thing. We're done here."

They hustled back toward the house, meeting up with Trey who had left Sophie and Robbie to finish up with their team.

"Something wrong?" Trey asked, reading her signals clearly.

"Just worried about Jose," Sara admitted, her pace quickening. Bongo quickly walking beside her.

"I'm sure he's fine," Trey said, but fell into step with her, sensing her upset.

She burst through the door of the house and seeing the room was empty, called out his name. "Jose. Where are you?"

He didn't answer.

"I'll check upstairs," Trey said, and took the steps two at a time while Mia checked the far rooms on the first floor.

Sara noticed that a side door in the kitchen was ajar and moved in that direction.

She stopped short at what looked like droplets of blood on the wooden floor.

Tugging Bongo's leash tight, she knelt and examined the floor more carefully. She had no doubt it was blood. Worse, she had no doubt it was Jose's blood.

As Trey came bounding down the stairs and Mia returned to the kitchen, they walked over.

Trey muttered a curse and said, "I'll call the rest of the team for help."

Sara held her hand up to stop him. "No. It'll be too many people mucking up the trail. Bongo and I will find him."

"With what?" Mia said, wringing her hands with worry.

Sara pointed to the drops of blood on the floor. "With that."

Urging Bongo close, she let her K-9 partner scent the blood, and said, "Find him, Bongo. Find him."

SHARP, JABBING PAIN jerked him back to consciousness.

"Good. I don't want you to miss anything," Guidry said, and stepped away, short bloody knife in his hand.

Jose peered at his side and the trio of wounds leaking blood.

Trey's words returned in a flash. *Some killers need to stick people to experience arousal.*

Glancing back at the other man, his joy was evident from the wide smile on his face and the brightness of his eyes, even in the dim light belowground.

"I want you to see how I'm going to kill your friends," Guidry said. He walked to a small table at one side of the space, and flipped on a lamp that spewed a circle of light over an assortment of wires, cans and batteries spread across the table's surface.

Guidry went to work at the table, but Jose wasn't about to let that happen.

He tried to sit up, but his hands were secured behind his back. His feet were also tied to keep him immobile.

That wasn't going to stop him.

He tucked his legs tight to his chest, ignoring the agony that ripped through his side.

Sucking in a few shallow breaths to contain the pain, he somehow managed to get his hands lower and close to his buttocks. Straining even harder, there was enough give in whatever tied them that he could slip his hands past his ass.

A chill sweat covered his body and dark circles swirled in his gaze as oblivion threatened to claim him again.

He inhaled deeply, marshaling his flagging energy, and pushed on. He would not let Guidry hurt his family.

Chapter Thirty-Two

Bongo led them across the narrow piece of woods near the road and then doubled back toward the fields leading to the Guidry farmhouse.

Fields where the only visible things were the stumpy stalks of corn that had been harvested a few weeks earlier. The dried stalks and scattered bits of leaves intermixed with vines, creating a tangle along the ground. Here and there bright spots of orange, pumpkins growing for a late fall harvest, dotted the fields.

They stopped at the edge of the field, searching for anywhere Guidry might be able to hide, but Sara couldn't see anything even though Bongo was pulling her toward the field and not the farmhouse.

Trey peered at the dog's actions. "There's nothing here but wide-open fields. He's probably at the farmhouse."

Bongo jerked at the leash, trying to urge her forward. "Bongo picked up a scent in the field."

"But if she's wrong—"

"Jose could die. Don't you think I know that?" Sara shot the words back at him, fear making her blood run cold. With a deep inhalation, she shook her head and said, "I trust Bongo. She's never wrong."

Trey hesitated, but then relented. "Then let's go."

GUIDRY WAS TOO busy planning his surprise to notice that Jose had somehow managed to bring his hands in front. That let him sit up and shimmy to the dirt wall of the space for support as blood loss made his head whirl again.

There was only a little light from the bare bulb hanging from a wire. It flickered uncertainly and as Jose traced the wire, he realized it was connected to a small device and then a car battery. By the base of the battery were red and black plastic clippings and a wire cutter.

Careful not to draw Guidry's attention, Jose scooted over a few inches and leaned down, reaching for the wire cutter. He grasped the tip of one of the handles and pulled it toward him soundlessly across the dirt floor.

Once secured, he had a difficult decision to make since he was sure the sound of the snip would alert Guidry to what he was doing.

Hands or feet? he asked himself, but the answer came immediately.

With a snip, he freed his legs.

SARA NEARLY RAN to keep up with Bongo as the dog jogged across the cornstalks and vines, hot on Jose's scent. Trey raced beside her, gun drawn in anticipation of a fight.

"Good girl, Bongo," she said in encouragement, hoping that the bloodhound was on the right track since the only thing she could see was a flattened field that led to the avocado and mango orchards in the distance.

They were midfield, surrounded by nothing except the cornstalks and pumpkin vines, when Bongo stopped running. She sniffed the ground, circling around a small area, before she dropped down to signal that she had found something.

Only it looked like nothing to her except dry cornstalks, leaves and pumpkin vines.

"This can't be it," she said, scanning the area and beginning to doubt Bongo for the first time.

Trey stood beside her, examining the area where Bongo had lay down. "Is she sure?"

Sara shrugged and said, "Bongo, please find. Please."

Bongo peered up at her, deep brown eyes almost accusing. She rose up, circled around the space, and then promptly sat again.

Sara muttered a curse and said, "We need to see what she sees."

GUIDRY'S HEAD WHIPPED AROUND, and Jose knew he had to act.

He jumped to his feet and faced the other man, his only weapon the wire cutter.

Guidry smiled and brandished his knife, clearly excited about the prospect of the fight he was sure to win.

Unless Jose had the element of surprise.

Reaching over, he snipped the wire leading to the light bulb, plunging most of the space into darkness. The lamp on the table still illuminated that space and cast light that limned Guidry's body, keeping him visible.

With another snip Jose freed his hands and pitched the wire cutter at the other man's head.

It landed with a loud thunk, stunning the man temporarily, but then Guidry launched himself at Jose.

With the advantage of darkness, he sidestepped the charge, bent, and heaved up the car battery to use as a shield.

Guidry swung out wildly with the knife and it connected with the battery casing, metal scraping against metal.

The other man cursed, giving Jose a clue as to where he stood, and Jose took advantage. He tossed the heavy battery in Guidry's direction.

The pained oomph he heard confirmed he'd hit his mark,

but a second later, Guidry barreled into him, propelling him across the room and into the table.

A wild clatter of metal echoed in the space as they fought across the surface of the table, sending cans, wires and batteries flying off its surface.

"DID YOU HEAR THAT?" Sara said and bent closer to the ground.

The noise came again, and Trey said, "I did."

He bent and jerked away leaves and vines with his bare hands.

She saw it then. An almost imperceptible line in the ground not far from where Bongo was sitting. A man-made line.

"There. Look there," she said, joining Trey as he furiously yanked away debris to reveal a rope handle.

He grabbed it and flung open the door, uncaring of whether there was a trap.

The noise of a struggle was evident now and as they peered down, she caught sight of a body flying across the room.

Guidry, his face bloodied, white hair in disarray. He had a wild look in his eye that turned to surprise as he peered toward her.

A second later, Jose came into sight. He was bleeding and held a large wrench that he swung to keep Guidry at bay.

"The cavalry's here, Pepe," Trey said, and scrambled down a ladder on one side of the space, gun drawn.

"Good to hear," he said, grinned and passed out.

LIGHT LEAKED FROM his half-open eyes as he struggled to open them. When he did, an unfocused picture slowly sharpened and became clear.

A family picture, like on *Noche Buena*. They took one every Christmas Eve, he thought, his brain muddled.

Only Sara was in this photo, he realized and tilted his head in her direction. "What are you doing here?" he said, barely able to muster a whisper.

She leaned close, smiling, tearful, and swept a stray lock of hair from his forehead. "You've been out of it since they brought you in a few hours ago."

"Brought me in?" he asked, and shook his head to clear the cobwebs, and finally realized he was in the hospital, surrounded by his SBS cousins as well as Trey's parents and his own mother and father.

"The knife nicked your lung. We had to make sure it didn't cause your lung to collapse," Sara explained, and danced her hand across his face again, her touch comforting.

"You're going to be okay," Trey said, and squeezed his hand.

"Easy for you to say," he teased, and was unprepared for the guilt that flitted across his cousin's face.

"I'm so sorry we pulled you into this, Pepe. We won't again," Trey said, voice filled with anguish.

"That's going to be hard to do, seeing as Sara and I are a thing. We're a thing, aren't we?" he said, smiling as he looked at her.

"We are, Jose. We're most definitely a thing," she said, tears of joy filling her gaze.

"Good," he said, and drifted his gaze across the family gathered around him before he closed his eyes and gave in to the rest he needed to get better.

DAYS LATER HE sat at the table with his SBS cousins, Tio Ramon, and most importantly, Sara and Bongo.

The Gonzales family. For too long he'd run away from them, but no longer.

Trey smiled and rose to give a report on the police investigation of Guidry.

"DNA analysis has confirmed that the man and older

woman found in the graves are related to Guidry and are likely his mother, Misty, and younger brother Thomas."

Sara shook her head and murmured, "He murdered his own family."

"And a dozen other women, but not before he and Metz had what they considered fun. Police were able to identify at least eight women, two of them raped before they were killed," Trey added to his report.

"What about the attack on Sara and the tractor incident?" Mia asked.

"General height matches him, but we don't have anything else to connect him to Sara's attack, but it makes sense it was him. As for the tractor, he wore gloves, but must have taken them off to hot-wire the vehicle since PD got a fingerprint that matches his."

"They have enough to charge him?" Sophie asked.

Trey nodded. "They do, and it looks like the district attorney is going to ask for the death penalty."

"So this is over?" Jose asked. He might not have wanted to be a part of SBS, but after all that had happened, he was a part of it now.

"You may need to testify, but you don't have to worry about Guidry anymore," Trey said.

Sara squeezed his hand, and he gripped it tightly and faced her, smiling. The nightmare with Guidry was over, but Sara would soon be a part of his family and no matter what came in the future, they would handle it together.

* * * * *

SECOND-CHANCE BODYGUARD

PATRICIA SARGEANT

To My Dream Team:
My sister, Bernadette, for giving me the dream.
My husband, Michael, for supporting the dream.
My brother Richard for believing in the dream.
My brother Gideon for encouraging the dream.
And to Mom and Dad, always with love.

Chapter One

"Ms. Archer, I'm Hezekiah Touré of Touré Security Group."
Hezekiah spoke gently, leaning toward the grieving widow.
"My brothers and I are so very sorry for your loss."

Jayne Archer huddled on a scarlet-cushioned dark wood
chair in the front row of the large Elizabethan-style salon
at Eternal Wings Funeral Home Friday evening. The carpet
was an abstract navy-and-scarlet pattern. The cloud-white
walls were framed in dark wood trim. Family and friends
who cared about the middle-aged woman surrounded her in
the stuffy room, holding her hand, rubbing her back, pat-
ting her arm. A hymn, "Blessed Assurance," played softly
on the funeral home's sound system. The comforting scent
of lavender floated around him.

The wake for Jayne's deceased husband, Dean Archer, had
just ended. Hezekiah had found it emotional but inspiring
and at times joyful. Random descriptives from family members' and friends' remembrances echoed in his mind: honor-
able, caring, professional and corny. The few times Hezekiah
had met with the older man, Dean had struck him as being
all those things, as well as having a quick, if corny, wit.

"Thank you." Jayne raised her head. Her voice was raw
from crying. Her large brown eyes were pink. Fat teardrops
rained down her round chestnut cheeks. "Touré Security."
She frowned as though searching for a memory. "Dean men-

tioned he'd hired your agency to provide security for the company. He'd been looking forward to working with you."

He smiled at her kind words. "My brothers and I had been looking forward to working with him, too."

Hezekiah's two younger brothers—Malachi and Jeremiah—were his equal partners in the family-owned security company their deceased parents had founded more than thirty years ago in Ohio's capital city of Columbus. They'd been shocked and saddened to learn of their newest client's sudden death a week earlier. Hezekiah had offered to attend the wake to represent their company and family.

None of them had attended a funeral since their mother had died two years earlier, three months after their father. He'd appreciated the expressions of sympathy from vendors and industry colleagues, as well as from friends, neighbors and their security contractors. He hoped to provide the same comfort to Dean Archer's widow.

Hezekiah pulled a business card from his black faux-leather wallet. "Ms. Archer, please call us if there's anything we can do to help you."

She accepted his card. Her smile trembled at the edges. "Thank you."

Hezekiah returned his wallet to the front pocket of his black suit pants. With a final goodbye and condolences, he turned to leave the stuffy salon. It was crowded with other mourners waiting patiently to express their sympathy. Many were drying tears, giving comfort, receiving comfort or all three. The scene brought back painful memories of his parents' funerals. Straightening his shoulders, he maneuvered his way out of the room and toward the business's exit.

"It was decent of you to come." The voice originated from somewhere behind him in the funeral parlor's lobby. Detective Eriq Duster, a forty-plus-year veteran of the Columbus Division of Police, approached him. Like Hezekiah, the homicide detective wore a tailored black suit with a bright white shirt. But instead of a broad black tie like Hezekiah's, Eriq wore a simple black bolo. The bronze slide clip was shaped like a trout.

Hezekiah retraced his steps to meet the older man halfway. "I'd hoped to get a chance to speak with you privately. I'm so sorry for your loss, Eriq. Dean told us you'd been friends for decades."

"Since high school." The wrinkles creasing the sixty-something's dark features seemed a little deeper. "He was like a brother. We were both only children. My late wife introduced him to Jayne. I wouldn't have made it through losing my Addie without them."

Hezekiah felt Eriq's sorrow like an expanding balloon, pressing against his chest. He searched his mind for words of comfort. "He spoke highly of you. I could tell he valued your friendship. Thank you again for recommending my brothers and me to his company. We appreciate your referral."

Having a veteran homicide detective recommend their security consulting company was a tremendous honor.

Eriq's smile didn't quite lift the clouds of sorrow from his jaded brown eyes. "You guys have earned it. Your parents would be proud of the way you've built on their legacy."

"Thank you." Hezekiah felt like a fraud accepting the compliment. How could his parents be proud of him when he'd dragged the business they'd created to the brink of financial ruin?

Eriq reached out to pat Hezekiah's shoulder. The detective's throat muscles worked as he swallowed. "You're welcome." His voice was husky. He dropped his arm. "I'm going to check on Jayne. Thanks again for coming." He turned toward the large salon.

Hezekiah stopped him. "Eriq, let us know if there's anything we can do to help. If you want to talk or anything, please call us."

Eriq's smile was a little more natural. "Will do."

Hezekiah watched him disappear into the salon before he turned toward the funeral home's exit. He'd left his black SUV in the adjacent parking lot. Pushing his way through the glass-and-metal door, he paused at the top of the five-step entrance. He closed his eyes and pulled in a deep breath, catching the scents of lilacs, fresh-cut grass and automotive fuel. He needed to break the bonds of grief that had shackled him since he'd walked into Dean Archer's wake. It had brought back the pain of his parents' deaths, which he'd shared only with his brothers.

His eyes snapped open. A prickly sensation crawled down his spine. Someone was watching him. He was sure of it. It was an unsettling feeling. From his vantage point at the top of the steps, he scanned both sides of the street. He stared at the dozen or so pedestrians on the sidewalk below. No one looked back. Most strode past at a brisk pace. A few meandered in groups, deep in conversation. He tracked the cars rolling down the avenue. Maybe the feeling was from an incidental encounter, a casual glance from a passerby. But it had felt like more than that. Hezekiah took another deep breath. The tightness in his back and shoulders had burrowed in. His black cap-toe oxfords tapped gently on the concrete as he jogged down the steps.

He strode the short distance over the sidewalk before turning left into the funeral home's black asphalt parking lot. The disturbing sensation of being watched continued. He glanced over his shoulder and around the nearby perimeter. Nothing. Hezekiah frowned. His father had often quoted to him a line from Joseph Heller's *Catch-22*: "Just because you're paranoid doesn't mean they're not after you." So true.

Hezekiah pulled his keyless car entry device from his right pants pocket and pointed it toward his SUV. Nothing happened. *Curious.* He continued forward and pressed the button again. No reaction. He knew he'd activated his car alarm before leaving the parking lot. Even if he hadn't, his alarm was set to automatically activate. Had his keyless-entry battery died?

He stopped beside his car and tested the driver-side door handle. It was unlocked.

What the...

His body chilled. He circled his vehicle, scanning every inch of it—body, windows, tires, muffler. Everything. He stopped beside the passenger door. A large manila envelope sat on the front passenger seat. He grabbed it, looking around the lot again. A few people were trickling out of the funeral parlor, but no one paid attention to him.

He opened the envelope and saw two eight-and-a-half-by-eleven sheets of paper. He pulled them out. The first was a plain white sheet. Two words were written in black marker. "You're next." The second sheet was a printout of a black-and-white image of him getting into his car that morning. His blood went cold. His father had been right: he may be paranoid, *and* someone was out to get him.

"EARTH TO CELESTE. Come in, Celeste."

Celeste Jarrett dragged her eyes from her laptop Friday evening. Anything to encourage her business partner to get to the point. Her attention settled on the other woman seated at her office's conversation table across the midsize square room. "What?"

Nanette Nichols, part owner of Jarrett & Nichols Investigations, rolled her big brown eyes. Beneath her shimmery silver shell blouse, her chest rose and fell in a sigh of disappointment. "I've been calling you for five minutes."

"No, you haven't." Celeste's tone was as dry as dust.

Nanette continued as though Celeste hadn't spoken. "If *I'm* the one planning my wedding, why are *you* the one having bride brain?"

Celeste sent a pointed look to the stacks of champagne-colored envelopes spread across her conversation table's blond-wood surface. "Why are you filling out your wedding invitations in my office?"

Nanette shrugged. "So we can keep each other company."

"Hmm." Celeste didn't recall saying she needed company. She returned her attention to her computer screen. "My brain hasn't checked out. I'm doing research for my case."

Nanette continued shuffling through the invitations. The event was less than three months away. Nanette's boyfriend of two years, Warren Collingsworth, worked in the marketing department of one of the top health insurance companies in the country. With Nanette's blessing, he'd applied for a promotion, which would mean relocating from Columbus, Ohio, to San Diego. As soon as he'd been offered the position, he'd proposed, and Nanette had been in her element, planning their San Diego destination wedding.

Celeste was happy for Nanette. Warren was perfect for her. But she was going to miss the other woman. They'd been patrol officers and then homicide detectives together with the Columbus Division of Police for a little more than a year. They'd taken a year to plan their investigations agency, which had opened almost three years ago. Nanette insisted Celeste could visit the couple in San Diego whenever she wanted, but it wouldn't be the same.

"Is this the case with the widow of the security-company owner who doesn't believe her husband committed suicide?" Nanette tapped her professionally manicured ebony-tipped nails on the table. It was a tell that she was biding her time before changing the subject. Nanette could only go so long without being the center of attention. That was probably one of the reasons they got along. Celeste preferred being in the background.

"Uh-huh." Celeste only half listened as she scrolled through her internet search result links. "Meryl Bailey, Arthur Bailey's widow. He'd founded Buckeye Bailey Security." She'd agreed to take the case after meeting the grieving widow yesterday morning.

"So? What do you think? Did he kill himself—or did someone do him in?" Nanette had wrapped up her final case two weeks ago yesterday. She continued to come into the office, allegedly so they could keep each other company while Warren was at work. But after nine years of friendship, Celeste knew the truth. Nanette needed attention. Celeste liked Nanette, but her business partner was high maintenance.

Celeste lifted her eyes from her screen again. She folded her arms under her chest and contemplated Nanette. The other woman looked photo-session ready. Her perfect makeup emphasized her wide, light brown eyes in her warm brown face. A wealth of long, shiny raven tresses framed her oblong face and pooled on her shoulders. Celeste was doing well when she remembered her lipstick.

"I don't know. He was under a lot of stress." Celeste counted some of the reasons for his tension on her fingers. "His business wasn't doing well. He'd lost another big account. And he was behind on his loan payments."

Nanette affixed a clear mailing label to another envelope. "Despite all those strikes against him, his widow doesn't think he committed suicide because he's Catholic?"

Celeste shrugged. Her job was to gather the facts, *not* debate her clients. "She said her husband had been afraid of losing his immortal soul. She claims he would've declared bankruptcy before he'd commit suicide. And she's adamant he wouldn't have wanted her to find his dead body. He wouldn't have wanted to upset her."

Meryl had indeed been very agitated when she'd found her husband in his car, locked in the garage, with the engine still running.

"Then who does she think killed him?" Nanette held an envelope in one hand and a stamp in the other.

Celeste reached for a sheet from her writing tablet. She

flipped it so Nanette could see both sides. "It's a long list... mostly competitor companies, employees, clients, vendors and a few relatives."

Nanette gaped. "It's sad that she thinks so many people would want her husband dead. Just sad."

"I know." Celeste set the list aside. Her internet searches focused on queries for connections that might reveal a common link. She was starting with Buckeye Bailey Security's competitor companies.

"So, have you decided who you're bringing as your plus-one to my wedding yet?" Nanette made it sound like an idle question.

Celeste knew that with Nanette, there were no idle questions. "For the half a billionth time, I'm not bringing anyone to your wedding. I'm traveling on my own. I will entertain myself on my own. Then I will leave on my own. I'm a capable, responsible person who can fend for herself, as you well know from our long and illustrious association. Don't worry about me."

Nanette gave another long-suffering sigh. "What about that hot security consultant you've been dating?"

Celeste gave her a second look. "How do you know he's hot?"

Nanette rolled her eyes. "I was curious about the man who finally convinced you to break your vow of celibacy, so I looked him up. His photo on his company website is H-O-T *hot*."

Celeste returned to her research. "We're not dating." And she was still celibate. "We had coffee and lunch."

She'd invited him to coffee on a Sunday, after which he'd asked her to lunch later that week. Both times, she'd remembered her lipstick. And she'd enjoyed his company. He'd been interesting, intelligent, charming and surprisingly funny. Apparently, she hadn't impressed him the same way.

He'd called her after their lunch date. It was as though

he'd known the exact moment she'd return to her office and settle behind her desk. Her heart had skipped a beat when she'd recognized his number. And then he'd explained why he was calling.

"Celeste, I don't think we're compatible. I enjoyed working with you during The Bishop Foundation case, but I don't think our personalities are the right fit for anything more. I wish you all the best."

She'd been too stunned to ask him what was wrong with her. That had been seven weeks ago today. It was still a sore spot.

Nanette tsked. "Why are the good-looking ones so hard to nail down?"

Celeste blinked. "What are you talking about? Warren's very handsome and he's been yours since the day you met two years ago. You're both lucky."

"Yes, we are." Nanette sighed. Celeste could almost see the stars in her eyes. "I'm excited about our future together, even though I know it'll be hard work starting an investigative agency on my own."

There she goes again. The lingering sentence. The side-eye. It was emotional extortion.

"You'll get plenty of references from past clients—and me. And you won't have to worry about money. You've got savings, and I'll be sending you regular payments for your share of Jarrett and Nichols."

Nanette set aside another completed invitation. "Or we could relocate Jarrett and Nichols to San Diego. Have you given that any more thought?"

Celeste sighed. "I've already said I don't want to move to San Diego. I've lived in Columbus for more than thirteen years. I don't want to uproot and start over in a new city where I won't know anyone."

"You'll know me and Warren."

"And I'm sure Warren would love to have me over every night for dinner and just to hang out."

Nanette shook her head as she sealed another envelope with tape. "All I'm saying is that you don't have anything to keep you here. What do you have to lose if you come with us?"

"That's not the compelling argument you think—" Celeste's hand froze on her touch pad. Her lips parted in surprise.

The headline for one of her search results triggered alarm bells in her head. "Owner of Archer Family Realty Remembered." Quickly scanning the article, Celeste learned Dean Archer had died unexpectedly of a heart attack in his office two weeks after Meryl Bailey's husband allegedly committed suicide.

And that had been less than two months after losing Dean Archer's contract—to Touré Security Group. She caught her breath.

Could that be their missing link?

"Earth to Celeste. Come in, Celeste," Nanette's voice sang out.

Celeste slowly rose from her seat. She held tenuously to the dots she was just starting to link. "I may have found our connection."

Nanette's brown eyes widened. "Did you find a motive for Arthur Bailey's murder?"

"Possibly." She looked down at her computer. "But I'll have to speak with Zeke Touré."

Her heart flipped with nerves—or perhaps nervous excitement?

"How was the wake?" Kevin Apple greeted Hezekiah from his seat behind his U-shaped gray-laminate reception desk Friday evening.

In the three months the twentysomething had been the

Touré Security Group's administrative assistant, he'd proven himself to be an asset to the agency. He was professional, intelligent, motivated and personable. Kevin had been up front about his goal of becoming a personal security consultant. Jerry had put him on a training schedule. They'd have to find a new admin soon. In the meantime, Hezekiah was enjoying the organization and efficiencies Kevin brought to the agency.

Kevin also had a bit of hero worship for Jerry. He'd recently gotten a similar haircut, and Hezekiah could swear his youngest brother also had the same bronze pullover and charcoal slacks that clothed the admin's gangly frame. He and Malachi had bets on when the two men would come to work wearing the same outfit.

"It was nice. Thanks." Hezekiah's fingers flexed on the manila envelope. He loosened his tie.

A movement in his peripheral vision brought his attention to the hallway that led to the agency's offices and conference rooms.

"Zeke." Malachi came to an abrupt stop beside Jeremiah in the reception area. He'd loosened his tie and rolled the sleeves of his ice-blue shirt midway up his forearms. "We thought you were going home after the service."

Hezekiah glanced at Kevin before responding. "I want to check on a couple of things before the weekend."

Malachi and Jeremiah exchanged a look. Hezekiah's tension eased. The gesture showed his brothers understood his subtle message. They sank into two of the four overstuffed slate gray armchairs that followed the reception area's perimeter. Malachi set his black briefcase on the floor beside his armchair and laid his steel gray jacket, a match to his pants, over its arm. Jeremiah dropped his tan satchel between his feet.

Kevin's dark brown eyes twinkled with humor. A wry smile creased his thin brown face. "That's my cue to leave."

He tugged his own tan satchel—a match to Jeremiah's—onto his shoulder. "I'm meeting my girlfriend for dinner. Have a good weekend." He waved over his left shoulder as he pushed through the Plexiglas doors with his right hand.

"You, too." Hezekiah echoed his brothers' farewell as he watched the younger man disappear down the staircase.

"What's up, Number One?" Jeremiah set his right ankle on his left knee. He was slim and fit, in a cobalt blue polo shirt and smoke gray slacks. "You've got that Houston-We-Have-a-Problem look."

Hezekiah offered the envelope to Malachi, who was closest to him, as he lowered himself onto the third armchair. "I found this on the front passenger seat of my car after Dean's wake."

Malachi pulled the two sheets of paper from the envelope, holding them so Jeremiah could also see them. They skimmed the first page, then the second. Their heads snapped up. Their nearly identical dark eyes widened with shock, then narrowed with fury.

Jeremiah exploded out of his chair. "You found this *in* your car? How is that possible?"

"The perp must have used a key jammer." Malachi's voice was low and controlled. His eyes scanned the printout of the image of Hezekiah climbing into his car that morning. "It blocks the signal from your key fob, preventing your door from locking and your alarm from activating."

Hezekiah gestured toward the papers in Malachi's hands. "How close does someone have to be for the device to work?"

"A few feet." Malachi moved his shoulders beneath his shirt. It was more of a flex to ease tension than a shrug.

Hezekiah looked between Malachi and Jeremiah. "Have either of you received any threats or suspicious packages or phone calls? Anything?"

"No." They shook their heads, echoing each other.

"We would've told you." Malachi lowered the printouts.

Hezekiah's tension eased a bit more. The furrows across his brow disappeared. His brothers hadn't been threatened. At least, not yet.

Jeremiah dragged both hands over his tight dark brown curls. He marched across the plush dark gray carpet to Kevin's desk, then back to his armchair. His movements were stiff. "How could they have known you were going to Dean's wake?"

"They couldn't have." Malachi sat back against the armchair. "They must've followed you from your house to our office and then to the wake. But how did they know where you lived? And what time you left for work?"

Jeremiah bit off a curse as he crossed back to Kevin's desk. "They've been following you for a while." He turned, pinning Hezekiah with an intense look. "Have you noticed a car or any vehicle hanging around?"

Hezekiah unfolded from his armchair. He shoved his hands into his front pants pockets and considered the carpet as he paced to the wall on the other side of Kevin's desk. "No, I haven't noticed any tails."

"They must be good." Jeremiah completed another round trip to his vacated armchair. "You would've noticed if someone had been following you."

Pausing with his back to his brothers, Hezekiah pinched the bridge of his nose with the thumb, and index and second fingers of his right hand. The office suite had seemed comfortably cool when he'd first entered. It had quickly become stuffy and oppressive. The tension blanketing the room added to his anxiety. There were too many unanswered questions. His mind had tried to fill in the blanks during the half hour commute back to the office from the funeral parlor. Who was targeting him? Since when? Why? What was their next move?

Are my brothers in danger?

Hezekiah lowered his arm. "I haven't noticed any tails,

but I did sense someone watching me as I left the funeral parlor." He turned to face his siblings. "I didn't see anyone looking back at me, but I couldn't shake the feeling I was being surveilled."

Jeremiah folded his arms across his chest. "That's it. You're staying with me until we figure this out."

Malachi narrowed his eyes at his younger brother. "He should stay with me. My house has the most secure system."

Jeremiah leaned toward Malachi. "*I'm* the one who's a trained personal security guard. I can better protect him if he's in physical danger."

Hezekiah reared back at the idea of his younger brothers coming to his rescue. He was the eldest. He was supposed to protect them.

Are they in danger?

"Hold on." He raised his arms. "First, Mal, your security system may be more advanced than ours because you're into the techy gadgets, but we all have high-quality systems. Second, we're all well trained in self-defense, thanks to Mom and Dad. I'll be fine on my own."

"That's crap, Zeke." Malachi's measured tone was misleading. Hezekiah could feel Malachi's temper emanating from him like a force field. "If this had happened to me or Jer, you'd relocate us to another country for our safety. Why are you any different?"

Because I'm the oldest.

Hezekiah dragged his hand over his clean-shaven head. "If I were to stay with you, I'd be putting you in danger. I'm not doing that."

Jeremiah set his hands on his lean hips. "So you think you can handle this on your own? I'm sick of your lone-wolf act, Zeke. There are three of us. Let us help you."

Malachi swept his arm out. "We don't even know where the threat's coming from."

"I may be able to help with that." Celeste Jarrett's voice came out of his dreams and into his agency.

The ground shifted beneath Hezekiah's feet. He turned toward the suite's entrance. His eyes swept her lithe figure. She stood in the threshold, wearing her usual black slacks and T-shirt. Her wide hazel eyes pinned him in place. A cool smile curved her full, heart-shaped lips. "Hi, Zeke. Long time, no speak."

He swallowed, easing his dry throat. *Ouch.*

Chapter Two

Celeste called on her better angels as she let the Touré brothers escort her to their conference room Friday evening. She needed them to keep her grounded. Every time she thought of Hezekiah Touré's final phone call, she wanted to go off.

She crossed into the conference room toward the rear of their office suite. Jerry held the black-cushioned chair on the right side of the large, rectangular glass-and-sterling-silver table for her. He took the seat beside her. Mal settled into the chair opposite Jerry, which left Zeke sitting right in front of her. Perfect. She schooled her features to keep even a hint of irritation from her expression.

The Touré brothers were ridiculously handsome, tall and athletic, with chiseled sienna features softened by full, sensual lips. Their dark, deep-set eyes could make you forget your inhibitions. Celeste had an out-of-body experience every time Zeke's almond-shaped coal-black eyes connected with hers.

The brothers had very different personalities, though. Zeke, the de facto head of the company, was in charge of corporate security. He projected an unmistakable air of strength and authority. Mal led the agency's cybersecurity division. He was the contemplative one who considered everything—what you wanted him to see and things you didn't want him to notice—before deciding on a course of action. Jerry oversaw the agency's personal security services. He gave the impression of being in constant motion, even when he was sitting still. He was impetuous and impatient, which tended to catch people off guard.

The conference room's chalk-white walls were decorated with beautiful oil paintings displayed in black metal frames. The subjects were well-known Ohio landmarks, including the Ohio Statehouse, the Cincinnati Observatory, the Paul Laurence Dunbar House, the Rock & Roll Hall of Fame and The Ohio State University Oval. Celeste remembered that they'd all been painted by Zeke.

The back of the room was a floor-to-ceiling window offering a portal for a wealth of sunlight. It overlooked the front parking lot and framed the treetops and a distant view of the city's outer belt, Interstate 270.

Celeste's eyes dipped to the manila envelope lying on the table in front of Zeke before returning to him. She ignored the way her heart vaulted into her throat. "May I see the contents?"

He slid the envelope across the table to her. Celeste withdrew the two sheets of paper. Her heart stopped. This was worse than she'd thought. She masked her battle to restore her composure by taking her time examining the printouts. Finally, she returned them to the envelope, then nudged the packet back to Zeke. Did he notice her hand shaking?

She swallowed the lump of fear in her throat and addressed Mal and Jerry. "Arthur Bailey died three weeks ago."

Mal nodded. "We were sorry to hear that. We sent a card and flowers to his family."

Of course they did. The considerate gesture, even toward a competitor, was in keeping with the Tourés' reputation in the community. "His death was determined to be suicide—"

"How did he die?" Zeke's deep, bluesy voice caused her heartbeat to skip.

Celeste steeled herself to meet his eyes again. "Meryl

found his body in his car. Their garage was locked, and the engine was running. According to the ME's report, his blood alcohol level was .12, legally drunk."

Zeke briefly closed his eyes. "I'm so sorry. I didn't know."

His brothers echoed his sentiment.

Returning her attention to Mal and Jerry, Celeste continued. "Meryl doesn't believe Arthur committed suicide. He'd been under a lot of stress, but he wasn't depressed. Most importantly, she's adamant he wouldn't have wanted her to find him like that. She's hired me to look into his death."

Jerry gestured toward Zeke. "What does that have to do with the threats against Zeke?"

Impatient as always. Celeste had noticed that about Jerry when she'd worked with the Tourés on The Bishop Foundation case. She could relate. She didn't like wasting time, either. "Arthur died less than two months after losing the Archer Family Realty account to TSG."

"Wait a minute." Zeke lifted his hand, palm out. "Do you think he committed suicide because we got the Archer account?"

Celeste looked at his large palm and long fingers. She could almost feel their warmth on her skin. She dropped her eyes to the table. "I don't think Arthur committed suicide. As I was saying, a little more than a month after losing the account, Arthur dies. Two weeks later, Dean Archer dies. Today, you received a threatening message." She inclined her head toward the envelope between them. It gave her the shivers.

Zeke's thick black eyebrows knitted together, and his eyes narrowed in a sexy frown. "You think Arthur's and Dean's deaths are connected to this message?"

Celeste spread her hands. "I don't think these are coincidences."

"Neither do I." Mal's tone was sharp, cutting off any possible denials.

Jerry's dark eyes hardened with determination. "At least now we have a possible motive for the threat. That will help us identify the killer."

Zeke arched an eyebrow. "Alleged killer." He pinned Celeste with a skeptical look. "Dean died of a heart attack. And I empathize with Ms. Bailey, but does she have concrete evidence that Arthur didn't kill himself? Did it look like a break-in? Were there signs of a struggle in their home or garage? Did he have defensive wounds from a fight?"

Celeste shook her head. "All she has is a gut feeling—and their forty-year marriage. I believe her suspicions should be taken seriously."

Mal rotated his swivel chair to face Zeke. "So do I. But if she's right, then the killer—or killers—was able to get close to the victims."

Zeke met Mal's eyes. "What about Dean's heart attack?"

Jerry tossed a hand toward his brother. "Come on, Zeke. You know as well as we do that there are poisons that can mimic a heart attack. We need to get you someplace safe while we look for the person threatening you."

"I'm not going to let someone send me running for cover." Zeke leaned into the glass-and-sterling-silver table. The shift brought him closer to Celeste. "We're a security company. How would that look?"

"Like we can take our own advice," Mal responded.

Zeke held his brother's eyes. "We're going to find the person behind this threat."

"We'll combine our resources." Celeste looked around the table. Working together, surely they would be able to keep the stubbornest Touré safe.

Zeke shifted his attention back to her. "With all due respect, Celeste, I'm not convinced our two situations are connected. My brothers and I will do some investigating of our own to see whether the deaths are suspicious."

Celeste blinked. Was he being cautious? Or was he trying to avoid her? The answer was ridiculously obvious to her.

"All right." With a mental shrug, she stood. The brothers rose with her. "I've got to get back to work. I have to catch a killer—and save your life."

Celeste wasn't certain how long her legs would support her. She turned to lead the men from their conference room without waiting to witness Zeke's reaction to her provocative claim. Yes, she'd made the statement to irritate him, but it was also true. Someone was targeting the people involved in the Archer Family Realty account. Zeke might not think the threat was serious, but she wasn't willing to bet his life on that.

"WE SHOULD WORK with Celeste." Jerry had a habit of repeating himself.

He and Mal followed Zeke back to his office after they'd said goodbye to Celeste Friday evening.

"We will, *if* Arthur's and Dean's deaths turn out to be suspicious." Zeke circled his heavy oak-wood desk and settled into his black-cloth executive chair. His brothers took the two visitors' seats in front of him.

Mal balanced his elbows on the arms of the black-cushioned chair and steepled his fingers. "Are you letting your past experiences with Celeste block your common sense?"

"I'd like an answer to that, too." Jerry looked from Mal to Zeke. "Didn't you guys go out a couple of times? What happened?"

"Nothing happened." Zeke tried to appear unfazed. He had the sense he wasn't fooling Mal. "This just isn't the right time for me to be in a relationship."

Jerry's face wrinkled with confusion. "Why not?"

Zeke pinched the bridge of his nose. "It's just not."

"The agency's doing better, Zeke." Mal's tone was low and somber. "Pretty soon, we'll be caught up on our debt and able to pay ourselves instead of living off our personal savings. And with Kevin's help, we're getting organized and processing new accounts faster."

Jerry gestured toward Mal. "He's right, Number One. Either way, you're allowed to have a life."

Zeke's lips curved in a half smile. "Thanks, Number Three, but I do have a life. A rather nice life."

Which could be even nicer if he spent more of it with Celeste. He might be able to pretend with his brothers, but he wouldn't lie to himself. He'd enjoyed their time together. Too much. She was smart, interesting, easy to talk with and sexy as hell. But he was wary of the distance he sensed her keeping between them. He wanted a relationship. But he suspected she was just after a casual fling.

"Nice?" Jerry spat out the word like it was rotten meat. "Listen, Zeke, I've been where you are right now, worrying about the agency and the two of you. But now that I'm with Symone, I feel better, not just because of her but because I have balance in my life."

Zeke knew his brothers were happier now that they were in relationships with people they cared about and who cared about them. Grace and Symone were wonderful. Both men had met their significant others while on assignments. Mal had been reunited with his ex-girlfriend, Dr. Grace Blackwell, when a serial killer was trying to steal one of her formulations. Jerry had met Symone Bishop when she'd hired Touré Security Group to protect her stepfather.

Zeke breathed past a pinch of envy toward his brothers. "I'm happy for you. I hope to be where you are one day, but this isn't that day."

Mal nodded, seemingly willing to change the subject. For now. "What's our next step?"

Zeke gestured toward his laptop. "I'll email Eriq. He and Dean had been friends since high school. He should know whether Dean or anyone in his family had a history of heart disease. I'll also ask him whether the ME found anything suspicious during his examination of Dean's body."

"Good idea." Jerry stood to pace the office. "Do you want to talk with Jayne?"

Zeke considered the question. "Not yet. She'd be devastated by the theory that someone took her husband's life. I'd rather not tell her unless we're sure Dean was killed and we know why."

"Good point." Mal lowered his hands. "But I meant what's our next step in keeping you safe. You should stay with one of us."

Jerry turned to Zeke. "Stay with me."

Zeke lifted his hands, palms out. "For the last time, I'm not bringing this danger to either of your doors. I have a security system and self-defense training, just like the two of you."

Mal crossed his arms over his chest. "There's safety in numbers."

"There's danger, too." Zeke gave them both a pointed look. "Suppose something happens and the danger spills out and touches Grace? Or Symone? That's not a chance I'm willing to take. Are you?"

Mal arched a thick black eyebrow. "Nice try, Zeke."

Jerry applauded. "Yeah. That was award worthy. But you know Mal and I would make sure Grace and Symone weren't involved with this. We'd keep them safe."

Zeke did know that was true. "Let's regroup after I hear from Eriq. Then we'll talk about a plan for how to handle this."

Another inquiry. Maybe they should ask for Celeste's help. Investigations were her specialty.

No. One distraction at a time.

Jerry spread his arms. "Regardless of whether your situation is connected in some way with either Dean's death or

Arthur's suicide—or both—you received a death threat. You can't pretend that didn't happen."

Mal stood. "We're going to protect you, whether you want us to or not."

He spun on his heels and strode from Zeke's office. His anger was disconcerting, especially since he never raised his voice or slammed anything. Zeke exchanged a look with Jerry.

His youngest brother jerked a thumb over his shoulder in the direction Mal had taken. "What he said." Then he disappeared through Zeke's office door.

Zeke couldn't blame his brothers for their reaction to the packet he'd received. As Mal said, if the situation had been reversed, he'd be acting the same way. Or worse.

But the situation wasn't reversed. Zeke clenched his teeth as his frustration tried to boil over. He was the one who'd received the threatening note. He'd do his best to protect the people he loved. An image of Celeste floated across his mind. He'd do his best to protect all of them.

"WHAT ARE YOU DOING?" Zeke spoke through the driver-side window of Mal's black SUV early Saturday morning.

He'd awakened about a half hour ago, shortly before dawn. From his bedroom window, he'd immediately spotted the vehicle nestled between two other cars a short distance from his house on the other side of the street. He should've known his younger brothers would pull something like this. Zeke had changed into his running clothes and shoes before rushing out to confront them.

Mal's almond-shaped ebony eyes were defiant. "Jerry and I are staking out your house."

Jerry leaned forward from the front passenger seat. His midnight eyes challenged Zeke to oppose them. "We haven't seen anyone or anything suspicious. Yet."

Zeke looked up and down his residential street. He didn't sense anyone looking back.

This early on a Saturday morning, there weren't many lights on in his neighbors' homes. A handful of cars had parked on either side of the blacktop. A few sat on concrete driveways. The sky was a soft gray as night eased into morning. The sun was only just starting to peek over the horizon. Birdsong intruded on the stillness of daybreak. The air was swollen with dew. Zeke smelled the moisture in the soil, on the grass and on the late-summer-turning-toward-early-autumn leaves.

His eyebrows met. "You spent the entire night out here?"

Good grief. While he'd been reviewing business reports, reading industry magazines, preparing for bed, both of his younger siblings had been guarding him and he hadn't known. That irritated him.

Mal gave a curt nod. "Right."

"We took turns sleeping." Jerry shrugged. "I don't need much, though. I feel pretty good now, like I can go another couple of hours. But I'll probably burn off that energy during our run. Don't worry, we packed our jogging clothes to save time."

Judging by his chatter, Jerry was probably more tired than he realized.

"I asked you not to get involved." Zeke's anger was stirring again. "You deliberately ignored me. I don't want you—"

"Fall back, Number One." Jerry cut him off. "Stop talking to us like we're your children. Mal's only two years younger than you, and I'm two years younger than him."

Mal leaned closer to Zeke, his head and shoulders partially emerging from the SUV's driver-side window. "We're a security firm, Zeke. If we can't protect our own, what good are we?" The fire in his ebony eyes was like a mini inferno, telegraphing the temper he was controlling. "More than that, we're brothers. If we don't take care of each other, who will?"

The confrontation sparked a memory of a conversation he'd had with their mother a little more than a year before her death. The recollection played like an old black-and-white film across his mind.

"Zeke, give your brothers a chance to lead once in a while. You love them. That's why you're so eager to help them. But they love you, too. Give them a chance to show you by letting *them* help *you*."

All these years later, he was still struggling with that lesson. *It's a lot easier said than done, Mom.*

Drawing a deep breath of the dew-laden morning air, Zeke straightened from the car. "Come in and get dressed. We need to hurry if we're going to meet Eriq by ten at Cakes and Caffeine."

Jerry jumped out of the SUV. "You've heard from him?"

Zeke led them to his home. "Yes, but the news isn't good."

Chapter Three

"Thanks again for letting me search your husband's offices here and at your home." Celeste sat on the navy-vinyl-and-silver-metal swivel chair behind Arthur Bailey's ash-blond-laminate desk late Saturday morning.

She pulled her denim jacket against her. The midsize room was cool and smelled like dirt. It wasn't surprising, considering a transparent layer of dust covered everything, including his desk, file cabinets and the bookcase on the far wall.

She and Meryl wore clear plastic gloves. Celeste had suggested the precaution in case they found evidence in Arthur's office that could support Meryl's belief her deceased husband hadn't killed himself. That he'd in fact been murdered. They'd taken the same approach when they'd searched Arthur's home office earlier. They hadn't found anything there, and it looked like they were about to strike out here as well.

Celeste sat back against Arthur's desk chair and surveyed his office again. The space was an organized mess. Folders were scattered across the desk and his ash-blond, faux-wood conversation table. Books and folders grew in messy piles from the table's two matching chairs.

"Anything to help learn the truth about what happened to Art." Meryl searched the bookshelves, shaking the books and binders stored there. The widow was a curvy sixtysomething with an unruly mass of salt-and-pepper curls. "It would help to know what we were looking for."

Celeste had gone through his desk and all the files in his drawers. She'd searched each folder in his cabinet. Some of the files had been sticky. A small bowl of individually wrapped hard candies gave a hint of how that could've happened. Celeste had even pulled out every drawer in the cabinet and desk in case he'd taped something to them.

She watched her client give a thick reference manual a rough shake, then replace it on the shelf before choosing another target. The older woman was dressed all in black, with a button-down blouse tucked into a narrow skirt and topped by a knit cardigan. Her black flats seemed to have a lot of mileage on them.

An image of the threatening note Zeke had received flashed across her mind. *You're next.*

"I'm not sure." Celeste stood, circling Arthur's desk on the way to the small conversation table. "Anything that seems suspicious or raises questions."

She didn't want to scare the other woman the way the note sent to Zeke had scared her. After finding her husband's dead body, the new widow was probably having nightmares, if she was sleeping at all. Celeste didn't want to add another frightening element to any of her dreams.

"What do you mean by *anything suspicious*?" Meryl returned a book to the shelf. Setting her hands on her full hips, she turned to Celeste. "We already know he wasn't shot or stabbed, so we're not looking for a gun or a knife. Are we looking for a bottle of poison? But if someone had drugged him, they would've done that at the house." She gasped. Her voice became thin, breathless. "Are we looking for a note? A threat?"

"Sit with me for a minute." Celeste removed a stack of folders from one of the chairs and placed it on the small table. She put the books from the second chair beside the folders. They'd already searched these items. Celeste sat while she waited for Meryl to join her.

The older woman pressed a small, chubby hand against her chest as she seated herself. She stared at Celeste with wide gray eyes. Her thin pink lips were parted as though she wanted to say more but words wouldn't come. The color had been leached from her white face.

"You think someone threatened my husband before killing him and that the threat is somewhere in this office or in our home." Her words were a statement.

"Meryl, if Arthur was murdered, I may have identified a motive. What did he tell you about the events that occurred before and after Archer Family Realty pulled their contract from Buckeye Bailey Security?"

The widow clenched her hands on her lap. "We talked about everything." She closed her eyes briefly. "Art was so upset. He was devastated after losing Dean Archer's contract. It was a big contract, and he'd provided their security for almost a decade."

"Why did Dean leave Art's company?" Celeste prompted.

Meryl pulled a dainty white-and-pink handkerchief from her cardigan pocket and dried her eyes. "It wasn't due to costs. I'm sure about that. Art's contracts were very competitive. Dean dropped him because the security guards assigned to their offices weren't professional. They arrived late. They left early." She briefly closed her eyes. "They even *slept* on the job. Can you imagine that?"

Celeste's eyebrows shot up her forehead. "Oh no."

"Oh yes." Anger flashed in Meryl's stormy gray eyes. "Dean complained to Art several times. Art tried talking to the guards, incentivizing them, reprimanding them. Nothing worked. They wouldn't listen." Her fist tightened on the handkerchief.

"Why didn't he fire them or assign different guards to Dean's account?" Celeste watched the other woman's body language and paid attention to her words. Meryl was holding back.

She dropped her eyes to the thin tan carpet. "Good guards are hard to find."

Especially when you were rumored to pay as poorly as Buckeye Bailey.

"So Archer Family Realty left Buckeye Bailey Security and contracted with Touré Security Group." Celeste sat back. Her eyes flicked around the office without focusing on anything. "How did Art react to Dean's decision?"

"He was angry, of course." Meryl's voice rose several octaves.

"With whom?" Celeste suspected the protective wife had been angry, too. "The guards? Dean? The Tourés? All of the above?"

Meryl shook her head. Her short curls bounced around her face in a frenzy. "No, no. Art didn't like Dean's decision, but he understood it. He wasn't happy that Touré Security got his contract, but he would've done the same thing in their position."

"Then he was angry with the guards." Which made sense. If they'd been more conscientious of their responsibilities, Art wouldn't have lost the Archer Family Realty account.

"Of course." There was a faraway look in Meryl's eyes. Celeste sensed the other woman had stepped back into her memories. "We took a big hit to our finances when we lost the Archer account. We had to find ways to shrink our monthly expenses. And Art had to let go of some of his contractors. It wasn't an easy decision, but in fairness, those guards had cost us the account. They had to go."

Yes, they did.

As a small-business owner, Celeste understood that, for the sake of his bottom line and his reputation, Art couldn't afford to keep those contractors on his books.

Celeste stood to walk the large room. Her suspicions that

Art Bailey's and Dean Archer's deaths were linked and that they were suspicious grew. And she was even more afraid that Zeke's threat was connected, too. But she needed proof. Tangible evidence to support her gut instinct and to convince one very stubborn Touré. She lingered beside Art's desk. What had she missed?

"How many guards did you let go?" Celeste looked at her client from over her shoulder.

"Four." Meryl answered without hesitation. She knew a lot about her husband's company. "There were three eight-hour shifts each weekday. Then the guards rotated the four weekend shifts, but they couldn't work more than forty hours in a week." She searched Celeste's features with wide, tear-filled eyes. "Do you think one of them killed Art?"

Celeste turned away. She needed to clear her mind, and she couldn't do that staring into Meryl's grief-stricken eyes. What did she have so far? A grieving widow's assertions, a dead Realtor and a threat against a security expert. If she was still a homicide detective, would she launch an investigation with that?

No.

Her eyes landed on the shelf above Art's computer. From this angle, she could see something lying beneath the row of dusty framed family photos and aging knickknacks. She went back to the conversation table, then carried her chair to Art's desk. It was more stable than the swivel chair he'd used.

"What is it?" Meryl's words broke on a sob.

"There's something on the shelf. I think it's an envelope." Celeste toed off her black loafers and climbed onto the chair.

"Careful you don't fall." Meryl sounded steadier. "That's a strange place for an envelope."

Celeste agreed. She leaned forward, collecting the knick-knacks standing on the shelf. She placed the treasures carefully on Art's desk. They didn't appeal to her, but the fanciful porcelain replicas of woodland animals probably meant a lot to Meryl.

She gathered the half dozen photos from the shelf. There were images of children, grandchildren, and a recent photo of Art and Meryl, which was different from the one beside his computer. They stood cheek to cheek, beaming at the photographer. Art had been a tall, handsome man. He was clean shaven. His gray hair was conservatively cut and thinning on the top. His ruddy cheeks and sparkling blue eyes suggested a good nature.

Finally, Celeste was able to grab the envelope. It was a nine-by-twelve manila carrier with the opening at the top. Its eerie similarity to the one Zeke had received yesterday gave her chills. She flipped it over. It was blank on both sides. Its metal clasp was sealed, but someone had ripped open the top. Celeste touched its jagged edges with a gloved finger. She glanced again at the shelf. A flood of investigative questions echoed in her ears.

How long had the packet been on the shelf?

Why had Art put it there?

Who'd sent it?

Hopefully, the envelope's contents would answer at least some of those questions. Celeste climbed off the chair and carried it and the packet back to Meryl.

"What is that?" Meryl gestured toward the envelope with the handkerchief clutched in her right fist.

"Let's see." Celeste sat before peeking inside. The contents confirmed her suspicions of what they were about to see. "Are you ready?" She held Meryl's eyes, searching for the answer before the other woman spoke.

Meryl filled her lungs with air, exhaled and straightened her shoulders. She nodded. Celeste pulled out two sheets of paper and laid them side by side on the table between them.

"Oh my—" Meryl gasped, covering her mouth with both hands.

Celeste studied the printouts. The first was a color image

of Art getting into a red pickup truck. The second was a note, a single sentence, two words: *You're dead.*

ERIQ DUSTER WAS waiting when Zeke, Mal and Jerry arrived at Cakes and Caffeine Coffee Shop on Old Henderson. The burly older man was wearing a gray Ohio State basketball T-shirt and shorts, and was nursing a large coffee. His casual dress was in keeping with Zeke's and his brothers'. They each wore dark shorts—navy blue, black and gray—with metal-hued pullovers—silver, bronze and rust.

The coffee shop was crowded with couples, families and friends enjoying a late-Saturday morning snack. Sunlight streamed in through its lightly tinted windows set into the stark, chalk-white walls. A stone fireplace stood in the center of the dark hardwood flooring. A handful of retirees and students were curled up on fluffy armchairs beside it, reading books or newspapers while sipping hot drinks. Scarlet-and-gray booth seating lined the café's perimeter. Cushioned gray armchairs and cozy dark wood tables were positioned around the room. Several customers occupying those booths and tables were working on laptops. Some were alone. A few collaborated in groups.

The veteran detective had taken a booth for four toward the back of the shop. The brothers joined him after buying their coffees.

Eriq lifted his tan disposable cup. "I could use something stronger." He offered the faintest of smiles. Grief had replaced the cynicism in his dark brown eyes.

"I think we all could." Zeke sat on the other side of the gray-laminate table from Eriq. Jerry was beside him.

"Dean didn't have hypertension." Eriq stared at the white plastic lid topping his cup as though it could provide the answers to his most pressing questions: Who'd killed his friend, and why? "His family didn't have a history of heart disease."

"You're sure?" Mal was seated beside Eriq.

Eriq looked up, nodding. "We grew up across the street from each other. Our families were more like extended relatives than neighbors. His family has a history of diabetes but not hypertension. Jayne verified that. During his last annual physical, Dean's numbers were fine."

Jerry spread his hands on either side of his coffee cup. "If his death certificate read *heart attack*, who signed off on it?"

"Dean's staff found him unconscious at his desk after lunch." Eriq leaned into the table as though it could hold him up. "The EMTs thought he was having a heart attack. That's what the attending physician told Jayne. That Dean had died of a heart attack. I didn't question it. Some homicide detective I am."

Zeke looked at his friend's clenched fist on the table. "You reacted as a friend first."

Mal cradled his cup between his palms. "Dean could've been poisoned with a toxin that mimics heart attacks."

Zeke nodded. "Like digoxin. It's highly lethal and difficult to trace."

Eriq frowned. "Since he was found at work, one of his staff must have poisoned him."

Zeke narrowed his eyes, calculating the possibilities of foul play. "Not necessarily. Digoxin could take up to two hours to kill someone, which gives us a wide window of opportunity."

"How do you know so much about this poison?" Jerry arched a thick black eyebrow. "Should we sleep with one eye open?"

"It was used in a James Bond movie." Zeke's tone was dry. He turned back to Eriq. "You know we need to ask. How were Jayne and Dean?"

Eriq nodded. "They were good. Solid. I spent a lot of time with them. They were happy."

Zeke nodded. The detective and the victim had been friends for decades. He would know if the couple was having marital problems. Dean would have told him. "We need to know all Dean's movements on that day. Does Jayne have any theories on who might have wanted to harm him?"

"I haven't told her about our concerns. Not yet." Eriq held Zeke's gaze. "First I want to know what made you question Dean's cause of death."

Zeke gathered his thoughts. "Did you know Arthur Bailey died?"

Eriq blew a breath. "Yeah. Suicide. I was sorry to hear it. He was a nice guy."

Zeke inclined his head. "His widow doesn't believe he killed himself. She's hired Celeste Jarrett to prove it."

"CJ?" Eriq raised his eyebrows. "If anyone can get to the truth, she can. She's as tenacious as a bulldog."

Zeke knew that to be true—although he wasn't convinced Celeste would appreciate the bulldog comparison. "Celeste began to suspect Meryl Bailey might be right when she read about Dean's sudden death. She became even more convinced when she found out about the threat against me."

Eriq's expression went blank with shock. "What threat?"

Zeke looked around the table at his brothers. They returned his regard with similar levels of deep concern. He addressed Eriq. "Someone got into my car yesterday while it was parked at the funeral parlor. They put a note on the front passenger seat. It just read *You're next*."

"There also was an image of Zeke getting into his car yesterday morning," Jerry added.

Eriq's eyes widened. "So CJ thinks there's a connection between you, Dean and—"

A strident bell interrupted their meeting. Zeke pulled his gray cell phone from the right-front pocket of his navy shorts. He bit off a curse. "My house is on fire."

Mal and Jerry shot out of the booth. Zeke rushed after them. He was already calling emergency services.

Celeste wasn't the only one who didn't believe in coincidences. Between the threats against him, and Dean's and Arthur's suspicious deaths, Zeke doubted this fire was an accident.

BY THE TIME they arrived at Zeke's home and had climbed out of Mal's car, firefighters had extinguished the fire and were securing the area. Before they left, the crew chief told Zeke it had been a grease fire. They'd been contacted in time. There wasn't much damage, and it was safe to enter the home. The chief also admonished Zeke not to leave his house when the stove was on in the future.

But Zeke hadn't used his stove that morning. After their run, he and his brothers had returned to his house. Since they only had an hour to change before meeting Eriq, he'd loaned Mal and Jerry clothes, and they'd agreed to eat at the coffee shop. He didn't bother to correct the firefighter, but his findings had confirmed Zeke's suspicion. The event hadn't been an accident. Someone had deliberately set his home on fire.

The flames had left a trail in the kitchen from the front-right burner, across the stove and over the counter. The window curtain above the sink was in tatters. His counters were scorched, and his flooring was damaged. Ignoring the sour stench of burnt wood, tiling and linoleum, Zeke packed a bag. He couldn't stay here tonight. He had to concentrate, and he needed to think. He led his brothers out of his home and locked the door.

"Could you take me to a hotel?" Zeke followed Mal across the street to his car. "I'll come back for my car later or tomorrow."

"A hotel?" Jerry's surprised question came from behind him. "That's a bad idea, and you know it. A hotel is the least safe place."

Zeke turned to face his youngest brother, who'd paused

on the curb. "Someone tried to burn my house down, probably hoping I was still inside. I'm not bringing that to your doorstep."

Jerry thrust his arm behind him. "The fact that someone tried to burn you alive is exactly the reason you need to stay with either me or Mal. Not in some all-access hotel where this killer could walk right up to you."

The sound of a revving engine competed with Jerry's voice. Zeke turned toward the noise. Before he could focus, Jerry had body-slammed him, sending him flying across the street and into Mal, protecting him from harm. But Jerry couldn't protect himself.

As if in slow motion, Zeke watched as the black sedan plowed into his youngest brother. Jerry became airborne, his arms and legs flailing like a discarded rag doll. His body spun up and over the car in a macabre somersault. Jerry landed on the asphalt with a sickening thud.

Zeke sprinted to him. "Jerry!"

"How's Jerry?" Celeste came to a stop less than an arm's length from Zeke. She was breathless from running up three flights of steps and down the hall. She'd been too upset to wait for the elevator.

Zeke was hunched over on one of the hard plastic gray chairs in the OhioHealth Riverside Methodist Hospital's waiting room Saturday afternoon. He looked up, frowning his confusion at her. "Celeste? What are you doing here?"

Celeste took another step toward him. She pulled the black denim jacket she'd shrugged on over her black T-shirt closer around her. It was cool in the hospital. "Eriq texted me. How's Jerry?"

Zeke stood. His navy knee-length shorts hugged his slim hips and exposed his long, powerful calves. His copper short-sleeved shirt stretched across his broad chest. "He has a mild concussion. His arm's broken, but the doctor said it's a clean break. Thank goodness. She also said the hospital will keep him a day, two at the most, to monitor his concussion. Symone, Mal and Grace are with him now."

Celeste glanced over her shoulder, wondering where Jerry's room was. She turned back to Zeke. "Then why are you out here?"

He shoved his hands into his pockets and flexed his shoulders restlessly. "I—He…" Zeke dropped into his chair. "I saw that car hit him. Jerry went flying. I thought I'd lost him." He turned his head and scrubbed his hands over his face. He bit off a curse. "That was supposed to be me. He pushed me out of the way. He risked his life to save mine. If I'd lost him, it would've destroyed me."

Celeste didn't know her half siblings, but she didn't need to to feel Zeke's pain. It was like a knife in her chest. It stole her breath. She sat in the matching chair beside him. Lifting her right hand, she stared at the broad expanse of his back in front of her. His muscles were taut beneath his shirt. Was it okay for her to touch him?

Unsure, she let her hand fall onto her lap on top of her black cotton shorts. Celeste spoke to his shoulder blades. "You didn't lose him. Stop thinking about what could've been and focus on what is. The doctor said Jerry will be fine. Believe her. You need to support him during his recovery. You also have to find the person who hurt him and tried to kill you."

Zeke straightened his back and squared his shoulders. "You're right." He shifted to face her. "I owe you an apology. I should have at least considered your theory that the threat I received was connected to Art's and Dean's deaths. I'm sorry."

He was close enough for Celeste to get a whiff of his soap-and-sandalwood scent. It had haunted her dreams night and day for weeks. She inhaled, and the fragrance brought her back to their lunch together. His sexy smile, quick wit and charming manners made her feel warm all over again. She'd accepted that he didn't want things to go any further between them, but she'd treasure the memories of their time together.

Celeste stood, shoving her hands in the front pockets of her shorts. "Even if you had listened to me, I don't know if it would've changed anything."

"I would've been more cautious. Will you help me?" He caught and held her eyes. "Please?"

At that moment, staring into his deep-set coal-black eyes, she thought she'd do anything for him. "Of course." The words left her on a sigh.

"Thank you." His broad chest expanded as he drew a breath. "Have you learned anything more about Art's case?"

"He'd received an anonymous threat similar to yours." Celeste pulled out her black cell phone and swiped through it, searching for the photos she'd taken of the sheets of paper. Sitting, she handed the phone to Zeke so he could see them. Their fingers brushed as he took the device. Zeke glanced at her before looking at the photos.

His face tightened. "Art's photo is almost identical to mine. I was getting into my car in the picture they'd taken of me."

"I remember." Celeste reclaimed her phone, shifting to face him. "I think Art was always meant to be the first victim."

Zeke frowned at her. "What makes you think that?"

She swiped back to the image of the note. "His message reads, 'You're dead.' Your message reads, 'You're next.'"

Zeke narrowed his eyes. "Why is that significant?"

"It suggests the killer has a stronger connection to Art than either you or Dean. Art seems to be the trigger. Meryl told me Art had fired four security guards after he lost the Archer Family Realty contract to you."

Zeke pinched the bridge of his nose with the thumb and

two fingers of his right hand. "I can't believe my brother was almost killed because of a vendor contract."

Celeste didn't care whether it was okay for her to touch him. She put her right hand over his left forearm. Beneath her palm, his muscles jumped, then relaxed. "*Almost*. That's key. He's going to be fine. And I'm sorry about your house." She squeezed his arm, then dropped her hand. "Meryl's pulling the personnel files of those four fired guards so I can research their backgrounds."

"We'll help." Mal's voice came from behind them.

Celeste and Zeke rose to face him. Mal's girlfriend, Grace, was with him. They exchanged nods of greeting. Celeste didn't know much about Dr. Grace Blackwell. She was a biomedical scientist with Midwest Area Research Systems. She was brilliant, tall and beautiful, with striking cinnamon eyes and long dark brown hair.

Zeke's tension stirred around him. "Jer's still okay?"

Mal nodded. "He has a whopper of a headache. He finally gave in and asked the nurse for painkillers. Symone's going to stay with him a while longer."

Jerry and Symone Bishop, chair of The Bishop Foundation, had met a little more than nine weeks ago when Symone had hired the Touré Security Group to protect her stepfather from a stalker. That was the first case on which Celeste had collaborated with the brothers.

Grace chuckled. "I don't know whether either of them noticed we'd left."

Celeste smiled her appreciation of Grace's attempt to lighten the mood.

Some of Zeke's tension dissipated like fog. "I'm glad she'll be with him."

"Me, too." Mal switched his attention to Celeste. "When will you get those personnel files from your client? I'd like to help you go through them."

Celeste checked her black smartwatch. It was a little past

noon. Meryl had just started compiling the records when Celeste had left her less than an hour ago. That had been right after Eriq had texted her about Jerry's accident and Zeke's home. "It'll take Meryl at least an hour to download those records onto a thumb drive. Maybe two o'clock? I'll text both of you when I hear from her."

"Great. Thank you." Mal arched an eyebrow, addressing Zeke. "How are we going to get you out of here? I'm sure the stalker followed you to the hospital."

"Mal's right." Grace scanned the lobby as though searching for the criminal in question. "They're probably waiting outside, watching for when you leave."

Zeke dragged his right hand over his clean-shaven head. "So what do we do?"

A light bulb came on in Celeste's head. "I have an idea."

Chapter Four

"I'm so sorry, Jerry." Zeke stood at the foot of Jerry's hospital bed late Saturday afternoon. Guilt and regret were heavy burdens on his shoulders.

Why had he been so pigheaded? Why hadn't he listened to his brothers? If he hadn't insisted on handling the situation on his own, Jerry wouldn't be in the hospital with bruised ribs and his right arm in a cast. He squeezed his eyes shut and bit back a string of curses.

You have to learn to accept help, Zeke. His mother's chastising words echoed in his ears. She'd always been after him for rushing in to fix other people's problems but not accepting help with his own. Because of his stubbornness, his youngest brother could've been killed.

"Knock it off, Number One." Jerry's voice was strained. His features were tight with the effort to handle his pain. "Or I'll get out of this bed and shake some sense into you."

Symone stood on Jerry's left, closest to the window. She rested a gentle hand on his shoulder. "No, you won't, tough guy. I'll do whatever I have to to keep you in that bed."

Her tone was playful, but Zeke saw the remnants of fear in her large chocolate eyes behind her black-framed glasses.

Jerry's lips curved into a faint smile as he looked at her. "*Whatever* you have to?"

Symone's blush almost matched the color of her floral

knee-length dress with three-quarter-length sleeves. The heat the couple generated made it clear the two had forgotten Mal, Zeke and Celeste were also in the room.

Zeke caught and held Symone's gaze. "I'm sorry for not doing a better job protecting Jerry."

Anger flashed in the back of Symone's eyes. She adjusted her glasses. "Were you the one driving the car that hit him?"

Zeke's eyebrows knitted in confusion. "You know that I wasn't."

"Then how is this your fault?" She paused as her breath hitched. Jerry took her hand. "I don't want your apology, Zeke. Don't you dare absolve this monster. Find them and have them thrown in jail."

Mal's words were quiet. "Symone's right, Zeke. Our focus is on finding the person responsible for hurting Jerry."

A bit of Zeke's tension eased with the knowledge his family didn't blame him even as he continued to blame himself.

"Come on." Celeste put a hand on Zeke's shoulder to push him from Jerry's room. "You've got your marching orders. You, too, Mal. Symone's got Jerry covered. We need to get Zeke out of here without being seen."

"I'm still on this case." Jerry's words carried a hint of panic.

"We haven't forgotten, Jer." Mal's tone was dry.

Zeke stopped to look back at him. "We're a team, Jer. I'm sorry I didn't act like it."

Celeste's hazel eyes twinkled with approval. "You can make up for it now. But first, we need a nurse."

Zeke gave her a quick look. "For what?"

Her grin didn't reassure him.

"MERYL AND I found the threat Art had received," Celeste said, addressing Zeke and Mal. They were seated on the other side of her desk at Jarrett & Nichols Investigations late Saturday afternoon. "It's similar to Zeke's. There's a note and a photo of Art, taken as he was leaving for work one morning."

Zeke accepted the printouts of the photos Celeste had taken of a manila envelope and its contents. He'd seen these images on her cell phone earlier, but that wasn't the reason he was distracted. His thoughts were still on the machinations Celeste had put into play so she and Mal could secret him out of the hospital.

Celeste had somehow convinced a nurse and an orderly to help them. The pair had gotten a wheelchair, blue surgical shoe covers and a sky blue robe for Zeke. He'd refused to change into the powder blue polka-dot cloth gown that tied in the back. Instead, he'd compromised by wearing the gown and robe over his street clothes. He'd had no problem slipping the pale blue disposable shoe covers over his white sneakers and rolling up his pant legs, but he'd had to be nudged into the wheelchair. He'd thought Mal had gotten off easy with the soft blue doctor's scrubs, complete with matching cap.

Once Celeste was confident their disguises would work, she'd wheeled Zeke to her car. She'd borrowed a bright blue nurse's uniform. It was the first time Zeke had seen her in anything other than black.

Dressed as a surgeon, Mal had exited the hospital several minutes later with the orderly. After dropping the orderly off at a local sandwich shop to be picked up by the nurse, Mal had met Celeste and Zeke at her office. The scheme had been complicated, but Zeke understood it had also been necessary. Lives were at stake—and not just his own. Despite the seriousness of their situation, he had the impression Celeste and Mal had enjoyed themselves. To be honest, so had he. It felt like going undercover.

Zeke brought his attention back to the case. A wave of sadness rolled over him as he reviewed the printouts. He and his brothers had liked Arthur Bailey. Whenever they'd run into the older man at industry events, they'd gotten along well. He couldn't imagine Art doing anything that would make someone want to kill him. Neither could he imagine the jovial security expert taking his own life.

The color printout was framed to show Art in profile as he climbed into his ruby-red pickup truck. The sixtysomething father of four had loved that truck like a fifth child. He was wearing black denims and one of his many scarlet-and-gray Ohio State Buckeyes jerseys. The second sheet carried a two-word typewritten message that read *You're dead*. Both the image and the note had been printed on plain white copy paper.

Zeke's skin chilled. He passed the papers and envelope to Mal on his left. "His wife hadn't been aware of this threat?"

Celeste shook her head. "No, Art hadn't shown it to her. We found it buried on a shelf above his desk."

This was the first time Zeke had been to Jarrett & Nichols Investigations. Celeste's cozy office carried a trace of her vanilla-and-citrus scent. He settled back onto the sterling-silver-and-black-vinyl visitor's chair and took a deep breath. His eyes swept his surroundings a second time. He was searching for something that would give him insight into the mystery that was Celeste Jarrett. It would be a challenge. She didn't have any personal items in the room.

On her L-shaped faux-maple-wood desk, everything appeared to be in its place. She seemed to have a penchant for black metal office supplies. Her pen-and-pencil holder stood beside her stapler. A fresh notepad lay beside it. The metal inbox on the corner of her desk sheltered a single glossy sheet of paper that looked like it had been torn from a magazine. A photo of a woman, posing in a pale lavender off-the-shoulder, low-cut gown with a full skirt, dominated the layout. He had a few questions about that. Beside it, the matching outbox contained several envelopes, topped by a utility bill. The shelf above her laptop on her left was empty, as were the surfaces of the file cabinets to her right. No photos. No trinkets. No hints about the woman behind the desk.

"Based on the angle of this photo, it wasn't taken from a car." Mal had changed out of his scrubs. He sat on Zeke's right with his left ankle on his right knee. His attention was glued to the printout. "The killer must have been standing down the block, waiting for Art. They must've been studying his routine for at least a couple of days."

Celeste frowned. "What makes you think that?"

Mal continued his scrutiny of the image. "It takes seconds for a person to get behind the wheel of their car. But this picture isn't rushed. It's sharp and almost perfectly framed. The photographer was ready. This wasn't their first attempt at taking Art's photo. They'd taken several practice ones beforehand."

Celeste's straight dark eyebrows stretched toward her hairline. "That's pretty impressive, Mal. Thanks."

Zeke fought back a proud smile. "We should ask Art's neighbors if they've noticed anyone new in the area."

"Either a new walker or jogger, with or without a dog." Mal placed his copy of the printouts into his black faux-leather portfolio, which he balanced on his left thigh.

"Great." Celeste added a note to her manila folder on her desk marked *Buckeye Bailey Security Case*. "While we're doing that, we can research our primary suspects. Meryl gave me a copy of the personnel files of the four security guards Art recently fired. I'll make copies of the files before you leave." She rested her right hand on the folders beside her.

Zeke's eyes drifted to the sterling silver ring she wore on her right thumb. Black infinity symbols encircled the band. Who'd given it to her, and why? Was that person still in her life?

"That'll be helpful." Mal looked up from his notes. "I'll do some additional background searches."

Celeste's eyes gleamed with determination "I'll help."

"So will I." Zeke looked from Celeste to Mal. "We should look into Meryl and Jayne Archer as well to see if they have any connections or suspicious people in their backgrounds."

"You're right." Celeste's sigh was distracting. "And we will, but I doubt either of them has anything shady in their pasts."

Mal's eyes narrowed on Zeke. His tone was firm. "You can't stay at your home."

"Especially since it's the scene of an arson investigation." Celeste's tone was dry. "We need to get you somewhere safe."

Zeke stood to pace Celeste's tiny office. Long strides carried him past her bookcase stuffed with law enforcement publications—industry magazines, legal reference books and technology manuals. A book on social media marketing barely visible among the business journals gave him pause. He couldn't imagine the cagey private investigator having a social media presence. She was as reticent as Mal.

Turning, he gestured toward his brother. "I can't stay with you or Jerry. I'd be putting you in danger. We don't know for certain the killer's only targeting me. Why would they?"

"If the killer's targeting all of us, that's even more of a reason for us to stick together." Mal's frown was familiar. It was an indication that his brother was immovable from his position. Zeke couldn't fault him. If their situations were reversed, his expression would be the same.

Celeste's grin seemed incongruous. "Stick together for what? To make it easier for the unknown assassin to hit all three of you at once? That's ridiculous, and if you were thinking straight, you'd see it yourself. Good thing I'm here. Zeke's right, Mal. He can't stay with either you or Jerry. Even if Zeke's the sole target, the killer probably has both of you on their radar."

Having Celeste on his side eased some of the strain from

Zeke's shoulders. "We don't know whether or when Dean received a threat. I found mine at Dean's wake. That fact, plus the wording—*you're next*—makes me think the killer wants to take us out one at a time."

"In which case, we won't know whether Mal and Jerry are in danger until the killer gets to you." Celeste's voice was brittle with concern. Zeke's eyes held hers.

Anger shook Mal's words. "Another reason to make sure they don't get to you."

"No." Zeke's voice was sharper than he'd intended. "Just because you haven't received a threat *yet* doesn't mean the killer's not looking for you."

Mal's frown returned. "My house has state-of-the-art, cutting-edge security systems."

Zeke matched his brother's expression. "I said—"

"Guys." Celeste extended her arms, palms out. "I have the perfect solution to this problem. The killer doesn't know about your connection to me." She pinned him with a challenging, taunting look. "You'll be safer staying at my place."

Zeke narrowed his eyes. That depended on her definition of *safer*.

"IT'S NOT MUCH, but it's mine." Celeste stepped aside to welcome Zeke into her home Saturday evening. She didn't have any reason to feel defensive. So why did she?

Celeste loved her little cottage in Worthington, a northern suburb of Columbus. The area was quiet. Most of her neighbors had either retired or were about to. Here, she was safe. She was accepted. It was her sanctuary. And she'd trusted Zeke enough to invite him to stay indefinitely, unlike her reaction to her previous boyfriend.

In the six months she'd dated He Who Would *Never* Be Named, Celeste hadn't even invited him over for coffee. The fact her subconscious had blocked her from making that gesture should have served as a warning. Maybe it would have if she hadn't been so desperate for affection. Celeste turned her back on that thought.

She dropped her house key into one of the small compartments of the yellow-and-black knapsack she used as a purse and waited for his reaction to her home. She was just curious. It wasn't as though she wanted his approval.

Did she?

The minute Zeke crossed her threshold, her thirteen-hundred-square-foot two-bedroom, one-and-a-half-bath residence felt like a one-bedroom condo. It wasn't just his six-foot-plus, two-hundred-thirty-some pound build. It was his commanding presence that filled the room and wrapped itself around her. That, and his soap-and-sandalwood scent. Not that she was complaining.

Zeke's eyes seemed to inhale their surroundings, taking in everything at once. "I like it. A lot."

The warm glow inside her grew a little bigger, a little warmer. "Thank you. So do I."

Zeke walked farther into her home. "It's so bright and welcoming."

Celeste followed him, trying to evaluate the open floor plan with the dispassionate eyes of a stranger. They'd entered through her attached one-car garage into a short, narrow hallway with white-paneled walls. To their left was the Honeywood staircase that led to the second floor. Behind them, overlooking the front of the house, was a cozy sitting room. She spent a lot of time curled up on its white-and-seafoam-green armchair and matching ottoman. The space was filled with leafy green plants that basked in the room's abundance of natural light.

Stepping past Zeke into the slate gray-tiled hallway, Celeste gestured to her left away from the sitting room. "This is the living room."

The hallway led to a modest room with maple-wood flooring. Its thick, cream faux-leather sofa and love seat surrounded a rectangular sofa table made of powder-coated iron and engineered wood. It stood on a tan-and-brown area rug in the center of the room. Potted plants congregated at the base of the two generous arched windows on the far wall. A large black flat-screen TV mounted beside the white stone fireplace dominated the space.

Celeste took him through an archway to the right of the TV. "This is the kitchen. You're in luck. I just went to the grocery store, so the fridge and cupboards are fully stocked."

"Thank you, Celeste." Zeke's words were sincere, but his tone was distracted. His eyes swept the cream cupboards, black appliances and slate gray tiling.

"Sure." Celeste hesitated. Zeke seemed dazed. What was he thinking? She shrugged off the awkward feeling and pulled her cell phone from the front-right pocket of her shorts to check the time. "I'll take you upstairs. The courier should be here with your luggage soon."

Zeke followed her up the staircase. "I'd only packed one bag, but I don't know how long I'll be imposing on you."

Celeste spoke over her shoulder. "You're not imposing. And you're welcome to use my washer and dryer, if it comes to that."

"You have a beautiful home." He sounded almost surprised. "It must be such a pleasure to return to it at the end of the day."

He got it. He understood what her sanctuary meant to her. Celeste's heart felt full. "Yes, it is. I love my job. I enjoy doing investigations whether it's corporate, government or personal cases. But my home is my favorite place on earth."

"I can tell." Zeke's tone was pensive.

Celeste reached the top landing and stepped into the room toward the back of her house. "This is my home office."

The cozy space had been designed as a second bedroom. Like the rest of her home, it was flooded with natural light. But she'd covered it with somber paint and filled it with darker furniture. She'd omitted the little calming touches like fluffy throw pillows, soft afghans and leafy plants. This space was meant to keep her focused on her work. Her small dark wood desk faced the lone rectangular window overlooking her backyard. The black faux-leather chair was similar to the one in her office at the agency. To the right of her desk, a black printer-cum-copier sat on top of a dark-wood-and-black-metal cabinet. Beside it was a smaller desk on which she assembled reports and spread out evidence. Above it was a poster board she used to track timelines and suspects. The maple-wood folding door to the wardrobe on the left was closed. It stored her treasure trove of undercover disguises.

Celeste looked up at Zeke beside her. He had about six inches on her. "You're welcome to work in here, if you'd like. I can bring up one of the chairs from the dining room."

Zeke's dark eyes sparkled with curiosity and interest. "Thank you. I'd appreciate that."

"No problem." She didn't have much experience hosting guests. She hoped she was doing okay.

Get a grip, Celeste.

This wasn't a sleepover or a staycation. It was a homicide investigation. They were after a serial killer who'd already murdered two people. Zeke Touré looked like he'd walked out of her wet dream and into her home office. But he was their sole surviving target, and his life was in her hands.

Get it together.

Besides, seven weeks ago, he'd told her he wasn't romantically interested in her. She stole a glimpse of him standing beside her. His shorts revealed his lean, well-muscled legs. His broad shoulders strained against his T-shirt. She'd have to box up those sexy fantasies in the farthest corner of her mind. At least for the time being. It wouldn't be easy, but she was a professional.

Swallowing a sigh, she looked away. "I have a treadmill, weight machine and other exercise equipment in the basement." She crossed to the closet. "But if you want to jog outside, I have a ton of disguises you can choose from." She opened the deep closet with an unintentional flourish.

Zeke stepped forward, stopping close enough for her to share his body heat. His eyes were wide as he scanned the contents. Celeste had acquired a variety of items for both women and men, including scarves, hats, wigs, eyeglasses, eye patches, jewelry, ascots and neckties. The wardrobe ranged from expensive-looking clothing and shoes to tattered attire. She also stocked materials to create sideburns, mustaches, beards, thinning hair and scars.

"Why do you have all of this?" Zeke sounded puzzled and awestruck.

"It's for undercover work and surveillance. If I always look the same, my target might become suspicious." Celeste took a clear silicon hair cap from a box on one of the shelves. "This is great. I use it to cover my hair, then apply a skin-toned latex mask. With a suit and mustache, I look like a man."

Zeke's eyes held hers. "Impossible."

A blush pricked her cheeks. Celeste made herself look away. "I'll show you the rest of the house."

Nearing the end of the short hallway, Celeste gestured toward a blond-wood door on their left without stopping. "The bathroom. I'll get you some towels." She pushed open the last door on the upper level. "This is the bedroom."

Celeste loved this space. It was one of the biggest rooms in her home. The white-paneled walls reflected the natural light flooding in from the two large windows in both the east and west walls. Gossamer-thin white drapes framed each window, stopping inches from the maple-wood flooring. Cream ceramic planters of pothos ivy were centered at the top of the four windows. A trace of lavender from the plug-in she'd attached to the outlet between the west-facing windows scented the air.

A white marble vanity table and natural white grain chair were partially visible beyond the half wall to the left behind the simple blond-wood chest of drawers.

A matching blond-wood dresser sat at the center of the front wall to her right. Matching nightstands stood on either side of the king-size bed in front of them. It dominated the room. Soft white coverlets and fluffy pillows in soft blues and greens swallowed the mattress. The pillows echoed the colors of the thick area rugs that surrounded the bed.

Celeste didn't mind silence. She'd been raised by her paternal grandmother, Dionne Eve Jarrett, who hadn't spoken much, at least not to her. But Zeke had had plenty of time to survey the room. Why wasn't he saying anything?

She glanced at him. "Is something wrong?"

"This could be a problem." He was hesitant.

"What?" Celeste scanned her bedroom.

Zeke turned to her as though in slow motion. "There's only one bed. Where do you want me to sleep?"

Celeste looked at her king-size bed. Those fantasies escaped her box and inflamed her body. She swallowed.

Chapter Five

Celeste's bed was giving Zeke an erection. It was the definition of decadence. A mountain of thick pastel pillows crowned it. A coverlet as soft and fluffy as summer clouds spread across its vast expanse, beckoning to him. Images of them naked beneath that cover, wrapped in each other's arms, were burned onto his mind. As he stood at the foot of her bed Saturday evening, Zeke could smell her all around him. He clenched his hands into fists and gritted his teeth, trying to focus on their life-and-death situation and not his body's reaction to her nearness. It was a losing battle.

"Where do you think you'll sleep?" Celeste seemed puzzled. She gestured toward the erotic fantasy masquerading as bedroom furniture. "On the bed. I'll take the sofa."

Zeke stiffened. "Excuse me?" He hadn't been raised by wolves. "I'll take the sofa. I'm not going to displace you from your bed."

Celeste gave him a once-over that made his knees shake. "You won't be comfortable on my sofa. You're too tall and too broad. I've fallen asleep on my sofa a bunch of times. I'll be fine."

Zeke became even more obstinate. "I can sleep anywhere. I've slept in my car when my brothers and I have done stake-outs."

"And how did you feel the next morning?" Celeste continued when Zeke remained stubbornly mute. "Please. Take the bed. You've made your point that chivalry is alive and well among the Touré brothers, but this is a matter of practicality."

"What about your office?" He swung his arm toward the room at the other end of the hall.

Celeste's lips twitched as she struggled against a smile. "I suppose you could put your head under the worktable, then angle your feet to fit beneath my desk."

She had a point.

Zeke surveyed her room again. An argument could be made that Celeste was even tidier than he was. It looked like she made her bed before she left for work, just like him. Her kitchen was spotless, without so much as a teaspoon in her sink. In her living room, her television remote controls had been neatly lined up in the center of her coffee table. Her throw cushions had been fluffed and strategically placed on her sofa and love seat. Every nook and cranny had been well organized.

The only thing left to work out was their sleeping arrangements.

Closing his eyes, Zeke pinched the bridge of his nose with his right hand. "What have you done in the past when you've had houseguests?" He lowered his hand and looked at her.

Celeste gave him a blank look, as though he'd spoken to her in an unknown language.

Zeke scanned her room again. As with other rooms in her house, her bedroom walls were decorated with mounted photographs of seascapes and mountain trails, and shelves of wood carvings and clay sculptures. But she didn't display photos of family, friends, coworkers or even herself in her house. Why was that?

He frowned at her. "Have you ever had friends or family come for a visit?"

Faint color darkened her high cheekbones. Her voice was

cool and perhaps a bit defensive. "You're the first houseguest I've ever had."

Zeke was gaining the first bit of insight into his host. "I'm not taking your bed."

"You're not sleeping on my sofa." Celeste was firm. "We'll share the bed. In deference to your chivalry, I'll roll a blanket down the middle."

Out of the frying pan, into the fire.

If he were a kettle, his body would be whistling. Zeke swallowed, easing the dryness of his throat. Thinking of being that close to her in a bed—even with a rolled blanket between them—made his heart jackhammer against his chest. "I'll sleep on the floor."

"Seriously?" Celeste planted her hands on her slender hips. "Do you see that hardwood flooring? You wouldn't be comfortable sleeping on that. If it makes you feel better, I'll add pillows to the blanket barrier. I have plenty of them."

That was an understatement.

Celeste checked the time on her cell phone. "Your suitcase should be here soon. I'll start dinner. I was planning on jerk-chicken stir-fry. Is that okay?"

"It sounds great. Thank you. I'll help."

Celeste turned to lead the way from her bedroom. "Great. There's still plenty we need to discuss. We can do that while you give me a hand in the kitchen."

"Of course." Anything to distract him from what was bound to be a restless night.

"IF I DIDN'T know you were a private investigator, I'd think you were the chef of a four-star restaurant." Zeke's crooked smile trapped Celeste's breath in her throat.

He continued to shrink the size of her home. Standing beside him at the kitchen counter Saturday evening, Celeste could feel him all around her.

The scents of jerk chicken and sautéed vegetables lingered in her kitchen as Zeke helped her clean up after dinner. He'd complimented Celeste on their meal several times. Either he'd been really hungry or she was a better cook than she'd thought.

"Thanks. Again." The warmth that rolled over her didn't come only from his praise. Celeste worked a little harder to push her attraction for the corporate-security executive to the back of her mind. "I hadn't realized how much fun cooking with someone else could be."

Or cooking *for* someone. Cooking and baking were more interests than hobbies. Culinary programs were her guilty pleasures. But the only other people she'd cooked for were Nanette and He Who Would *Never* Be Named, the first man she'd stupidly given her heart to. She'd cooked both meals in her old apartment. Neither of them had been to her sanctuary.

Zeke nodded as though he was mentally filing her statement away. "I'd like to interview Meryl. Can we meet with her in the morning?"

She nodded as an image of the security company owner's widow popped into her mind. "I get it. You have your own questions and want to get your own read on her and her marriage to Art. No problem. I'll arrange a time with her. In the meantime, I've got a few questions for you. You know the drill, hotshot. Anyone new come into your life in, let's say, the last six months?"

Like a love interest you met maybe seven weeks ago?

"The only new relationships I've had in the past year are professional." Zeke stacked his dishes on top of hers in the sink. "You know what it's like to run your own company."

"So the only new people you've met are related to your work?" Celeste loaded the dishwasher. She hoped she sounded more nonchalant than nosy.

"That's right." Zeke disappeared into the dining room, then returned with the pitcher of fresh lemonade. "Our company's starting to grow."

"I've noticed. Congratulations."

"Thank you." Zeke tossed her a smile that conveyed his relief. "We just hired an administrative assistant, Kevin Apple. We did a thorough background check on him. And you and I have just started collaborating on cases, but we've known each other for years."

With her peripheral vision, Celeste watched Zeke find space for the pitcher in her refrigerator. There wasn't another woman in the picture. She just wasn't good enough. Again. Celeste's mood nose-dived.

She continued packing their dishes into the dishwasher. There were twice as many place settings as she was used to having. "Tell me about your new clients. Who are they? Do you have any concerns or suspicions about them?"

"Why are you asking me these questions?" Zeke circled Celeste where she stood at the sink, prewashing the dishes. "You said Art was the trigger for these threats and murders."

Celeste shoved aside the fresh hurt from the reminder that Zeke didn't think she was good enough. "That's my theory. But we can't overlook the possibility—slim though it may be—that I'm wrong and something else triggered the attacks."

Zeke chuckled. "All right." He began transferring the pots from the stove to the sink. "Mal does a complete background check on all our new clients and their principals. It's part of our client-onboarding process. He hasn't turned up anything suspicious on any of them. If he had, we wouldn't work with them."

She recalled Mal's background reports. "Mal's incredibly thorough."

"Yes, he is. He flags anything even remotely questionable about our clients."

Celeste heard the pride in Zeke's voice. What was it like to be part of such a close-knit family? She could only imagine it would be wonderful to have people to lean on when you were in trouble, celebrate with when you achieved success, comfort you when you were down. Someone to just be with when you didn't want to be alone. Celeste shrugged off her regrets. She couldn't do anything about her past, but she was happy with her present. And although she was losing her business partner, her future still looked bright.

She started the dishwasher, then turned to watch Zeke scrub her pots and pans. She ignored the way his T-shirt wrapped around his biceps, which flexed and relaxed with his every move. "The new person in your orbit may not have made direct contact with *you*. They may have connected with someone close to you."

"That's a good point." Zeke's thick, dark eyebrows knitted over his broad nose.

"I'm more than just a sparkling personality." Celeste rolled her eyes. "Who's managed to breach your inner circle?" She took the dish towel from the rack beside the refrigerator and used it to dry the newly scrubbed pots and pans as Zeke set them on the drainboard.

Zeke's chuckle was a low rumble that played on her stomach muscles like pebbles skipping across a pond. "You mean, besides you?" Celeste arched an eyebrow at him. Undaunted, Zeke continued. "As you know, Mal reunited with Grace a little more than five months ago. And Jerry started dating Symone about two months ago. But they were both clients first, so we did thorough checks on them."

"You've checked out Grace, Symone, Kevin and all of your clients." Celeste straightened from putting the final pot in a lower cupboard. "Are you sure there isn't someone who could've slipped through the cracks? A vendor? A new tenant in your office building or new neighbors on your block?"

Zeke shook his head at every suggestion, but Celeste sensed him combing through his thoughts. She led him into her living room and settled onto her soft white faux-leather love seat.

"Kevin has a new girlfriend." Zeke dropped onto the matching sofa to Celeste's left.

Celeste mulled that over. "Have you and your brothers met her?"

Zeke shook his head again. "They've only been dating a few weeks, a little more than a month. But I'd better let Mal and Jerry know about our suspicions." He pulled his cell phone from his front-right shorts pocket and typed into it.

Celeste's attention drifted to the cold, stone fireplace across the room. Votive candles and framed scenic photos were arranged on the simple blond-wood mantel. She gave them only a cursory look as her thoughts tumbled around in her mind. "So to your knowledge, she's never been to your agency. Would Kevin give her a tour without telling you?"

"No." Zeke's cell phone buzzed, claiming his attention. He checked the device, then returned it to his pocket.

She waited for Zeke to expand on that. Her lips trembled with amusement when he didn't. For Zeke, the matter was closed. "How can you be so sure?"

"We're a security agency." Zeke spread his arms. "We use the same procedures and protocols we recommend to our clients. Our offices have surveillance cameras and alarm systems. If Kevin was giving tours of our agency, we'd know."

"That's a little creepy."

Zeke gave her another crooked smile. "The cameras aren't everywhere, just the common areas—reception, kitchen, supply closet. Not in our offices or the conference room. We keep sensitive information about our clients and their businesses. We have to take precautions to keep them safe."

"Hmm." She considered her own client files. "Maybe I should take those precautions, too."

"I'd be happy to set up a system for you."

Zeke was willing to work cases with her. He'd asked her to help Touré Security Group with Symone's investigation. He'd accepted her help with this matter. And now he'd offered to install a surveillance system for her. But as far as a personal relationship, well, Zeke just wasn't into her. Until that moment, she hadn't realized how much she'd looked forward to getting to know him better. Disappointment was a bitter taste in her mouth.

Did her smile look as unnatural as it felt? "Thank you. I'd appreciate that." Celeste pushed herself to her feet and locked her knees. She spoke over her shoulder as she circled the love seat on her way to the stairs. "I'm going to work for a few hours before bed. Do you need anything?"

"No, thank you." He sounded as though he'd been caught off guard. "I'll bring my suitcase upstairs. Is it all right if I store it in your closet?"

"Of course." Without a backward glance, she mounted the stairs. "I'll clear some drawers and closet space for you."

"I don't want to inconvenience you." His voice was tentative.

"It's no trouble," she called over her shoulder.

At least one mystery had been solved. Zeke would never consider her anything more than a colleague. Knowing that, she could concentrate on catching the serial killer and stop thinking about her broken heart.

"I STILL THINK I should sleep on the floor." Hezekiah Touré could test even the patience of a saint.

Celeste wasn't a saint.

Zeke had emerged from the bathroom, where he'd changed into baggy navy shorts and a gray Ohio State Buckeyes T-shirt that hugged his torso like a lover's arms.

She sat up in bed, tucking the sheet under her arms to provide an extra cover over her chest in addition to her short-sleeved, scoop-necked sapphire pajama top. "I promise you'll be perfectly safe sharing this room with me."

A smile brushed across his lips. "And I promise the same."

"I know." Pity.

She sensed he wanted to say something more. His eyes lingered on her, but then he shifted his attention to the space between the bed and the vanity.

Zeke gave a decisive nod. "I'll be fine on the floor."

Celeste glanced down to her right. She'd spent at least half an hour changing her bed sets, including the six pillowcases, making sure the pillows and covers were evenly distributed, and rolling the comforter into a narrow border, perfectly centered on the king-size mattress. She'd placed the makeshift divider beneath the bedsheets. She'd even added the pillows. The barrier ran the length of the bed, starting from between the two sets of pillows. But still, the arrangements weren't good enough for him. Fine. It was late Saturday night. She needed to get some rest before they met with Meryl Sunday morning.

With a mental shrug, she pulled the comforter from beneath the sheets and pushed it to the right side of the mattress. "Suit yourself. There are extra sheets and blankets in the linen closet. You can have those three pillows." With that, she lay back down.

"Thank you." Zeke crossed to the bed. After taking the comforter, he spread it on the floor, close to the chest of drawers. He set the pillows in place on top of it before leaving the room.

Celeste folded her arms behind her head and watched him stride down the narrow hallway, presumably to the linen closet to collect those sheets and blankets she'd mentioned. Seconds later, the light came on in the passageway, spilling into her bedroom. The closet's folding door opened with a soft swoosh. There was a faint rustle of cloth as Zeke searched for the items he needed. Celeste frowned. Was he messing up her storage system? No, she could relax. He was too tidy and respectful to do that.

She was tempted to roll over and pretend to be asleep. It was late. She was an early riser. But what was the point?

They'd both know she was faking. No one would be able to sleep while someone was building a nest on the floor beside them. The linen-closet door closed with a muted snick. Seconds later, Zeke came into view.

He glanced at her before kneeling on the floor to arrange the sheets and blankets. "I'm sorry to keep you up."

She freed her arms from behind her head and curled onto her right side. "Did you get enough blankets?"

"Yes, thank you." He reached across the comforter to spread a seafoam green sheet over it. His movements were stiff and awkward. Was he deliberately avoiding looking at her?

She stared at the back of his head. "And pillows? Will three be enough?"

"I'm sure they will be." There was a smile in his voice. That was better. "I'm sorry to deprive you of your usual half dozen fluffy pillows."

She feigned a sigh of disappointment. "I'm glad you recognize my sacrifice."

"Thank you." He finally looked at her. His dark eyes twinkled with amusement. "I usually get up at four forty-five a.m."

"That's fine." Celeste shrugged beneath the sheets. "I'm an early riser, too."

"Thanks." Zeke stood to turn off the overhead light. "Ready?"

Celeste stretched to turn on the lamp on her right nightstand. "Ready."

Zeke turned off the top light, plunging the room into shadows and seduction. Celeste watched his silhouette walk to his makeshift bed, then disappear from her line of sight. She turned off the lamp.

"Perfect." His sigh floated up from the floor, pulling another smile from her.

Celeste loved that about Zeke. With him, her smiles were

spontaneous. Her laughter was real. She felt almost playful. Years of loneliness evaporated when she was with him, and she was happier. She wanted to hold on to this feeling and this moment. But that wasn't a good idea. She and Zeke wanted different things from their relationship. He wanted a colleague. She wanted so much more.

"Why didn't you want to share the bed with me?" *OMG!* Had she actually said that out loud? Judging by the funereal stillness coming from the other side of the room, she had. "Never mind. Forget it. I didn't—"

"It wouldn't have been a good idea." Tension was palpable in his voice.

Celeste rolled onto her back and scowled at the ceiling. Moonlight and streetlamps eased the dark shadows across the white spackle. What did he mean by that? She'd placed a blanket down the center of the mattress, for pity's sake. Their platonic relationship would have survived the night.

Her eyes widened. Did he know how she felt about him? She was mortified.

Celeste forced herself to draw a slow, calming breath. "Zeke, why did you decide to stop going out with me?"

The silence was long and impenetrable. Celeste squeezed her eyes shut. She clenched her hands into fists at her sides. *Please just tell me. Just tell me.*

Her eyes popped open when he finally spoke.

"I wanted to get to know you, Celeste." His words were like foreplay, stoking a fire within her. "But you wouldn't let me."

"What do you mean?" Memories from their coffee and lunch dates played across her mind like a movie trailer. What was she missing? "We talked."

"Yes, but it was always about *me*." He'd managed the perfect note of frustration. "I wanted to get to know *you*. I wanted our dates to be a give-and-take. But I was doing all the giving, and you were doing all the taking."

Celeste's lips parted with shock. That wasn't what she was doing. She rose up on her right elbow and turned to his silhouette in the dark. "Men like talking about themselves." He Who Would *Never* Be Named certainly did.

"You're doing it again." This time, his sigh was a soft note of disappointment. It pierced her heart. "Instead of telling me why you don't talk about yourself, you're turning our conversation back to me. Do you even realize you're doing that?"

Celeste fell back onto her pillows. No one had ever accused her of not talking about herself. Now she was the one who didn't know what to say. She'd expected Zeke to break her heart. She hadn't expected him to also make her head spin. "You know everything about me. I'm from Chicago—"

"Why did you leave?"

"I was a homicide detective—"

"Why homicide?"

"I co-own a private investigation agency."

"Why didn't you return to the department? I know they wanted you back." A rustle of cloth gave the impression Zeke had turned onto his side. "I've asked you these questions before. Remember? If you don't want to tell me, I'll respect that. But I'm looking for a relationship, Celeste, not casual encounters."

"I'm not interested in casual encounters, either." Her mind was still reeling.

"But you don't seem to want me to get to know you." He sighed when she didn't respond. "Good night, Celeste." Zeke's makeshift bed rustled again as he settled in to sleep.

Celeste curled onto her side. "Night."

He was asking her to let him in. She wanted to, but how did she even begin to take down her protective walls? There were so many of them.

And the scariest thought of all, the one that was going to keep her up all night: What if she opened herself up to him and he didn't like what he found?

Chapter Six

Zeke's alarm went off at 4:45 a.m. on Sunday. His room was still dark.

Wait. It wasn't his room. It was Celeste's. His arm shot out to slap his alarm into silence. He didn't want to disturb her. He sat up and looked over toward her mattress. Although his eyes were still adjusting to the dark, he was pretty sure there wasn't a body in that bed.

He whispered her name. "Celeste." Silence. A beat later, he tried again, louder this time: "Celeste?" Still nothing.

Zeke tossed off the bedding and stood to cross the room. His body was stiff from sleeping on the floor despite the nest of blankets and pillows he'd used for his makeshift mattress. Turning on the overhead light, he looked to Celeste's bed. It was empty. It was also made. His lips parted in shock. If he hadn't seen her before they'd fallen asleep, he would've thought she hadn't gone to bed last night.

What?

How?

His eyes swept the room. A plain sheet of paper was taped to the door. He pulled it free to read it. *Good morning, sleepyhead! Gone for a run. Back around 5 AM. Make yourself at home.—C*

He read it again. She'd gone for a run and would be *back*

in fifteen minutes? How long had she been up? And how had she managed to make her bed, get dressed and leave the house without his hearing her? He was a light sleeper and a security professional. He was trained to react to every out-of-place sound. How had he slept through her movements? He laid the note on the nearby dressing table. Apparently, he'd have to wait fifteen minutes for his answers.

Zeke pulled black running shorts and a brown wicking T-shirt from a drawer Celeste had cleared for him. He collected his black running shoes from her closet and added a gray baseball cap to help mask his face. He dressed, then hurried downstairs with minutes to spare. The front door opened as he reached the entryway. Celeste was early.

She locked the door before turning to him. Her beauty froze Zeke in place. Her face glowed with energy and enthusiasm. Sweat dampened her brown skin. Her cheeks were flushed with exertion. Her hazel eyes twinkled up at him like sunlight on the river.

"Good morning! How'd you sleep?" She grinned, and Zeke's knees went weak.

He grabbed the staircase railing to steady himself. It took a moment to register her words. "I must have slept very well. I didn't hear you moving around at all."

Celeste wiped her upper lip with the back of her hand. "Inquiring minds want to know. Do I snore?"

"Not that I heard." Zeke gave her an answering smile.

Celeste pumped her fist as she strode past him. "Yes!"

Zeke stepped off the stairs and followed her. "Do *I* snore?"

Before today, he'd considered himself to be a morning person. He had nothing on Celeste. Who would've thought the cynical private investigator with the Johnny Cash wardrobe would greet the morning with so much vigor and excitement?

Celeste spoke over her shoulder. Long strides carried her into her kitchen. "More like a deep breather."

Zeke chuckled. "I'll take that. You must be a morning person."

She stopped beside the pass-through window. Her lips parted, and her eyes widened as she feigned surprise. "You're not?"

"It's not even five. Give me a moment." Zeke smelled the sharp, salty tang of her perspiration. "What time did you leave?"

"About four." She pulled a glass from the cupboard. Her limbs were long and slender in knee-length black biker pants. She wore a sleeveless orange-and-silver reflective jacket over her black wicking T-shirt, which was heavy with sweat. "I did a little more than six miles. Would you like a glass of water?"

"Yes, please. You left the house at four?" Zeke shrugged his eyebrows. "But you didn't set an alarm. Did you have trouble sleeping?"

"Slept like a baby." She offered him a glass of water, nodding when he thanked her. "It occurred to me that we should ask the guards if they've received threatening messages or if anyone new has come into their lives. If the motive is revenge for the murderer being fired, wouldn't they be upset with the people who came in late or slept during their shifts? They're the ones responsible for the killer being out of a job. Right?"

"That's a good point." Zeke was impressed. "In fact, if the killer is one of the guards, I'm surprised they wouldn't have already taken their revenge on their ex-coworkers."

Celeste gave him a considering look as she took another deep drink of cold water. "Are you going for a run?"

Zeke drained his water before answering, giving himself time to think. Once again, she'd changed the subject each time he'd asked something personal. She was a master at deflection. He tried a more direct approach. "Do you always wake up before 4:00 a.m.?"

Celeste started to answer, then paused. Her expression shifted. Her bright hazel eyes darkened with caution. "I've been waking around three fifteen, three twenty for as long as I can remember. That's why I don't need an alarm clock. I just get up when my body tells me to."

Zeke was like a sponge, eager to soak up as much as she was willing to share about herself. But he had to move slowly. Her tense voice and jerky movements let him know she was uncomfortable talking about herself.

He approached Celeste, putting his empty glass in the dishwasher beside her. "And that's usually three fifteen? Why so early?"

"I don't know." She shifted her stance. "I grew up with my paternal grandmother. It drove her crazy that I'd get up and start moving around so early. She'd make me go back to bed, but I couldn't sleep. I taught myself to move quietly so I wouldn't bother her. At college, I kept up the habit so I wouldn't bother my roommates. As a police officer, moving quietly was a valuable skill."

"I can believe that." Zeke had dozens of other questions, but the strain in Celeste's eyes urged him to wrap up his interview. "Thank you for telling me about yourself."

She rewarded him with a relieved smile. "Sure."

"And to answer your question, yes, I'm going for a run. I don't think the killer has any idea I'm here. And the cap masks my features." He tipped his brim.

"Hmm." Celeste finished her drink. "It does, but you should still wear one of my fake mustaches. You can never be too careful."

Zeke arched an eyebrow. She must enjoy playing dress-up. She also had a good point about being careful. "Do you have a particular one in mind?"

"Yes, I do." Celeste's smile gave Zeke an uncomfortable sense of foreboding.

"Why do I have the feeling I'm not going to like your choice?"

Once again, Celeste strode past him, this time on her way upstairs. "Maybe you have trust issues. I hear that's going around."

Zeke arched an eyebrow behind her back. He was entrusting his life to someone with trust issues. That suspicious nature made Celeste an ideal person to keep him safe. But it was an impediment to having a personal relationship with her.

Fortunately, all he needed was a bodyguard. That's what he kept telling himself. The problem was, he wanted so much more.

"I'VE BEEN TRYING to understand why Art hadn't told me about the threat he'd received." Tension orbited Meryl as she sat on the overstuffed warm-gold-cloth sofa in her living room late Sunday morning. Anger entered her voice. "I've been going round and round about it in my head, and still I can't understand it. I was his *wife*. Why would he withhold that information from me? If he'd told me, maybe I wouldn't be his widow now."

Her voice choked on her last sentence. Meryl's eldest child, Katie Bailey-Smith, was on her left. She put her right arm around her mother's shoulders to hold her close.

"I'm so sorry, Meryl." Celeste's voice was husky with empathy. "The most logical explanation is that Art hadn't wanted to worry you."

Zeke sat beside Celeste on the lumpy matching love seat on their host's right. The scent of the herbal tea Katie had served them floated up to him from the large blue ceramic mug cradled in his hands.

Meryl's wide gray eyes were pink with tears as she looked

to Celeste. "You can see how that further supports my conviction that Art didn't kill himself. Can't you?"

In her voice, Zeke heard the unspoken pain of not being able to remove the image of her loved one's dead body from her mind.

"Of course they can, Mom." Katie's voice was firm. Her eyes, identical to her mother's, were dark with anger and frustration. "Why would my father kill himself if he didn't want to worry my mother? That makes absolutely no sense."

Katie looked like her mother, just twenty-plus years younger. Both women were dressed in almost identical simple black long-sleeved dresses. It was clear to Zeke that the Baileys' first child was their protector. Katie's younger siblings remained in the kitchen. Low, somber voices occasionally drifted out to him. He couldn't make out what they were discussing, but the clang of steel pots and pans and the clatter of porcelain indicated they were making lunch.

Meryl's eyes were stormy as she pinned Zeke with a look. "I know what I must sound like—a hysterical woman who's in complete denial. But when you've been together for as long as Art and I, and when you love each other as completely as we did, you know each other inside and out. You know what the other would and wouldn't do and why. You know the other's intentions regardless of the results. Art and I were together since we were kids. Now our children have children. That's a long time, Mr. Touré. That's why you'll never be able to convince me that my Art killed himself. Someone murdered him."

"Please, call me Zeke." He shared a look between mother and daughter. "And I believe Art was murdered, too. It's too much of a coincidence that Art would kill himself after receiving a message threatening his life."

Zeke's words seemed to take Meryl's and Katie's tempers down a notch or two.

Meryl's sturdy shoulders lowered on a sigh of relief. "So you'll find whoever killed my husband?"

Zeke glanced at Celeste before returning his attention to Meryl. "Yes, we will. We believe Art wasn't the killer's only target. Dean Archer's death was also suspicious. And I was threatened as well."

"Oh, no." Meryl's words were muffled behind her hand. "I'm so sorry."

Katie gasped. "Oh, my gosh."

"You were right to be concerned, Meryl." Celeste's tone was somber. "Art is the first victim we're aware of, but his killer has a bigger agenda."

Katie addressed Zeke. "If the police had listened to my mother, Dean Archer would still be alive, and you wouldn't have been threatened."

"We don't know that." Zeke was certain the killer wouldn't be that easy to find.

Katie and Meryl stared at him as though he was a dead man walking. Their fatalism wasn't helpful. Zeke looked away, taking a visual tour of the living room. The walls were a dingy cream. They were a few shades lighter than the worn, wall-to-wall carpet that extended past the archway and into the dining room. A simple, scarred dark wood coffee table stood in front of the sofa. A thick warm-gold armchair was off to the side.

Warm-gold curtains were open, framing the narrow windows on either side of a redbrick fireplace. Part of a train set and several colorful building blocks had been abandoned beside them. The dark wood fireplace mantel was teeming with family photos. Zeke set his mug on the coaster Katie had provided, then crossed to the fireplace for a closer look. Images included Meryl and Art alone and together, and pictures of their children and grandchildren through various stages of their lives: births, baptisms, graduations and weddings.

More murmurings carried from the kitchen, joined by the

scrapes of chairs across linoleum and the whir of a blender. He recalled a comment he'd made to Celeste. *I didn't know Art well. We only saw each other at business functions. But he always seemed happy.* Zeke realized now that joy came from his family.

"The logical place to start is the connection between Art, Dean and Zeke." Celeste's usual gruff manner was on a break. Her gentle tone and manner as she spoke with Art's grieving family impressed Zeke. "Dean canceled his contract with Buckeye Bailey Security and hired Touré Security Group. According to the time stamp on the photo of Art entering his car, it was a few weeks later that he received the threat."

Zeke turned away from the fireplace. "After Dean's wake Friday afternoon, I found a note in my car that stated 'You're next.' Based on the connection between Art, Dean and me, and the fact Art fired the guards assigned to Archer Family Realty, we're investigating the guards first. Can you offer any insights into them?"

Meryl and Katie exchanged a look. Zeke could feel their tension, as well as their desperation to find the person who'd taken their loved one from them.

"I didn't know Art's employees well." Meryl spread her arms. Her right fist clutched a used facial tissue. "I have my own job and didn't spend much time at his company. All I knew about his employees is what he told me, which wasn't much." She gestured toward Celeste. "I gave you the employee files on the guards who'd been assigned to Dean's company."

"We were hoping for more personal impressions." Celeste set her blue ceramic mug on a coaster beside Zeke's. She pulled her notepad from her knapsack. "Had Art complained about one of them in particular? Did he argue with any of them? How were his relationships with them before Dean canceled the contract?"

"Even a seemingly minor argument." Zeke resumed his seat and retrieved his portfolio from his attaché case.

Meryl frowned at the carpet as though searching her memories. "No, he didn't blame one above the others. He blamed them all equally—as well as himself."

"Dad blamed himself?" Katie let her arm slide from her mother's shoulders. "Why?"

Meryl used the tissue she clutched to wipe her nose. "Your father said he should have acted sooner and taken more drastic steps to address Dean's concerns about the guards. I remember him saying if he'd removed one of the guards, he'd still have the Archer account."

"'One of them'?" Zeke and Celeste asked in unison.

"Do you remember which one?" Zeke continued.

Meryl shook her head. "But I can still hear his voice. 'If I'd just removed that guard, I'd still have the bleeping account.' Except he didn't say 'bleeping.' Art had been very upset. Losing Archer had been a devastating blow to his company. It was a big account, and he'd had it on contract for years."

"I'm sorry." Having just signed the contract with Archer Family Realty, Zeke was aware that it was a significant account. They requested guards stationed at their company office as well as their holdings. Plus, Touré Security Group was providing cybersecurity services.

"There's nothing for you to be sorry for." Meryl looked at him with wide, startled eyes. "My husband understood you didn't take Archer from him. He lost the account. He never blamed you or your brothers. He liked and respected your family."

Meryl had removed a weight Zeke hadn't realized had been on his shoulders. "Thank you for telling me that. Had anyone new come into Art's life? Guards, clients, colleagues?"

Meryl began shaking her head even before Zeke finished

his question. "No, no one new. He couldn't afford to hire new guards, even after firing those four. And there weren't any new clients, although he was hopeful he'd find someone to replace Archer." She stretched her shoulders. "And he didn't mention new colleagues."

"What about you, Meryl?" Celeste searched the widow's face as though trying to read her mind. "Have you met anyone new? Perhaps in the neighborhood, at work or church?"

"Or through a friend?" Zeke added.

"No, no one." Even as Meryl said the words, Zeke sensed her struggling to draw even a crumb of a clue from her memory. "I've known most of my friends since the kids were young. We don't have any new hires at work—at least, none that come to mind."

"What about me?" Katie leaned forward, catching Zeke's eyes. "Would it be significant if someone came into my life?"

"It could be." Celeste's pen was poised over her notepad, ready to record anything her client's daughter shared.

Katie switched her attention to Celeste. "I met a woman at the gym. She seemed a little strange. She made me uncomfortable. And now she's gone. It's like one day she makes herself part of the group of people I hang out with at the gym, then a week or so later, she drops off the face of the earth."

Zeke exchanged a look with Celeste. She seemed to have the same reaction he was having. That was textbook suspicious behavior.

Celeste sat back, studying Katie. "What made her seem strange?"

Katie spread her hands. "Well, first, she invited herself into our group like some kind of parasite. She ignored every clue we gave her—subtle and not so subtle—that she wasn't welcome. She asked a bunch of nosy questions, then she vanished without a trace. Doesn't that seem strange to you?"

"Very." Celeste nodded. "What's her name?"

"That's the thing." Katie exhaled a heavy sigh. "I wasn't paying attention. Heida or Gretchen or Hannah. Something like that. I'll ask my friends if they remember." She retrieved her cell phone from the coffee table.

"Where's your gym?" Zeke asked.

"A few blocks from my house." Katie typed a quick message into her phone before returning it to the table. "I live in Delaware." She named a city north of Columbus.

"What do you remember about her?" Zeke hoped she recalled something helpful. Anything.

Katie looked at her mother. "Now that I think about it, she asked a lot of questions about our family." Her cell phone beeped. She took it from the table to read the screen. "One of my friends from the gym thinks her name is something like Annie or Allie or Alex. Sorry." She sent a reply, then set the device on the table again.

"No problem." Celeste shook her head. "It's probably an alias. If she was involved in your father's death, she wouldn't have given her real name. But even an alias gives us a start."

Celeste was right. For that reason, Zeke recorded the six possible names on the writing pad in his portfolio. "What kinds of questions did she ask about your family?"

"She wanted to know if my parents lived nearby. Whether we spent a lot of time together and where we liked to go." Katie's memories seemed to stoke her temper. "She always looked like she was about to work out, which was really strange. I mean, she had her hair in a ponytail, and she always wore shorts and T-shirts. But she never did anything. She was never sweaty or anything. Who goes to a gym if they're not going to exercise? I've heard of people joining a gym but not going. I've never met anyone who gets up early, goes to the gym, but doesn't work out."

"Could you describe her for me?" Zeke turned to a blank page in his writing tablet. "Was her face thin or was it rounder like yours?"

"I wish I'd taken a picture of her with my phone." Katie frowned at the redbrick fireplace across the room. "Her face was fuller, but it wasn't quite round. She was about my height, five foot ten, and stocky. Her hair was light brown or a dark blond. She wore it in a ponytail, but she had bangs that covered her forehead and her eyebrows."

"What about her eyes?" As he spoke, Zeke sketched a round face fringed by heavy bangs, with hair swept back as though in a ponytail. "Was there anything special about them? Were they close together? Wide? Small?"

"Her eyes were unremarkable. I can't remember if they were blue or green." Katie shrugged helplessly. "They might have been brown. And she had a small, thin nose and thin lips."

"That's *really* good." Celeste's voice was low. She'd leaned closer to watch him work. "You're *really* talented."

Zeke could feel her warmth seeping into his clothing, getting under his skin. "Thank you." He looked at her, and their eyes locked. He didn't want to break their connection, but he had to. Summoning all his willpower, he pushed himself to his feet and crossed to Meryl and Katie on the sofa. He held out his portfolio to show them the sketch. "Is this what she looked like?"

Meryl's lips parted in surprise. "This is wonderful. Celeste's right. You're *very* talented."

"Yes, you are." Katie spoke the words on a breath. "I think her eyes are a little farther apart. And her bottom lip was fuller. And her cheekbones… I think her face is shaped more like a heart."

Zeke made the alterations to the sketch. He caught Celeste's vanilla-and-citrus scent as she came to stand beside him. He wanted to wrap an arm around her waist and pull her closer. Instead, he focused on moving Katie's Mystery Woman's eyes farther to the sides and making her bottom lip fuller and her cheekbones more prominent.

He turned the notepad back to Katie and her mother. "What do you think?"

Katie's jaw dropped. "Oh my gosh. That's her!" She jabbed her index finger toward the sketch. "That's her!"

Meryl looked from Katie to the notepad and back. "Are you sure?"

"I'm positive." Katie's voice hitched. She looked up at him. Her gray eyes were wide and dark with pain. "Do you think she killed my father?"

Zeke exchanged a look with Celeste. The caution he felt was reflected in her eyes. "There may not be a link between her and your father's death. The only way to know is to find her."

Katie's eyes returned to the sketch. "You've given me hope that my father's murderer will be caught."

Zeke tried to share her optimism. There was a lot at stake: his life, and his brothers' and Celeste's lives. He had to find the killer for all their sakes.

"JERRY'S APPETITE'S BACK." Mal's image appeared in the center of the camera during the videoconference Sunday afternoon. "But then, how long did we really expect his appetite to be gone?"

Zeke's responding quicksilver smile eased the tension from his features and captivated Celeste. He'd carried his clean laptop from her home office to her dining room. The table there provided enough space for them to sit together.

Zeke turned his smile to her. "Jerry's like a human garbage disposal."

Celeste didn't think the youngest Touré would appreciate their description of his eating habits, but she enjoyed being clued in on the joke. "But he's so fit."

"For now." Mal snorted. "Symone will bring him home from the hospital. Fill me in on your meeting with Meryl Bailey. Did she give you any insights on the guards?"

Zeke tapped his pen against his portfolio. "Meryl and her daughter, Katie Bailey-Smith, couldn't tell us anything about the guards—"

Celeste interrupted. "It sounded like Art didn't tell Meryl much about his employees."

Zeke nodded. "We'll have to rely on the personnel files she gave us."

Mal rested his right hand on a small stack of manila folders beside him. "I've started going through them. Art was very thorough."

"Good." Zeke turned to the page with the sketch of the Mystery Woman he'd redrawn and cleaned up. "Katie mentioned meeting someone recently at the gym she belongs to. Did you get the sketch I emailed earlier?"

Mal tapped a few keys on his computer. "You think this woman from Katie's gym could be involved? She doesn't match any of our four suspects, not even if they wore a disguise."

"That's true." Celeste leaned closer to Zeke, ostensibly to get a closer look at his sketch. She breathed in his soap-and-sandalwood scent. "But Katie said this woman had attached herself to her and her gym friends, and asked several questions about her family, then disappeared. She described her as 'creepy.'" Using both hands, Celeste made air quotes for "creepy."

Mal grunted. "I'd describe that as 'creepy,' too."

Zeke frowned at his illustration. "The woman's about five ten and average build. Katie couldn't remember the color of her eyes but said her hair was either brown or dark blond."

Celeste leaned back against her chair. "Neither Katie nor her friends could remember the woman's name. If she's the killer, she would've given them a fake one anyway."

Zeke looked up at his computer monitor. "If I send you a more detailed sketch on unlined paper, do you think you can run it through your fancy facial-recognition program?"

Still seemingly looking at the photo file of the sketch, Mal arched an eyebrow. "*Our* facial-recognition program isn't that fancy. It's a basic trial membership. It'll recognize photos, but I'm not sure it'll recognize the photo of a sketch. It's worth a try. Send me the new image as soon as you have it."

Zeke nodded. "I'll get on that once we're done here. Also, I gave Meryl and Katie your business card and told them to contact you if they think of or hear anything else that could help identify the killer or an accomplice."

Mal switched his attention from the file to Zeke. "So you definitely think we're looking for more than one person? An accomplice?"

Zeke's shrug was a restless flex of his broad shoulders. Tension pulsed like an invisible force field around him. "If she were planning to kill Art, why did the Mystery Woman make contact with his daughter in Delaware? She must have known Art lives and works in Columbus. What purpose would it serve to connect with Katie?"

Mal rested his forearms on the table in front of the computer. "Maybe she was hoping Katie would tell her parents, making her contact with their daughter seem like a subtle threat. 'I can reach your family anywhere.'"

"I don't think that's it." Celeste's thoughts raced. Zeke was onto something. "Katie didn't tell her parents. Even if she had, why would they give the encounter a second thought? But if one of the guards wants revenge for being fired, why didn't they make both deaths look like either a suicide like Art's or a heart attack like Dean's? The killer wouldn't have reason to suspect the police would have questioned those deaths. Such elaborate staging makes it seem as though more than one person's involved, which begs the question: do we have the right motive."

Mal spread his hands. "If not revenge, then what?"

"I don't know. Yet." Celeste sighed. "But in case our killer isn't one of the guards—or if one of the guards is working with an accomplice—we need to cast a wider net. We're asking everyone about new acquaintances they've made within the last six months. So, Mal, besides Grace and Symone, have you made any new friends?"

Mal narrowed his eyes in thought. "I haven't but Kevin has. I'll do a background check on his new girlfriend."

"Great." Celeste loved action-oriented people like the Tourés. She pushed her chair back from her desk. "You do that. In the meantime, Zeke and I will chat with Jayne Archer."

She pulled her cell phone from the front pocket of her black jeans and used it to check the time. The widow of the recently deceased Realtor Dean Archer was expecting them in just over an hour. Would she or members of her family also have had an encounter with Katie's Mystery Woman? If so, the connection would elevate the Mystery Woman from creepy gym stalker to a certified suspect for murder. Celeste slipped her cell back into her pocket and glanced at Zeke. The urgency of their situation was like a punch to her chest. They needed to find this Mystery Woman before she found him.

Chapter Seven

"Eriq said you think my husband was murdered." Jayne Archer sat across from Zeke and Celeste at her rectangular blond-wood kitchen table late Sunday afternoon. She looked and sounded as though she'd been crying for days. Her voice was raw. Behind her small, rimless glasses, her dark brown eyes were pink and puffy. "That would explain this letter."

She pushed a simple manila envelope across the table toward Zeke, handling it gingerly, as though it was hazardous waste. Seated beside him, Celeste squeezed his forearm before he could accept the packet. Reaching for her knapsack on the hardwood floor beside her chair, she pulled two pairs of disposable gloves from one of its many zippered compartments. Celeste gave one set to Zeke. She donned the other.

He tugged on the gloves, grateful she'd thought to bring them with her. Dean's full name was written in cursive across the front. "Do you recognize the handwriting?"

"No." Jayne's voice quivered, breaking the word into multiple syllables.

Zeke hadn't thought so, but he had to ask. His eyes dropped to the used tissue Jayne clutched in her right fist. He wished they didn't have to put her through this interview while her grief was still so fresh. He regretted having to question both mourning families. But in criminal investigations, time was of the essence.

He returned his attention to the envelope. He had a sick foreboding about what they'd find inside. Zeke glanced at Celeste before pulling out the two plain white pages. He laid the papers on the table between them. The first sheet contained a two-word threat: *You're next.* The second was a full-color image of Dean getting into a gleaming bronze sedan.

Celeste stiffened. "Where did you find this?"

"In Dean's home office." Jayne removed her glasses before using her tattered tissue to dry her eyes.

"Did you ask him about it?" Reaching out, Celeste slid the box of facial tissues closer to their hostess. Jayne murmured her thanks.

"Of course." Her scowl was furious. Her brown cheeks were flushed. "He claimed it was a joke. I pushed him on it. I mean, who keeps a *joke* made in such poor taste? But he wouldn't change his story. He must've thought I was as dumb as a rock."

"No, ma'am." Zeke's response was firm. "He didn't think you were stupid. He was desperate to protect you."

"Zeke's right." Celeste drew the letter closer to her. "Never forget that Dean loved you very much. A love like that is rare."

Celeste sounded wistful, as though she was grieving a lost lover. Zeke frowned. Was he the one who gave her the ring she always wore on her thumb? Was that the reason she was reluctant to get involved with him? His heart tore a little.

He took a breath, then addressed Jayne. "Does Eriq know about this threat?"

"I'm giving it to him tonight." Jayne put her glasses back on. "He's joining my family and me for dinner. Would you two like to join us?"

Celeste blinked as though surprised. "Oh, no. But thank you." She pointed at the papers and envelope. "May I photograph these?"

Jayne glared at the items. "Of course."

As Celeste used her cell phone to capture the evidence, Zeke surveyed the kitchen. Thin white curtains were closed over both windows, blocking some of the sunlight and casting the cheery room into shadows. Pot holders along the stove, hand towels beside the refrigerator, and place mats on the table added colorful accents that eased the sterile backdrop of stainless steel appliances and snow-white walls. Half a dozen mugs, cups and partially filled glasses seemed forgotten on the white-and-yellow marble counter.

Zeke sipped the coffee Jayne had given them when they'd arrived. It had cooled. He set the white porcelain cup on its matching saucer. "Had Dean mentioned being worried about anything, or had he seemed preoccupied?"

"Yes." Jayne removed her glasses again and used a fresh tissue to dry her tears. "He had trouble sleeping. He was barely eating. He'd lost a lot of weight that he didn't need to lose. That's why I didn't question his having a heart attack. He'd been under so much stress."

"I understand." Celeste put the threat and the printed image into the envelope before sliding them across the table. "Had he given you any idea what was bothering him?"

Jayne shook her head, glaring at the packet. "He'd become so secretive. Maybe even paranoid."

"Paranoid?" Celeste glanced at Zeke.

"What makes you say that?" Zeke asked.

Jayne's frustration swept across the table like a gathering storm. "He'd stopped jogging outside and used the treadmill instead. He said he'd switched because of the heat. But it hadn't been that hot, and he *loved* running outdoors. He'd also started working from home more often and wouldn't tell me why." Her words came faster until they were almost running together. "Since he was being so mysterious, I decided to search his home office." She stabbed her finger toward the manila envelope. "That's when I found that vile message."

Zeke frowned, considering the package. If Dean's reclusiveness had been in reaction to that threat, why hadn't he brought it to Eriq? He wished the older man were still alive so he could ask him. Eriq might have been able to prevent Dean's death.

Celeste's voice refocused Zeke's wayward thoughts. "Had you or Dean made any new acquaintances in the past six months or so?"

Jayne's still-smooth brow furrowed. She dropped her eyes to the table. "None that I can think of at the moment." She rubbed her arms as though she'd felt a chill. She was wearing an oversize red T-shirt and loose-fitting navy shorts. Were they her husband's?

Celeste rotated the ring on her right thumb. "How about your children? Have they met anyone new?"

"I'll ask them." Jayne split a look between Celeste and Zeke. "Do you think the threat could be from someone we've recently met?"

"It's possible." Zeke pulled one of Mal's business cards and a manila folder from his briefcase. "If you think of anyone who's recently been introduced to you or if you learn of someone new in your children's lives, you can call my brother, Mal." He gave Mal's card to Jayne, then opened the folder to reveal the sketch of Katie Bailey-Smith's Mystery Woman. "Do you recognize this person?" He slid the sketch across the table to Jayne.

Jayne slipped her glasses back on and drew the image closer. "Oh, this is very good. Whoever drew it is very talented."

Celeste looked at Zeke. "Yes, he is."

The admiration in her eyes made Zeke's cheeks warm. He tugged his gaze away. "Thank you. Does the woman in the sketch look familiar?"

"Nooo." Jayne drew the syllable out with uncertainty. "Wait." She laid the sketch back on the table and placed her long, slender left hand over the top of the head. It sounded as though her words were being pulled from her. "She might, but I'm not sure. About a week before…his death, I went to Dean's office. He'd been so depressed. I wanted to surprise him with a lunch date. I'd styled my hair and took extra time with my makeup. And I wore my favorite dress with heels." She smiled softly at the memory. "When I arrived, he was talking with a young woman who claimed to want to list her house with him. But she had short red hair—too short for a ponytail."

"Why did you say she *claimed* to want to list her house with Dean?" Celeste asked.

Jayne glanced at the sketch again before raising her eyes to Celeste. "The woman was in her mid-to late twenties. I would have expected her to fill out the agency's online form rather than coming into the office. For someone in that age group, that seemed odd to me."

"That does seem weird." Celeste glanced toward Zeke before returning her attention to Jayne.

"Why are you covering the top half of the sketch?" Zeke inclined his head toward Jayne's hand. She seemed to have forgotten it still lay on the paper.

"There was something else that was odd about her." Jayne lifted her left hand and turned the sketch toward Celeste and Zeke. "She wore very large dark sunglasses that she kept on the whole time she was meeting with Dean. Who does that?"

"You were in Dean's office during the entire meeting?" Celeste asked.

"They weren't discussing state secrets." Jayne shrugged one shoulder. "And I used to help Dean at the agency when he first opened it. Anyway, I remember thinking the sunglasses were too big for her and that they drew attention to the lower half of her face. She had a small, pointed chin, and her lower lip was fuller than her upper lip, just like in your sketch. I can't swear it's the same person, but it's quite a coincidence."

Zeke reached for the sketch at the same time Celeste did. He positioned it between them.

Celeste looked up at Jayne. "Your attention to detail is amazing. I can't believe you caught that."

Jayne smiled at Zeke. "The praise belongs to the artist. You're very talented, Zeke. You put so much detail into the image it looks almost lifelike."

"Thank you." Zeke returned his attention to the drawing. There was now a possible connection between this Mystery Woman and both of their victims, despite her obvious efforts to conceal her identity. Who was she, and what was her connection to Archer Family Realty, Buckeye Bailey Security and Touré Security Group?

"If Jayne's right, Katie's Mystery Woman is another connection between Art and Dean." Celeste felt Zeke's energy beside her at the dining table Sunday evening. They were videoconferencing with Mal. Fresh from the hospital, Jerry had also joined them. "Which supports our theory that the connection between Archer Family Realty, Buckeye Bailey and TSG is the Archer contract, and that the motive is revenge."

"That makes the most sense." Jerry looked uncomfortable in what appeared to be his home office. The cast on his left arm was too prominent to ignore. The scarlet T-shirt beneath the gray hooded sweat jacket emphasized the pallor of his tense, chiseled features. When they'd asked, he'd said he felt fine. Obviously, he was lying.

Mal had rolled up the sleeves of his lightweight smoke gray sweater. "While we're on the subject of the Mystery Woman, Kevin's girlfriend broke up with him. She told him she was going home to Toronto."

"Well, that's not suspicious much." Jerry's response was as dry as dust. "Another person who mysteriously enters, then mysteriously disappears from the life of someone connected to a target in this case."

Mal grunted his agreement. "I'll show him the sketch tomorrow. I didn't want to text it to him in case his ex cloned his phone—"

Jerry interrupted. "Good thinking."

Zeke nodded. "Yes. Thanks for taking care of that."

Mal moved some files around on his desk. "Unfortunately, the facial-recognition program we have isn't able to work with the sketch."

"Thanks for trying." Celeste rotated the sterling silver ring she wore on her right thumb.

"Yeah, nerd. It was worth the effort." Jerry's attempt at humor was strained. "Mata Hari keeps showing up all over our case, but we don't know how she could be connected. Is there another angle with the contract?"

"Or for a second killer?" Mal's voice was tight, as though he was struggling under the pressure of having his brothers in danger.

Zeke rubbed the back of his neck. "Do you think there could be two killers with two different motives for murder?"

Celeste looked to Zeke, trying not to get lost in his coal-black eyes. "It's a solid theory and would explain why she's partnering with one or more of the guards, *if* that's what she's doing."

Zeke turned back to his brothers. "Are there possible connections between our Mystery Woman and the fired guards?"

Mal tapped on his laptop's keyboard. "Two of the four guards assigned to the Archer account were women. Agnes Letby, sixty-two, and May Ramirez, sixty."

"Jayne said our Mystery Woman is in her twenties." Jerry's tone was pensive. "I'm doing the background check on Ramirez now. She has three daughters. All in their thirties. None of them live in Ohio."

Celeste didn't see that as an obstacle. "They don't have to *live* in Ohio. One of them could be visiting. And maybe they're in their thirties but look like they're in their twenties."

"So we're searching for two killers." Zeke pinched the bridge of his nose. "Right now I can't think of an alternative motive that connects our three companies."

"Unless it's a case of hell having no fury like a woman scorned." Jerry raised his uninjured right hand, palm out. "Hear me out. Are we sure one of the widows isn't involved? Maybe Meryl killed Dean for canceling his contract with Art, then killed her husband because his failing business was putting a strain on their finances."

Celeste folded her hands on the desk in front of her. "That's an interesting theory. But why would Meryl hire me to find her husband's killer? That's like hiring me to find herself. Why wouldn't she just confess?"

Zeke's soft laughter stirred the butterflies in Celeste's abdomen. "Don't go soft on him just because he's injured. Even in pain, Jerry can dish insults as well as take them. Don't let him fool you."

"Thanks for letting me know." Celeste flashed him a grin and watched the light spark in his eyes.

"Whatever, man." Jerry gave them a crooked smile. "What about Jayne?"

Zeke spread his hands. "Victims' spouses are usually the top suspects, but we don't have a motive for Jayne. Eriq said they were happy and had a strong marriage."

Jerry ran his right hand over his tight curls. "I had to ask."

Zeke closed his portfolio. "In the morning, Celeste and I will start our interviews of Art's former guards with Damien Rockwell. We'll try to find out if he's connected to this woman without pushing her farther underground."

Celeste gave Zeke a warning look. "We also don't want

to give away too much about our investigation and lose our edge."

Mal sat back against his chair, shrinking his image on the computer screen. "You'll have the background report on Rockwell within the hour."

"That'll be great. Thank you." Zeke shared a look between Mal and Jerry. "I wish we knew for certain neither of you were targets. Are you sure you haven't received threatening messages, either written or recorded?"

Mal arched a thick black eyebrow. "We'd know if we'd received one of those. I haven't."

"Neither have I," Jerry said.

Celeste crossed her arms under her chest. The answer seemed obvious to her. "You're in charge of TSG's Corporate Security Division. You worked on the contract with Dean. That's the reason the killer's identified *you*, not your brothers." She turned to Mal's and Jerry's images on the screen. "But that doesn't mean you guys are in the clear. Stay sharp. Zeke's the primary target, but the killer could come after *you* to get to *him*."

If Meryl hadn't asked her to investigate Art's suspicious death, Celeste wouldn't have realized Zeke was the target of serial killers. She hadn't believed Art had been murdered—not at first. But now she knew Meryl had been right. Someone had killed her husband and made it look like suicide. The same person—or people—appeared to have killed Jayne's husband. Now they were targeting the man she... What? All right, she had feelings for Zeke. Very strong feelings. Celeste wanted justice for both widows and their murdered spouses. But her sense of urgency was focused on Zeke. She had to keep him safe. She had to find the people who were threatening him. At any cost.

IF HE REACHED OUT, his fingertips would almost touch Celeste's mattress. Zeke's palms tingled with that thought late

Sunday night. His makeshift bed lay between Celeste and her chest of drawers. He turned his head against the pillow and stared at the ceiling. An image of Celeste as she'd looked before he'd turned off the light was superimposed over its shadows. She'd pulled her fluffy white coverlets over her chest. Thin cream ribbons of material wrapped her slender shoulders. Curiosity and desire had branded a question on his mind: What did Celeste Jarrett wear to bed?

After reading Mal's report on Damien Rockwell, the former Buckeye Bailey Security guard whom he and Celeste would interview in the morning, Zeke had needed a mental break. He'd wanted to clear his mind so he could approach the case from a fresh perspective. But filling his thoughts with Celeste would not help him get a good night's sleep.

"Are you worried about your brothers?" Celeste's soft whisper was like a jolt of electricity.

Zeke started. He turned his head toward her voice. His eyes had adjusted to the dark. He could make out the bed, but from this angle, he couldn't see her lying on it. That was for the best.

Trails of light from the moon and nearby porch lamps slipped into the room from the edges of the window's curtains. The constant chirp of crickets from her yard and the occasional swoosh of cars rolling down her street created their background music. The faint scent of Celeste's vanilla-and-citrus perfume was everywhere.

Zeke frowned. "How did you know I was awake?"

"Are you kidding?" Her low chuckle caused the muscles in his gut to tighten. "I can feel your tension way over here."

He rolled onto his left side. "You can sense my tension, but in the mornings, I can't hear you make your bed or leave your house."

Her sheets rustled as though she was shifting on her mattress. Was she deliberately being noisy to pile onto his confusion?

"I'm a trained investigator." She kept her voice low, as though she didn't want to be overheard by…whom? "I'm adept at being undetected."

"Well, lady, you've got mad skills. Not even my parents were as talented."

Her low laughter tied his abdominal muscles in knots. "I'm flattered. Your parents are still highly regarded in the security and law enforcement communities."

He forced himself to breathe. "I mean it."

"So do I." Celeste hesitated. "I know you wouldn't say something like that if you didn't mean it. So thank you."

"You're welcome." Zeke rolled onto his back, searching for a way to fill the awkward silence.

Celeste threw him a lifeline. "I understand your concern for your brothers' safety. But, Zeke, they can take care of themselves. That's their job, taking care of themselves and other people."

"I know. But I don't even have the words to describe how scared I was when that car struck Jerry." He rubbed his eyes with the heels of his hands as though he could erase the memory. "Standing there, all I could do was watch his body roll over the car, then fall onto the street. I never want to feel that afraid or useless again."

"I understand." Her words were soft sympathy. "You and your brothers are so close. And you're used to being in control. That attack took that security from you. Thankfully, Jerry will be all right."

"Thank God for that." Why did she think he was controlling? His brothers often accused him of the same thing. "And thank you, for listening."

"Of course." Her sheets rustled again, almost as though she was making a big performance of rolling back over on the bed. A trace of amusement entered her voice. "Will you be able to sleep now? If not, I'm happy to switch places with you. Maybe you'd sleep better on a real mattress."

Zeke chuckled. "My father's ghost would haunt me for the rest of my life if I were to toss a woman out of her own bed." He lay still and let her laughter caress him.

"If you're sure." Celeste's voice rolled with amusement. "You need your rest."

"As do you." He was reluctant to bring their conversation to an end, but it was getting late. "Good night, Celeste. Sleep well."

"See you in the morning, Zeke." Her sheets rustled again.

Yes, you will. Bright and early.

Zeke smiled at the ceiling. She wasn't going to leave her home undetected for a second morning in a row. His pride was on the line.

Chapter Eight

"Thanks for meeting me so early." Damien Rockwell glanced at his silver Timex Monday morning. His thin dark brown features were tight with tension. "My shift starts soon, and I don't want to mess up this job, especially after what happened at Buckeye Bailey."

Zeke and Celeste stood with Damien near the parking lot behind the glass-and-metal building that housed the offices of Damien's new employer. According to Mal's background report, it had taken Damien six weeks to find a new job. The post with the investment company appeared to be a step up for him.

"The appointment time is fine. We're morning people." Zeke gave Celeste on his left a pointed look.

Hours later, it still stung that, for the second morning in a row, Celeste had made her bed, gotten dressed, and left her home for a predawn jog and he hadn't heard her. How did she do it?

"I don't know if I can really help." Damien's almond-shaped dark brown eyes shifted between Zeke and Celeste. Beneath his security guard uniform—white shirt with a black tie, blazer, pants and loafers—he had the long, wiry build of an avid runner. "You really think someone killed Art? That's cray. Who would do that?"

"We think his death is connected to the Archer Family Realty account." Zeke wondered about the twentysomething's agitation. Was it all due to his need to get to work on time? Or was something more behind it?

Damien frowned his confusion. "Why would Dean Archer off Art?"

Celeste shook her head. "Dean Archer was also killed. We're looking into both murders."

"But you two aren't cops?" Damien waved a hand between Zeke and Celeste.

Celeste shrugged her knapsack off her left shoulder and set it on the sidewalk between her black loafers. "We're investigators, but we're working with the police."

Damien looked around, then lowered his voice. "To be honest, I don't like talking about the past, you know? I'm still embarrassed about getting fired. I didn't really know what I was doing, all right?"

"What does that mean?" Celeste frowned up at the guard. He was a few inches shorter than Zeke but several inches taller than Celeste. "You didn't know you were sleeping on the job?"

"Shh! Keep your voice down." Damien's cheeks flushed pink. He tossed furtive glances behind both narrow shoulders before continuing. "That's not what I meant. I'd just, you know, graduated from college. I was still kind of transitioning from student to, you know, responsible adult. But I've got my act together now. Being unemployed has a way of forcing you to get serious and really grow up."

It wasn't yet seven o'clock, but already more than half a dozen employees had arrived at the investment firm. The company followed the same procedures Touré Security Group recommended to its clients. Zeke observed the staff using identification cards to access its secure entrance. He'd seen two guards at an identification-screening station in the center of the lobby.

"At least you landed on your feet." Celeste gestured toward him. "And you must be making more money here than you'd made with Buckeye Bailey." She surveyed their surroundings.

A dozen or so vehicles—dark SUVs, bright compact sedans, and dark gray or silver hatchbacks—stood in the asphalt parking lot. Black mulch beds nurtured young burning bushes and small evergreen shrubs. In the distance, rush hour traffic congested US Route 23. The scents of moist earth, cut grass and engine exhaust surrounded them. Zeke focused on Celeste's vanilla-and-citrus perfume.

Damien stiffened. His eyes narrowed with suspicion. "Yeah. New job, new company, more money. There's nothing wrong with that."

Zeke frowned. "No, there's not." Then why was the younger man defensive? "As we explained when we contacted you yesterday, we just have a few questions about your time with Buckeye Bailey Security and Archer Family Realty. Was there tension between any of the guards and management?"

Damien hesitated. "I don't know if I'm comfortable talking about other people."

"This is a homicide investigation." Celeste shoved her hands into the front pockets of her black slacks. She wore them with a black button-down shirt and black jacket. "If you've seen or heard anything that could help our investigation, you're compelled to share it."

"So how about it, Damien?" Zeke shrugged, trying to cut some of the building tension. "Were there any conflicts between Art and your colleagues?"

Damien's expression eased from wariness to resignation. "All right. I did overhear Art arguing with a couple of people about their payroll deposits. But you didn't hear it here."

"What about their deposits?" Zeke prompted to get Damien talking again.

"They were late." Damien's eyes stretched wide with horror. "You know, I think Art was having cash flow problems. One guy said his pay had been late *twice*." He held up two fingers as though emphasizing the gravity of the situation. "Yeah, Art must've *really* been having *a lot* of money trouble."

Zeke made a mental note to fact-check Damien's theory about Art's money. If his competitor were having financial challenges, what was the source? "Which guard had more than one late payroll deposit?"

Damien's expression conveyed his reluctance to give up the name. Zeke sensed Celeste's impatience. "Cooper. Chad Cooper. That's one guy I wouldn't want to cross. Dude looks like he's straight out of Rikers."

Chad Cooper was also on their suspect list. But according to Mal's preliminary report, Chad was in prison for aggravated assault and robbery. His sentence had started days before Art's murder. That was an airtight alibi.

Unless Chad was working with someone on the outside. Katie's Mystery Woman, perhaps?

"Did you ever hear Chad threaten Art?" A cool breeze played with Celeste's wavy dark brown tresses. She brushed the hair from her eyes.

"Nah." Damien shook his head. "He was furious, but he never really took it *that* far. The closest he got to a threat was saying something like, 'This better never happen again.' You know? I mean, you can't blame the guy for being angry that Art stiffed him. Everyone's got bills. And if you do the work, you need to be paid."

"What about you?" Celeste watched Damien closely. "Did you ever get stiffed?"

"Nope." Damien's chest puffed out with pride. "Not once."

"Really?" Celeste's straight black eyebrows flew up her forehead. "If everyone else's checks were bouncing, why didn't yours?"

"Not *everyone's*. Just a couple of people." Damien's response carried a thread of irritation. Annoyance glittered in his dark eyes. "Or maybe it was just Chad's. I don't remember."

Celeste glanced at Zeke before addressing Damien. "If your memory comes back, please call us. The payroll issues could be an important point."

Zeke shared Celeste's frustration, but he wouldn't pile on to Damien. Instead, he took a calming breath before asking something else. "Where were you August 22?"

Damien's expression went blank. Zeke sensed him sifting through his memories. "I don't know. Wait. That was a Friday. The Guardians were playing." The guard referenced Cleveland's Major League Baseball team. "I was at a sports bar, watching the game with friends."

They could ask Eriq to confirm that later, if necessary. Zeke pulled the sketch of their Mystery Woman from his inside jacket pocket. "Do you recognize her?"

Damien took the sketch from him. He frowned as he studied the drawing before giving it back. "No. Sorry. She's cute, though. Who is she?"

"That's what we're trying to find out." Zeke folded the sheet and returned it to his pocket.

Celeste gave Damien a considering look. "You don't seem overly concerned that Art was murdered."

"Art was okay, even though he fired me." Damien crossed his arms over his narrow chest. "We weren't friends, but I didn't have anything to do with his death, if that's what you're getting at."

"And how was your relationship with Dean Archer?" Zeke asked.

Damien shook his head and spread his arms. "I don't think I ever spoke two words to Mr. Archer."

"Have you received any threatening messages?" Celeste's abrupt change of topic surprised the younger man.

Damien rocked back on his heels. "No." He glanced at Zeke before turning back to Celeste. "Do you think I will? Should I be worried?"

"If you get a note, yes." Celeste looked at Zeke. "Do you have any other questions?"

Zeke understood Celeste's tough approach, but the surprise on Damien's face got to him. He couldn't walk away when the younger man looked so unsettled. He pulled a generic Touré Security Group business card from the same inside jacket pocket that secured the sketch of their Mystery Woman. He didn't want to leave his or his brothers' information all over Franklin County. "We don't believe the killer is targeting you, but if you have any concerns—or if you think of anything else—call us."

He and Celeste thanked Damien for his time, then strode back to her car. "Do you want me to drive?"

She frowned at him. "It's my car, control freak."

He heard Jerry's voice in the uncomplimentary nickname. Shaking off the memory, he veered toward the passenger door of Celeste's black four-door sedan. "Maybe you could go a little easier on the next suspect."

She paused, meeting his eyes across the hood of her car. "We get more information when one of us plays tough and the other is empathetic. If you'd like, next time you can be the empathetic one."

She must be kidding.

Zeke gave her a skeptical look. "You're not as gruff as you pretend to be."

She arched an eyebrow as though challenging him. "You don't think so?"

"No, I don't."

"I'd hate to disappoint you." Celeste disappeared through her driver-side door.

Zeke folded himself onto the passenger seat. "Tough as nails or soft like bread, you could never disappoint me."

Something in Celeste's expression shifted. She blinked and the moment was gone. "I'll hold you to that."

Why did he have the sense she was only half joking? Celeste navigated her car out of the parking lot, leaving him with another mystery to solve.

"KEVIN RECOGNIZED THE woman in Zeke's sketch." Mal made the announcement during their videoconference. He and Jerry were in the Touré Security Group conference room Monday morning.

Celeste didn't know why she was surprised, but she was. She'd suspected the serial killer had found a way into Zeke's inner circle the same way she'd made contact with Art's daughter.

"Who is she?" Zeke sat beside Celeste at her dining room table.

"His ex." Mal flexed his shoulders. "She told him her name was Anne Castle. It's probably an alias."

"Kevin said she's a green-eyed brunette." Jerry seemed to be getting used to the cast on his left arm, which was fortunate. His doctor had told him he'd have to wear it for at least six weeks, until the end of October. "She must have been wearing a disguise for at least one of these identities."

Celeste rotated the ring on her right thumb as she shifted through her memories. "She was a blonde with Katie, a redhead with Dean and Jayne, and a brunette with Kevin."

Mal crossed his arms over the ice blue shirt that stretched across his broad chest. He wore it with a navy tie. "Kevin said she was curious about TSG. She told him she wanted to be a police officer, but if that didn't work out, her fallback was security—"

Jerry grunted. "That's hurtful."

Mal ignored the interruption. "Fortunately, Kevin didn't tell her anything. It's against policy to share processes and procedures."

Celeste shivered with a sudden chill. She found and held Zeke's eyes. "That rule saved your life." She tore her eyes from his. "Did she give him a number, email, address?"

Jerry ran a hand over his tight dark brown curls. "Kev tried her cell. The number's no longer in service. And the address she gave him is a furniture store on the east side."

"What about a photo?" Zeke's voice was starting to reveal his frustration. Celeste understood.

"Nothing usable." Mal rubbed the back of his neck. "She didn't like having her picture taken. In the few images Kevin has, she's covering her face."

"If I were a serial killer, I wouldn't want anyone taking my photo, either." Jerry's deep sigh expanded his chest and lifted his shoulders. "Poor Kev."

Celeste winced at the painful memory of her own love-stricken mistake. That had been five years ago. She'd been older than Kevin appeared to be. All things considered, Kevin's situation had turned out well. His circumspection had prevented real harm from coming to the Touré family. Celeste hadn't been as lucky.

Zeke's right shoulder brushed Celeste as he sat back against his dining room chair. Heat spread across her chest, and up and down her arm. "Kevin may know more than he thinks. She may have let some comment slip that could tell us where she likes to hang out or where she's really from or even where she went to school."

Jerry jumped on that. "I'll follow up with him."

"Thank you." Zeke's impatience once again seemed under control. "In the meantime, Damien Rockwell thinks Art was having financial trouble. Mal, could you dig around to see if that's true? If it is, we need to know what was straining his accounts. Did he owe someone money?"

"I'm on it." Mal typed something into his electronic tablet in front of him.

Celeste shifted to face Zeke. "Meryl didn't say anything about money being tight."

Jerry drummed the fingers of his right hand on the conference table. "Are we sure she's not a suspect?"

Celeste turned to Jerry's computer image. "Didn't we have this conversation yesterday?"

"Hear me out." Jerry raised his right hand, palm out. "What if she and Jayne agreed to kill each other's husband?"

Zeke's thick black eyebrows knitted. "You mean, like the plot of *Strangers on a Train*?"

Jerry jabbed his index finger toward Zeke. "Exactly."

"No." Zeke's tone was final. "Seriously, Jer. Let this one go. There's no *there* there."

Celeste said a prayer that Jerry listened to his brother. "Damien should stay on our suspect list."

"I agree." Zeke finally looked away from her as he considered his brothers' images on the monitor. "Why was he the only guard whose pay was never late?"

Jerry shrugged his uninjured right shoulder. "Maybe he's lying about Art having cash flow issues."

"Or about his deposits never being late," Mal suggested.

Celeste felt a rush of adrenaline. Brainstorming investigations with the Tourés was like running mental sprints. She enjoyed the way the brothers worked their cases together and advanced—or dismissed—ideas and suggestions. She also appreciated being treated as though she'd always been part of their team.

With Nanette, she often felt as though she was doing the heavy lifting on her cases as well as her partner's. Another confirmation that she was making the right decision by remaining in Columbus. As much as she liked her business partner, she didn't want to start fresh with Nanette in San Diego just to continue the same pattern of behavior. She'd rather continue their agency on her own.

"We need to set up our next interview." Zeke's statement was a call to wrap their meeting.

Jerry tapped a command into the laptop with Mal's help. "Next up is May Ramirez. I've just sent both of you a copy of the background report on her. Mal and I have already gone over it. May's close to retirement. She's divorced. She has four children, two grandchildren and perfect credit. After being fired from BBS, she took a job as a security guard at the Deep Discount Mart in Dublin. Her work contact information's in the report."

Zeke was already uploading the file onto his smart tablet. "Great work. Thanks."

"And with one arm. Thank you." Celeste exchanged a teasing smile with Jerry before printing the file from her laptop. She heard the faint hum of the printer in her office upstairs.

Jerry grinned. "Don't mention it."

Mal's fingers danced across his tablet. "Jer and I are working on the final two guards: Agnes Short and Chad Cooper. Agnes is retired and remarried. She and her new husband recently moved to North Carolina. You can take her, Jer."

Jerry leaned closer to Mal's tablet. "Her being out of town doesn't clear her, though. She could be working with Kev's ex, Anne Castle."

Mal inclined his head toward his screen. "So could Chad Cooper. His prison sentence started in June, two months *before* Art's murder."

Zeke stared across the dining room, as though the resolution to their case was written on the far wall. "They'd both have perfect alibis if we hadn't stumbled across the Mystery Woman."

"We didn't stumble. That was solid investigative work." Celeste rolled her eyes. "I'm more than just a sparkling personality."

Zeke's grin banished the lines of fatigue from his chiseled features—and dazzled Celeste. "You're right, of course. Please forgive me."

Celeste was pretty sure he was mocking her. She ignored him. "To your point, the Mystery Woman could be working with any of our suspects. Or all of them."

Jerry shook his head in disbelief. "So instead of reducing our list of suspects, we've actually added to it?"

"It seems like it." Celeste shrugged. "We'll interview Agnes and Chad but prioritize the two suspects who are local and not in jail." She stood. "I'll ask May if we could meet with her this afternoon. We need to keep up the momentum of our interviews."

The sooner they completed these interviews, the sooner they could solve this case. Hopefully. Then Zeke would be safe—and so would her heart.

"LUNCH IS READY." Celeste spoke from the doorway of her home office Monday afternoon. "I also got a hold of May Ramirez. We're meeting her at four."

Her words pulled Zeke from the draft of his business plan. He'd been building out charts, notes and calculations since he and Celeste had ended their videoconference with Mal and Jerry almost two hours ago.

He stood and stretched, finally registering the aromas of spicy chicken soup with fresh vegetables, including onions, tomatoes and peppers. "I'm sorry. I meant to help cook. I lost track of time."

Celeste waved a hand toward the stacks of printouts beside his laptop. "What are you working on?"

He flexed his shoulders to ease their stiffness. "Updates to TSG's business plan."

Celeste turned to lead him downstairs. "It looks like you're struggling with it."

Zeke followed her into the dining room. She'd set the blond-wood dining table. Lunch was served on matching brown-and-white cotton crocheted table mats. Both settings contained a medium-sized cream porcelain bowl filled with chicken-vegetable soup, a smaller matching bowl of garden salad and a clear acrylic glass of lemonade.

"I *am* struggling." Zeke held her chair before circling the table to his seat. "This looks and smells wonderful. Thank you so much. If you don't mind my using your kitchen, I can cook dinner. It's not fair that you do all the cooking."

On the center of the table, three vanilla votive candles stood to the right and three more to the left of a large, round brown-tinted glass bowl filled with vanilla potpourri. The bowl was centered on another brown-and-white cotton crocheted table mat.

"I don't mind your using my kitchen at all. I'd like to try your cooking." Celeste tossed him a teasing smile as she spread a brown napkin on her lap. "What's your specialty dish?"

"That would be my blackened chicken with asparagus spears." Zeke dug into his salad. It was a meal by itself. Celeste had filled it with baby spinach, cucumbers, celery, carrots, raisins, mushrooms, onions, and cheddar and mozzarella cheeses. He appreciated a salad that was more than a bowl of lonely iceberg lettuce.

They talked about the entrees they enjoyed cooking, their comfort foods, favorite restaurants and go-to desserts. Time flew. Zeke felt himself relaxing, as he always did in her company. And this time she didn't dodge his questions. If they'd talked about cooking during their coffee date, could they have worked up to more personal questions over lunch? He'd never know. Anyway, that was in the past. Whether they had a future was up to Celeste.

Collecting her place setting, Celeste turned toward the kitchen. "I understand what you're going through with your business plan. Those things are the worst."

Zeke stacked his dishes and followed her. "It would be easier if I weren't worried about these threats against my family."

"It also would be easier if you weren't doing it on your own." Celeste looked at him over her shoulder. "There *are* three of you, you know. Why don't you let your brothers help?"

He set his dishes on the counter near the dishwasher, then returned to the dining room to continue clearing the table. "We're equal partners, but I've been the de facto director since our parents died."

Celeste was silent for a beat or two. "You and your brothers expanded your marketing beyond the small companies that have been your agency's bread and butter. You're reaching out to medium and large businesses."

"That's right." Zeke shrugged his shoulders, trying to ease his sudden tension. He carried the pitcher of lemonade to the fridge. "I'm worried about industry trends. We need to be proactive, anticipating changes, instead of reactive."

Celeste's expression was thoughtful as she loaded the dishwasher. What was she thinking? "You've been getting a lot of press lately, too, because of the high-profile cases you've been involved in." Her grin was sheepish. "I've been a little jealous."

A smile replaced his frown. "Is that right?"

"A little bit." She lifted her left hand, measuring perhaps half an inch with her index finger and thumb. "But my point is, aren't the marketing changes you've made and the press you've been getting enough? At least for now? Do you think it's a good idea to add a lot of new services at the same time?"

"We've got to try something." Zeke closed the refrigerator door and clenched his fist around its handle.

"What does that mean?" She straightened to look at him. Her voice was brittle with concern. "What's going on, Zeke?"

Zeke released his grip on the refrigerator. He pinched the bridge of his nose. "I told you I took the lead on the operating decisions for TSG."

"And?" She finished packing the dishwasher.

Shame swamped him. "My decisions haven't always been strategic. In fact, a couple of them have been pretty stupid and have hurt the company."

"Hurt the company?" Celeste stilled, frowning at him in disbelief. "What are you talking about? TSG is solid. It has a great reputation, not just in the security industry but in the business community as a whole."

"Maybe from the outside looking in." Zeke blew out a breath. "We're running the agency. We're paying our bills on time. We're making payroll for our contractors. But we haven't paid ourselves in months." He risked a look at Celeste. Her expression of surprise made him clench his teeth.

"Well, that won't continue for much longer." Celeste spread her hands. "You've been getting so many calls you've had to hire an office assistant for the first time in TSG's history."

Zeke moved the soup pot from the stove to the sink and filled it with water. "How did you know that was the reason we hired Kevin?"

"I'm an investigator, remember?" She arched an eyebrow and looked at him from under her long, thick eyelashes. "I can add two and two and get to four. Why else would you hire an admin when your thirty-year-old agency has never had one before?"

Her indignant tone made him smile. "I apologize. I didn't mean to offend you."

"Apology accepted." Celeste inclined her head.

Zeke finished scrubbing the pot, then rinsed it. Steam rose from the faucet. "Do you really think I'm a control freak?" He braced himself for her answer.

"You're with me because you don't want your brothers taking care of you." She leaned against the kitchen counter and crossed her arms under her chest. "You're beating yourself up over business decisions your brothers must have approved. So yes, I think you're a control freak. You think so, too, otherwise you wouldn't be asking."

Zeke couldn't deny a word of what she'd said. "What's wrong with my wanting to keep my brothers safe?" He placed the pot on the drainboard.

Celeste straightened from the counter and circled him. She took the pot from the drainboard and dried it with a dish towel she'd taken from a hook near the stove. "I'm confident things will get better soon for you and your brothers."

"I hope so." He dried his hands with a paper towel from the roll suspended above the counter. "I've been thinking about what Damien Rockwell said about Art and Buckeye Bailey. TSG's finances are on shaky ground. I can see myself in Art's position. One bad decision, one lost client could damage our company. I've got to find a way to stabilize our finances."

"You can't compare TSG to Buckeye Bailey." Celeste bent to return the pot to the lower cupboard. "Your agencies are very different. You provide annual training to your contractors and hold them to a higher standard. I don't mean to speak ill of the dead, but Art was well-known for cutting corners."

Zeke wanted to hold on to her encouraging words with both fists. But she didn't have the full picture. "We're still paying off debt from the cabin construction. It was originally intended as a secluded vacation spot for high-profile clients who wanted their privacy. We aren't getting as much use out of it as I'd hoped."

"At least you're able to pay it off." Celeste propped herself against the refrigerator. "You and your brothers will figure it out. Take a breath and step back. The answer's probably right in front of you. Right now you're just too busy to see it."

The tension in his neck and shoulders untangled. The way she listened to his concerns soothed him. Her reassurances encouraged him. But it was the expression in her wide hazel eyes that drew him to her. She believed in him even as he doubted himself. Before he realized it, he'd drawn Celeste into his arms and lowered his lips to hers.

Chapter Nine

Celeste's breath caught in her throat. She'd seen the light in Zeke's coal-black eyes shift. She'd felt the air between them sizzle. Yet his kiss surprised her. In a good way. A very good way, like waking from a wonderful dream and realizing you hadn't been asleep.

She leaned into him, deepening their kiss. Zeke's arms wrapped around her waist, drawing her even closer. Her muscles trembled. Her mind blanked. She parted her lips on a sigh. Zeke's tongue pressed against them, urging her to open wider, then swooping in. He teased and caressed her, tasting her and allowing her to sample him. Celeste mimicked his actions. Zeke groaned in response. His large hands slid down her back and cupped her hips to his. Celeste melted. Her blood heated. She raised up on her toes to fit herself more closely to him. She wanted more. She wanted now.

She wanted him.

Her cell phone screamed. Celeste flinched. Her eyes sprang open. They locked with Zeke's. The heat in their dark depths set her body on fire. Her cell sounded again. Its vibration was trapped between her right derriere and Zeke's left hand.

"You should get that." The pulse pounding in her ears muffled Zeke's voice. He released her hips. His warm, rough palms moved over her arms, drawing her hands from his shoulders. "It could be related to the case."

Before she could stop him, he'd turned from her and strode out of the kitchen.

Darn it.

Celeste pulled her phone from the back pocket of her black jeans. She checked the caller ID. It was Nanette, the human prophylactic. "What's going on?"

"I thought you were ignoring me." Her partner sounded confused.

"I couldn't even if I'd wanted to." *And I had.*

"You don't sound happy to hear from me." Her voice betrayed her pout.

If only you knew. Her abdominal muscles tightened with residual yearning. "It's this case. I've got a lot on my mind." *Like the way Zeke tasted on my tongue.*

"Oh. How's it going?" Nanette seemed distracted.

Was she counting the RSVPs to her wedding reception? Reviewing the menu options? Checking her seating plan? Whatever Nanette was doing, Celeste knew her partner wasn't interested in her murder investigation, so why had she called?

"We're checking leads, but what do you need?" Celeste stopped in front of the bay window in her living room.

She scanned her surroundings through its sheer curtains. Her neighborhood didn't have sidewalks, and the narrow two-way street in front of her home didn't invite cars to linger. In other words, it wasn't a hospitable surveillance environment for serial killers. But she wasn't taking any of that for granted with Zeke's safety at stake. She craned her neck west and east. Any pedestrians nearby? Cars moving slowly? Items displaced on her walkway? No, no and no. The tension in her shoulders eased a bit. Celeste refocused on Nanette's voice.

"Have you reconsidered moving to San Diego with me?"

Beneath Nanette's voice, papers rustled and tape dispensers screeched.

"You mean you *and* Warren?" Celeste spun on her bare heel and strode through her living room, dining room and foyer.

"Of course that's what I mean. We're getting married."

Celeste's patience was straining. "And I've already told you I'm not moving to San Diego."

Earlier, she'd opened the venetian blinds over the tinted glass of the French doors that led onto her rear deck. Both her ten-by-six-foot oak deck and her yard, which stretched beyond the structure, were empty. *Good.*

"But I'd really like you with me." Nanette's voice bordered on a whine. "We make a good team. Won't you reconsider?"

Celeste scanned as far as she could see beyond her yard. "Nanette, I'm investigating a serial killer, remember? The person I'm protecting is another target. I don't have time to think about anything else, including your wedding." *Or the way Zeke's body felt pressed against mine.*

Nanette's heavy sigh trudged down the satellite connection. "I know you're on a case, CeCe—"

"Please don't call me that." Celeste had been making the same request for six years. Another example of her partner not listening to her.

Nanette continued. "You're always on a case, but my whole life is on hold until you make your decision. I won't know what I'm going to do until you know what you're going to do."

Celeste tucked her left thumb into her front jeans pocket and drummed her fingers against her hip. How was Nanette's life on hold? She was on the cusp of a new journey with someone she loved to distraction. They were planning their wedding and relocation. If anything, her life was moving at warp speed.

"I've already made my decision. You don't want to accept

it." Satisfied that her backyard was secure, Celeste paced back to her living room.

Nanette exhaled. The frustration in the sound was thick enough to cut with a knife. "How could you not want to move to San Diego? It's a bigger market than Columbus. We could be even more successful there."

"I don't want to start over." Irritation tightened Celeste's grip on her phone. "Take me off your to-do list. You have enough going on with your wedding and your move."

Nanette was still talking. "I do have a lot going on, including worrying about launching another investigative agency all by myself. It would really be a big help if I knew I could count on you."

And there it was: the real reason Nanette wanted her to move to San Diego. She wanted Celeste to do the heavy lifting with the business launch the same way she'd done the bulk of the work opening Jarrett & Nichols Investigations in Columbus.

Celeste stilled. She wasn't alone in the living room any longer. Zeke was behind her. His steps were almost silent on the stairs. She turned. Zeke had changed into a lightweight gunmetal-gray suit, pale blue shirt and dark blue tie. In a moment of insecurity, Celeste wondered whether she should change her jeans and blouse. She decided against it.

Holding Zeke's eyes, Celeste responded to Nanette. "You'll be fine. I have confidence in you. You should have confidence in yourself."

"But, CeCe—"

"*Please* don't call me that." Celeste checked her watch. She and Zeke needed to leave now if they were going to meet May Ramirez at the Deep Discount Mart on time.

"—how can I concentrate on my wedding or relocation or new house when I don't know what's going to happen to me?"

She turned her back to Zeke to clear her mind. "Nanette,

you and Warren are going to live happily ever after in San Diego. It doesn't matter whether I join you. I've got to go. I have a meeting."

"I really, really want you with me in San Diego." Nanette sounded like an overtired child. "It's not as though you have anything or anyone keeping you here."

That may be true, but it still hurt to hear. "Goodbye, Nanette."

Her business partner tsked. "When will your case be over?"

Celeste started. "Are you serious right now? As soon as the *serial killer* gives us their timeline, I'll share it with you. Bye." She ended their call and turned back to Zeke where he stood on the stairs. His shoulder was propped against the wall. "Sorry about that. Are you ready to go?"

Zeke straightened. "Are you leaving Columbus?" His voice was quiet and devoid of inflection.

Why did she want to hide from his question? Celeste briefly closed her eyes. Because that question made her remember she didn't have a home. She had a house she loved, a business she was proud of and a community she wanted to serve. But where was home for her? Where was the community that stood with her when she was in trouble? Where were the people who didn't want anything more than friendship from her? She'd been asking those questions her entire life.

Celeste grabbed her knapsack from the closet beside her front door. Her movements were impatient, like her mood. She spoke with her back to Zeke. "My business partner, Nanette Nichols, is getting married."

Zeke interrupted. "Are you in the wedding?"

Celeste frowned at him over her shoulder. "Why are you asking?"

A ghost of a smile played around his lips. "I noticed a

torn page from a magazine in your inbox. It had a picture of a purple bridesmaid dress."

"Yeah." Celeste shivered and turned away to close the closet door. "Nanette asked me to be a bridesmaid. I declined. I'm pretty sure she was trying to fix me up with another one of Warren's friends."

"Warren's her fiancé?"

"Yes." Celeste dug out her car keys from a compartment in her knapsack. "He accepted a promotion to a position in San Diego. Nanette wants our business to relocate there."

"What do *you* want?" Zeke's deep, bluesy voice soothed her fraying nerves. His seemingly sincere interest in her answer eased her tension.

"I'm staying in Columbus." She lifted her knapsack onto her left shoulder. "Nanette's having trouble accepting that."

Zeke descended the stairs. "What's preventing you from moving to San Diego?"

Celeste stilled. It was weird—in a good way—to have someone ask her that question, as opposed to hearing Nanette's repeated assertion that she didn't have anything keeping her here. She hadn't realized before how lonely and alone hearing that made her feel.

She took a moment to consider her response. "I suppose it's the lesser of two evils. I'm not looking forward to running the agency by myself. But I don't want to uproot my life and move across the country, either."

"I wouldn't want to do that, either." Zeke stopped at the base of the staircase. "Are there other reasons you've decided to stay here?"

Was it her imagination, or was he fishing for something? She searched his eyes for the answer to that question. Either Zeke Touré had a really good poker face or his question didn't have any hidden agenda. "Like what?"

"That's what I was wondering." Zeke crossed his arms. "Where does your family live?"

Celeste stiffened. "I told you. I'm from Chicago."

Zeke inclined his head. "I remember. But what about your family?"

This confiding thing was even harder than she'd thought. "My paternal grandmother raised me. She and her family are in Chicago. We aren't close." He could probably hear that in her voice. "My mother died in childbirth."

"I'm so sorry." Zeke's tone was thick with empathy.

"Thank you. I'm named after her." She'd never confided that to anyone before. She shoved her fists into the front pockets of her jeans.

He broke the short, tense silence. "Thank you for sharing that with me."

Celeste stretched her shoulders to release some of her tension. "I've lived in Columbus for more than a decade. I don't have family here, but I have a home I love, places I enjoy visiting and professional networks that help me with my business."

"And there are plenty of people who'd miss you if you left."

Celeste realized her snort of disbelief was less than gracious. "Like who?" *You?* Her toes curled in her loafers as she remembered their kiss.

Zeke held her eyes, raising her body's temperature. "Plenty of people. Eriq, for one. You're like a daughter to him. My brothers, Symone, Grace and I enjoyed working with you on The Bishop Foundation case."

He enjoyed working with her. Seriously? She so wanted to challenge him on that. *What about that kiss, Zeke? Do you remember sliding your tongue into my mouth? I sure do.*

But she couldn't summon the nerve. "I enjoyed working with you, too." She checked her watch again. "We'd better get going. We don't want to keep Ms. Ramirez waiting."

"It helped me to talk with you about TSG's business plan." Zeke crossed to the door that led to Celeste's attached two-car garage and held it open for her. "I'm happy to be your sounding board about your future plans for your agency."

"I may take you up on that." Celeste entered the garage, breathing in Zeke's soap-and-sandalwood scent as she passed him.

She didn't have the courage to admit it—not even to herself—but Zeke was one of the reasons she was staying in Columbus. As pathetic as it might sound, she wanted to be part of his life. A colleague in their adjacent industries. A partner on future cases.

And after that kiss…well, perhaps the door hadn't been completely closed on something more.

"I HAVE NEVER been late to work. Not a single day in my *life*." May Ramirez shook a small, angry finger at Zeke and Celeste. Her petite body trembled in her gray-and-orange Deep Discount Mart security uniform. "And I've *never, ever* slept on the job. But I was fired because *other* people did. How is that fair?"

"It's not." Zeke's response was reflexive. He hadn't meant to say anything. But the tiny woman was an imposing figure.

He cradled a disposable cup of coffee between his palms as he sat with Celeste and May in the discount store's mini coffee shop late Monday afternoon. The three matching small, circular blond-wood tables near them were empty. That, and the cacophony of sounds from the customers, clerks and pop music playing over the audio system provided cover for their meeting.

Zeke had offered to buy the refreshments. He and Celeste had chosen small coffees. May was on her lunch break. She'd ordered a sandwich combo with chips and an allegedly fresh apple turnover for dessert. According to their background check, May was in her midsixties, but she looked much younger. Her tan features were smooth, and her thick, simple bob was still a glossy dark brown.

As he lowered his coffee to the table, Zeke's right arm brushed against Celeste's where it rested on the table beside him. She scooted her chair farther away, giving him more room. "You're still angry about being let go from Buckeye Bailey Security even though the separation occurred almost two months ago."

A blush darkened May's cheeks. She straightened on the hard plastic cream chair as though trying to appear taller than her five foot one-or-two inches. "Of course I'm still angry. I'll be angry for the rest of my *life*. I was fired because the guards on other shifts were unprofessional. Why was *I* punished for *their* bad behavior?" The older woman took another bite of her roast beef sandwich.

Celeste sipped her coffee. "You think Art Bailey fired *you* because of what other guards did?"

"I don't *think* it. I *know* it." May's cherubic features were strained. Even her hair seemed to vibrate with tension. "Art told me I should've told him the other guards were coming in late, leaving early and sleeping on the job. Why would I do that? I'm not their supervisor. We didn't even work the same shift."

Zeke frowned. Had he heard correctly? "Art only assigned one guard to each shift? Since when?" The security industry's general rule of thumb called for one guard for every one hundred people. Archer Family Realty employed between one hundred and fifty to two hundred people.

May's bowed lips tightened. "That's right. It was another one of his brilliant cost-saving ideas." Her sarcasm was hard to miss.

A memory played across Zeke's mind like a movie trailer. Years ago, Buckeye Bailey Security had surprised the corporate-security industry by reducing his staff to one guard per shift at each of their contracted locations. This had occurred while Zeke's parents had still been alive. They'd commented to him and his brothers that they thought this was a bad idea.

And it had been. Art had laid off a number of guards, and several more had quit. His company also had lost a few clients. Those were the reasons his parents had believed Art had gone back to staffing two guards per shift. Now one of his former guards was telling them that Art had once again reduced his shift staff. How much financial trouble had the other business owner been in, and why?

Zeke tried digging a little deeper. "We understand Buckeye Bailey had trouble making payroll. Did you have that experience or know anyone who did?"

May snorted. "No. Art paid garbage to begin with. If he'd stiffed me even once, I would've left. The job wasn't that great. I mean, the hours were good, and the work wasn't demanding. But I could've gotten another job." She spread her arms, indicating the discount store. "I got this one."

Zeke exchanged a curious look with Celeste. Damien Rockwell, the first guard they'd spoken with, made the payroll problem seem like a regular thing, although he admitted he'd never had a problem with his paycheck. According to May, there weren't any payroll issues at all. Why would either guard lie?

May gestured toward Zeke. "You know, I considered applying for a job with TSG. You guys have a good rep, and you pay well."

"Why didn't you?" He genuinely wanted to know.

May wrinkled her nose and shook her head. "You have that physical fitness test, and your contractors have to know CPR and basic first aid. That's too much."

Celeste gestured toward May with her paper coffee cup. "Do you keep in touch with any of the other guards from Buckeye Bailey?"

May's eyes widened with surprise. "No. Why would I?"

Celeste shrugged her slender shoulders under her scoop-necked black cotton blouse. "Curiosity. Spite."

"I like you." May's features relaxed into a smile that transformed her appearance. She looked younger and more approachable. Celeste blinked at the other woman's response. May split a look between Zeke and Celeste before continuing. "I did hear Chad Cooper's in prison. I could've predicted that. He had the weekend hours and filled in during the week when other guards called off. I don't know how he got a job in security in the first place."

Celeste's straight eyebrows knitted. "Why do you say that?"

May shook her head and expelled another breath. "He's one scary guy, and he hangs out with scary people. I mean, is that the kind of person you want representing you to your clients? What was Art thinking?"

Zeke recalled the mug shot Mal had provided with his preliminary file on Chad. He could understand why May would describe him as "scary." His Buckeye Bailey personnel file indicated he was in his early twenties, but his scowl made him look much older. He had a bony, square face framed by a wealth of dirty-blond tresses that grew past his shoulders. But his ice blue eyes, with their dead, flat stare, had left the strongest impression on Zeke.

"Do you know why he was arrested?" Zeke finished his coffee.

May checked the time on her cell phone. "I heard he got drunk and got into a fight. I told you, he and his friends are really scary, like they'd kill you as soon as look at you."

Celeste moved her coffee cup aside and folded her forearms on the table. Her shoulder brushed Zeke's upper arm. She shifted her chair farther away. "What was Chad like to work with?"

"Angry and lazy." May looked uneasy, as though the memory of Chad was disturbing. "Like I said, I didn't see him often. He was a floater and a weekender. But I remember he acted like he was untouchable, like he could do whatever and would never lose his job." She snorted. "Once he had the nerve to ask me for money. Can you believe it? Of course, I said no."

Zeke's eyebrows lifted. He was equal parts surprised and impressed. "You weren't afraid of him?"

May scowled. "Of course I was afraid, but I know people like that. You give them money one time, they'll keep coming. It's like a slow death. If he was going to kill me over money, it would be better for him to do it quickly and get it over with."

His surprise faded, leaving him only impressed. May seemed to be more courageous than she thought.

"Do you remember where you were August 22?" Celeste's question cut through the brief silence. Had she meant for it to be jarring?

May's thin eyebrows stretched toward her bangs. "That was three weeks ago. Do you remember where *you* were?"

Celeste spread her hands. "Zeke and I are working with the police to investigate Art Bailey's and Dean Archer's murders."

"What?" May jumped as though her exclamation startled even her. She looked around the mini dining area. They were still the only customers. She lowered her voice to a stage whisper. "*Murdered?* I'd heard Art committed suicide at the end of August and Dean Archer died of a heart attack. What was it? Two weeks ago?"

"It's been ten days." Zeke mentally shrugged. Whether it had been fourteen days or ten, the family wouldn't have closure until the killer was brought to justice. "Where were you Friday, August 22, May?" He considered the petite woman as he waited for her answer. How could she have forced Art into his car? Did she own a weapon?

"I was here." May waved a hand around the store. "I work noon to nine, remember? And I didn't know where Art lived until I read his obituary."

Zeke looked at Celeste. He could tell they were thinking the same thing. They'd need to verify May's alibi with her supervisor. He'd ask Eriq and his partner, Taylor Stenhardt, to follow up on that. But based on this interview, May Ramirez had moved to the bottom of their suspect list.

He turned back to the former guard. "May, have you received any anonymous messages—either letters, emails or phone calls?"

"No, I don't think so." May shook her head, still seeming to search her memories. She stiffened. Her eyes leaped between Zeke and Celeste. "Wait. Are you saying *I* could be in danger? Why would anyone kill me? What have *I* done?"

Celeste waved her hands in front of her. "If you haven't received any messages yet, you're probably in the clear—"

May scowled. "That doesn't sound as encouraging as you seem to think."

Celeste held the other woman's eyes. "You're probably in the clear, but stay vigilant."

Crossing her arms under her chest, May leaned back against her chair. "Well, thank you for letting me know there might be a threat out there with my name on it."

Zeke unzipped his black faux-leather portfolio. He pulled out the sketch of their Mystery Woman and turned it toward May. "Do you recognize this person?"

May leaned into the table for a closer look at the image. Her hands were flat on the table, as though she didn't want to get her prints on the paper. After a few seconds of silent scrutiny, she responded, drawing out each word. "No, I don't think I've seen her before." She pulled her eyes from the sketch and pinned Zeke with a look. "Is she the killer?"

Zeke returned the sketch to his portfolio. "We believe she's connected to Art's and Dean's murders." *And the threat against me and, possibly, my brothers.* He drew out a generic Touré Security Group business card and gave it to May. "If you think of anything else that could help identify Art's and Dean's killer, or if you have any concerns about your safety, please call us." He stood, holding the back of Celeste's chair as she rose to stand with him. "Thank you again for your time and insights, May."

"Thanks." Celeste nodded at May before turning toward the store's exit.

Zeke matched his pace to her shorter but fast steps. He lowered his voice. "We need to find the source of Art's financial problems and how they're connected to Dean and TSG."

And they needed the answer sooner rather than later. His brothers' safety depended on it.

Chapter Ten

"I'll ask Eriq to verify May's alibi with her supervisor."
Zeke shifted on the smoke gray passenger seat of Celeste's
older black sedan to look at her as they drove out of Deep
Discount Mart's parking lot Monday evening.

"May doesn't seem like a strong suspect, but we need to
look under the surface." Celeste braked at the parking lot
exit to check traffic.

Zeke leaned forward to get a better look at the congestion.
Rush hour was in full swing. Time seemed to stand still before they were able to exit onto the street.

Zeke relaxed against the cushioned bucket seating. Like
his SUV, Celeste's sedan was spotless. The carpeting was
vacuumed. The dashboard and console were dusted. The
windows were clear. And the interior smelled like vanilla
and citrus. He drew a deeper breath.

Zeke's eyes traced the clean line of Celeste's elegant profile. "I think it's time to interview Chad Cooper and Agnes
Letby. We've agreed either or both could be working with the
Mystery Woman, which means they could be part of these
murders even though she's out of state and he's in prison."

"That's true." Celeste checked her rearview and side mirrors. Her words came slowly, as though she was considering
her response. "One or both of them could have planned the

murders, then told the Mystery Woman what to do—who to make contact with, how to kill Art and Dean, and when. You know, I'm really getting tired of referring to her as the 'Mystery Woman.' I hope we get an ID on her soon."

Had Chad or Agnes also told their Mystery Woman who to get close to in his world, and how and when to kill him and his brothers? No matter how many times Celeste, Mal and Jerry told him his brothers weren't the target, Zeke couldn't get past the fact that TSG was a family-owned company. The three of them were a unit.

He forced those dark thoughts from his mind. "Both May and Damien said they'd seen Chad's temper. And we know he has financial troubles because he asked May for money."

"His money issues must be pretty bad if he's asking co-workers like May for a loan." Celeste brought her car to a stop at the traffic light before the Ohio State Route 315 North on-ramp. "May said they barely knew each other. He must have been pretty desperate to ask her for money."

Celeste studied her side and rearview mirrors again before returning her attention to the traffic light. Was she avoiding making eye contact with him? "If his situation was already desperate, Chad could have lost his temper over being fired."

Imprisonment during the time of the murders was usually an airtight alibi for homicide suspects. But the addition of this unknown person and her connection to the murders raised doubts about Chad's and Agnes's alibis. Based on information from Damien and May, Chad's motive could be money. And both former guards referenced Chad's temper. But the fact she'd retired and remarried seemed to indicate Agnes had moved on with her life. Was that her attempt at misdirection? Could she still be harboring a grudge against Dean and Art?

"He has a history of striking out when he's angry." The traffic light turned green. Celeste eased the car forward toward the state route on-ramp. "His arrest record shows a pattern of assaults, but we don't have any examples of his being involved in homicides."

"Point taken." Zeke inclined his head. "I still don't think we should rule him out. And despite his repeated arrests, he hasn't learned to control his temper. It's not hard to imagine his crimes escalating."

Celeste checked her blind spot before merging onto the state route. "I'm not ruling him out. It's just Chad's record shows he's an impulse guy. I can see him more as the kind to beat up Art when Art fired him. I don't see him as taking a year to plot multiple elaborate murders. Do you?"

Zeke considered her words. Her arguments were solid, but he couldn't give up on his theory of Chad as a viable suspect.

"You've made good points. Here are a few of mine." He counted each on his fingers. "Chad is our only suspect with a criminal record. His financial problems give him the strongest motive. He has a temper. And, according to May, he has 'scary' associates."

"All right. I'll arrange a meeting with Chad." Celeste retrieved a pair of large sunglasses from the compartment above her rearview mirror. She put them on without taking her eyes from the road, then once again changed lanes. She positioned her sun visor to cover the top half of her side window.

The sunlight wasn't that bright.

She sped past two cars before working her way back into the middle lane. She studied her rearview and side mirrors again. This time, her scrutiny was even longer. She was staring at those mirrors like they were crystal balls and she needed to read her future. Straightening on his seat, Zeke faced forward. He searched his passenger-side mirror.

"We're being followed?" He already knew the answer.

There was no other explanation for her erratic driving and the tension snapping in the space between them.

"Yes." Celeste was grim.

Zeke clenched his teeth. "Our cover's been blown."

OUR COVER'S BEEN BLOWN.

Celeste sat straighter in her seat. She'd come to that same conclusion. The navy blue SUV had pulled in behind them from a side street several blocks before the entrance to Ohio State Route 315. Maybe it was a coincidence that it had merged onto the route also. But the hairs on the back of her neck disagreed. And they were never wrong.

The driver wasn't trying to be inconspicuous. Either they wanted her to notice them shadowing her in the middle lane or this was their first tail. Celeste didn't believe the driver had firearms. This wasn't a John Wick movie. It was more likely that they were driving close because they wanted to get a good look at her. She hoped her sunglasses and sun visor would prevent that.

"What's the plan?" Zeke's voice was deep and tense.

Adrenaline pumped into her system. The pulse at the base of her throat was leading the stampede. Most people had a fight-or-flight response to danger. Her response had always been fight-or-fight-harder.

Celeste tightened her grip on the steering wheel. "Text Eriq. Have him and Taylor meet us at the substation on Red River Road. That's where we'll lead our stalker."

Zeke started texting before Celeste had finished speaking. "Done."

"Great. Now I'll describe the car for you. We'll give the description to Eriq and Taylor. Tell me when you're ready." She waited for Zeke to launch a clean page on his smart phone's Notepad app.

"Ready," he prompted her.

Celeste squinted at her rearview mirror. "Navy blue Ford

Expedition. Older than 2020. And the license plate is H-R-
S, maybe eight, one, maybe three, four. No distinguishing
stickers or marks." *Darn!* "But it has the name of the rental
company on the plate's frame." She gave it to him.

"Eriq and Taylor are on their way to the substation." Zeke
tapped his cell phone screen. "You must really know cars to
be able to estimate their model years."

Celeste looked over her shoulder to make sure the right
lane was clear before moving into it. "No, but I'm familiar
with the Ohio law that states after 2020, cars no longer need
front license plates. Since it has a front plate, it must be 2020
or older. Our stalker just switched lanes."

From the corner of her eye, she noticed Zeke clench both
fists. As someone used to being in control, it must be frus-
trating to be a passenger while they were being tailed.

"Can you make out the driver?" His voice was tight.

Celeste was glad he wasn't turning around to look himself. She didn't want the tail to see him or have further confirmation Zeke was her passenger.

In reflex, Celeste glanced at the rearview mirror. "I can't
make out the driver. He or she is wearing a ballcap and
sunglasses. It could be our Mystery Woman. Or it could be
someone I ticked off in traffic and this is a road rage incident."

"I think you'd be able to tell the difference." His tone
was dry.

Celeste took the Henderson Road exit off the 315 North
and turned toward the substation a few miles away. "The
driver couldn't possibly think we haven't spotted them."

Zeke grunted. "I think they want us to see them. They're
probably trying to intimidate us."

"Why?" Celeste glanced at him before returning her attention to the traffic. "So we could stop trying to identify
them and instead wait docilely for them to kill you? As if."
A rush of fear formed a lump in her throat.

Frequent glances in her rearview mirror assured her the SUV continued to shadow them as they wound their way through the northeast Columbus neighborhoods. Traffic was snarled with commuters impatient to make their way home. The SUV stayed with them through every stop light, intersection and turn until they got to the substation.

Celeste turned into the asphalt parking lot in front of the police substation, then glanced in her rearview mirror. "The SUV's moved on." She pulled into a space on the left side of the visitor's lot close to the substation's entrance, then put the car in Park. Spaces for law enforcement vehicles were in the rear. "Let's wait for Eriq and Taylor inside. Hurry."

Zeke climbed out of the vehicle and waited for her. "We're going to have to leave your car behind since they've identified it. I can't figure out how, though."

Celeste walked with him to the substation. She had no trouble ditching her car if it would help ensure Zeke's safety. "Our stalker knows we're investigating the case. The question is, how did they know we'd be interviewing May this afternoon?"

The police substation was a square, three-story redbrick-and-tinted-glass building. It smelled of old carpeting, burnt coffee and stale doughnuts. It had taken years for Celeste to enter a police building—any police building—without being triggered by memories of the betrayals that had caused her to give up her career in law enforcement.

She'd loved being a police officer and then a detective. Her role allowed her to ensure justice for neighbors who'd been wronged. Her childhood experiences gave her a greater dedication to protect her community from bullies and other threats to their safety. But those dreams ended in heartbreak when He Who Would *Never* Be Named had used her, framing her for his corruption and turning the department—her found family—against her.

Those memories shook her, causing Celeste to stumble

on the stairs as though someone had once again pulled the rug from beneath her feet.

Zeke caught her arm with catlike reflexes, keeping her from stumbling. "Are you all right?"

Celeste was mesmerized by the concern darkening his eyes. She blinked, breaking her trance. "Yes. Thank you." She offered him a weak smile, hoping to dispel the doubts she read in his expression.

She strode through the substation's glass door as Zeke held it open for her. Celeste squared her shoulders as she shoved the poisonous memories of the past back into the far corners of her mind. At the desk, she gave their names to the officer on duty and explained they were waiting for Eriq and Taylor. While they waited, Zeke updated Mal and Jerry via text. Based on the way his cell lit up, it was safe to say his brothers were more than a little concerned.

Zeke pinched the bridge of his nose. "*This* is the reason I hesitated to update them. Even though I told them we're meeting with Eriq and Taylor, they act like I can't handle myself."

Celeste gave a bark of startled laughter. "Look who's talking. You're the dictionary definition of an overprotective older brother."

Was that a blush of embarrassment darkening his chiseled cheeks? Celeste's heart melted a little.

Fortunately for Zeke, Eriq and Taylor strode into the substation in time to save the eldest Touré from coming up with a defense.

"CJ!" Eriq wrapped her in a bear hug that eased her final knots of tension and lifted her from the floor. "It's been way too long."

Celeste laughed as she hugged him back. "We had lunch last week, crazy man."

The older detective was a father figure to her. That was

the reason he was the only person in her life allowed to give her a nickname.

"You work too hard." Eriq stepped back and turned to Zeke. He gave the younger man a firm handshake and squeezed his shoulder. "It's good to see you, Zeke."

Taylor's greeting was warm, though more subdued. "It's good to see both of you are safe. We hope it stays that way."

"Absolutely." Eriq turned to lead them into the bullpen. "Let's get a meeting room. We've checked up on Jerry a couple of times. Sounds like he's on the mend. Thank goodness." He stood aside near the doorway of a closet-sized conference room toward the front of the bullpen.

Taylor led Celeste, Zeke and Eriq into the cramped space. The scent of burnt coffee and stale pastries followed them in. A midsize rectangular table dominated the room. The dark gray conference phone in the center of its smooth blondwood surface reminded Celeste of a Star Wars Wing Fighter. Six matching chairs surrounded it, two on each side and one at each end. Thin pale gray wall-to-wall carpeting—the same carpeting that ran through the bullpen—muted their footsteps. Black-framed photos of the mayor of Columbus, division of police leadership and police headquarters downtown seemed intended to bring color and dignity to the dingy surroundings. They didn't.

Circling the table, Taylor took one of the two chairs on the right. "Zeke, you texted us about the tail."

Zeke sat beside Celeste on the left side of the room and pulled out his cell phone. "Celeste gave me a partial description of the SUV." He read from his notes.

Taylor jotted down the characteristics of the navy blue Ford Expedition, including the estimated year and partial license plate. "Good job, Celeste." She stood and crossed to the door. "I'll run this through the system and see what we get. Be right back."

Celeste watched Taylor disappear beyond the threshold, leaving the door open. She wanted to will the detective to come back with good news. The sooner they found the stalker, the sooner Zeke would be safe. But it didn't work that way. She forced her muscles to relax. While they waited for Taylor, Celeste and Zeke filled Eriq in on their impressions of their first two security guard suspects, Damien Rockwell and May Ramirez.

After listening to their summaries and observations, Eriq sat back on his blond-wood chair. "Do you think one of them could have been tailing you?"

Zeke crossed his arms over his chest. "I don't know how. May went back to work after she met with us. And how could Damien have known where we'd be this afternoon? Celeste made the appointment with May only a few hours ago."

Reading the question in Zeke's dark eyes, Celeste shook her head. "We weren't followed to Deep Discount Mart. But if someone knew we were investigating the case, they'd know we were going to interview May. They just wouldn't know when."

Eriq nodded. "And our Mystery Woman is unaccounted for. She could have had May under surveillance, waiting for the two of you to show up."

Taylor returned in time to hear Eriq's response. "She's not a mystery anymore." She set two printouts on the conference table. The first was a copy of a driver's license. The other was Zeke's sketch of the anonymous woman. "Look familiar?"

Zeke leaned forward, brushing his right arm against Celeste's left shoulder. She was beginning to think he was doing such things on purpose.

He drew both printouts closer. "She's a definite match." He looked at Celeste. "What do you think?"

She nodded. "Absolutely."

Taylor glowed with satisfaction. "Meet Monica Ward.

She rented the Expedition when she came into town from North Carolina."

"North Carolina?" A memory stirred in the back of Celeste's mind. "Isn't that where the retired guard, Agnes Letby, lives?"

Eriq grumbled. "Along with about eleven million other people, but it's a good start."

"A very good start." Celeste picked up the sheet of paper and studied the driver's license image. "Who are you working with, Monica, and what's your connection to this case?"

"OUR MYSTERY WOMAN has a name—Monica Ward." Zeke felt a surge of satisfaction in being able to share that information with his brothers. They were one step closer to keeping his family and Celeste safe. "Taylor was able to identify her using Celeste's description of her rental car."

Zeke, Celeste, Eriq and Taylor had called the Touré Security Group from the police substation's meeting room early Monday evening.

"Impressive." Jerry's praise was stuffed with excitement. "And, Celeste, quick thinking taking Zeke to the substation. We knew you were the right person to watch our brother's back."

Mal's response was less enthusiastic. "This feels like a trap."

"And there's Mr. Buzzkill." Jerry's tone was dry.

Mal continued as though Jerry hadn't interrupted him. "Why would Monica Ward get close enough to be identified?"

Zeke glanced around the table. Across from him, Eriq and Taylor frowned at the phone, deep in thought. Beside him, Celeste returned his regard as though waiting for his response. Zeke felt himself being pulled into her hazel eyes. He broke their contact.

"Mal has a point." Zeke focused on the phone, imagining his brothers sitting together in their company's conference room. "Celeste noticed Monica wasn't trying to remain undetected."

Celeste leaned closer to the conference phone. "It was obvious from the beginning she was following us."

"That just means she doesn't have experience tailing someone." Jerry's response was a verbal shrug.

Celeste looked at Eriq seated across the table from her and shook her head. "It was more than that, Jerry. She wanted us to know she was there."

"She's taunting you." Mal's voice was grim. "She's tired of trying to flush you out. She wants you to come after her instead."

Zeke's eyes widened. "You may be onto something."

"Well, you two aren't going to do that." Taylor inclined her head toward her partner seated beside her. "Eriq and I will track down Monica Ward. I've already put out a BOLO for her and her car. We'll let you know when we bring her in for questioning."

Be On the Look Out. Celeste nodded, folding her arms on the table in front of her. "Hopefully soon. The sooner we bring her in, the sooner Zeke will be safe."

Zeke looked at her in surprise. It felt strange having someone other than family voice their concern for his safety. Usually, people expected him to take care of them as well as himself. It felt odd—in a good way—to have someone so invested in his well-being.

He swallowed to ease the dryness in his throat. "I'm not the only one in danger. Let us—Eriq, Taylor, my brothers and me—handle the case from here. The threat level has surged. I don't want you caught in the middle of this. *We* don't want you in the middle of this."

Zeke ignored Eriq's snort of derision, Taylor's sigh and the snickers coming through the phone.

"Excuse me?" Celeste's eyebrows jumped up her forehead.

Zeke glanced at Eriq and Taylor. They seemed almost pitying of the situation he'd created for himself. No help there. He returned his attention to Celeste. "Celeste, I've put not only my family but you in danger. I'd feel better if you left us to investigate this case without you."

Celeste shifted on her chair to better face him. She tapped her right index finger with her left one. "First, I've been in law enforcement for almost ten years. I was a homicide detective before becoming a private investigator." She tapped her right middle finger. "Second, this is *my* case. Meryl Bailey hired *me* to find her husband's killer. I'm not walking away." She tapped her ring finger. "And third, *I* invited *you* to this questionable party to keep you safe when *I* deduced that you were the killer's next target. You're welcome."

Zeke started to argue, but the expression in her eyes gave him second thoughts. "All right. Points taken. And thank you."

Celeste still seemed to be bristling. "Besides, Monica Ward already knows about me. Just as I was taking down her license plate, I'm sure she was taking mine. If she has my plate, she has my address."

"We need to move you." Mal's voice came over the phone. "Both of you."

"We'll go to the safe house." The idea of staying alone in the secluded cabin in the middle of the woodland resorts with Celeste Jarrett put his body on a slow burn.

"Good." Mal's approval was short and to the point. "Jerry and I will get a couple of burner cells and clean laptops to you. They'll be waiting for you at the resort's main office."

"That's a good idea," Jerry said. "The system will alert you if you're being tracked."

"It's going to be tricky getting you to this safe house." Taylor jerked her head toward Zeke and Celeste on the other side of the table. "Monica could be waiting for you to leave the substation."

"I've got a plan for that." Celeste's words sparked a battle between hope and dread in Zeke.

He shifted on his seat to face her. "What are you thinking?"

Celeste gave him one of her rare smiles, the one that touched her eyes. "I'm putting out a call for disguises."

Zeke sighed. Dread overpowered hope.

Chapter Eleven

"Should I put your Halloween costumes back in the storage closet?" Nanette steered her BMW coupe into the left-turn lane onto Morse Road. She was taking Celeste to the car-rental center Monday evening.

"They're not Halloween costumes. They're disguises." This wasn't the first or even fifth time she'd explained that to Nanette. The fact she'd bought most of these outfits from Halloween costume stores notwithstanding. "And no, thanks. I'll take the trunk with me."

In response to Celeste's call, Nanette had paused her wedding planning to deliver Celeste's second-hand green-and-brown trunk to the substation. The oversize luggage was outfitted with wheels and a handle and was stuffed with a myriad of disguises. Not costumes. Despite the variety, Zeke had proven to be a difficult customer. Most of the outfits were sized for Celeste's smaller frame. Zeke was built like a professional football tight end. In addition, he didn't have any imagination when it came to undercover disguises.

Zeke hadn't even entertained her "wealthy Texan" idea. He'd responded with a flat stare when she'd explained a successful disguise was both subtle and unexpected. His preference had been a fedora, fake sideburns and mirrored sunglasses. *Boring!*

He'd borrowed Eriq's tan blazer to distract from his clothing. Celeste shook off her exasperation. In the end, all that mattered was that Zeke's appearance was sufficiently altered to enable them to move him to safety. His outfit—although unimaginative—had accomplished that.

Celeste had used the "wealthy Texan" disguise herself. Why waste a good idea? She'd changed into a man's wine red shirt, black bolo tie and gray suit coat. She'd stuffed her hair under a silver Stetson, added lifts to her oversize black boots and hid behind silver-rimmed sunglasses. Presto chango, she hoped. Celeste had walked out of the substation's front entrance with Nanette. She wore the Stetson and sunglasses even in her partner's bright red Beemer. Zeke and Taylor had exited through the rear, where Taylor's police-issued vehicle was waiting. The detective was taking Zeke to the car-rental company, where Celeste would meet him.

Touré Security Group had had a corporate account with the rental company for years. An account with a rental-car company, a safe house at a cabin resort… Those were things she hadn't even considered aspiring to for her business. She couldn't fathom why Zeke would think his family's agency wasn't doing well.

Nanette kept her eyes on the traffic signal, waiting for the left-turn arrow. "What are you going to do about your car? It's still at the substation's visitors' parking lot, right?"

"Eriq's taking it back to headquarters." Celeste knew Nanette understood she was referring to the police headquarters off Marconi Street in downtown Columbus.

Nanette snorted. "I wonder what Monica Ward will make of that."

"*If* she's still waiting for Zeke and me." Celeste abruptly shifted topics. "Could you lend me some clothes to wear while I'm at the safe house?" She studied the passenger-side mirror. She didn't think they were being followed.

It wouldn't be hard to tail Nanette. Celeste was half convinced she could do it on foot. Her partner's bright red

BMW stuck out in traffic. She also drove like a snail. Celeste glanced at her from the corner of her eyes. She suspected Nanette drove slowly so people could admire the way she looked behind the wheel. In fairness, she looked great, but they were on the clock. Celeste checked her watch. It was already after six.

"Of course." Nanette bounced with excitement. "You know I don't wear black, right? I embrace *all* the bright colors. But no problem. I'll have the suitcase delivered to the safe house." Nanette pulled forward as the turn light activated. "Where is it?"

"You know I can't tell you that." Celeste knew her business partner didn't have any black items in her wardrobe other than the obligatory little black dress. But then, beggars couldn't be choosers. She adjusted her Stetson and sunglasses. "The fewer people who know where we are, the safer we'll be. Have the courier take it to TSG. And thank you. I promise to be careful with your belongings."

"I know you will." Nanette turned left onto High Street. "But come on, now. Do you think the killer will track me down and torture me to find out where you are or something?"

"This is serious, Nanette." Celeste shifted on the soft silver-and-black leather seat to face her partner's profile. "We aren't keeping tabs on an unfaithful spouse or tracking leads in some white-collar crime. Two people have already died under suspicious circumstances, and a third has been threatened." Celeste faced forward. "If you have an emergency, call or email me. But only in an emergency, Nanette. Please don't call me to talk about your wedding or your move. Okay?"

Nanette's sigh was sharp with impatience. "Celeste, I wouldn't have to call you if you'd hurry up and answer my questions."

"What questions?" Celeste was equally impatient.

"For example, what about your plus-one for my wedding?" Nanette stopped at a red traffic light. She gave Celeste a sly smile. "Are you and Zeke back on?"

Celeste unclenched her teeth. "I told you, I'm coming alone."

She checked the side mirror again. She didn't detect any suspicious activity. The killer probably wouldn't expect her to be traveling in a flashy bright red car.

"Urgh! You're so stubborn." The traffic signal turned green. Nanette guided her car across the intersection. Slowly. "What about San Diego?" The words seemed to have been dragged from her, as though she worried they would trigger Celeste.

They did.

"Really, Nanette?" She shifted on the passenger seat again. "Now? I just told you a serial killer followed Zeke and me to the substation. But you want me to set that aside and plan the rest of my life for you? Right now?"

Nanette scowled. "I know, Celeste. And I'm sorry. But I'm worried about my financial future. I love Warren and I'm so proud of him. He earned this promotion. But what about *me*? What am *I* supposed to do?"

Celeste took a deep breath, then exhaled. She heard the panic in Nanette's voice. She could almost taste her fear. "Nanette, you and I started our own private investigation agency. You can do it again on your own in San Diego. You're a good businessperson and a great investigator. You'll be fine."

"But I want you to start the agency with me." A slight whine entered her voice.

Translation: *Nanette wants me to handle all the paperwork and promotion needed to launch the business, just as I did in Columbus.*

"And I told you, I'm happy here in Columbus."

"But there's nothing keeping you here."

An image of Zeke slipped into her mind, but Celeste remained silent. Fortunately, Nanette didn't push the issue.

Pulling into the turn lane, her partner waited for a break in traffic before guiding her BMW into the car-rental company's parking lot. Celeste surveyed their surroundings for anything suspicious or seemingly out of place. Nanette snagged a space near the nondescript building and put her vehicle in Park.

Celeste looked at her in surprise. "What are you doing?"

Nanette's thin eyebrows knitted. "I want the man you'll be staying with for heaven knows how long to meet me. That way, he'll think twice if he has any ideas of foul play because he'll know at least one person will be coming after him."

Celeste paused. That was kind of sweet. With a mental shrug, she climbed out of the coupe and crossed briskly into the one-story smoke-glass-and-silver-metal structure. She sensed Nanette following close behind her. Celeste pushed through the glass entrance and spotted Zeke waiting for her toward the back of the customer service waiting area. He was still wearing the fedora and fake sideburns, but he no longer had Eriq's tan blazer. He must have given it to Taylor to return to her partner.

She stilled as Zeke removed his mirrored sunglasses. His eyes swept over her as though making sure she was unharmed. Celeste nervously adjusted the Stetson and pushed her dark sunglasses higher up the bridge of her nose.

Zeke's attention shifted to Nanette behind her before he recaptured her eyes. "Everything all right?" His deep, bluesy voice wrapped around her.

"Yes, everything's fine." She sounded breathless. Celeste stopped a little more than an arm's length from him. "Nanette Nichols, Hezekiah Touré."

Nanette offered him her right hand. "You're even more attractive in real life. Why did you and Celeste stop dating?"

Oh. My. Goodness.

Celeste froze. She could feel the blood rushing into her cheeks. She tapped the floor with her left foot, hoping it would trigger the ground to open up and swallow her. It didn't.

She pivoted to her partner. "Thank you for your help, Nanette. You can leave now."

Nanette held on to Zeke's hand. "Are you free the first Saturday in December?"

Zeke glanced at Celeste before turning back to Nanette. "What's happening the first Saturday in December?"

Nanette beamed at him, still holding his hand hostage. "I'm getting married. You—"

"Nanette." Celeste's voice was a low hiss. "There's a serial killer after us. Please leave. *Now.* We'll talk later."

Her partner scowled at her. "I'm going to hold you to that." She released Zeke's hand and stepped back. "Take good care of my girl." She turned on her heels and disappeared through the front door.

Celeste saw the car fob in Zeke's large right hand. "Let's go. And this time, you can drive."

She marched toward the rear exit without looking at him. As she pushed through the door that led to the rental-car parking lot, she sensed Zeke's confusion but gave thanks for his silence. If she expended a bit more effort, she might be able to forget the humiliation her soon-to-be former partner had visited upon her and focus on keeping Zeke alive.

THE SAFE HOUSE rose from a fantasy. Celeste's eyes widened as she took in the two-story log cabin. The dark-pine-and-red-cedar post-and-beam structure glowed in the waning sun as Zeke approached its attached garage Monday evening. It stood among the evergreen pines and ancient oak trees toward the back of the sprawling resort owned by one of Touré Security Group's long-time clients.

Celeste had first learned of it when she'd helped the Touré

brothers on The Bishop Foundation case a couple of months ago. She'd heard the notes of relief and pride that they'd had the facility in which to secure Symone Bishop, the nonprofit organization's chair.

Touré Security Group guards protected the resort's buildings and grounds. To the west and south, sturdy, old oak and evergreen trees sheltered the cabin from a distance. Craning her neck, Celeste thought she spied a hiking trail in the distance. Ah, it would be such a pleasure to jog that trail. A healthy, active river provided additional protection to the east. The nearest cabin was perhaps five miles north of them.

Zeke activated the garage door opener he'd received from the front desk—along with one set of keys, she'd noticed. What was that about? Was it his way of making sure they never left each other's side? He didn't have to worry about that. Until she was convinced he was safe, she was going to stick to him like gum on his shoe.

The heavy red-cedar door rose slowly as Zeke crept the car forward. He put the dark gray sedan in Park and pulled the emergency brake before giving her a wry half smile. "I haven't been here since Jerry and Symone used it. But I've been told it's in good shape."

That was intriguing. What had he expected? "Are you saying one of the Touré men isn't perfect?"

Zeke gave a startled bark of laughter. "We're all far from perfect."

Celeste's eyes moved over Zeke's shoulders, back and hips as he climbed out of the sedan.

There was at least one Touré who was pretty close to perfect in her book.

Zeke unlocked the breezeway door that connected the garage to the cabin. To the left was the dark pine entry door and straight ahead was the cabin's great room. The space was decorated in muted tones: warm tan, soft brown and moss green. A stone fireplace stood in the front of the room. The pine flooring gleamed. Beneath the cedar-wood coffee table, an area rug picked up the room's accent colors. A matching overstuffed brown sofa and two chairs with ottomans surrounded the table. A dining room was set at the edge of the great room with a kitchenette beyond it. Both areas continued the great room's colors. The whole cabin smelled of cedar pine.

Symone had mentioned during more than one videoconference how beautiful the cabin was. Seeing it for herself was something else. Celeste felt her tension ebbing. She sensed Zeke relaxing little by little as well. This would be a great spot for a long weekend vacation. For now, with a killer after them, there was only so much relaxing they could do. It helped to have a space in which she could take a breath and think clearly, though.

Zeke's voice broke into her thoughts. "Which would you prefer to do first: make dinner or take the tour?"

She continuing to admire her surroundings. "The tour."

Zeke nodded, crossing to the stairs. "Hopefully, our clothes will arrive soon."

He'd asked Mal to lend him clothes just as Celeste had asked Nanette to pack her a bag. They weren't willing to take the chance that Monica Ward hadn't found Celeste's home address yet. The delay in receiving luggage was a small price to pay for safety.

Celeste mounted the staircase behind Zeke, momentarily distracted by the sight of his flexing glutes. She clenched her hands to keep from reaching out. Squaring her shoulders, she took a deep breath and inhaled his warm soap-and-sandalwood scent. It was going to be a long stay at the resort.

"This cabin is basically one big panic room," Zeke said over his shoulder. Celeste heard pride as well as wariness in his tone. "We set up security cameras around the cabin's perimeter and in the trees closest to the grounds. All the windows are covered with a tint sheet. We can see out, but if anyone's skulking outside, they can't see in. Of course, we shouldn't go outside. And Mal will include a clean laptop and cell phone for both of us when he sends over our luggage." He stopped at the top step and turned to face her. "You know the rules. No personal devices while we're in hiding at the safe house."

Celeste looked up and felt herself being drawn into his coal-black eyes. She forced herself to blink, turning her attention away. "I've got it." The sooner they located Monica Ward and identified whoever she was working with, the sooner they could leave the safe house and get back to normal life. That's what she wanted.

Wasn't it?

At the top-floor landing, Celeste counted four rooms.

Zeke turned to his right. "We use this room as the operations office. The computers here manage the security systems. I'll show you how it works later." He stepped toward the next room. "I'll sleep here. It's closest to the stairs."

Celeste crossed the room's threshold. It wasn't a big space, but it was clean and comfortable. It had the same soothing decor as the rooms downstairs. A patterned coverlet in moss green and soft brown covered the queen-size bed. It matched the area rugs that surrounded it. An ornate cedar carving of a landscape had been placed on the snow-white wall behind the bed above the headboard. The bed frame, nightstand and dressing table were made of the same wood. Celeste changed direction and wandered to the bed across the room. She trailed her fingertips over the coverlet. The cotton material was soft.

She stopped in front of one of the tinted windows and assessed the cabin's layout in relation to this room. It was closest to the stairs, meaning it was closest to any potential danger. In operational terms, this was the space in which the protector would set up in the interest of shielding the protectee. Zeke appeared to have forgotten which one of them held which role.

She turned to confront him. "Since you're the killer's target, I should take this room."

Zeke stepped back into the hallway as though distancing himself from her words. He must know she was right. "No, I'll show you to your room."

Okay. Enough was enough.

Celeste straightened to her full height, which was six inches shorter than his. She squared her shoulders and pushed her fists into the front pockets of her black jeans. She took a calming breath, filling her lungs with the cedar-scented air. "Let's get something straight, Zeke. *You* are the one who needs protection. *I* am your bodyguard. I'm more than qualified for the role. I was on the force for six years. I've broken up riots, disarmed attackers, arrested murderers. I've proven I'm capable of taking care of myself and others. If you're not prepared to let me do my job, then what am I here for, Zeke? Your entertainment?"

She held his eyes as he absorbed her words. She sensed the turmoil in him as he considered her challenge. He'd been raised to protect those who couldn't protect themselves. Celeste admired that. But he needed to remember she wasn't in that category. Like Zeke—and like Zeke's mother—Celeste had been trained to protect herself and others. She was *not* going to let him get away with treating her like she needed saving.

Finally, he nodded his acquiescence. The motion was jerky with reluctance. "You're right. This will be your room. I'll take the one down the hall."

Celeste relaxed and followed him to the room in question. It was almost identical to hers. The patterned coverlet on the queen-size bed and the area rugs that surrounded it were warm tan and moss green. The intricate cedar carving above the headboard depicted maple leaves that seemed to be floating on an autumn breeze.

Zeke turned, nudging his chin toward the door behind them. "There's only one bathroom."

Celeste flashed a grin. "You must be thrilled to have your own room again. And to be sleeping in a bed. You get your privacy back."

Zeke grinned. "You weren't such a bad roommate. You were neat and quiet. I'd still like to know how you were able to leave every morning without waking me."

"I'm sure you would." Celeste arched an eyebrow and moved toward the stairs. "I'm hungry."

That was one way to change the subject. The sound of Zeke's footsteps behind her reassured Celeste that he was willing to follow her lead—at least for now.

"How did you know TSG would need a safe house? Do you have a crystal ball?" Celeste posed the question after dinner Monday night.

Zeke stood in front of the sink, scrubbing a skillet. Memories of their meal were kept alive by the aroma of the blackened chicken and garden salad that lingered in the air and danced on his taste buds.

A few chuckles rolled past his lips in self-deprecating humor. "I wish we did have a crystal ball. I could use one right now. I certainly could've used it a year ago." He pitched his voice above the sound of the running water. "As I mentioned, we'd originally planned to offer it to high-profile clients and their families who needed to disappear from the media for a while. We have a couple of guards on retainer who maintain the cabin and its grounds at a moment's notice, including stocking groceries. They're discreet. My brothers and I regularly come out to check on it."

"Does it get a lot of use?" Celeste added the final dishes and silverware to the dishwasher.

"Not as much as we'd hoped." Zeke winced as he dried one of the pans. His stomach muscles clenched as he thought of how much money they'd sunk into this unicorn—and how little return they'd had on their investment. An example of his mismanagement of their company's money. "On the one hand, you want high-profile clients to know the space is available. On the other hand, publicity would compromise its security."

"I see your point." Celeste took the dishcloth from him to continue drying the pans and trays as he returned the items to their cabinets. "But it's been a good investment. Twice now, you've been fortunate enough to have it to keep someone safe, this time yourself."

"I guess." Talking about the safe house always made him tense. Zeke wouldn't add using the cabin for his own protection to their company's profit column.

"Don't sound so gloomy." Celeste turned to lead them into the great room. "It's not as though people can walk onto the resort from the street. There's security, including your own guards. If you promote it only to your exclusive clients, this safe house will pay for itself in time."

"Why hadn't I thought of that?" She'd given him hope.

"Sometimes you have to let go of control and ask for input." Celeste threw up her hands. "You should get a hobby."

Zeke gaped at her back as he followed her into the great room. "Have you been speaking with my brothers? They've started nagging me about my lack of social life."

Celeste snorted as she curled into the far end of the overstuffed brown sofa. "I wouldn't do that to you. I don't like it when Nanette meddles in my personal life."

Zeke settled onto the other end of the sofa. "Nanette's taken it to another level. Did you know she was going to ask me to be your date for her wedding?" Although it wouldn't take any persuasion.

"No, I did not." Celeste briefly covered her face with her

hands. "How embarrassing was that? You'd think after all these years, I'd be used to her doing that, but I'm not."

"Does she try to fix you up a lot?" Zeke didn't like the sound of that.

"Yes." Celeste sighed. "I've told her a million times I don't need a date for her wedding. I can make my way to the church and reception with GPS."

Zeke was uncomfortable with the sense of relief he felt that she wasn't bringing a date. He covered it with a smile. "At least Mal and Jerry aren't trying to set me up."

"Yet." Celeste lifted her right index finger. "Trust me. That'll be their next step." She let her hand fall back onto the sofa.

He hoped she was mistaken. "So you declined to be in the wedding party because of the dress?" Zeke tried to imagine her in the fussy lavender gown. He couldn't. "I've never seen you in anything other than black pants or jeans."

Celeste didn't move, but Zeke sensed her stiffen. The warmth in her eyes cooled just a bit. "Wearing black clothing usually allows me to blend into the environment. People tend to overlook me."

That would be impossible. No one could overlook Celeste Jarrett. She was a presence that was hard to miss. He didn't correct her, though. Zeke was too surprised by the personal information she'd shared with him. That was the second time she'd shared something so intimate about herself. It gave him hope that maybe she would let him past the walls she hid behind and allow him to get close to her.

Zeke set those hopes aside for now. "Will you take on a new partner when Nanette moves to San Diego?"

"I don't know yet." Celeste stood and wandered across the room to the cold fireplace. "I think I'd like to run the agency by myself for a while." She turned back to him. A wisp of a smile curved her full heart-shaped lips. "Taking on a partner is a big decision, and I don't make big decisions lightly."

Zeke nodded his understanding. She'd already made the big decision of remaining in Columbus. He'd take that win and the opportunity to build on it.

Chapter Twelve

Jogging indoors had felt weird. Celeste preferred to run outside, rain or shine, hot or cold. But Zeke was right. Even on the relative safety of the wooded resort grounds, they should remain indoors as much as possible. They couldn't risk bumping into someone they might know. A couple of innocent, casual conversations later, their cover could be blown.

Their luggage had arrived last night. Celeste had insisted on going with Zeke to get their bags from the resort's management office. Even though they were staying in the Touré Security Group safe house, she was still his bodyguard. The thought may not sit well with him, but facts were facts.

Judging by Zeke's reaction, Mal had packed well. He'd seemed pleased with the clothing, shoes and toiletries his brother had loaned him.

The jury was still out on Nanette. Her business partner had been very generous in providing her with outfits and other items to get through the next few days. Celeste really appreciated her generosity. But after she'd pulled out the bright business casual clothing and bold exercise wear, she'd found sheer baby doll nightgowns, barely there lingerie and booty shorts. In September. Nanette's message was loud and clear. Her friend might as well have labeled the bags *Attire to Help You Get Your Groove Back*. The last thing Celeste remembered was a cherry red thong. She'd decided it would be best to keep washing her sensible undergarments.

This morning, moving around undetected in a strange environment had been a challenge. But Celeste had had eighteen years of growing up with her paternal grandmother, Dionne, to develop her technique and another thirteen years to perfect it. Zeke hadn't found her in the exercise room—otherwise known as the basement—until after she'd run a mile on the treadmill, proving she still had mad ninja skills. She'd completed her five-mile run while he'd worked the strength-training machines. Then they'd switched places. The camaraderie had been nice, with easy conversation and laughter. It had continued as they shared breakfast, adding a few accidental—maybe on purpose—touches. Very nice. But for the past hour plus, she and Zeke had been closeted in their separate bedrooms, working.

A chord sounded from the clean laptop Mal had provided to her, indicating a new email had entered her Jarrett & Nichols Investigations account. The notification jarred her out of those enjoyable morning memories. Seated at the little pinewood desk centered between the two windows on her bedroom's far wall, Celeste checked her messages. Her eyebrows stretched upward in surprise. The sender was someone she hadn't seen or thought of in years, Sterling Jarrett. Her biological father.

The only thing Sterling had given her was life. After her mother had died in childbirth, he'd dumped the day-old Celeste with his mother and walked away. Correction: he'd also given her the obligatory annual visits on her birthday and Christmas, taking time away from his new family. What a guy. Celeste wondered again what kind of person had her mother been to have wanted anything to do with someone like Sterling?

His email's subject heading read, "Important Message about Your Grandmother." Celeste narrowed her eyes. Why was Sterling contacting her about Dionne? Her muscles were weighted with reluctance as she pressed the keys to open the email. His salutation caused a wave of nausea to wash over her.

My dearest daughter, It's been a long time. Please call me. I need to discuss your grandmother. With affection, Dad.

Affection? What was he up to?

Despite her aversion to any contact with him, she felt a fission of concern. What was wrong with Dionne?

Celeste grabbed her clean burner phone from the desk and tapped in the number he'd provided in his email. Her call connected on the second ring.

"Hello?" The sound of Sterling's voice triggered a flood of negative emotions from her childhood and youth.

Celeste braced herself, schooling her voice to be cool and in control. "Hello, Sterling. I got your email."

"Good morning, Celeste. I wish you'd call me 'Dad.'"

Celeste's eyes stretched wide. *Seriously?* She remained silent through the awkward pause.

Sterling continued. His voice was warm and caring. "How are you?"

Celeste went on immediate alert. She lurched out of her chair and paced the room. Her muscles were stiff with tension. She already felt out of sorts. She'd chalked it up to wearing someone else's clothes. Nanette's royal blue knee-length skirt and deep gold blouse were giving her an out-of-body experience.

This rare call from Sterling was making it worse. Celeste hadn't heard from him either by phone, mail or email in almost five years, since he'd sent her an email congratulating her on becoming a homicide detective. The message had read like a form letter. She suspected he'd been directed to send it.

Celeste drew a breath and kept her voice steady. "What can I do for you?"

Sterling cleared his throat. The sound seemed awkward, as though he wasn't comfortable with the distance between them. That was almost laughable since he'd created it. Celeste pressed the phone more tightly against her ear as she turned away from the pinewood dressing table and paced toward her queen-size bed. Through the phone, she heard a male news anchor announcing stock price gains and losses for Tuesday morning.

"Celeste, I'm sorry to tell you this." His voice was muted with grief. "Your grandmother has died."

Dionne was dead?

Celeste dropped onto her bed. She stared blindly across the room through the windows. She'd spoken with the elderly woman less than two weeks ago. Celeste had gotten into the routine of calling Dionne on the first and third Saturday of each month, outside of obligatory calendar dates like the older woman's birthday and holidays. Dionne had sounded tired, but otherwise she was her usual grumpy, negative self. After every call, Celeste wondered why she bothered keeping in touch with the bitter woman. But she knew the reason. She may not have liked Dionne, but she'd been grateful that the elderly woman had taken her in rather than packing her off to a foster home. Other than surprise, Celeste didn't feel anything at the news. Shouldn't she have a sense of loss and grief? Shouldn't she have the same reactions that Meryl Bailey and Jayne Archer were experiencing?

"What happened?" Celeste filled her left fist with the soft cotton green-and-brown coverlet that lay beneath her.

"She had a heart attack." A thin thread of grief made Sterling's words seem heavier.

Celeste had been aware of Dionne's hypertension. The older woman had been managing it all Celeste's life. During each call, Celeste would ask about her health. She'd scheduled semiannual visits so she could take Dionne to her doctors' appointments. Had something unusual happened to trigger the attack?

Or was this investigation getting to her?

"That doesn't sound right." Leaning forward, Celeste rubbed the spot on her forehead between her eyebrows. "She'd been taking her medication and getting regular checkups. When did this happen?"

Sterling paused. "Wednesday."

Celeste jerked upright. It was like she'd been slapped. "Wednesday? As in, almost a week ago?" And Sterling was only telling her now? She tightened her hand on the fistful of the coverlet as though it were someone's throat.

"We've…" Sterling cleared his throat. "There was a lot to take care of."

With an effort, Celeste purged the emotion from her voice. "I'm sorry for your loss. Is there anything else I can do for you?"

A muted knock sounded on his end of the call. Was he at work? "Hold on, Celeste. Come in." His voice became muffled. He must have put his hand over the receiver. A minute or two later, he returned to their call. "It's your loss, too, Celeste."

"Is it?" A trace of bitterness escaped into her tone. She couldn't blame herself too much. She was almost choking on the emotion. "Then why am I the last to find out?"

It hurt to always be the afterthought. Or not to be considered at all. After thirty-one years, you'd think she'd be used to it. But she wasn't. That was one of the reasons Celeste hadn't known how to respond to Zeke's accusation that she'd closed herself off. She hadn't known she was doing that. She wished he'd told her sooner.

Sterling's words broke into her self-reflection. "Mother told me you often called and visited with her. She said you'd sent her birthday and holiday cards." His smile came through the phone. "That's more than my children ever did."

His children. Did he realize *she* was one of his children? Probably not. He'd treated her as an obligation. A charity case. Her stomach muscles clenched at the painful memories. She forced herself to block out the past and focus on this call.

Sterling wasn't telling her anything new. Dionne had complained constantly that Sterling and his children had never called, emailed, or sent her letters or holiday greetings. They didn't seem aware that she had a birth date. The only time they visited was when they wanted something from her. Her tirades weren't meant to praise Celeste for spending time with the older woman. Celeste had the sense Dionne wanted Celeste to commiserate with her. The old woman seemed to forget she'd never given Celeste a greeting card.

She flexed the muscles in her neck and shoulders, hoping to ease her tension. "Is there anything else?"

Sterling's sharp breath echoed in Celeste's ear. "You don't sound upset at the news of your grandmother's passing. You should be grateful to her for raising you."

Wow. How dare he?

Celeste stood from her bed. She strained to keep her voice low. Zeke was working in his room, which was on the other side of the wall from hers. Or was he? Awareness swept down her spine like a warm evening breeze. Without turning toward the door, Celeste knew Zeke stood there, watching her.

She forced the image of him from her mind and struggled to stay focused. "*You* should be grateful as well. If your mother hadn't taken me in, you would've had to raise me yourself." Or perhaps he would've stuck her in foster care. "Her taking me in allowed you to pretend I didn't exist outside of holidays and birthdays." She regretted allowing her father to trigger her temper. She wanted more than anything to end this call. Right. Now.

He drew another audible breath, this time exhaling noisily. His displeasure didn't impress her much. "Your grandmother's funeral will be here in Chicago this weekend."

"Is there anything else?" Celeste's voice cooled.

Sterling's voice heated. "Are you going to attend?"

Celeste had no desire to see Sterling with the family he'd abandoned her for, the family he'd never let her be part of. She'd stopped yearning for relationships with them years ago.

Celeste straightened her spine. "I'm on a case. In fact, I have to get back to work now."

"Are you still a homicide detective, or are you running the place now?" His attempt to sound like a proud father missed the mark by a lot.

Celeste rubbed her eyes with the thumb and two fingers of her left hand. "You never cared about my career before. Why are you asking about it now?" She sensed tension in the silence on the other side of the call.

When Sterling finally spoke, his words were clipped. "Mother's death has reminded me how little time we have. I wasn't there for you as I should have been when you were growing up, but I want to be there for you now. And I want you to meet your siblings."

Was he kidding? She was a successful entrepreneur with a home and good credit. "I don't need you now."

Sterling's sigh was the sound of defeat. "Celeste, you're named in Mother's will."

All the pieces of the puzzle dropped into place: his call, the kind words, his interest in a better relationship with her. Celeste pictured her grandmother's modest home and her few belongings. She didn't think the elderly woman's estate would inspire this newfound paternal interest. Still, she was calling BS.

"Thank you for letting me know." Celeste ended the call. She was more drained now than after her hour-plus workout earlier in the morning. But she couldn't give in to the temptation to rest. There was still one matter to deal with.

She spoke without looking around. "Do you need something?"

HOW DOES SHE do that? How did she know I was here without looking around? And how does she walk around the cabin without my hearing her?

Zeke crossed the threshold into Celeste's bedroom. His steps were hesitant. "I'm sorry, Celeste. I didn't mean to pry. I wanted to ask when you might have time to discuss the case."

"We can talk now." She turned to him.

Celeste stepped forward, swaying a bit as though her legs were trembling. She came to an abrupt stop. Her features were pale and stiff. Zeke sensed her struggle to mask her emotions. His arms ached to wrap around her and offer comfort. She seemed uncertain and vulnerable.

"Are you sure?" He gestured toward the cell phone still in her grip. Her knuckles were white with tension. "Your call sounded upsetting."

Celeste looked at her phone as though she didn't remember she held it. She tossed it onto the bed beside her. "How much of that did you hear?"

Zeke's face warmed with embarrassment. "Most of it. I'm sorry, Celeste. I don't know why I didn't walk away."

That wasn't true. He'd stayed because he'd wanted to learn more about her. And he'd stayed because he'd wanted to comfort her, if he could.

Celeste nodded. Was that a gesture of acceptance? Forgiveness? Or a reflexive response?

"That was Sterling Jarrett. My father." Her eyes drifted to her cell phone. "His mother died. Six days ago."

"I'm very sorry for your loss, Celeste." Why had her father waited so long to tell her of her grandmother's passing?

You know what? Forget it. He couldn't imagine a reason that would justify such a delay. Zeke would've been furious if someone had waited that long to let him know a relative had died.

"Thank you." She wandered the room. Her movements seemed restless and random.

Zeke tracked her steps. "How do you feel?"

"I feel fine. As I've told you, Dionne raised me, but we weren't close." Celeste was breathless, as though she'd been running. "So I don't know why she named me in her will."

"She cared about you." Zeke crossed his arms over his chest and braced his legs. Should he be worried that she was aimlessly wandering her bedroom?

"No, she didn't." Celeste paced in silence for several seconds. "I called her twice a month and visited a couple of times a year." She paused as though trying to catch her breath. "Why did I call her? Why did I keep in touch with her?"

She wasn't asking him, but Zeke answered anyway. "She was your grandmother. You cared about her."

"No, I didn't." Celeste shook her head, emphasizing her point. "I kept in touch with her because she lived alone, and I felt obligated to check on her. The last time we spoke, she accused me of calling to see if she was dead. I told her she was too evil to die. And I meant it. Apparently, I was wrong." She gasped, covering her mouth as if trying to take the words back.

"You were angry and hurt, Celeste." Zeke lowered his arms and stepped to the center of the room. He felt the emotions battering her: shock, anger. Sorrow. "You didn't mean it."

"Yes, I did." Celeste turned her back to him. She brushed a hand across her cheeks, then folded her arms beneath her chest. Her words were tight. "Dionne Jarrett had been hateful to me my whole life. She made me feel like I had to apologize for my existence every day. There were days she made me wish I'd never been born."

Her words were knives impaling his chest. "Celeste—"

"So why does her death make me feel so bad?"

Zeke caught her before she crumbled to the floor. He lowered them both to a seated position on the patterned rug. His back pressed against the foot of the bed. Wrapping her in his arms, he searched for words to comfort her.

"I'm so sorry, Celeste." He whispered the words against her hair. "I'm so sorry she hurt you."

"She made me feel like trash." Her voice was muffled against his chest. "So why do I care that she's dead?"

Her pain was his pain. Zeke swallowed the lump in his throat so he could speak. "Because you care about people, Celeste. That's who you are. It's the reason you went into law enforcement. It's the reason you rushed to the hospital when you heard Jerry had been hurt. It's the reason you volunteered to put your life in danger to protect me."

Celeste tightened her arms around him. She spoke into his chest. "I don't want anything to happen to you."

The intensity in her voice shook him. Zeke stopped breathing. Was she speaking strictly professionally—or did she feel something more? "I don't want anything to happen to you, either." His voice was so rough he didn't recognize it. "You have a big heart, Celeste." Why hadn't he realized that before?

She leaned away from him. Her hazel eyes were wet with tears. With jerky motions, Celeste drew her sterling silver ring from her right thumb and raised it so he could see the infinity circles on the band.

"My mother gave Sterling this ring before I was born." Her voice was a whisper he could barely hear. "It's the only thing I have of hers. Well, I guess it's not hers." She put the ring back on her thumb. "It belongs to him, but my mother bought it for him."

Zeke swallowed the lump in his throat and held her closer. "I'm so sorry." He wished he could think of something more meaningful to say but he felt overwhelmed. She'd already had so much pain in her life. Was this the reason she had trouble letting people get close to her?

Celeste pulled away and pushed herself to her unsteady feet. She resumed her pacing with tentative steps. "Sterling left me with his mother to raise me. Dionne was an angry person. She yelled all the time. All the time. She claimed my mother deliberately got pregnant to force her son to marry her. She'd hated my mother and transferred that hate to me. She hated everything about me, especially how much I reminded her of my mother."

Outrage propelled Zeke to his feet. He was shaking with it. "That was a cruel thing for your grandmother to do. Your parents' relationship had nothing to do with you. You were a child. She should *not* have taken her anger and resentment out on you."

Celeste's eyes were wide with surprise. "I—I appreciate your saying that." She turned away from him and scrubbed her face with her hands. "You've asked me how I was able to get out of my house without your hearing me and about my being able to sense when someone's near me." She faced him again. A faint smile touched her lips, but it didn't reach her eyes. "Those are some of the survival skills I learned growing up with Dionne. If she didn't know I was in her house or if I could tell where she was, then I could avoid her." Her smile spread. "Sometimes, I could go for days without seeing or hearing her. Those were wonderful days."

"I hate that your childhood was so miserable." Zeke clenched his fists at his side. "I wish I could go back in time to do something—anything—to bring you some joy."

Celeste shrugged. "You're bringing me joy now. I know we're on a life-and-death case, but honestly, you've made me laugh and smile more these past three days than I have in years."

Zeke closed the distance between them and drew her into his arms. "Then let me bring you more."

Chapter Thirteen

Zeke lowered his head and pressed his lips to hers. Celeste shook in his arms as though she'd touched an electrical current. He groaned low in his throat and held her more closely. He loved the feel of her body in his arms, the touch of her lips against his. The scent of her. She raised up on her toes. Her body was warm and firm as she pressed herself against him. Zeke's heart began a slow, steady pounding against his chest. He opened his mouth just enough to sweep his tongue across the seam of her lips. Celeste parted for him with a sigh. His heart beat faster.

He swept inside, caressing her tongue with his own. Her arms slid up his torso and over his chest. Her small, soft palms cupped his face as she deepened their kiss. He burned from the inside out. Using his body, Zeke guided Celeste back toward her bed. His fingers fumbled as he tugged his wallet from his front pocket and tossed it onto the mattress. His hands shook as he worked to remove her clothing and coaxed her to take off his. When they were naked, standing in pools of their discarded garments, he stepped back. She was beautiful. Long, toned limbs; full breasts; tight waist and rounded hips. Her skin glowed in the late-morning sunlight leaking through the window blinds.

Celeste raised her right arm and drew her fingertips down his chest to his abdomen. "You're incredible."

Zeke shook his head. He could barely breathe, much less form words. "You're amazing."

Her smile seduced him as she pushed him onto the mattress behind them. She crawled onto the bed, balancing herself on her arms and legs over him. She closed her eyes and parted her lips as she lowered her head to kiss him again. Zeke held her waist, drawing her down to him as he deepened their kiss. Her skin was soft and warm against his palms. She tasted like peppermint and smelled like vanilla and citrus.

Zeke smoothed his hands down her sides and cupped her hips, pressing her against him. Celeste gasped at his touch. He drank in the sound, enjoying the feel of her against him. Her full breasts pressed to his chest. Her long legs tangled with his. He sent his tongue deeper into her mouth, mimicking the way he wanted to bury himself inside her. Celeste drew him even deeper. She rocked her hips against his. Zeke heard his blood rushing in his head. He felt his heart thundering against his chest. Or was it hers?

Celeste freed her mouth from his. She whispered against his neck. "You're making my head spin."

"You're making me burn." Zeke rolled them onto their sides. Drawing her back against his torso, he spooned behind her. He pressed his right knee between her thighs. "Part your legs for me, sweetheart."

Zeke paused, sensing her desire—and confusion.

CELESTE'S SKIN WAS WARM. Fires burned across her breasts, within her belly and between her legs. Zeke trailed kisses down the side of her neck.

His voice, deep and seductive, whispered in her ear. "Part your legs for me, sweetheart." His right knee pressed against her legs, parting her thighs.

This was unexpected. "Zeke, I—"

He lowered his knee and wrapped his arms around her.

He drew her closer to him. He nibbled, licked and kissed the curve of her neck. His hand caressed her thigh, her torso, her breasts. Long, slow strokes that fueled the fire inside her until Celeste thought she'd explode. Her hips rocked back against his, her body pleading for him.

Zeke whispered against the shell of her ear. "Do you want me, Celeste?"

"Yes. Oh yes." She gasped for air.

"Do you trust me?"

"Yes," she sighed.

"Part your legs for me, sweetheart."

Celeste raised her right leg. He pressed his knees between hers. Zeke slid his right hand across her hips and between her thighs to touch her there.

"Zeke." She moaned low and long. His fingers moved over her. Sweat broke out on her skin.

"I'm here." His voice was husky. "Let me hold you, sweetheart." His left hand caressed her breast as his right hand cast a spell.

His moved against her, matching her rhythm as her body took control. He trailed kisses down the back of her neck and across her shoulder. She shivered against him, and he held her tighter.

"Zeke." Celeste's movements became more desperate. She strained against him. "I can't."

"Yes, sweetheart, you can." He breathed the words against her ear. Her nipples pebbled against his palm. Zeke squeezed her breast gently. "I'm right here."

Celeste felt her tension building, tightening her muscles to a breaking point. The pressure was centered between her legs. She writhed and strained against Zeke's magic fingers as he coaxed awake a desire she thought was in a permanent coma. His other hand was molding her right breast, stroking and teasing her. Strange sounds came from her: raw groans, deep moans, thin whimpers. Her body burned and melted under his touch. Her thighs quivered. Her muscles trembled. Her pressure built and drew tighter, and tighter, and tighter. And then she erupted. Zeke held her. He kissed her shoulder and neck as wave after wave of pleasure crashed over her.

Celeste lay back with her eyes closed. She drew a deep breath and collected her scattered thoughts. Opening her eyes, she took Zeke's wallet. She turned her head and caught his eyes. They were dark and heavy with desire.

She gave him his wallet and a smile. "Want to join me this time?"

He pulled a condom from his wallet. "Very much so."

Celeste took the packet before he could open it. "Let me."

She straddled his thighs. Her body still hummed with arousal. She held his erection and stroked her tongue over its length. His deep, broken groan stoked her desire further. Celeste fitted the condom onto him, then took him into her. With one strong move, he slid into her moisture. Zeke lifted his hips, driving himself even deeper inside her. Celeste gasped, rocking her hips forward. She arched her back as she moved with him. His thrusts filled her, stroking the embers of her passion into another inferno of need. He lowered his hands and grasped her hips, moving her on him as he pressed against her. Celeste could feel the perspiration covering her body.

"Roll with me, sweetheart." Zeke wrapped one arm around her. He rose up, then tucked her under him.

His body was a delicious weight on her. Celeste wrapped her legs around his hips and pressed herself harder against him. Zeke kissed her shoulders, nibbled her neck, teased her nipples. He covered her mouth with his. He rocked with her, kissing her deeply, endlessly. Celeste floated weightless on a wave of desire. Her legs strained as he pressed against her. Her back arched as he cupped her hips. Her blood rushed in her head. Her heart thundered in her chest. Her breath came in short, sharp gasps. Her muscles drew tighter and tighter. Then he touched her. Her body snapped. Celeste tightened her arms and legs around Zeke as he stiffened above her. Their bodies shook against each other as together, they soared over the edge.

CELESTE DRIFTED UP to consciousness. She was so relaxed. More relaxed than she could remember ever feeling. A steady beat like a heavy tapping echoed in her head. What was that? What time was it? What day was it?

Where was she?

Stretching her arms and legs, she drew a deep breath, filling her head with the clean scent of soap and sandal-wood. The tapping sped up, sounding more like a locomotive. The warmth seeping into her bones came from the warm, muscled, naked body beneath her. She opened her eyes and found herself staring across the broad expanse of Zeke's chest. She was snuggled against his left side. His arm was wrapped around her with his hand cupping her hip. Her left thigh lay across his narrow hips. Her palm rested over his heart close to her cheek.

Her body vibrated. Her skin burned. It all came back to her. It was Tuesday afternoon. She was in bed with Zeke in his cabin safe house. And they'd just made love. Her fin-gertips combed through the short hairs sprinkled across his chest.

Zeke's low, sleepy voice echoed in her ear. "Am I for-given?"

"For what?" Celeste was aware they were lying above the sheets of his bed, naked. There was nowhere to hide. She gingerly removed her thigh from his hips.

Celeste had never felt this way before. Her heart ballooned in her chest. It struggled to contain its flood of emotions: joy, hope, excitement and something more that she didn't have the courage to identify. Yet. Were these feelings a result of the powerful physical connection they'd just shared? Or were they real? Did Zeke feel them, too?

Please let him feel them, too.

"For eavesdropping on your conversation with your father." Zeke opened his eyes. His voice sped up as though he wanted to share everything on his mind before she interrupted him. "It was inexcusable. I know I shouldn't have done it, and I'm very sorry for invading your privacy. But I heard the pain in your voice and couldn't walk away from you."

He'd stolen her breath. He'd stayed because he couldn't walk away from her while she'd been in pain. With those words, Zeke Touré continued to tear down the walls she'd built around her. He was making it harder for her to hide. Part of her didn't want to crouch behind those barriers anymore. He was dispelling the darkness and tempting her into the light. She felt seen. She felt valued. For the first time in her life, she felt neither the compulsion to apologize for being nor the instinct to battle for the right to exist.

It was a miraculous realization.

Celeste swallowed the lump of emotion threatening to choke her. Her voice was husky. "I think I can be persuaded to give you another chance."

"I appreciate that." Zeke sounded relieved. "And I want to say again how very sorry—and outraged—I am over the way your family has treated you."

"Thank you." Celeste took a moment to savor the feeling of having someone on her side. "That first night you were in my home, you said you wanted me to talk more about myself. I didn't want to."

"I could tell." Zeke rolled onto his side to face her. His voice was soft.

Celeste's hand drifted from his chest. "I'd never done that before. I didn't even know if I could." She gave him a weak smile. The words weren't easy for her to say. "But I've never walked away from a challenge."

He smiled into her eyes. "I didn't mean it as a challenge."

"I know. But I'm glad I took it that way, otherwise I would never have opened up to you. And I'm glad I did." Celeste took a breath, briefly lowering her eyes. "Having someone I feel safe confiding in, someone I can trust and who listens without judgment, makes a difference. Thank you."

"You're welcome. And I feel the same about you. Beneath your gruff exterior, you have a big heart, and you're easy to talk with." He flashed the grin that made her toes curl. "We make a good team."

A good team. As they lay in bed, naked, facing each other. A teammate wasn't the first comparison she would hope he'd think of. What had she wanted him to say? That she was the love of his—

"Yes, we do make a good team." Celeste found a smile.

Zeke rolled off his side of the bed, then turned to offer her his hand. "Let's hit the showers." He gave her a sexy wink.

Celeste smiled, letting him help her to her feet. The teammate analogy had great perks.

Chapter Fourteen

"If revenge is the motive for Dean's and Art's murders, Damien Rockwell and May Ramirez don't fit." Zeke sat next to Celeste at the cabin's dining room table Tuesday afternoon. His palms itched with the urge to hold her hand. "They both have new jobs. They're doing well and have moved on. Damien's doing better now than when he worked for Art."

After getting dressed, he and Celeste had put together a quick lunch of salad and grilled-cheese sandwiches before joining Mal and Jerry for their case-status meeting. He hoped his inability to look away from Celeste wasn't too obvious to his highly observant younger brothers.

It wasn't only his strong feelings that drew his eyes back to her again and again. It was also the very un-Celeste outfit she was wearing. Celeste's and Nanette's fashion preferences couldn't be more different. All the times their paths had crossed, Zeke had never seen her in anything other than black. But today, Celeste was wearing Nanette's lime green capris and pink-white-and-gold blouse. She looked confident, vibrant, amazing. The blouse's square low-cut neckline framed her collarbone. Zeke could still feel her skin against his lips. His eyes strayed toward her again.

"Zeke's right." Celeste met his eyes, then looked to the laptop. The screen showed Mal and Jerry seated together in the Touré Security Group conference room. "Damien accepted responsibility for sleeping on the job. May still seems irritated that Art apparently held her responsible for her coworkers' bad behaviors. But I don't think she would've killed him or Dean for that."

"Which leaves us with Chad and Agnes." Zeke stared hard at Jerry, looking for signs of pain or fatigue. He seemed better today. "We have to speak with them. They're part of this. Even if it turns out that they aren't viable suspects, they might have helpful insights."

"I agree." Celeste rotated the sterling silver ring on her right thumb. "I was going to arrange an interview with Chad, but that tail from our meeting with May distracted me."

"One or both of them could be working with Monica Ward," Mal added.

Jerry held up his right hand, palm out. "Slow your roll, cybersleuth."

Mal shrugged. "It's too early to rule out anything."

"Agnes is doing well also." Jerry wore another loose-fitting short-sleeved dark pullover. This one was copper. He must have bought several of them to accommodate the white plaster cast, which extended from his palm to halfway up his bicep. "She got married and retired to North Carolina with her very wealthy husband. Chad's the only one who isn't doing well."

Mal made a note in his smart tablet. "I'll look for any connections Chad may have to Monica Ward."

"That will be helpful. Thank you." Zeke was still restless. There was something they were missing. What was it?

Mal's words interrupted Zeke's stressing. "One of our personal security consultants is helping with surveillance."

"Good thinking." But they were still missing something.

Celeste sprang from her chair and paced past Zeke. "Agnes and Chad don't fit the revenge motive, either. We're missing something."

Jerry raised his voice. "You know we can't see you, right?"

"We're talking to an empty chair." Mal sounded almost amused.

Zeke shifted in his seat to track her movements as she paced from the dining room to the kitchen and back. Her strides were long and stiff with temper. Tension and impatience shot from her and battered against him. He felt her presence in the room with him, but her thoughts seemed miles away. It was as though she was running various scenarios in her mind.

Celeste ignored his brothers' comments as she marched back and forth beside him. "Where's the harm? As a result of their losing their job, what harm did any of the former guards experience? The loss of a house or medical insurance or the end of a marriage? It's not enough that Agnes, May, Damien and Chad lost their jobs. What harm did their job loss cause to trigger their killing spree?"

"The Invisible Woman makes a good point." Jerry referenced one of the characters from the Fantastic Four superhero comics, Dr. Susan Storm, a.k.a. the Invisible Woman.

Zeke and Mal exchanged smiles.

Celeste continued as though she hadn't heard the youngest Touré. "May and Damien got better-paying jobs with better benefits. Agnes remarried."

Jerry was right. Celeste was making very good points.

Zeke picked up her train of thought. "And Chad has been in prison for months. If he'd planned this elaborate revenge, would he have committed a crime that would have landed him in prison?"

Jerry shrugged his healthy right shoulder. "Prison would give him an airtight alibi—except for Monica Ward's connection to the case."

Celeste stilled. "This is about something more than someone's job. We probably have the right motive—revenge. But we have the wrong reason."

Zeke felt a chill blow through him. "You think the killer wants revenge for something else? Like what?" He searched his mind for the answer.

"I don't know. Yet." Celeste reclaimed her seat. She seemed to have worked off most of her tension. "We need to find other links between TSG, Buckeye Bailey and Archer that could be a motive for murder: professional or social connections, organizations, cases. Something."

"I'm on it." Mal tapped the keys on his smart tablet.

"I can do it." Jerry tossed his right arm. "Zeke and Susan Storm are questioning suspects. You're already looking deeper into Chad's background. I'll search for other connections between our three companies."

Mal glanced at Jerry's cast. "We'll discuss that later." He turned back to the computer. "You should know someone may be following me."

Zeke straightened in his chair. "Excuse me?"

Celeste leaned into the table. "Wait. What?"

"Why didn't you lead with that?" Jerry shifted to face Mal.

"Because of your reactions." Mal gestured toward the monitor. "We needed to review the case—"

Zeke interrupted him. "Have you received a threat?"

"No." Mal turned to Jerry. "Have you?"

"No, I haven't." There was an edge to the youngest brother's voice. "And we're not done talking about this."

"Why do you think you're being followed?" Zeke balled his hands into fists, straining to keep his voice even and fear from clouding his judgment.

Mal switched his attention from Jerry back to Zeke. "I've sensed someone watching me. And the same car keeps driving past my house."

"Is Grace all right?" Celeste asked.

"Yes." Mal ran his hand over his clean-shaven head. "It

took some persuading, but I've convinced her to keep her distance from us until this case is over."

Zeke briefly closed his eyes. How many people had he endangered with his actions? He wasn't even certain what he'd done wrong. He'd responded to a request for a bid for a corporate-security account, and his bid had been accepted. Was that the transgression that had led to two murders and endangered his friends and family?

He opened his eyes and saw Celeste. He wouldn't let anything happen to any of them. "Have you assigned a consultant to yourself?"

Mal's eyes flared briefly in surprise. "No."

"I'll keep an eye on him." Jerry's words were grim.

Zeke's eyes dropped to Jerry's cast. "All right."

He recognized the uncertainty in his voice, but he needed to let go of some control. He trusted his youngest brother knew what he was getting into and what he was doing. Besides, Jerry was starting to moderate his impulses and taking more time to think things through. Symone was a good influence on his brother.

"We'll see." Mal's skepticism was a little louder.

Zeke shook his head. They needed to solve this case yesterday. He scowled. "Both of you be careful out there."

Jerry gestured toward the screen. "That's good advice for all of us, Number One."

Mal looked from Zeke to Celeste and back. "Watch each other's back."

After ending the videoconference, Zeke sat staring at the keyboard. What was he missing? What more could he do to keep his brothers safe?

A soft, warm weight settled on his right shoulder. Zeke looked up into Celeste's troubled hazel eyes.

"They're not helpless." Her voice was soft. "And neither are you."

"Thank you." Zeke covered her hand with his own. "Please keep reminding me of that."

CELESTE FELT THE tension in the hard muscles of Zeke's broad shoulder course through her palm, up her arm and lodge in her chest. He was a man tormented, and her heart hurt for him. What could she do to help him carry this burden? What could she say to reassure him that, just as they had with The Bishop Foundation hostile takeover attempt, they'd bring the murderer to justice and his brothers would be safe. His brothers. The inseparable Touré trio.

She squeezed his shoulder, then let her arm drop to her side. "One thing the killer didn't take into account is how close you and your brothers are and how well you work together. In less than a week, they've moved you to safety, identified the top suspects and revealed the stalker."

"We couldn't have done any of that without you." Admiration shone in his eyes. It made Celeste uncomfortable. Or maybe it was Nanette's clothes.

She stood and wandered the dining area, forcing herself not to fidget. "I'm happy to help. Problems are usually easier when you can share them." Zeke's silence was deafening. Celeste struggled against nervous chatter. It was a losing battle. "Besides, we're helping each other. The sooner we solve this case, the sooner we can tell my client who killed her husband and why."

"Who do you share your problems with?" Zeke's curiosity carried from the dining table behind her. "Is it Nanette?"

Celeste turned to him. She could feel that her smile was crooked. "I thought you didn't like it when people changed the subject from themselves."

"You didn't ask a question." Zeke's grin chased the tension from his chiseled features and revealed perfect white teeth. His voice was warm with humor. Had she helped to ease his burden?

Celeste shook her head, expelling an exasperated breath. "I'm never going to get the hang of this emotional sharing stuff."

"You're doing fine." He closed the laptop and rested his forearms on the table in front of him. "Is Nanette the one you confide in when you're troubled?"

Why was he asking? She'd like to know the reason for his curiosity, but she'd follow up about that later. For now, she wanted to keep the shadows from returning to his eyes.

Celeste wandered from the dining area into the great room. She admired the room's gleaming pinewood floor with its warm soft-brown-and-moss-green area rug. Her eyes lingered on the fluffy brown sofa and matching chairs with ottomans. The cabin was beautiful, but she preferred her bright, whimsical little home in Worthington.

"Nanette is a good friend, but she's not much of a problem solver. I can't strategize with her the way you can with your brothers." Celeste walked past the cedar-wood coffee table and paused in front of the stone fireplace.

"Why did you go into business with her?" Zeke's chair squeaked against the flooring, as though he was leaving the table.

"She asked me to." Celeste drew a breath, filling her senses with the fragrance of cedar pines. And with Zeke's soap-and-sandalwood scent. He was so close. "When I told her I was opening my own agency, she asked to join me. She was a good detective, and we could split the start-up costs. So I figured why not? Honestly, during these past almost-three years, she's been great at promoting the agency and bringing in clients."

"Celeste, why didn't you return to the department? Your lieutenant wanted you and Nanette back. Why did you turn him down?"

She faced him. This was the second time he'd asked that. His tone was more caring than curious. That was a point in his favor. If he was just being nosy, she wouldn't tell him the time of day. But there was something in his voice, his eyes, that made her want to tell him things she'd never told another soul.

Her smile was unsteady. "It's a long story."

His eyes smiled back. "Start at the beginning."

Celeste paced past him, gathering her thoughts. "Nanette was promoted to detective a couple of years before me. She was dating a detective in the robbery division. She and Roger kept saying his partner, Lee, and I should go out. Lee was handsome, intelligent and charismatic. So when he finally asked me out, I said sure."

Big mistake.

"Lee Martin." Zeke didn't ask.

Celeste frowned over her shoulder. "You knew him?"

Zeke shoved his hands into the front pockets of his gray pants. "I know he and Roger Strand were convicted and sentenced for the crime you and Nanette were charged with."

Celeste searched Zeke's features. His face was unreadable, but his tension reached her across the room. He was angry. With whom—and why? Was he angry with her? She had flashbacks of the reactions from some of the officers and detectives with whom she'd served. They seemed to think she and Nanette should've taken the fall for their "brave brothers in blue." They'd acted as though she and Nanette had done something wrong in defending themselves. Their betrayal had felt like a physical attack.

She turned to face the fluffy brown sofa again. It was easier than looking at Zeke and wondering what was going on in his very agile mind. "I thought I was in love. And Nanette, she was over the moon. She'd been practicing her authentic reaction to Roger's anticipated proposal. She was convinced he was going to ask her to marry him. And then Internal Affairs called. Nanette and I were accused of stealing property from the evidence room—money, drugs, jewelry. They had log sheets with our signatures and footage of us handling the evidence boxes. Even our union lawyers urged us to take a deal."

Zeke prompted her when she stopped. "How long had you and Lee been dating by this time?"

"Six months." Celeste marched to the bay window. "He was my first call after Internal Affairs, but he said he didn't want anything to do with me. He said associating with a dirty cop would be bad for his career. That's when I realized he'd set me up."

Shame enveloped her. Six months. She'd given him her heart, her mind and her body. If they'd been together much longer, she was sure she would've given him even more. She'd wanted forever with him. But their relationship had been a lie from the start. Anger, pain and humiliation were ripping her apart from the inside just as they had back then. Her muscles trembled from the effort to keep herself together. Willpower alone kept her on her feet. Celeste took deep breaths to combat the nausea.

"I'm so sorry, Celeste." Beneath Zeke's gentle words, she heard an edge of anger. "With all the evidence against you, how did you find the courage to fight them?"

"I owe everything to Eriq." Thinking of Eriq's steadfast belief in her helped Celeste breathe. Her relationship with the veteran detective was the best thing to come out of her time with the Columbus Division of Police. "Everyone in the department thought we were guilty—except him. He's been my mentor since the day I walked into the department. He's what I imagine a real father would be."

"He's very proud of you."

"That's nice to hear." Relief and gratitude washed away the residual feelings of anguish and shame. Celeste turned away from the window. "He'd warned me to be careful. He said Lee was too slick. But again, I thought I was in love. So when I was charged, I was ashamed to ask him for help.

Before I could get my courage up, he was knocking on my door, helping me figure out what I needed to do to clear my name. Nanette and I fired the union lawyers and hired a defense attorney to represent both of us. Then we started our investigation. It wasn't easy."

Zeke took his hands out of his pockets and stepped away from the fireplace. "What did you do?"

Celeste allowed her mind to travel back to those planning sessions with Eriq and Nanette. Being proactive and involved in her defense had protected her sanity. "Lee and Roger must have been selling the stolen items. We found their fences. The ones who were willing to talk met with our attorney and linked Lee and Roger to the thefts. A forensic technician proved the footage was fake, and a handwriting expert testified that our signatures had been forged."

A glint of satisfaction lit Zeke's eyes. "And now Lee and Roger are in prison where they belong. I'm so proud of you for having the courage and strength to defend yourself. You constantly impress me."

The look in his eyes made Celeste believe she could do anything. "You're pretty impressive yourself, which is how I know we're going to keep your family safe and take down Dean's and Art's killer. We make a good team."

Zeke grinned as though she'd given him a gift. "Yes, we do."

After Lee, Celeste didn't think she'd trust anyone ever again. She'd envied Nanette for being able to find real love with Warren. Maybe like Nanette, she could trust again. Zeke wasn't Lee. He wasn't a slick, showy charmer. He was a sincere, caring, albeit controlling, protector. She trusted Zeke with her life, just as Zeke was trusting her with his.

Then why was she so afraid to trust him with her heart?

CELESTE'S EYES WERE crossing after her third review of Jerry's report on Chad Cooper. Her frustration rose as she sat at the desk in her bedroom in the safe house late Tuesday afternoon. Her attention drifted away from the laptop Mal had sent her toward the shared wall between her room and Zeke's. Had he found anything they may have missed the first two times they'd read Chad's file? Perhaps she should ask him. She closed the computer as she rose from her chair.

Her cell phone rang, stopping her in her tracks. Celeste checked the caller ID. Nanette. She'd never before noticed how very bad her partner's timing was. "Hi, Nanette."

"Hey, is everything okay?" Nanette sounded suspiciously concerned.

"As well as can be expected, considering an unidentified serial killer who's already killed two people is after my protectee." Celeste strained to catch background sounds. She wanted to know from where her partner was calling.

Nanette sighed. "Do you have any new leads?" Was she settling back onto her office chair or her living room sofa?

"Not yet." Celeste wandered her room. "We're going a little deeper into our known suspects' backgrounds. But that's not why you're calling." *Please don't let her try to convince me to move to San Diego again.*

"You've got mail." Papers rustled under Nanette's announcement. "I stopped by the office since you're, shall we say, on location, to check on the mail and messages."

"I appreciate that." So the other woman was probably calling from their office. One of the many benefits of having a partner: they could check the mail when you couldn't.

"Sure," Nanette continued. "You have a letter from a law firm. I don't recognize the firm's name but it's in Chicago. I thought it might be important. Don't you go to Chicago a couple of times a year?"

"Yes, I do." Celeste searched her mind for clues as to why a Chicago law firm was sending her a letter. "It's probably the firm handling Dionne's estate."

"Dionne who?" Nanette sounded confused.

"She's—she *was*—my paternal grandmother."

"Your *grandmother*?" Surprise boosted the volume of Nanette's voice.

Celeste winced as her eardrum took the punishment. "Sterling, my father, called this morning to tell me his mother had died." It still rankled her that he'd waited almost a week to tell her. Although why should she be surprised? She'd bet the only reason he'd called was that he'd known the law firm was going to contact her. He'd wanted to run interference.

"Your *father*?" Once again, Nanette's surprise was like a cymbal ringing in her ears. "Mind. Blown. Why haven't you ever told me your grandmother and your father were still alive?"

Celeste shrugged although Nanette couldn't see it. "You never asked, and I don't have a relationship with either of them."

Their exchange reminded her of the discussion she'd had with Zeke. He hadn't wanted to make assumptions about her life. Instead, he'd cared enough to ask her about her family. A warm feeling enveloped her.

Nanette's impatient breath brought Celeste back to their phone call. "It's obvious you're not close since you refer to them by their Christian names. I talk about my family all the time. And I call them 'Mommy,' 'Daddy' and 'Nana.' I figured all your family must be dead. I thought those Chicago trips were mental health vacays. You're pretty intense."

Memories of those biannual trips to check on Dionne played across her mind. "No, those weren't vacations."

Those four-day stays were the exact opposite. They were packed with doctors' checkups, dental exams and pharmacy trips for her grandmother. Celeste also checked the condition of her grandmother's house to make sure it was safe and in good repair. And the whole time, she endured her grandmother's familiar suspicious stares and hostile silences. What had compelled her to make those visits? She would rather have spent that time in her own lovely little home. In fact, from the minute she packed up her car for the six-hour drive, she was looking forward to the day she returned.

HBO's *The Wire* said it best. Every situation had two days: the day you get in and the day you get out. The stuff in between didn't matter.

"Anyway, Celeste, I'm sorry for your loss." Nanette's words were awkward and muted. "I remember when my maternal grandmother died. We'd been close. Her death was hard on me."

"Thank you." Celeste left it at that. She didn't want to explain that Dionne had been a virtual stranger to her.

"Of course." Nanette sighed. "Now, what should I do with the lawyer's letter? You're probably right about it being about your grandmother. I could scan it and email it to you. You know you can trust me not to read it. Unless you want me to?"

Nanette's insatiable curiosity was her superpower. It made her a great investigator.

Celeste shook her head in amusement. "I don't care if you read the letter."

"In that case, I'll read it to you now." Nanette's voice bounced with excitement. "But I'll still email a scan of it to you before I leave."

"Thanks, but I don't know why you're so excited. It's probably just an official announcement about Dionne's death." Celeste imagined Nanette reaching for her letter opener during their brief silence. In the other woman's opinion, there were few things worse than a papercut.

"Oh, girl, this is more than an announcement." Nanette inserted a dramatic pause. "According to this letter, you're your grandmother's sole beneficiary, and she's left you her, quote, 'sizable assets,' end quote. The lawyer asks that you contact them, quote, 'at your earliest opportunity,' end quote."

"*Sole* beneficiary?" Celeste massaged her brow. "Well, that solves the mystery of Sterling's phone call."

What were these assets, and how much were they worth?

Chapter Fifteen

"Are you police officers?" Agnes Letby's image was projected onto Zeke's clean laptop early Wednesday morning. She removed her overly large red-rimmed sunglasses and squinted at the monitor.

The retired Buckeye Bailey Security guard and serial killer suspect looked like she'd joined the videoconference straight from the salon. Her hair was skillfully dyed a rich honey blond and swept high onto her round head, giving her a regal appearance. Her makeup was perfect. It took at least ten years from the sixty-two recorded on her employment files.

Agnes craned her neck as though trying to identify where she and Zeke were. This made Celeste doubly grateful to Eriq for securing permission for her and Zeke to use the same small meeting room at the police substation where they'd spoken with the detectives before taking refuge at the cabin safe house.

Mal and Jerry had vetoed Zeke and Celeste interviewing Agnes via videoconference. They'd raised the possibility of Agnes circumventing Mal's cybersecurity systems and tracking them to the safe house. This would be especially bad if Agnes was working with the serial killer.

Celeste accepted they had a point. But Zeke had a good

argument as well. She and Zeke had conducted every other interview. They'd questioned Damien and May. They'd spoken with Dean's and Art's families. The information they'd personally collected could prove useful when meeting with Agnes. With their personal experience, Celeste and Zeke might think of follow-up questions or notice inconsistencies in Agnes's responses that Mal and Jerry wouldn't catch. The two overprotective younger brothers weren't completely sold on Zeke and Celeste's plan to interview Agnes from the substation, but they conceded it was better than sending Agnes a virtual invitation to the safe house.

"We aren't officers, but we're working with the police." Celeste sat beside Zeke, sharing the laptop screen with him.

Although she was wearing the most subdued items her partner had packed, she was still uncomfortable in Nanette's clothes. Judging by Zeke's reaction to her appearance, she'd chosen well. The emerald scoop-necked blouse had long flowing sleeves. The pencil-slim cream skirt was a little loose in the hips and a little short in the knee-length hem. Her black loafers didn't enhance the outfit, but wobbling around in Nanette's four-inch stilettos would've made her motion sick.

"Why did you decide to retire after you left Buckeye Bailey Security?" Zeke looked very handsome in his smoke gray suit, navy shirt and tie.

Agnes's chuckle was raspy, as though she was battling a cold. "I don't know who your sources are, but I didn't leave Buckeye Bailey. I was fired." She spread her arms, balancing her sunglasses in her right hand. "And at my age, I didn't think any decent security company would hire me. So when my lover suggested I retire and that we get married and move to North Carolina, I thought, 'Why the heck not?'"

Celeste didn't want to like Agnes, but there was something about the older woman that was drawing her in. "Congratulations."

"Best decision he's ever made." Agnes's big blue eyes twinkled. "How long have you two been together?"

Celeste blinked. She decided to let Zeke handle that question.

He responded with confidence. "This is our second case together."

Ah. Good one. "Yes, we're colleagues." *With benefits. Very nice benefits.*

"Really?" Agnes arched a thin brown eyebrow. "Did you forget I was a security guard? We're very observant." She winked. "Don't worry. Your secret's safe with me. You make a good-looking couple."

Celeste's eyes widened. It was time to regain control of the interview. "Ms. Letby—"

"Call me Agnes, hon." Agnes put her sunglasses back on. The large black lenses covered two-thirds of her face.

"Agnes." Celeste inclined her head. "How was your relationship with Arthur Bailey?"

"I wouldn't call what we had a *relationship*." Agnes's words held a thin layer of dislike. "I only saw Art when I collected my paycheck twice a month. We barely spoke. If he'd moved the agency into the twenty-first century and implemented direct deposit like we'd all asked him to I can't even count the number of times, I wouldn't have had to see him at all."

"How did you feel when he fired you?" Zeke asked.

Agnes removed her sunglasses again. She cocked her head as though in confusion. "Mr. Touré—"

Zeke interrupted. "Call me Zeke."

Agnes glowed. She glanced at Celeste, wiggling her eyebrows in approval. "Zeke, how would you have felt if someone had fired you unjustly?" She held up her hands. "I know Art lost the Archer account and couldn't afford to keep all of us, but May and I had been complaining about Damien and Chad for *months*—"

Zeke stopped her again. "You and May complained about Damien's and Chad's unprofessional behavior?"

Celeste was surprised as well. May hadn't mentioned that.

"You bet we did." For the first time, anger surfaced in Agnes's voice. "May's shift was between Sleeping Beauty—that's Damien—and Mr. No-Show, Chad. She told me she'd start her shift and find Damien sleeping, sometimes at the front desk. And Art had called me more than once to relieve May when Chad was late. He called it 'bonus shifts.'" She made air quotes with both of her hands. "I called it 'not hiring qualified people.' I'm sixty-two years old. Do you think I want to spend every day of my life at work?"

Celeste crossed her right leg over her left. Startled by how high the skirt rode up her thigh, she immediately put both legs flat on the ground. "Did you notice any tension between Art and either Damien, May or Chad?"

"May?" Agnes laughed. After her outburst, her temper seemed to dissipate. She put her glasses back on. "She was too busy looking for another job to waste energy on Art. So was I." She sobered. "But something was going on with Chad. More than once, when I went in to get my check, I heard them arguing."

Beside Celeste, Zeke tensed. "Did you ask him what it was about?"

Agnes was shaking her head before Zeke finished speaking. "I never asked. I didn't want to get involved. But Chad saw me outside of Art's office once as he was storming out. He claimed he and Art were arguing because Art didn't have his paycheck *again*."

Celeste caught the suspicion in Agnes's tone. "You don't sound like you believed him."

"That's because I didn't." Agnes crossed her arms over her ample chest. "Chad had worked for Art for what? A cou-

ple of months? I'd worked for him for years. In all that time,
I'd never had any trouble with my pay. Not once. But he'd
missed Chad's paycheck multiple times? And only Chad's?
No one else ever complained about not getting paid. I know
that for the last couple of years, Buckeye Bailey had been
leaking money like a sieve. But I still didn't buy it."

Celeste held Zeke's eyes. If Agnes didn't buy Chad's story
about missing paychecks, why should they? They couldn't
put it off any longer. They had to speak with Chad. He may
be the key to the motive behind the murders.

"Why hadn't May told us she and Agnes had been complaining to Art about Damien and Chad for months?" Zeke
directed the question to the image of his brothers projected
onto his computer monitor.

Mal and Jerry were in the Touré Security Group conference room. Even to his concerned eyes, they looked fine.
Jerry didn't seem to be in as much pain over his broken arm.
And they both appeared to have made it into the office without running into the stalker. He breathed a sigh of relief.

Seated beside him in the police substation's meeting room,
Celeste seemed unusually quiet, as though more than this
case was on her mind. Did it have anything to do with Agnes's comments about their body language?

Zeke hadn't been aware that he'd been telegraphing anything, although he wouldn't mind if people knew they were
together. Now that she trusted him enough to open up to him,
he wanted another chance with her. He'd thought he'd made
that clear. Was she uncomfortable with the idea of their relationship becoming public knowledge?

Jerry shrugged his uninjured right shoulder. "The only
way to know why is to ask her."

Mal rubbed the back of his neck. "Neither Damien nor
Agnes had problems with their paychecks. May didn't mention any issues with her pay, right?"

"She didn't mention that she and Agnes had complained about Damien and Chad, either," Jerry muttered.

Zeke considered Celeste. She was so still. Almost pre-occupied. Should he be concerned? "What do you think, Celeste?"

She was rotating the ring on her right thumb. Her mother's ring. "I think Chad was blackmailing Art. I think his missing 'paycheck' wasn't for his work. It was for his silence."

"What now?" Jerry frowned. "Where are you getting that from?"

"Of course." A light bulb went off in Zeke's mind. He addressed Jerry. "Agnes claimed Buckeye Bailey Security had been leaking money like a sieve. Is there a connection between Art's financial problems and his arguments with Chad?"

Mal ran a hand over his head. "Chad was showing up late to the point that Agnes and May complained about him, but Art wouldn't fire him. Maybe that's because of the black-mail material Chad was holding over Art."

Jerry spread his arms, looking from Celeste to Zeke and Mal. "But in the end, Art did fire him. And what does Chad's blackmail scheme have to do with us or Dean?"

"That's what we have to find out." Zeke was grim.

"I'll follow up with Meryl this afternoon." Celeste sounded terse. "I have a feeling she's still holding out on us."

"I'm afraid you're right." Zeke held her eyes. "We have to meet with Chad as soon as possible."

"Hold on, Number One." Jerry held his right hand up, palm out. "Mal and I have been talking. We think you going to the prison is a bad idea."

Zeke frowned at the monitor. "Why?"

"What?" Celeste spoke at the same time.

Mal gave Jerry the side-eye. "You can't go without security."

Celeste burst out laughing. "There are literally security guards in prison."

Jerry's scowl was stubborn. "If Chad's working with Monica Ward, they could set a trap for you if they know when and where you'll be. That could've been what happened the last time you were followed."

"What do you mean *the last time*?" Celeste lifted her right index finger. "We've only been followed *once*. *One* time."

She was right, but Zeke opted to stay out of it. He kind of enjoyed having someone defend him. Having Celeste defend him.

Mal broke the impasse. "Eriq got permission for the two of you to videoconference with Chad tomorrow afternoon. You can use that same room."

Celeste chuckled again. "You Tourés, you really look out for each other. It's nice."

"We're brothers." Zeke turned to Mal. "That reminds me. Are you still being followed?"

Mal looked thoughtful. "I don't think so, but I'm being vigilant."

Zeke was reassured. Mal's idea of vigilance was everyone else's definition of extreme paranoia. He had the best home-security system of anyone he'd ever known. Mal should be safe. He hoped.

Zeke checked his watch. "We might as well head back." He saved the notes they'd made on his computer. "We'll call you after our interview with Chad tomorrow."

Jerry inclined his head. "All right. Be careful getting back."

"Stay alert." Mal split a look between Zeke and Celeste before leaving the meeting.

"You and your brothers make a great team." Celeste's tone was thoughtful.

"I agree." Zeke studied the faraway look in her eyes. "And you were right. I need to get their input on TSG's business plan earlier. I'll talk with them about it." Although, like his brothers, Zeke didn't like admitting to failures.

He stood, extending his right hand to Celeste. She took it, sending heat up his arm. He didn't want to let go. One of the officers escorted them to Zeke's rental car. Eriq's orders.

Zeke navigated the car out of the parking lot and braked at a red light. "Is everything okay? You seemed quiet during our meetings."

Seconds that felt like minutes ticked by in silence. Zeke thought she was going to ignore his question or change the subject. The impression that, even after what they'd shared that morning, she was still putting up walls between them hurt. Then she spoke, and he breathed again.

Celeste's voice was low. "The attorney for Dionne's estate sent a letter to my office. I asked Nanette to read it to me. I'm not just named in her will, as Sterling had told me. I'm her sole beneficiary. That's why he called me. He's panicking."

Zeke's temper spiked on Celeste's behalf. "He pretended he wanted a better relationship with you, but you believe he's panicking because he was left out of his mother's will."

"I do." Celeste's voice carried to him in the cozy confines of the rented sedan. "Dionne constantly complained Sterling and his children were always asking her for money."

"Was your grandmother wealthy?" The traffic light turned green, and Zeke moved the car forward.

Celeste shrugged. "She didn't talk about her finances, and I didn't ask. I haven't asked her for money since I was sixteen. I left her house when I was eighteen, and I've been taking care of myself ever since."

That wasn't pride he heard. It was determination and resolve. Celeste Jarrett was her own person. She could take care of herself and wasn't willing to count on anyone else. Zeke was impressed. He was also concerned. Had she convinced herself that she didn't need anyone? Not even him?

She continued. "I'm not surprised he had an ulterior motive for calling me. But I am upset he thought I'd fall for it. He must think I'm a fool."

"Then he doesn't know you at all." Zeke regretted his sharp tone. He softened it. "What do you want to do?"

Celeste rotated the ring on her thumb. "I'll email the lawyer tonight. Let her know I'm in the middle of a case and ask what she needs from me."

Zeke took the Route 315 North on-ramp. "I'm here for you if there's anything I can do to help. You shouldn't have to go through something like this on your own."

"Thank you. I may take you up on that." Celeste's voice held a weak smile.

Zeke turned his attention back to the road. "Of course. I want to help you."

As much as you'll let me.

"AGNES LETBY'S WORDS keep echoing in my mind." Zeke finished packing their bowls, plates, glasses and silverware into the dishwasher and straightened away from the machine Wednesday afternoon.

"Which ones? She used a lot of them." Celeste dried the large saucepan they'd used to make the lentil soup they'd had for lunch. She returned it to the dark wood cupboard beside the oven.

The kitchen was redolent with the scent of lentil and onions, as well as the vinaigrette and olive oil from their salads. As they'd prepared lunch, they'd moved together as though they'd shared scores of meals before. It was funny the way little things like that could ease a loneliness Zeke hadn't even known he'd felt.

"The ones about Buckeye Bailey Security's financial challenges." He rested his hips against the white-and-silver-marble counter and crossed his arms over his chest. "Agnes's specific words were 'For the last couple of years, Buckeye Bailey had been leaking money like a sieve.'"

Celeste's cell phone rang. She checked the ID screen before sending the caller to her voicemail. "Why can't you get that out of your head?" She strode past him on her way to the great room.

Had she brushed against him deliberately? He hoped so.

Zeke followed her. "I've told you before the similarities between Buckeye Bailey and TSG make me nervous. It's like watching my family's company in the future, if we aren't able to turn things around."

Celeste folded herself onto the far end of the sofa. "But TSG isn't leaking money like a sieve."

Wincing on the inside, Zeke paced the great room. Should he remind Celeste of the business mistakes he'd made? She must think he's a loser to have so badly steered his family's company. He felt sick, thinking of the decades of hard work his parents had put into their legacy, only to have him, in a handful of years, bring their investment to the edge of collapse.

"No, but as I've said, we haven't paid ourselves in months." He paused in front of the bay window. Instead of the rolling lawn and magnificent trees, he pictured his parents and his brothers. "We're working to pay our bills. That's not what my parents had planned for us."

"That's not the *aspiration* your parents had for you. But running a business is hard. Some days, you think you'll never see another client. Never get another paid invoice. I get it. And I'm sure your parents had those same feelings as they built their company."

His parents had mentioned more than once there were months when the company had struggled. Zeke had thought they'd hoped he'd learn from their experiences. Instead, he'd recreated those experiences, putting his own spin on them.

Zeke pinched the bridge of his nose as frustration swamped him. "Adding Archer Family Realty has helped, but we've got to do more to rebuild. And to protect ourselves in the future. If we were to lose even one client, it could destroy us like it destroyed Art."

"What are Mal's and Jerry's ideas?" There was a soft rustling from the sofa, as though Celeste had shifted to keep him in sight as he resumed his pacing.

Zeke paused again. "I haven't discussed it with them yet." He sensed the shock in Celeste's silence.

"Why not?"

Zeke expelled a heavy breath. "This isn't exactly an easy conversation to have."

"Yet you're having it with me." She broke off. Her voice stiffened. "Is that because my opinion doesn't matter?"

Shocked, Zeke spun to face her. Her eyes held his with an intensity that mesmerized him. "That's not true. In fact, it's the opposite. I want your opinion. You're a small-business owner, too. You know how challenging it is trying to forecast how the markets are going to affect our incomes. But I don't want you to think less of me because of bad decisions I've made."

Celeste's eyebrows leaped toward her hairline. "Now, that's just ridiculous, almost as ridiculous as you not having this conversation with your brothers."

Zeke paced toward the fireplace. "This was on me. And I've learned from my mistakes, but I don't want to let my brothers down again."

"I thought the three of you were equal partners?"

"We are."

"Then this was actually on *all* of you." She stood from the sofa and crossed to him. "Listen, I know you love being in control, but I'm sure you didn't implement your expansion plans without input from Mal and Jerry."

Zeke frowned. "Of course not. We discussed those business decisions."

Celeste braced her hands on his biceps. "You need to have this conversation with them, too. *Now.* Give Mal and Jerry bigger roles in developing your company's business plan.

I'm sure they want to help. And you shouldn't take this on by yourself."

Zeke shook his head. "They haven't said anything to me about wanting to help develop the plan."

Celeste's eyes twinkled with amusement. "That's because you're a control freak and they probably didn't want to argue with you. They love you. You're very lucky."

"I know." Zeke's sigh was less burdened this time. "And you're right. They were probably picking their battles. We tend to do that."

"You guys are phenomenal when it comes to brainstorming. You build off each other's ideas. I'm sure you can come up with some great strategies for keeping TSG thriving."

"Thank you." Zeke gave her a considering look. "Do you really think I'm controlling?"

Celeste's hazel eyes darkened. "Yes, but I love a challenge."

"And I love…challenging you." He pressed his lips to hers to keep from confessing what was in his heart—he was falling in love with the prickly private investigator. In fact, he may have already fallen.

Chapter Sixteen

"You've been waiting for the business plan." Zeke was videoconferencing with his brothers in his cabin bedroom early Wednesday evening. "It's taken longer than expected. I've come up against a wall and don't have a clear idea of where to go from here."

His brothers, who were seated in the Touré Security Group conference room, watched him in silent anticipation. It was as though they expected him to say something more.

Jerry glanced at Mal before returning his attention to Zeke. "Is this where you finally ask for our input *before* you finalize the plan?"

Zeke rubbed his right hand across his eyes. "I deserved that."

Jerry expelled a breath on a broken laugh. "Yeah, you did, control freak."

Mal smiled. Zeke recognized the expression. His middle brother agreed with Jerry but didn't want to hurt Zeke's feelings. Celeste was right. He was a control freak—and it was past time he shared the responsibility of developing their business plan with his brothers.

Mal gestured toward Zeke. "I know you think you've made some bad decisions. Your previous ideas were ambitious, but we've benefitted from them, including recruiting contractors in other states—"

"Mal's right." Jerry interrupted. "Those contractors came in handy when we had to go to Florida to protect Grace's grandmother."

Mal inclined his head. "That's right. And we've hired a couple to keep tabs on Agnes. They haven't turned up anything suspicious on her. The safe house was a good investment, too."

"Yeah, it was a good idea to use it now and when we were protecting Symone." Jerry nodded again. "Mal's making a lot of good points. And using words instead of grunts to make them. So you need to stop kicking yourself over those decisions. They may not have turned out the way you intended, but they were good investments."

Zeke pinched the bridge of his nose. "I just wish we were making a return on these investments." He dropped his hand. "However, our priority—I think—should be finding a way to protect the agency from future market shifts. I need your help with that."

Mal and Jerry exchanged another look before Mal responded. "We've had a 57.7 percent increase in cybersecurity requests, and we've increased our client retainers almost a third over last year by 31.4 percent."

Jerry gave them a sheepish grin. "I can't rattle off numbers like the human spreadsheet, but personal security requests are up at least thirty percent. As you know, we've had to increase the number of training classes to keep up with demand without sacrificing quality—or our reputation."

Although encouraging, the news didn't ease Zeke's concerns. Those numbers reflected their current business. How sustainable was that income? It was impossible to tell.

Zeke straightened in his seat. "Those numbers are great. Corporate-security requests have increased a bit, too. But what about the future? What if corporate, cyber and personal security requests all drop? We need a feature of our agency that will help shield us from that type of market turn."

Mal's thick black eyebrows knitted in an expression similar to Jerry's. "We can monitor trends, but we can't forecast the future."

"Yeah, we'd need a crystal ball for that." Jerry shook his head. "Things are going well now. We're paying down our debts. We'll be able to pay ourselves again soon and, hopefully, put away extra savings in case cash flow gets a little tight again."

Why couldn't his brothers understand his concerns for the agency's future? "What if we aren't able to set aside extra savings before the market shifts? What if AI replaces our corporate security or cybersecurity or personal security services? Or all three?"

Artificial intelligence was one of the market trends Zeke considered a very real threat to Touré Security Group's business. Not everyone would choose the personal touch over automated systems, especially if the price tag was lower. Zeke didn't want to cut costs to bring in more customers. He didn't think his brothers would be interested in that strategy, either. It hadn't worked for Arthur Bailey.

Mal pinned Zeke with an intense stare. "Art's financial challenges are a cautionary tale." It was as though his middle brother had read his mind. "He tried to build his business by underbidding projects to bring in clients. Mom and Dad didn't do that. Neither do we."

Zeke ran a hand over his clean-shaven head. "I know that—"

"Do you?" Jerry interrupted. "Then why are you panicking? We're doing well. That doesn't mean we can sit back on our laurels, but we don't need to run around like the sky is falling, either."

It was a struggle to remain seated when his body was vibrating with impatience. "I'm not panicking. I want to explore options that could help stabilize the company if technologies or market trends make things more challenging for our industry."

Mal spread his hands. "We can't add a division every time we need to supplement our business income. At some point, we'll become a jack of all trades, master of none."

Jerry raised a hand. "Wait a minute, Mal. Number One may be onto something." He lowered it again. "I've been giving this some thought. This is our third case involving an investigation. We were successful with our first two cases. I'm praying we're successful with this one, too. What do you think about adding investigative services to our agency?"

Mal lowered his head as though considering the idea. "We would be competing against Celeste's agency. She's more established and has better credentials. It also feels disloyal."

Jerry shifted toward Mal. "We wouldn't have to move into investigations. What if we asked her to collaborate with us? She could refer us to her clients who need services like personal, cyber or corporate security. We could refer her to our clients who need investigations like fraud, lawsuits, corporate espionage."

"That's a good idea." Mal nodded his agreement. "We could still collaborate on some cases. Investigations is a natural offshoot of security. And partnering with another company would help expand our client base."

Zeke sat perfectly still as his thoughts raced. "What if we asked her to join us?"

Jerry frowned. "You mean, like merging our two agencies?"

Zeke leaned forward, lowering his voice. "Her partner's getting married and moving to San Diego. Celeste doesn't want to relocate, but she doesn't want to run the agency by herself, either. What if we ask her to join TSG?"

Jerry's expression brightened. "Why not? The four of us make a good team. It could be the Touré Security and Investigations Group—TSIG."

Mal looked dubious. "Do you think that would interest her?"

Zeke spread his arms. "What wouldn't she like about the plan? She enjoys working with us. We enjoy working with her. She'd be the head of her division. She wouldn't be giving up anything."

"Except her independence." Mal arched an eyebrow. "Right now she's working for herself, making her own decisions. Collaborating on a case is one thing. Would she be interested in collaborating on her livelihood?"

Jerry shrugged. "You have a point, but we should at least ask her."

Zeke gestured toward Jerry. "I'll ask her. The worst that could happen is that she says no."

The idea of partnering with Celeste to take TSG to the next level the way his parents had worked together made him more excited about the future than he'd felt in years. He hoped this was a vision she could share with him.

"Meryl, tell me about Art's financial problems." Celeste had called her client on the burner phone Mal had prepared for her. She sat cross-legged on her bed in the safe house early Wednesday evening.

"What do you mean?" the widow asked. But Celeste heard something in the other woman's voice that told her Meryl knew what she was talking about. From the beginning, Celeste had the feeling her client was keeping secrets. Now she was certain of it.

Celeste called her bluff. "Buckeye Bailey Security was operating in the red. Art had had to cut guards even before he fired the four who were assigned to Archer Family Realty. What was behind Art's financial trouble?" She sensed Meryl debating whether to tell her the truth or continue to feign ignorance. "Meryl, this might have something to do with Art's murder."

"Art was sued." The words rushed out of Meryl. "Two years ago."

Celeste's hand tightened around the cell phone. "By whom?"

Meryl hesitated. The pain of this topic transmitted over the satellite connection. Celeste empathized with her client, but she had to keep pushing. Art and Dean had already been killed. Now Zeke's life was on the line.

Celeste held the phone even tighter. "Meryl, who sued him?"

Meryl sighed. "The children of the guard who was killed on duty."

Oh no. "What happened?"

The sound of running water in the background gave the impression of Meryl pouring herself a cool drink. The faucet shut off, and Meryl spoke. "It was the middle of March two years ago. I'll never forget it. It was a beautiful day. Or at least, it had started that way. Then Art called me late that morning. He'd gotten a call from a police officer. One of his guards had been shot multiple times while on duty. Art had gone to the hospital immediately, but he was too late. The guard, Sally Jaxx, had died."

Celeste briefly closed her eyes. Grief tried to drain her energy. She took a breath and kept going. "I'm so sorry. Did they catch the killer?"

Meryl's sigh shook. "It was domestic violence. The husband of one of the employees killed Sally and his wife before shooting himself. Sally had two children. Art met them at the hospital. They were devastated."

"Of course." Celeste's heart broke, imagining Sally's children's distress. "How old were they?"

Meryl hesitated as though trying to remember. "I think they were in their late teens or early twenties."

Celeste had seen enough tragedies as a police officer and a homicide detective to understand that saying that final goodbye to a parent was hard at any age, whether you were a tween, teen, young adult or middle aged. She'd never known her mother, but she still felt her loss. "Do you remember their names?"

"No, I'm sorry. I could look through Art's files to see if there are any papers with their names on it."

Celeste nodded. "Thanks, Meryl. That would be helpful. What about their father? Was he there?"

Another call was trying to come through Celeste's cell phone. She checked the screen. It was Sterling again. She'd sent his call to voicemail earlier. This time, she rejected it, then returned to her conversation with her client.

Meryl hummed. "I think Art had said their father had died. I'd asked because Sally had a different name from her children. She'd remarried, but I don't think their stepfather was in the picture, either. I don't remember what happened to him. But her children sued Art for negligence."

Celeste stood from the bed and started pacing the room. "On what grounds?"

"Art used to assign two guards to every shift. But he'd reduced those staffing levels to stay competitive. Sally's children claimed his lack of appropriate training to the contractors and inadequate staffing contributed to Sally's death. The court agreed with them and awarded them damages. They also wanted Art to go back to assigning two guards per shift. The cost of the additional staffing, plus his attorney's fees, were a big hit to the company's finances."

Celeste turned to walk back to her bed. Through the wall behind the headboard, she heard the periodic murmur of Zeke's voice. She knew he was having a videoconference with his brothers to discuss their business plan. She couldn't make out their words, but the lack of tension in their exchange indicated the meeting was going well.

She turned to pace away from the wall. "Is that the reason Art eventually went back to only one guard per shift?"

"That's right. Art didn't actually tell me much about the lawsuit. He said he didn't want to *burden* me with the company's problems." For the first time, anger entered Meryl's voice.

In Meryl's position, Celeste would've been irritated by Art's attitude, too. She was sure Art's business's assets affected their personal finances. Because of that, Meryl had a right to know and understand the things that impacted Buckeye Bailey Security.

"But you think the lawsuit was the reason Art's business suffered financially?" Celeste asked.

"I know it was." Meryl's tone was firm. "He had a hard time making payments to Sally's children. Operating expenses had increased, and a couple of his clients went out of business."

"Wow. That's a lot." As a small-business owner herself, Celeste could imagine the stress Art was under.

"Yes, it was. He was having trouble sleeping and eating. He'd lost a lot of weight. But he *didn't* commit suicide." Meryl was adamant.

Celeste believed her. Meryl said Art would have reorganized under bankruptcy protection before he ended his life. Based on their decades of marriage, Celeste was certain Meryl was right. She knew her husband. And there had been that threatening letter.

Celeste stopped pacing and stared blindly through the window. Beyond the maple trees and evergreens, past the rolling grass, she could see the river and the late-evening sunlight dancing on its surface. "Meryl, why didn't you tell me about this lawsuit when I first took your case?"

Meryl gave a tired sigh. "As I explained, Art didn't tell me much about the lawsuit. And if I'd brought it up, you might have considered it more evidence that Art had killed himself."

"I still would've investigated your case."

"I know that about you now." There was a smile in the older woman's voice. "You're not the kind to be dismissive like some people. You check the facts yourself."

Celeste was proud and a little embarrassed by the compliment. "I do my best."

Meryl hesitated. "And to be honest, Sally Jaxx's death was a dark time in the company's history. It wasn't just the lawsuit. Sally had been with the company for years. She was a really good person. Art was devastated. I just didn't want to relive that. I wanted to protect Art's legacy."

Was protecting her husband's legacy more important than finding his killer? Celeste didn't bother to ask Meryl that question. In the end, she'd been forthcoming about the lawsuit, and that was all that mattered.

Celeste turned from the window and paced back toward the wall behind her bed. "You said Sally had been shot on assignment. Where was she assigned to work that day?"

Meryl gasped, a short, sharp explosion that echoed in Celeste's ear. "She was working at Archer Family Realty."

Celeste stilled on her way to the dressing table. What were the odds? Sally had been murdered while working for Buckeye Bailey Security, which had assigned her to Archer Family Realty. Two years later, someone kills Art and Dean. "Sally's children sued Art for negligence. Do you know whether they also sued Archer Family Realty?"

Meryl spoke after a beat of silence. "No, I don't. Celeste, do you think… Could this be a coincidence?"

Celeste dragged a hand over her hair. "I don't believe in coincidences. I think we may have identified the real trigger that links Art's and Dean's murders." She turned toward her bed and the wall she shared with Zeke.

How does he fit into this?

"You want to know about Arty's death?" Chad Cooper fixed his eyes on Zeke. His image appeared through the lens of a computer in the prison's library Thursday afternoon. "Suicide, right? Was sorry to hear about it." He didn't sound sorry.

Zeke returned the other man's flat stare. "It wasn't suicide. Someone killed him."

He was seated beside Celeste. Her outfit today was a bright red miniskirt and a silk pearl white long-sleeved blouse that flowed over her curves like water. Zeke had enjoyed one long look at her before leaving the cabin, then consigned himself to keeping his attention on her beautiful hazel eyes.

They were using the same police substation meeting room in which they'd videoconferenced with Agnes the previous morning. They'd chosen to set up their laptop facing a wall without windows or framed photos, making their location more difficult to pinpoint.

The former Buckeye Bailey Security guard's appearance had changed a lot since he'd entered the prison system. He'd shaved his head, getting rid of the dirty-blond tresses that had rolled past his shoulders. He'd also added a couple of tattoos and a thick mustache with a three-quarter beard. If Zeke were estimating correctly, he'd also added about ten pounds of pure muscle.

"Someone killed Arty? Really?" Chad's eyes lingered briefly on Celeste before moving back to Zeke. "Are you sure? What's the motive?"

Celeste crossed her arms. "Why don't you tell us?"

"What?" Chad let out a surprised laugh. His brown eyes sparkled with it. "You think *I* killed Arty? How? If you haven't noticed, I'm already in prison."

Zeke narrowed his eyes as he tried to read the other man's body language, which was difficult on a videoconference. The camera framed Chad from the top of his tattooed head to the middle of his chest covered by the orange-twill prison uniform. He sat straight in his chair, with his hands apparently folded on his lap. His posture indicated openness. Still, Zeke believed Chad was lying.

Part of his skepticism was based on the revelations Celeste had shared with him and his brothers after her conversation with Meryl yesterday evening. The four of them—Celeste, Mal, Jerry and he—suspected Chad was Sally Jaxx's son. They were waiting for Mal to confirm it.

"How would you describe your relationship with Art?" Zeke wondered if he'd seen a spark of anger in Chad's eyes. It had disappeared too quickly to be certain.

The fired guard shrugged. "He was my boss. I mean, we were friendly, but we weren't friends."

"How friendly were you after he tried to stiff you twice on your pay?" Celeste lobbed the question at their interview subject with taunting aggression.

"He didn't stiff me." Chad leaned toward his computer monitor. "The checks were late, but he paid me what I was owed."

Celeste shrugged. "They were still late. And then he fired you."

"He didn't fire me." Chad's features tightened as his temper built. He switched his attention back to Zeke. "Arty laid off a bunch of guards because TSG took the Archer Family Realty contract from him."

Zeke shook his head. "We spoke with the guards who'd been fired along with you. They confirmed that Dean Archer had complained about your unprofessional behavior. *You're* the reason Art lost the Archer contract."

Chad's nostrils flared with anger. "That's bull—"

This time Celeste laughed. "Are we supposed to believe everyone's lying *but* you? Just admit Dean Archer accepted TSG's contract *after* leaving Buckeye Bailey Security because of *your* sloppy behavior."

A muscle flexed in Chad's jaw. "You're pretty bold talking

to me from behind a computer screen. Would your tongue be as sharp if we were face-to-face?"

Celeste leaned closer to the monitor. "You're pretty bold having other people do your dirty work for you. People like you don't intimidate me."

"Is that right? Then why aren't you here?" Chad spread his arms, indicating the prison. "When I heard you wanted to talk to me, I thought they meant in person. I don't get that many visitors."

"You're right. You don't." Zeke drew a printout of the prison's visitors log for the past three months. "In fact, you've only had one person visit you in the past three months. She's visited every week, though, at least once a week. Monica Ward."

Blood drained from Chad's face. Zeke felt a rush of satisfaction. *We've got you.*

He spoke when Chad remained silent. "Is she your sister?" It was a wild guess. After all, they had different surnames. But it was a gamble worth his life—or death.

Chad narrowed his eyes. "I don't know who you're talking about."

"I'll take that as a yes." Zeke held up the sheet of paper, angling it so Chad could read it through the camera. "Her signature's on this form. She's written your name and identification number on the visitor log. Does that help your memory?"

"I'm not denying that she's been here." Chad's voice cooled. He gestured toward his computer monitor. "You have the log. But what's that matter? You seem to think that's evidence. Evidence of what?"

"Conspiracy to commit murder." Celeste's voice was expressionless, but Zeke sensed her anger and impatience. "We can connect Monica to you, Arthur Bailey, Dean Archer and Zeke Touré."

No, they couldn't. At least not yet. Connecting Monica to the three of them would be a challenge, considering she wore disguises when she met with Dean, with Art's daughter and with Kevin. But Zeke remained silent because Celeste's bluff was a good one and could come in handy.

Chad sneered. "You're lying."

Zeke shrugged. "How else do you think we were able to identify her? Your sister was dating one of TSG's employees."

Chad swallowed before trying his own brand of bravado. "I still don't know what you're talking about."

"We're talking about murder and attempted murder." Celeste leaned back against her chair. She was generating enough frost to freeze every pipe in the substation. "You must really like it in prison, Chad. Your stay is going to be extended for a very, very, very long time."

Chad looked away, then back. "Obviously, I won't be able to change your mind. You're not listening to me. You're only willing to believe what suits your vision of your case. Well, good luck with that." His eyes held Zeke's. "You'll need it." He ended the meeting, turning the screen to black.

Celeste sighed. "We've got them, both of them. And he knows it."

Zeke shifted in his seat to face her. "You were brilliant to follow your instincts with Meryl. The information she gave you about the lawsuit connected all the dots: Chad and Monica as the killers, and revenge against Art and Dean for their mother's murder as their motivation."

Celeste frowned at him. "But how do *you* fit into that?"

Zeke rubbed his eyes with his left hand. "That's the missing piece. Hopefully, Mal will find something."

Celeste looked at the black screen. "How much do you want to bet Chad's warning Monica right now?"

Zeke's muscles tightened with tension. "If he is, how will she react?"

ZEKE'S CELL PHONE rang as he stepped out of the shower early Friday morning. He and Celeste had just finished their workouts. It wasn't yet 7:00 a.m. The call could only be from his brothers. Hopefully, they'd discovered more information about Monica Ward or Chad Cooper.

He dried his hands and grabbed the phone on its third ring. "Hey, wh—"

Jerry's voice was sharp with panic. "Mal's been shot."

Chapter Seventeen

"Lean on me!" Celeste hissed as she tugged him closer to her, further impeding his movements as they crossed the hospital parking lot early Friday morning.

"Hurry up. I've got to get to my brother." Zeke struggled to keep from shouting his panic and frustration. He was sweating. It was from a combination of anxiety and the ridiculous costume Celeste had forced him into.

"That's exactly what Monica's looking for." Celeste had altered her gait, taking longer—albeit slower—strides. "Someone running across the lot toward the emergency room entrance. Perhaps to check on someone with a gunshot wound?"

After receiving the bare minimum details from Jerry about the shooting, Zeke had flown out of the cabin's bathroom. He'd found Celeste and explained why they needed to get to the Riverside Hospital Emergency Room. Right. Now.

Celeste had slowed things down. She suspected Monica had shot Mal at least in part to flush Zeke out of hiding. In case she was right, she'd insisted they wear disguises to the hospital. She'd been firm that Zeke wear her overweight old man's costume. She'd dressed as a gangly young man, stuffing her hair into a natural wig and attaching an adhesive and makeup that gave her chin and upper lip stubble.

Zeke gritted his teeth. "Have you considered your obsession with disguises is your subconscious need to hide from the world?" He felt her stiffen and regretted his comment.

"Listen, Gramps, that kind of talk is going to get you dropped in this parking lot." The spunk in her response reassured him that Celeste wouldn't hold his amateur psychology against him.

"This is killing me." Zeke was forced to waddle due to the extra padding he was carrying around his stomach, waist and hips, and Celeste's pressing down on his arm.

"I know, and I'm truly sorry. But this is for everyone's well-being, not just yours." Celeste was tapping the keys on her cell phone with her thumbs.

Was she staying in character as a gangly youth, or was she communicating with someone? "Who are you texting?"

"Jerry." Celeste dropped her cell phone into the front pocket of her baggy, faded blue jeans and used both hands to pretend to help him walk. "He and Mal are waiting for us in one of the examining rooms. Eriq and Taylor are with them. We're supposed to ask for Nurse Becky Hardy at the desk."

"Great," Zeke said on a grateful sigh. He tried to speed up, but Celeste held him back. It made for a long journey to the emergency room entrance.

The waiting area was packed. Zeke didn't sense any hesitation in Celeste's movements as he leaned on her. She set a course for the registration desk. Her gait remained steady and deliberate, much to Zeke's impatience.

She stopped in front of one of the nurses seated behind the desk. Her name tag read *Becky Hardy*. Becky had a warm, welcoming expression. Her brown eyes sparkled when she smiled. A wealth of thick red curls framed her peaches-and-cream face but clashed with her hot pink short-sleeved top. Zeke instantly felt that he could trust her.

Celeste lowered her voice. "We're here to see Detectives Duster and Stenhardt, please."

Becky's expression became more serious. Her big brown

eyes considered Zeke before returning to Celeste. She stood and circled the desk. "Please come with me."

To Zeke's relief, the young nurse set a brisk pace to the examination room. Her curls swung around her head as though in a panic. Arriving at one of the closed doors, she knocked twice before pushing it open and stepping back.

Celeste inclined her head. "Thank you."

"Thank you, Nurse Hardy." Zeke tried to smile past the fake gray beard and mustache Celeste had affixed to his face, before following her across the threshold into the room.

Jerry sat in a chair beside the examining table. Mal was seated in the chair facing the table. Eriq and Taylor stood on either side of him. The middle Touré wore a sweat-stained slate gray wicking jersey and black running shorts. A white bandage was wrapped around his right upper arm. His face was stiff with anger, some of which eased when he saw Zeke.

"What are you both wearing?" Jerry split a look of humor and bemusement between Zeke and Celeste.

"They're disguises," Celeste responded before Zeke could. "Don't tease. It was hard enough convincing your brother to wear one."

Zeke gave Jerry a quick visual scan. He looked worried, but physically he was fine, except for the cast that was still on his left arm. He said he'd been walking laps around Antrim Lake in northwest Columbus while Mal was jogging. Zeke was grateful the two had been together and that Mal had only sustained a flesh wound.

Mal looked to Celeste. "You think Monica Ward shot me to get to Zeke. I agree. Thank you for taking care of our brother."

Jerry cleared his throat. "Yes. Thanks, Cece."

"Celeste is fine." She stepped aside, giving Zeke a clearer path to Mal.

Zeke heard the fear in Mal's voice. His brothers' care and

sincerity humbled him. Zeke crossed to him, clenching his fist to keep from grabbing Mal in relief.

"How are you feeling?" He heard the scratchy tone of his voice.

"Angry." Mal looked up at him. "But I'll be fine. You should've stayed in the safe house. That's what it's for."

Zeke's eyebrows—the real ones—flew up his forehead. "Would *you* have stayed at the safe house?"

Mal's eyes never wavered. "No."

Zeke looked at Eriq and Taylor. "I'm surprised to see you two here so early, but I'm grateful."

In his dark gray suit, Eriq looked like he'd been up for hours. Today's bolo clip was silver and shaped like a white bass. "A friend was shot. Where else would we be?"

Taylor looked around the room. She appeared fresh and wide awake, in a trim black pantsuit. Her honey-blond hair was balanced on the crown of her head. "Are we sure Monica Ward didn't just mistake Mal for Zeke? Your family resemblance is pretty darn strong."

"I'm positive." Celeste's response was firm.

"How?" Taylor asked.

Celeste pointed to Mal. "Because Mal's still alive. If Monica mistook him for Zeke, the outcome would've been very different."

Eriq crossed his arms over his broad chest. "I agree with CJ." His tone was somber, bordering on funereal. "This means you three have been under surveillance for some time. Probably months."

Taylor crossed her arms. "The killer knew about your regular runs at Antrim, and when and how often you jog there. You may want to stay away from the lake and otherwise alter your schedules for a while."

"You're right." Mal looked disappointed.

Jerry groaned. "We've got to close this case. It's bad enough that I can't jog for the next six weeks because of this cast, but walking indoors on a treadmill is not my idea of a good time."

Mal looked around the room. "Based on the information Celeste got from Meryl on the lawsuit against Art, I was able to dig deeper into Monica Ward. Zeke and Celeste were right. She's Chad Cooper's sister and Sally Jaxx was their mother."

Celeste took a few minutes to fill Eriq and Taylor in on Monica and Chad's lawsuit against Art's company.

Mal continued. "Sally Jaxx was murdered two years ago on March 15."

Jerry interrupted. "So that's two and a half years ago."

"Correct." Mal nodded. "Which was three months after her application for employment with TSG was denied because she failed the physical fitness test." His eyes met Zeke's. "Your name and signature were on that declination letter."

Celeste blinked. "That's the missing piece that connects the revenge motive to Art, Dean and Zeke. Monica and Chad blame Art for not providing backup for their mother. They blame Dean because their mother was killed at his company. And Zeke because they believe that, if you'd hired their mother, she'd still be alive today."

"She very well might have been." Zeke scrubbed his hands over his face, surprised when he felt the fake beard against his palms.

"Don't blame yourself." Taylor was adamant. "She didn't pass the fitness test."

"You *can't* blame yourself." Celeste's eyes were wide with concern for him. "There are too many variables in life. Let's stay focused on the case." She turned to Mal. "Do you have an address for Monica?"

Mal rubbed the back of his neck. "I'm working on it."

Eriq rested his hand on Mal's left shoulder. "We'll give you a hand with that." He scanned the room. "With your help, we're closing in on the person who killed my friend. Thank you."

"No thanks necessary." Zeke dropped his eyes to the white bandage on Mal's sienna bicep.

For his part, Zeke didn't think he'd be able to sleep again until the serial killer was finally caught.

"I HAVE A proposal for you." Zeke's words broke their companionable silence late Friday afternoon. He took a breath, stretching his emerald pullover across his chest. "My brothers and I want you to partner with us. We want to offer our clients your investigative services. In exchange, we'd ask that you refer our security services to your clients."

Celeste's skin warmed as her temper ignited. They'd finished lunch hours ago. She'd been thinking about the apples and grapes in the fridge. Snacks she could eat with one hand—or pitch at Zeke's handsome head.

With an effort, she kept her voice flat, without inflection. "You want me to bail you out."

"What?" Zeke's eyes widened. "No, it would be a collaboration. We'd refer each other to our prospective clients."

Celeste could barely hear his words above the buzzing in her ears. She knew he'd said something. Whatever it was, it wouldn't have made a difference. "Your company's finances are unstable. Your words. You said TSG's finances were on shaky ground. You need a source to protect your agency in case of a market shift. You see *me* as that source."

He was using her. Like others before him. Sterling. Dionne. Lee. Nanette. To name a few. Now, with a broken heart, she could add Zeke to the list. She'd thought what they had was real. He wasn't with her because he *needed* her. He was with her because he *wanted* her. At least, that's what she'd thought.

Zeke stood from the dining table to pace. "You're misunderstanding our intent. This would be a mutually beneficial partnership. The referrals would help each of us to grow our client base."

Celeste wanted to stand as well, but she was afraid she'd pummel him. He'd hurt her. She wanted to release at least a little of that pain. "And if your client used me, you'd take a percentage of the case."

Zeke stopped to frown at her. "That's right. Just as you'd get a percentage of any case we got from your referrals."

She still couldn't stand. Her knees were trembling. From nerves or temper? *When he looks at me, does he see his future—or his finances? And how pathetic was she? What made her think someone as intelligent, successful, kind and caring as Hezekiah Touré would have any interest in her?*

Fool! Fool! Fool!

"I appreciate the offer." That was a lie. She winced as she swallowed the bile in her throat. "But I don't need more referrals. I have as much work as I can handle from client referrals and law enforcement contacts. Besides, Nanette's leaving, remember? I'm taking on her clients. All of them."

Zeke dragged his hand over his head. He expelled a breath. "I hadn't thought of that."

He hadn't thought of her at all. He'd thought only of himself. And maybe his brothers. What he wanted. What he needed. She'd thought he'd cared about her. He'd said he'd wanted to get to know her. He'd wanted more than a physical relationship. Had anything he'd said been sincere? Or had it all been part of his plan to get close to her so he could use her? Like Lee had. And Nanette. And like Sterling was trying to do.

"No. You hadn't thought of that." She was growing numb. Good. She pushed herself off her chair and locked her knees. "Is that what this seduction was about?"

Zeke's dark eyes flared with anger. His body stilled. "What?"

"Were you trying to make me more amenable to your

persuasion to stay and help put your family's company back on solid ground?"

"Never." His voice was gruff. Tight. "How could you think that?"

She arched an eyebrow. "You wouldn't be the first."

His sharp cheekbones flushed. "Don't compare me to Lee Martin."

"Don't make it so easy." She collected her case files from the table, then stormed past him toward the stairs. "My whole life, people have been getting close to me just to use me." She spun back to face him, anger strengthening her limbs. "And you've been the worst of them."

"Celeste, that's not—" He tried to interrupt, but she wouldn't let him.

Celeste verbally bulldozed past him the same way he'd trampled all over her heart and soul. "All that crap about wanting to get to know me. Wanting me to share my thoughts, my feelings, my past with you." She stalked toward him, jabbing her finger into his chest. "Those were all lies! But I have to hand it to you. You put more effort into your act than the others did. Bravo."

Zeke took hold of her wrist to stop her attack. "It wasn't an act."

"Save it!" She jerked her hand free. Spinning on her heels, she headed back to the stairs, clutching her files to her chest.

"My feelings for you are real, Celeste." He aimed the words at her back.

It was like someone slid a blade between her shoulders. Was she bleeding? Celeste breathed through the pain.

Grabbing the banister, she pulled herself onto the first step. "Ah, so that's the reason you're asking me for referrals. Your *feelings*."

"Celeste, one has nothing to do with the other."

She looked at him over her shoulder. "Doesn't it? I'm done

with being used." She marched up the steps on stiff legs, without another word.

Zeke's eyes drilled into her back. Let him look. She'd learned her lesson. This time was much more painful than all the others combined and multiplied by infinity. This time, she'd fallen in love. Zeke had broken through all her barriers. She'd never wanted to share her thoughts, her fears, her past with anyone before. But she'd allowed Zeke to get close to her. She'd thought he was opening himself to her in return. Instead, he was lulling her into a false sense of security. And she'd let him.

Fool! Fool! Fool!

At the top of the stairs, Celeste paused to let the pain pass through her. She crossed into her room, and with all her willpower, refrained from slamming her door shut. Instead, she closed it quietly behind her.

Celeste pressed her forehead against its cool surface, inhaling its cedar scent. She'd given Zeke her heart. He'd asked for her business contacts. She'd never make the mistake of letting anyone close to her ever again.

Chapter Eighteen

"How did you mess this up so *badly*?" Jerry asked the question Zeke's mind had been shouting since Celeste had walked out of the great room minutes before.

They'd each retreated to their rooms, separated by a shared wall. Through that barrier, Zeke could hear her, speaking softly to someone. He couldn't decipher her words. With whom was she speaking? Were they discussing his colossal error in judgment? Did he have any hope of fixing his mistake? That's what he hoped his brothers could help him figure out.

"You or *we*?" Mal broke his silence. He was almost eerily still, seated beside Jerry at the Touré Security Group conference table. He'd loosened the black tie he wore with the pale gold long-sleeved dress shirt.

Since Zeke had texted asking them to join this video-conference call, his middle brother had been silent. Mal's dark eyes had seemed to assess Zeke's every movement and expression as he'd recounted his disastrous exchange with Celeste. Jerry had been the one to interrupt with commentaries and verbal nudges, prompting his narration. Anyone who didn't know the brothers would think Mal was silently gloating that he'd warned Zeke and Jerry that their offer wouldn't be as well received as they'd hoped. But unlike Jerry, Mal wasn't prone to gloating. He wouldn't take pleasure in I-Told-You-Sos. At least, not in the moment. That boast might come later. But right now, Zeke could sense Mal was trying to figure out what could have gone wrong and what Zeke wasn't telling them. Zeke could attest that there was a lot he was holding back.

"What does that mean, 'you or we'?" Jerry interrupted. The white cast on his left arm seemed to glow against his dark bronze short-sleeved shirt. Both brothers must have left their jackets in their respective offices.

Zeke kept his voice low. "Mal's asking whether she thinks all three of us are taking advantage of her or just me." He stood to pace. "She only accused me."

"Why are you walking away from the camera? You know we can't see you, right?" Jerry continued after Zeke ignored his exasperated question. "Why would Celeste think you were using her?"

"Because she has feelings for him." Mal's response exposed what Zeke should have realized himself. What he should have considered before he blundered in with his grand offer of working together.

"Oh." The light bulb came on for Jerry. "Do *you* have feelings for *her*?"

Zeke spoke with his back to the monitor. "I'm in love with her."

"So that's a yes." Jerry broke the brief silence. "Which means you've really screwed this up."

Zeke returned to the small wooden desk. His movements were stiff and jerky as he claimed his seat in front of the clean laptop. "That's right, Jer. I have. So how do I fix it?" His words dripped with sarcasm and impatience.

Jerry shrugged his right shoulder, glancing at Mal, then back to Zeke. "Just tell her how you feel. That worked for me and Mal."

Mal hadn't moved during their videoconference. "If he does that now, Celeste will think he's trying a new strategy to get her help with our company. She won't believe he's being sincere."

"Exactly." Zeke sank back against his chair. "I told her my personal feelings for her don't have anything to do with our professional lives, but she didn't believe me. She basically told me to take a flying leap into a shallow pond."

"Harsh." Jerry winced. "Look, we should scrap the referral plan. Celeste doesn't need our help. Once Nanette leaves, she'll be drowning in clients. She's probably going to have to contract with other detectives to help her."

"Jerry's right," Mal said.

Jerry frowned. "Why are you surprised?"

Mal ignored him. "Zeke, what's more important to you—building the company or building a life with Celeste?"

"Celeste." He felt guilty, but he owed his brothers the truth.

He wanted Touré Security Group to succeed. He owed it to his parents for the legacy they'd built for him and his brothers. He owed it to his brothers because it was their inheritance, too. And he owed it to himself. His parents had taught him to always give his best effort to every endeavor. But seeing his brothers' happiness after falling in love with exceptional women had made him realize their company's success alone could never fulfill him. He needed a partner. Someone who could help him see through the dark times. And someone with whom he could share the brighter days. His brothers had that. He wanted it, too.

"Good answer, Number One." Jerry's dark eyes twinkled with the mockery only younger siblings seemed able to manifest.

"Agreed." Mal nodded. "When Celeste's ready to listen, lead with that."

"Cyborg's right." Jerry inclined his head toward Mal on his right. Mal's shoulders rose and fell in a silent sigh. "Celeste needs to know that you meant it when you said your personal relationship with her doesn't have anything to do with our two companies. The best way to prove that to her is to take our companies out of the equation."

Zeke closed his eyes briefly in gratitude. "Thank you. Both of you. That's good advice."

"Good luck." Mal held his eyes through the computer's camera.

Zeke could tell he was remembering when he'd faced a similar turning point in his relationship with Grace. Zeke was heartened by the fact that things had worked out for the medical researcher and his brother. Hopefully, he'd also be able to fix things between himself and Celeste.

"We'll send you our bill and encourage you to let your friends know about our services, if they need similar help." Jerry gave him a cocky grin.

Zeke echoed Mal's anguished groan.

Jerry split a look between Zeke and Mal. "Too soon for the referral joke?"

Zeke leaned toward the laptop's keypad. "I'll catch up with you later." He ended the meeting then stood to wander the room.

When Celeste's ready to listen, lead with that.

He glanced toward their shared wall.

When would she be ready to listen to anything he had to say outside of the case? Would she ever be ready?

CELESTE'S CELL PHONE rang minutes after she'd secluded herself in her bedroom. She pulled it from the front-right pocket of Nanette's scarlet linen pants. Maybe it would be a welcome distraction. She checked the screen. It wasn't. It was Sterling. Again. He'd already left several voicemail messages for her, all of which she'd ignored. She was tempted to ignore this one as well. But she was in a bad mood anyway. Perhaps she should just get this conversation over with.

She rotated her neck to ease the tension there and filled her lungs before exhaling. "Hello."

"Celeste. I'm glad I finally caught you." The irritation was evident beneath his words.

She didn't owe him any explanations. She didn't owe him anything. *Let's just get to the point and get this over with.* "Why are you calling?"

"As I've explained on the numerous voicemail messages I've left for you, we need to discuss your grandmother's estate." Sterling's patience seemed on the verge of unraveling.

Welcome to the club.

"I've already heard from your mother's lawyer." Celeste kept her voice down.

She was aware Zeke had entered his room shortly after she'd come upstairs. She could barely hear his voice through their shared wall behind her headboard. Was he speaking with his brothers? Were they discussing their failed plan to use her to help increase Touré Security Group's revenue base? What were they planning now?

Sterling's voice was loud in her left ear. It shattered her concentration. "What did she say?"

Startled, Celeste jumped. "Who?"

Sterling's sigh was short and sharp. "The lawyer. What did she say about Mother's estate?"

She hadn't said anything. Instead, Celeste had emailed the lawyer to explain she'd received her letter, but since she was working a case, Celeste wouldn't be able to meet with the lawyer right away. In the interim, they'd have to do as much as they could via emails and, when possible, phone calls until Celeste closed the case. But that wasn't the information Sterling was after. Even if it was, Celeste wasn't inclined to share those details with him.

She roamed the spacious bedroom. Her steps took her past her dressing table to the window in the front half of the room. The view overlooked the main entrance to the cabin. "What do you want to know about the estate?"

Sterling hesitated, as though her question had confused him. "Well, we should know what kind of condition she left her estate in. Is it carrying any debt? Is she up to date with her payments like her taxes, insurance and utilities? Does she have any liens against her home?"

Celeste mentally filed everything Sterling said to reference later. Experience had taught her that people hid their goals and motivations within their words.

"I'll be sure to ask the lawyer." Celeste moved on to the window on the left near the back of the room. "Anything else?"

She wanted to linger near the shared wall to catch any stray words that penetrated it. But it was a two-way street. If she drifted too close to the wall, Zeke would be able to hear her as well.

Sterling sighed again. He did that a lot. He'd recorded several sighs on his voicemail messages. "Celeste, surely you realize this isn't right."

She froze. She'd known those words were coming. And still they hurt—almost as badly as Zeke had hurt her. But not quite.

Her mother had been Sterling's first wife. Allegedly, he'd married her for love, and Celeste had been his first child. Despite that, Celeste wasn't a real member of his family. She was an outsider. Dionne had never accepted Celeste's mother so Sterling wouldn't accept Celeste.

Yet in the end, Dionne had left her…everything. "Why do you think your mother made me the sole beneficiary of her estate?"

"Who knows why my mother did anything?" Sterling's words had a bite to them.

"You do." Celeste resumed her walk about her room. She turned away from the windows and wandered toward the closet. She considered the colorful and admittedly pretty outfits Nanette had loaned her. Maybe it was time to rethink her all-black wardrobe. Hiding from people hadn't shielded her from harm. "If you had to guess, why do you think she left everything to me?"

"I don't know." Now Sterling was just being stubborn.

"Then let me try to guess." She let the sleeve of the soft pink silk blouse slip through her fingers. She propped her right shoulder against the wall beside the closet and stared blindly at the dressing table. "You and your children live near your mother in Chicago. Despite that, you rarely visited, and the only time you called was when you needed something. You didn't spend much, if any, time with her during the holidays, and you never helped her celebrate her birthday."

The silence was deep and tense.

"What gives you that idea?" Sterling sounded as though he was chewing glass.

"Your mother gave me that idea. In fact, I'm practically quoting what she'd tell me every time I called and visited." Celeste's gut burned with satisfaction.

"You only have her side of the story."

"It's her estate. Her side of the story is all that matters."

Sterling blew an irritated breath. His silence was longer this time as he apparently tried to work out his next steps. Celeste used the quiet time to try to make out what Zeke was saying, but his voice was too low and too deep. She knew he was speaking with his brothers and suspected she was the topic of their conversation. Since they were working this investigation together, if they were discussing the case, they would have asked her to join them.

The next time she saw Zeke, she'd have to play it cool. And she'd have to keep her guard up.

"We just want our fair share, Celeste." Sterling brought her focus back to their conversation.

"And that's what your mother believed she left you—your fair share."

"She left us nothing," Sterling snapped.

"Exactly." Celeste straightened from the wall. "I have to get back to work, Sterling."

"I don't even know where you live." Sterling's remark surprised her.

Celeste frowned. "Are you planning a visit?"

She'd been eighteen years old the last time they'd spoken in person. It was the morning she'd moved out of his mother's house, in a car she'd bought herself. She'd been on her way to Ohio to attend Franklin University. She'd wanted to go to college but had known she couldn't count on financial assistance from the adults in her life. Instead, she'd gotten a job, earned scholarships and applied for grants. But Sterling had still shown up minutes before she'd left. He'd tried to give her a paternal speech and take credit for the success she'd worked for. She'd driven off before he'd finished and had never looked back.

"I have your phone number, but I don't have your address." He was breathless. Was he climbing stairs? What was he doing? "Do you have my address?"

Time to cut this conversation short. "If I need to get in touch with you, I'll call."

"What are you going to do, Celeste?" Sterling caught his breath.

"I'm going to settle your mother's estate. After that, I don't know." She disconnected the call. With any luck, Sterling would wait to hear from her and stop leaving messages every other day.

Celeste's eyes strayed toward the far wall. Lately, it didn't seem as though luck was on her side.

Zeke's knock on her door made her jump. Slipping her cell phone into the front pocket of her borrowed slacks, Celeste crossed to the door and yanked it open. She took mean-spirited satisfaction in Zeke's surprised expression.

"I'm sorry to interrupt." His words were low. His eyes were wary. "Eriq and Taylor want to meet."

"SHE'D LISTED THIS address on her rental-car application." Taylor led Celeste and Zeke down a narrow hallway on the third floor of a three-story redbrick apartment building early Friday evening. She wore pale gray slacks and a boxy-cut navy blue jacket.

The building was in northwest Columbus, not far from Zeke's neighborhood. That was unsettling. He'd noticed the two police cruisers parked across the street. Were they waiting for Monica Ward's return?

Music, television programs and conversations carried into the hallway from the apartments they passed. If he spread his arms, Zeke suspected he could touch the walls on either side of the hall. The building must have been built in the early twentieth century. It smelled of mold and dust. Eriq's, Taylor's, Celeste's and his footsteps were silent on the thin moss green carpet. At the end of the hall, narrow French doors opened onto what appeared to be a stacked black-framed balcony. Natural light streamed through the glass doors, supplementing the hallway's fluorescent lighting.

Faux-maple-wood doors alternated along the paper-white walls. Taylor led them across the threshold of the door third from the end of the hallway. "We came to bring Monica in for questioning, but she was already gone. She must have realized we were getting close to her."

Zeke stepped aside for Celeste to enter. "Chad may have tipped her off after our videoconference with him yesterday."

"The apartment manager let us in." Eriq's voice carried from behind them. Zeke glanced back at the older detective. Eriq wore a dark brown suit. A copper clip in the shape of a walleye held his bolo tie in place. "It looks like Monica packed in a hurry. She's either moved to another location or she's left the city. We've put out a BOLO for her."

There was no way to predict how long it would take to get results.

Celeste stood a little more than an arm's distance from him. Zeke ignored the deep freeze wafting from her despite her warm blue blouse and red slacks. He turned his attention to the worn and faded efficiency unit Monica seemed to be using as her base of operations. He listened to Eriq's and Taylor's recount as he surveyed his surroundings. A shabby navy blue-cloth sofa bed dominated the space. It was open and unmade. Monica looked like a restless sleeper. Her plain white sheets lay tangled in the middle of the thin mattress beneath the single pillow. A chipped and scarred dark wood nightstand was positioned beside the bed.

Zeke started to cross toward it. Celeste grabbed his arm, stopping him. She released her hold just as abruptly and pressed disposable gloves into his chest.

He took them from her. "Thank you."

She turned away without a word. She still wasn't ready to listen. That was okay. He could be patient. She was worth the effort.

Zeke pulled on the thin, blue latex gloves as he approached the nightstand. His eyes moved over the moss green porcelain lamp. It was missing a shade. There were three quarters, two nickels, a dime and three pennies beside it. A five-by-seven-inch color photo was balanced against it. The image was of Chad Cooper and Monica Ward hugging a middle-aged woman who stood between them.

Off on their own were two contact lens cases. On a hunch, Zeke opened them. Each had a different tinted pair of lenses. In one case, the lenses were blue. In the second, they were green. He turned to find Celeste searching the closet. Two mannequin heads—one wearing a red wig, the other an ebony one—waited on a shelf.

"It looks like we've found Monica's disguises." Anger rolled over him. Zeke tightened his hands into fists to control it.

He met Celeste's eyes before she turned away to unload the model heads. Taylor and Eriq helped her bag them. Zeke moved on to the kitchen.

That's when the stench hit him. The unmistakable, nauseating stink of dishes left too long in the sink. His eyes stung as he surveyed the cramped space. Coffee-cup stains dotted the off-white linoleum counter. Cupboard drawers and doors were left partially open. Dirt tracked the off-white flooring.

Zeke turned and hurried out of the kitchen so he could breathe again. "She hasn't left."

"Sure she has." Eriq swept his arm around the room, bringing Zeke's attention to the clothes strewn across the thin carpet. "She must have been in a panic when she packed up and raced out of here."

Zeke tracked Eriq's gestures. "I don't think that's what we're looking at. Monica's apartment isn't a mess because she packed in a rush. It's a mess because she's a slob."

Taylor's thin blond eyebrows knitted. "What?"

"Monica's not missing. She's just not home." Zeke pictured Jerry's room when they were growing up and his home before he started dating Symone. Yes, there were definite similarities between what he was looking at now and the nightmarish memories of his childhood. This was the room of a slob. "Her clothes aren't flung across the room. They're pooled on the floor."

Zeke thought of the police officers parked out front. They were an extra layer of protection. They could also be a deterrent. Monica would be spooked if she noticed them before they saw her. Then what would she do? Where would she go? Zeke briefly closed his eyes. He needed to close this case. As long as Monica was who-knew-where, his brothers and Celeste were in danger.

"I agree that Monica hasn't left." Celeste closed the closet doors. "She could be out looking for us. She could be anywhere. But she's coming back."

"What makes you so sure?" Taylor wore a plain white blouse under her navy jacket.

Zeke pointed toward the picture of Monica with her mother and brother. "Because she left that photo behind."

"And Zeke's still alive." Celeste appeared beside him. Frost still rolled off her. "She's not going to leave until she's accomplished what she's here for, regardless of what happens to her."

Zeke shrugged his eyebrows. "And there's that, too."

"You've convinced me." Eriq checked his watch. "In which case, we should get you back. We don't want you here when she returns." He stepped back and gestured for Celeste and Zeke to proceed him.

"All right," Celeste said over her shoulder. "We'll wait for your update."

Zeke followed her from the apartment. "Hopefully, we'll hear something soon."

They were steps away from the exit beside the French doors, which led to the stairwell, when something—or someone—snatched Celeste and dragged her out of sight around a corner.

Zeke's heart was in his throat as he rushed after her. The scene that greeted him almost caused his heart to stop. Monica Ward had found them. One of her arms was wrapped around Celeste's neck. Her other hand held a gun to Celeste's throat.

She caught Zeke's eyes and gave him an evil grin. "I knew if I waited, *you'd* find *me*."

Zeke didn't think he'd ever take another breath.

Chapter Nineteen

"Wait!" Zeke's heart galloped like horses through a storm. "I'm the one you want. Let her go, and I'll come with you."

"You'll come with me anyway." Monica's brown eyes gleamed with malice. "I'm taking her for insurance." Her smile blinked away. Her pink lips thinned. Her voice snapped. "Go on. All of you. Lead the way."

Zeke hesitated. He didn't want to turn his back on Celeste. He knew Monica was capable of hurting him by hurting the people he loved. What could he say to make her let Celeste go?

Eriq's voice moved past him like a frigid wind. "We're not letting you take anyone."

Monica shielded herself behind Celeste's body. "Take your best shot." She arched a thin brown eyebrow. "I didn't think so. Now, *move*!"

He looked back at Eriq and Taylor. They both had their guns drawn, but everyone knew they wouldn't use them. They were in the narrow hallway of an occupied residential building. They couldn't risk a stray bullet penetrating one of the units and hurting—perhaps killing—someone. This wasn't a safe space to stage a shoot-out.

Zeke's heart slammed against his chest. He was sure they could all see his shirt waving against it. He glanced at Celeste again. She returned his gaze and rolled her eyes. Slowly.

Deliberately. Twice. He could hear her in his mind: "I'm more than just a sparkling personality."

Did she have a plan? A better question: Would it work? There was so much at risk. Too much. Her life. Zeke took a steadying breath. She was a trained professional. And they were out of options. This was a situation that was out of his control. He had to step back and give her a chance.

Zeke turned and led the other four into the stairwell that exited into the rear parking lot. Like the hallway, the stairwell was narrow. And it smelled old. The walls and stairs were made of concrete and had been painted a utilitarian gray. There was a window at each landing that allowed in a meager amount of sunlight to supplement the fluorescent bulbs affixed to the walls and ceiling.

Zeke descended the first set of stairs. He was alternately cold with fear and hot with anger. He held fast to the gray metal railing to support his unsteady knees. Beneath the muted sounds of their footfalls, the silence was oppressive. Zeke stopped beside the fire engine–red door that opened onto the second floor and glanced over his shoulder. Taylor was a step behind him. Eriq followed her. Monica and Celeste were at least an arm's distance behind Eriq.

Monica held a fistful of Celeste's blouse to anchor them together. She seemed tense, as though she anticipated some eventual resistance. Celeste's features were expressionless. He couldn't tell what she was thinking. Was she nervous? Did she have any doubts about what she was planning to do?

What was she planning to do, and how could he help her?

"Don't even think about walking through that door." Monica pressed her gun into the back of Celeste's head.

Zeke's heart took a painful pause before trying to bulldoze its way out of his chest. He clenched his hands and continued down the stairs.

Another small window and another red door marked the first-floor landing. Zeke didn't have any illusions that the officers stationed on the street to keep watch for Monica would happen to glance toward that window and see them in the stairwell with their target. They were on their own. That's what they had to plan for.

Zeke had reached the ground level. The exit was perhaps three paces ahead of him. They'd run out of time. His mind raced through possible scenarios to get them out of this situation. Could he signal the officers? Eriq and Taylor both had guns. Could they shoot out the tires of whatever vehicle Monica used for her getaway? In doing so, would any harm come to Celeste?

He pushed through the exit and stepped out into the parking lot. It was empty except for the dozen or so cars standing in what appeared to be assigned spaces. He'd left their rented smoke gray sedan in a visitor's spot. Zeke tightened his fists as he walked into the lot. If Monica hurt Celeste in any way, he'd dedicate the rest of his life to making her life a living—

Behind him, he heard a muffled, "Oomp" and then a thud. Zeke spun toward the noise. Celeste stood above a prone Monica, with the killer's gun in her hands.

Her legs were braced apart on the asphalt. She pointed the weapon at the other woman. "Eriq, could you cuff her, please?"

Eriq grunted. "It took you long enough."

Zeke watched the other man wipe his upper lip with the back of his wrist. His hand shook slightly as he holstered his weapon before pulling out the handcuffs.

Celeste engaged the gun's safety before turning it over to Taylor. The detective secured the weapon in an evidence bag as Eriq read Monica her Miranda rights.

With two strides, Zeke crossed to Celeste. He locked his hands around her upper arms and searched her face. "Are you all right?"

Her crooked smile melted his heart. She rolled her eyes.

"How many times have I told you, I'm more than just a sparkling personality?"

Zeke wrapped his arms around her and held her tight. "Thank God you're safe."

He could have lost her today. If that had happened, he would have lost himself. It was going to take him weeks to banish from his mind the image of her with a gun to her head. He held her even closer to him and breathed in her scent.

As ugly as this day had been, it had taught him one very valuable lesson: he needed Celeste Jarrett in his life. He had to find a way to make that happen.

"YOU DIDN'T HAVE to come into the agency." Celeste led Nanette into her office to retrieve her partner's suitcase and colorful wardrobe Saturday afternoon. "I told you I'd bring it by. It's the least I could do after you loaned me your clothes for a week."

Minutes before, Celeste had been at the Bailey residence, debriefing Meryl and her children on the investigation and capture of the person responsible for killing Arthur Bailey and the charges that were, at that moment, being brought against her co-conspirator. The meeting had been painful. Many more tears had been shed, but at least the family had closure and had received some peace in knowing their husband and father had not committed suicide.

Celeste wheeled the pastel purple suitcase out from beside her modular faux-maple-wood desk and turned it over to Nanette.

Nanette waved a dismissive hand. "I was out doing bridal stuff anyway. Besides, I wanted to know if the clothes worked."

Celeste frowned, tilting her head to the side in confusion. "Worked?"

"To turn up the heat with the sexy security consultant."

Nanette grinned as she made herself comfortable on one of the sterling-silver-and-black-vinyl chairs at Celeste's small glass conversation table. "Tell me *everything*."

Celeste shook her head as she rounded her desk and took the black-cloth executive chair. "You do, of course, remember this was a homicide investigation and not some sort of reality-TV love connection? Someone was trying to kill my protectee." Even though they'd solved the case and the killer was in custody, that phrase still made Celeste's blood run cold.

"I know, I know." Nanette crossed her right leg over her left. She smoothed the material of her grape knee-length skirt over her right thigh. She swung her deep purple wedge-heel shoe above the thin gunmetal-gray carpet. "But you solved the case, and he's safe now. How did you solve the case?"

Celeste gave Nanette a summary of the past week, hitting only those points that were relevant to the investigation. She watched her friend's eyes grow wider as she described the events of the last twenty minutes of the case.

Nanette interrupted as Celeste got to the part when Monica had grabbed her in the hallway. Her words were partially muffled behind her right palm. "Have mercy, Celeste! She held a gun to your neck?"

Celeste was glad she was seated as she remembered that moment. She didn't think she'd ever been that scared. "Yes. She'd seen the officers in their patrol cars and known they were looking for her. She avoided their notice by climbing the fire escape to the roof of the building and entering the third-floor hallway through the French doors."

Nanette shook her head. "That's crazy. What did Eriq and Taylor do?"

Celeste spread her arms. "They drew their guns. What else could they do? Monica was using me as a human shield. And we knew that many, if not all, the apartments were occupied at the time. We didn't know if other people were on their way up the stairs. We had to get out of the building before we tried anything."

"That's terrifying," Nanette said on a breath.

"Yes, it was." Celeste shivered as her mind played flash-backs of what seemed like the never-ending descent into the parking lot yesterday evening.

Monica had gripped the pearl white blouse so tightly against her that Celeste thought the buttons would pop. The cool metal of the gun's barrel had bitten into the skin between her shoulder blades.

She'd kept a steady pace as they'd walked the three stories to the building's ground floor. All the while, she'd held two thoughts in her mind. The first was that she'd only have one chance at getting the gun away from Monica and that would be when they stepped out of the stairwell into the parking lot. She'd remembered stepping up to the threshold sill when she and Zeke had entered through the rear door. She'd hoped that step would force at least some distance between her and Monica's gun. It had.

Celeste had taken a large step across the threshold and down into the parking lot. Moving as quickly as she could, she'd grabbed Monica's gun hand, twisting the wrist to make her drop the weapon, then continued twisting her arm to flip her onto the asphalt.

"What did Zeke do?" Nanette's question blessedly drew Celeste from the memory of that confrontation.

"He'd offered to take my place." That was the second thought she'd held in her mind.

Zeke hadn't hesitated. His first thought had been ensuring her safety, apparently at any cost. The fear and anguish in his eyes couldn't be mistaken. Celeste doubted he had a plan when he'd told Monica to release Celeste and take him instead. He couldn't have put something together that quickly.

Still, he was prepared to turn himself over to someone determined to kill him in order to keep her safe.

"What?" Nanette pressed a hand to her heart. "Celeste, that man *loves* you."

Hope stole her breath. "Do you really think so?"

"Of course he does!" Nanette gaped at her. "The whole reason the two of you went underground in the first place was to keep him safe from that homicidal maniac. But as soon as she got her hands on *you*, he volunteered to give up his life for yours. *That* is love."

Celeste rose to pace her cramped office. "But that's the kind of man Zeke Touré is. He and his brothers. They're protectors. It's not just their business. It's in their blood."

Nanette huffed. "Girl, if all he was interested in was 'protecting' you—" she put the word in air quotes "—he could've said, 'Wait, let's talk about this.' Or, 'There's no way you're getting out of this.' But you said he offered to take your place. That's love."

Celeste leaned back against her desk. Her knees were shaking with nerves, hope and excitement. "I hope you're right. Because I'm in love with him."

Nanette screamed her joy. "I knew it! I knew it! I've never seen you as mopey as you were when you and Zeke stopped going out. So when are you going to tell him how you feel?"

Celeste tightened her grip on her desk behind her to keep from dropping to the floor at the idea of telling Zeke she loved him. "I don't know. I haven't thought about that. I mean, suppose you're wrong and I'm right, and he was just being chivalrous or something?"

Could someone as decent and kind as Hezekiah Touré fall in love with a misfit like her?

Nanette rose and crossed to her. She took her hands and held her eyes. "Celeste, I know you have trust issues. I have no idea what happened between you and the family you never talk about. But I realize what Lee and Roger did to us did a job on you. It did a job on me, too. If it weren't for you, I would be in prison."

Celeste shook her head. "We solved that crime together."

Nanette squeezed her hands. "No, girl, that was all you. And I know I've been leaning on you ever since. You carried the lion's share of opening this agency. You even helped me close the majority of my cases and never once asked for a share of my profits."

Celeste shifted with discomfort. "Where are you going with this?"

"You're worthy of being loved, Celeste." Nanette tightened her grip on Celeste's hands when she tried to pull free. "No, listen to me. Zeke is the first person you've shown any interest in since that punk Lee five years ago. I've lost count of the number of times I've tried to fix you up over the years, and you wouldn't give any of those prospects a chance. And they were good ones. Zeke is a good man. Eriq likes him, and he has a good reputation in the community. If there's any chance of having a relationship with him, take it. You deserve it."

Celeste tossed her a grin. "That's good advice. This bridal thing is giving you second sight."

Nanette gave her a shaming look. "It's more like you're finally listening to my excellent advice."

Celeste straightened from her desk. "Before I talk with Zeke, I think I'd like to add some color to my wardrobe. I enjoyed the way I felt wearing your clothes. The brighter colors made me feel seen. I liked that."

Nanette raised her fists in the air and screamed. "This is fantastic!" She spun toward the table to grab her handbag. "Quick, before you change your mind." She laughed. "Goodbye, Johnny Cash. Hello, Rihanna."

Celeste stopped mid-stride. "Wait. What?"

"DON'T KNOW HOW you did it, bro." Jerry lowered himself beside Mal on Zeke's steel gray leather sofa Saturday afternoon. Like his brothers, he wore dark knee-length shorts. His bronze short-sleeved cotton accommodated his cast. "I would've passed out if I had to lead someone down three flights of stairs while they held a gun on Symone."

Zeke sank into his matching armchair to the right of the sofa before his knees gave out. He wore rust-colored shorts with a black jersey. "I've already had one nightmare about it. I suspect there will be a lot more."

The brothers had just finished a celebratory lunch. Since Zeke's kitchen was out of commission because of the fire, Jerry and Mal had brought over sodas, salad and an extra-large, extra-cheese-and-pepperoni pizza. They'd claimed it was to celebrate successfully closing the case yesterday. That was probably partly true. But he believed it was mostly to do a reconnaissance of the area to make sure there weren't still threats lurking around him. That was fine. He'd done a similar surveillance of both of their neighborhoods as well as Celeste's yesterday and planned to do one again today.

"You didn't see what she did to disarm Monica?" Mal sat on the corner of the sofa closest to Zeke's armchair. He had on coffee-colored shorts with a cobalt shirt.

"No, but whatever she did, she moved quickly." Zeke gripped the chair's padded arms to keep at bay the fear and anger he'd felt yesterday afternoon. "I heard Monica cry out, but by the time I turned around, she was already on the ground and Celeste had her gun."

Jerry shook his head. His eyes were wide with amazement. "Celeste has some scary skills."

"When are you going to see her again?" Mal asked.

Good question. Zeke swallowed a sigh. "I don't know. I'm trying to work up my courage. She was furious with me after I asked her to partner with us."

Jerry spread his arms. "But she stuck to your side like a shadow the whole time we were at the precinct."

"It was the other way around." Zeke tightened his grip on the chair's arms. "*I* was sticking to *her* side."

Celeste had been physically unharmed after the ordeal. She hadn't sustained a bump, bruise or scratch from the encounter with Monica. But it had taken hours to convince him she was okay. He couldn't stop touching her—her arms, shoulders, back and neck. He'd even checked the back of her head where for one horrible moment Monica had held her gun.

"I saw the way she was looking at you, Zeke." Mal looked from Jerry, who nodded his agreement, back to Zeke. "I think she's ready to talk with you again."

Jerry leaned forward, balancing his elbows on his lap. "Zeke, I know how scary it is to tell someone how you feel."

Mal interrupted. "So do I."

Jerry glanced at Mal before continuing. "But Celeste is worth the risk. She's good for you."

Mal nodded. "She makes you laugh. You're happier—and less controlling."

"She's a miracle worker." Jerry's voice was dust dry. "And she's a bad—"

The doorbell interrupted Jerry's praise. Zeke unfolded himself from the armchair and strode toward the front door. He sensed his brothers trailing him, as though they wanted to make sure danger wasn't on the other side. He checked the peephole. His heart stopped. His breath caught in his throat. It took him a moment to remember to open the door.

"Celeste." Was he dreaming?

She stood on his porch wearing an apricot pencil-slim, knee-length dress with cap sleeves and soft cream ankle boots with one-inch heels.

Celeste looked over Zeke's shoulders. She must have noticed Mal and Jerry behind him. "Is this a bad time?" She took a step back when he didn't respond. "I could come back later."

Jerry walked forward and offered her his hand. "Celeste, hello. It's good to see you. Ignore my brother." He drew her past Zeke and into the house. He moved back to stand between Mal and Zeke. "Sometimes I think he was switched at birth. This is a good time. Mal and I were leaving."

Zeke's brain started working again. "Yes, they were just leaving."

Mal gave Celeste a big hug. "Thank you for protecting our brother."

Celeste's eyes stretched wide with surprise. She patted Mal's shoulders. "You're welcome."

Jerry gave her a one-armed embrace. "Yes, thank you so much for taking care of Zeke. You're amazing."

"I couldn't have done it without you guys. We make a good team." Celeste patted Jerry's right shoulder, then stepped back. She looked from Jerry to Mal. "Please tell Grace and Symone I said hello."

"We will." Mal gave her a smile before he and Jerry disappeared through Zeke's front door.

Zeke locked the door behind them, then faced Celeste. His heart was running seventy miles an hour. "You look beautiful."

"Thank you." A blush filled her cheeks. She smiled at him and his heart beat even faster.

"Please come in." He gestured with his right arm that she should proceed him. "Can I offer you something to drink?"

"No, thank you." She lowered herself to the right corner of the sofa. "I had lunch with Nanette."

Zeke was relieved. He'd forgotten that all he had was water and milk. He reclaimed his armchair. "How are you?"

"I'm better." Celeste rotated the ring on her thumb. "I met with Meryl and her children. They're very grateful to you and your brothers for helping to find Art's killers."

Zeke nodded. "Jayne sends her thanks as well."

"That's nice." Celeste looked around his living room. Zeke wondered what she thought of his decorating skills. She returned her attention to him. "Now that the case is over, I had a chance to speak with Dionne's lawyer. She's going to settle the estate, including the sale of Dionne's home. Her estate's worth a little more than a million dollars. Imagine my surprise."

Zeke's eyes widened. His eyebrows rose up his forehead. "Wow. Are you going to share it with your father?"

"No, that's not what Dionne would have wanted. If she had, she would have named him in her will."

"That's true. Are you going to keep the money?" A million dollars was tempting, but Zeke couldn't imagine Celeste having anything to do with her grandmother, including inheriting her estate.

"No." Celeste shook her head decisively. "I haven't taken money from Dionne since I was sixteen." A slow smile curved her lips and brightened her eyes. "I've decided to donate all her money, including the proceeds from selling her house, to The Bishop Foundation."

"What?" Zeke's jaw dropped. "That's wonderful, Celeste. Symone's going to be thrilled."

"The foundation does important work, supporting medical research." Her smile grew into a grin. "I'm excited about the donation."

"So am I." Zeke smiled. "I'm glad you told me. Thank you."

Her grin faded and her uncertainty returned. She straightened her shoulders and drew a deep breath. "Zeke, I owe you an apology."

"For what?" He frowned his surprise.

"I misjudged you. I jumped to conclusions when I should have trusted you." Celeste started to stand, then sat back down, as though her legs were unsteady. "It wasn't until

Monica grabbed me and you offered to take my place that I realized you really do have feelings for me."

Zeke held Celeste's eyes. She was at least as nervous as he was. Knowing that gave him courage to bare his heart. "Celeste, I'm in love with you."

Celeste's eyes widened. The blood drained from her face. Her shoulders slumped. She buried her face in hands and sobbed.

Zeke leaped from his chair. He sat beside Celeste and took her into his arms. "Celeste, sweetheart, what did I say?"

Celeste slumped against him and continued sobbing into her palms.

Zeke was near panic. "Sweetheart, what's wrong? Please tell me."

Her voice was muffled behind her hands. Her words came in short bursts. "My whole life, no one has ever said those words to me. My whole life. Until you just did, I didn't realize how much I needed to hear them."

She was breaking his heart. His arms tightened around her. He wished he could go back in time and take all her pain away. He couldn't. There was nothing he could do about her past, but he could do his best to make sure her future was full of joy and love.

Zeke kissed her temple. "If you let me, I'll tell you I love you so often you'll get tired of hearing it."

Celeste chuckled. "Impossible." She drew back from him and looked up into his eyes. "I'm in love with you, too, Zeke. I'm sorry it took a near-death experience for me to realize it."

He smiled. "Let's not think about that now. I've never been so afraid in my life." He wiped the tears from her cheeks. "I understand you've had experiences that have made you reluctant to trust people, but I promise I will never do anything to betray you."

Celeste nodded. "I believe you. And I would never, ever do anything to betray or hurt you, either."

"I know." Zeke's eyes drank in her delicate features. Her beautiful wide hazel eyes, heart-shaped lips and high cheek-bones. "I love you, Celeste, and I'm going to spend the rest of my life making sure you know that."

He kissed her, catching his breath when she parted her lips for him. He swept his tongue inside her, tasting her sweetness. He raised his head to take a breath.

Celeste whispered against his ear. "Say it again, please?"

He smiled. "I love you, Celeste."

"That will never get old," she said on a sigh, and kissed him again.

* * * * *

COMING SOON!

We really hope you enjoyed reading this book. If you're looking for more romance be sure to head to the shops when new books are available on

Thursday 19th December

To see which titles are coming soon, please visit

millsandboon.co.uk/nextmonth

MILLS & BOON

LET'S TALK

Romance

For exclusive extracts, competitions and special offers, find us online:

f MillsandBoon

X @MillsandBoon

⟲ @MillsandBoonUK

♪ @MillsandBoonUK

Get in touch on 01413 063 232